D0442865

INDIGO

Be Sure to Seek Out These Recent Works from the Authors of *Indigo*

KELLEY ARMSTRONG

The *City of the Lost* series

The *Cainsville* series

CHRISTOPHER GOLDEN

Ararat

Snowblind

CHARLAINE HARRIS

All the Little Liars

The *Cemetery Girl* trilogy

TIM LEBBON

Relics

The Silence

JONATHAN MABERRY

X-Files Origins: Devil's Advocate

Dogs of War: A Joe Ledger Novel

SEANAN McGUIRE

The *October Daye* series

The *InCryptid* series

JAMES A. MOORE

The *Seven Forges* series

The *Tides of War* trilogy

MARK MORRIS

The *Obsidian Heart* trilogy

Albion Fay

CHERIE PRIEST

Brimstone

The Family Plot

KAT RICHARDSON

The *Greywalker* series

The Death of All Things

INDIGO

a mosaic novel

CHARLAINE HARRIS

CHRISTOPHER GOLDEN

KELLEY ARMSTRONG

JONATHAN MABERRY

KAT RICHARDSON

SEANAN McGUIRE

TIM LEBBON

CHERIE PRIEST

JAMES A. MOORE

MARK MORRIS

ST. MARTIN'S PRESS ⚏ NEW YORK

INDIGO. Copyright © 2017 by Charlaine Harris, Christopher Golden, Kelley Armstrong, Jonathan Maberry, Kat Richardson, Seanan McGuire, Tim Lebbon, Cherie Priest, James A. Moore, Mark Morris. All rights reserved. Printed in the United States of America. For information, address St. Martin's Press, 175 Fifth Avenue, New York, N.Y. 10010.

www.stmartins.com

The Library of Congress Cataloging-in-Publication Data is available upon request.

ISBN 978-1-250-07678-6 (hardcover)
ISBN 978-1-4668-8835-7 (e-book)

Our books may be purchased in bulk for promotional, educational, or business use. Please contact your local bookseller or the Macmillan Corporate and Premium Sales Department at 1-800-221-7945, extension 5442, or by e-mail at MacmillanSpecial Markets@macmillan.com.

First Edition: June 2017

10 9 8 7 6 5 4 3 2 1

INDIGO

1

———

Nora could have vanished into the shadows, but she didn't need to. The people crowded around the sidewalk memorial for Maidali Ortiz were so lost in their grief she might as well have been invisible. Normally she had to work a little harder to hide in plain sight, but not today. It made her job much simpler.

The girl's body had been dumped at the top of the steps that connected Heath and Bailey Avenues, a broad set of concrete stairs with black wrought-iron railings, shaded by lush oak trees. Fall had arrived at last, and a cool breeze rustled the leaves of those trees. During the day, the long descent from Heath to Bailey would be pleasant enough, but at night, with streetlamps that were constantly broken, the stairs would be dark and forbidding.

She wove through the crowd to get a better look at the steps. Stout, middle-aged Dominican women clustered together, keeping mostly to themselves, but the high school and middle school kids weren't so discriminating. The Irish and Dominican and Cuban kids stood together, girls holding each other, while others added flowers and stuffed animals and framed photos to the memorial that had grown up around the graffiti-covered US mailbox to the left of the stairs.

Nora listened to the quiet weeping and the words of comfort and shock spoken by those around her. Inhaling the scent of the flowers, she glanced around at the homes on either side of the stairs. The small, three-story apartment house with a façade of tan bricks and the squat little single-family row house had only two things in common: each had a small patio in front and bars on all the windows. This was Kingsbridge. While other Bronx neighborhoods were being gentrified, Kingsbridge had been sliding in the other direction for years.

"Did you know her?"

Nora blinked and frowned at the man who'd appeared beside her. Early thirties, sweater pushed up to his elbows, facial scruff, and two-tone brown wing tips. She marked him as a former hipster who missed his glory days, but he was handsome. Odds in Kingsbridge suggested Cuban or Dominican, but she wasn't going to guess.

"Not at all," Nora admitted quietly, turning aside to move the conversation away from the gathered mourners. "I'm new to the neighborhood. Just out for a run, to be honest, but it seemed disrespectful not to at least stop and offer up a prayer."

The former hipster cocked his head, brown eyes warm. "That's kind of you."

"It's a horrible thing." Nora hugged herself with a shudder. "I know it's not the safest neighborhood, but I never expected something like this. Three kids in a row."

Though she had her magenta-streaked hair tied back and was dressed for it, the out-for-a-run story was only a cover. The shudder, however, was real.

"It's awful, no argument," he said. "But you just got here. Don't give up on Kingsbridge yet. There are a lot of good people here, families that go back generations—"

"Yours?"

A news van pulled up at the curb and the crew began to climb out. The former hipster scowled at their presence and nodded to a spot farther up the sidewalk, away from the crowd and the cameraman. A police car rolled silently up the block, and Nora could see a competing news van approaching as well.

"Both sides of the family, yeah. Half–Puerto Rican, half-Albanian, but a hundred percent Kingsbridge." He offered his hand. "I'm Rafe Bogdani."

They shook, and she lied, "Shelby Coughlin."

Rafe commented on her Irish name, how down on Bailey Avenue there were still clusters of Irish families that went way back, but she wasn't paying much attention now. Church bells were ringing inside the Dominican church at the bottom of the steps, echoing out across the bright autumn morning, and the people at the top of the stairs moved to either side, waiting for the procession they knew was coming.

Nora saw pain in Rafe's eyes. "You knew her?"

Rafe glanced at her, hesitant. But then he nodded. "I teach history at the high school. I had Maidali in class last year. She was a smart kid, thoughtful in a way so few of them are."

Nora forced herself not to look too interested. She shifted to get a better view past the crowd and down the stairs, where a procession ascended from the church on Bailey Avenue. "What about the other two?"

"The boy was an eighth grader, I hear. Never met him. Supposedly the other girl, Corinna-something, was from Yonkers. Down staying with her cousins, was it?"

Nora nodded. "Sounds right."

Corinna's last name had been Dewar. A fifteen-year-old ginger with more freckles than there were stars in the sky. The eighth grader had been Tomas Soares, a future track star, tall for his age and un-afraid of running at night.

Nora and Rafe stood in the midst of the crowd on the Heath Avenue sidewalk, watching as Maidali Ortiz's parents and grand-father and little brother climbed the stairs. The fall breeze had stilled as if the morning held its breath, and the murmuring on the side-walk also fell silent. The only sounds were the quiet sobs of the family members and their dearest friends, the people who had been in the church for this morning's memorial. The police wouldn't re-lease Maidali's body yet, but the family hadn't wanted to wait any longer to offer up prayers, both in the girl's memory and in search of some comfort. Some small bit of grace that might alleviate the screaming pain in their hearts.

Nora wondered if they had found even a sliver of that grace, of peace. She hoped so, but from the looks on their faces as they were confronted by the neighbors and spectators waiting, she doubted it.

"How could someone do that to a child?" Rafe whispered.

She didn't have to ask what he meant. Nora had seen a couple of the crime-scene photos thanks to her police contacts. Maidali had been mutilated, her face and body marked with a knife, her eyes removed postmortem. The girl had been murdered elsewhere, her body dumped down the steps sometime between 2:00 and 3:00 a.m. on Wednesday morning. Whoever had killed Maidali had returned her to her neighborhood, dumped her seven blocks from her house, like some car thief who'd gone for a joyride and then left the car nearby in apology.

Not an apology, Nora thought. *They were done with her. Tossed her back where she'd come from.*

The idea made her clench her fists. Whoever had killed Maidali had to be stopped before doing it again. The police might find the killer, but if they didn't . . .

Nora hadn't yet been able to get her hands on the autopsy reports for Corinna Dewar and Tomas Soares—she had no informants in the Fiftieth Precinct—but Maidali's killing had made the murders a serial crime, which bumped the whole thing up the ladder. The entire city was paying attention now. Nora expected to get access to the complete file eventually, but today it had been important for her just to be here, to get a feeling for the crimes.

Nora stuffed her hands into the pockets of her fitted hoodie and made herself small, hoping to draw as little attention as possible. Some of the relatives of the first two victims were on the stairs as well, and she had already spoken to several of them while working on the larger story. At thirty-one, she had already paid her dues as a journalist, both in print and digital media. Early on, she had written about her generation and its place in American culture, about social justice and modern media, and occasionally about New York City itself. Over time, New York took over, with Nora focusing more and more on crime and corruption. For the past two years she'd worked as an investigative reporter at *NYChronicle*, the premier urban-news source in the region, and one with a global readership.

The job was perfect for her for other reasons also, but those were after-dark reasons, not thoughts for the bright of day.

The priest reached the top of the stairs just as Maidali's mother saw the sprawl of flowers and mementos and photographs that had been placed around the graffitied mailbox. Somehow the graffiti added to the beauty and the pain of the memorial. Lit candles burned in tall glass cylinders, their flames dancing as the late-September breeze kicked up again.

The dead girl's parents held hands and lowered their heads. The two news teams crowded in at the edges of the mourning circle, cameras rolling. Some of the spectators took out their phones, and only then did Nora do the same. Rafe frowned at her, a ripple of distaste crossing his features, but she forced herself to ignore him, taking thirty seconds of video and then snapping a few quick photos of Maidali's little brother—*You don't know his name, Nora . . . you should know his name*—kneeling by the mailbox and picking up one of the flowers there. A white-and-purple lily, its head fat and wilting.

The past year had seen a growing concern about children going missing in New York. Statistics suggested a certain percentage of them were runaways—some kids' day-to-day nightmares were too dark, or dreams were too big, and they wanted to find their own corner of the sky. But every law enforcement source she'd spoken to off the record had indicated that the past few years had seen a slow but steady rise in these numbers that could not be attributed to runaways. The other options were abduction and murder. Her ex-colleague, ex-boyfriend, and current friend-with-benefits, Sam Loh, had been working on an in-depth series on human trafficking in the northeastern United States, and how traffickers—so long unpunished for the thousands upon thousands of immigrants they'd tricked or stolen and sold into slavery—were now feeling bullet-proof and had been expanding their business, snatching children who were sure to be missed. Children the police were going to make a real effort to find.

Those kids never came back.

As Nora stood and let the grief of Maidali Ortiz's family wash over her, she wondered if it would have been better if Maidali had never been found. Was it better to have a missing child, one you could imagine might in time have escaped harm, might have found a way back into the sunlight . . . or better to know for certain that the baby you'd held swaddled in your arms, the one whose every fever had filled you with fear, the one whose laughter had filled your heart to bursting . . . was it better to know that child was dead?

God help her, she thought it might be. It was the ugliest question, and the most hideous answer, that had ever planted roots in her mind.

Nora snapped several more photos with her phone, pictures of the people gathered in that mourning circle, even a few shots of the news teams that filmed the scene. She avoided taking a shot of Rafe, mostly because of the guilt she felt pinking her cheeks, knowing he must think her just another vulture.

The priest cleared his throat, sighing heavily before he launched into a prayer. Nora had thought Maidali's father might say something to those who had come out to honor the memory of his daughter, but she could see the pain in his eyes and realized that he barely registered the presence of others.

Rafe lowered his head while also shifting slightly away from her. She saw his disapproval, the wrinkle of his brow, and she wanted to speak to him—tell him she wasn't as heartless as he thought, that her photos weren't gruesome souvenirs but a vital part of telling Maidali's story. The feeling frustrated her, that need to apologize for who she was and what she did, and she felt herself drawing away from him, too. At least she wasn't crowding the dead girl's family with a TV camera, van parked at wrong angles against the curb, turning their daughter's murder into a ratings grab, with a warning that if you didn't watch their report on the killings, the same thing might happen to *your* child. The media didn't like to do stories about human trafficking because those stories never had an ending. Murder, though, was an ending of its own. Even without answers to the who and why of it, people could understand mourning. But a missing child . . . those stories haunted. Lingered. The public didn't like those stories.

The priest finished his prayer. He put a hand on the father's shoulder and faced the crowd, offering a blessing to them for their support of the Ortiz family in their time of need. The boy handed the mother his wilting lily and she took it, eyes wide with such pain that she must have slipped into a world of numb incomprehension.

Nora had wanted to blend. To get the story from inside the sorrow, not merely as an outside observer. Now she wished she were anywhere else.

Rafe gave her another disapproving glance, and she moved away from him even farther, barely even aware of the priest's intonations. Circling behind Rafe and the rest of the onlookers, she moved toward the stairs. She had left her car down on Bailey Avenue, thinking she'd return to it when the family was gone and the crowd had mostly dispersed. Now she did not want to wait. She had the information and the photos. The one thing she didn't have was the only thing that mattered—answers.

The sun had shifted in the sky, moving the shadow of the house to the top of the stairs so that she could not avoid passing through it. Five steps from the summit, adjacent with the first lamppost, she entered the shadow and faltered, sucking in a tremulous breath. Her limbs felt leaden and cold, and a sharp pain stabbed at her eyes. A dreadful stink washed over her, along with a wave of nausea.

Just go, she told herself, and staggered down two or three more steps.

Pain lanced through her skull again, and her knees felt weak. The shadow around her seemed to breathe with malice. Angrily, she pushed it back, casting the shadow away so that it clung to the wall of the house and left the stairs in full sunlight for an eye blink before she allowed the shade to return to normal.

The shadows were hers.

She refused to fear them.

The block of Seventy-Fourth Street between Columbus and Amsterdam was lost in time. The sidewalks were broken and uneven and interrupted at regular intervals by old trees whose branches created a canopy over the street, their leaves rustling pleasantly three seasons a year. Cars parked on either side narrowed the one-way street to the bare minimum needed for vehicles to pass. Despite its location in a busy part of Manhattan's Upper West Side, that block tended toward a kind of quiet much of the city never achieved. Nora always imagined that her little block had changed hardly at all in the past half century. Only the cars gave it away.

She lived in a third-floor studio in a building that looked even narrower than the street. Three flights of stairs kept her in decent shape, but she nearly always stumbled on the way to her floor, as if the stairs conspired against her, with steps taking turns being the one that unaccountably grew in height on a given day. An extra inch or so, just enough to catch the toe of a shoe. The banister had saved her many bruised shins.

The original advertisement for the apartment had described it as a "loft," but she'd quickly discovered that this was code for "studio so small that you'll put your mattress in a loft space not much bigger than the top shelf of a closet." Still, for all the time that she spent at home, the studio suited her needs well enough. A bathroom, a tiny galley kitchen, a closet, and a high-ceilinged living room complete with a ladder that let her climb up to the shelf above the kitchen. Her mattress smelled like food 24-7. A tiny space, but enough room for Nora and her three cats.

Kelso, Red, and Hyde had been named after her three favorite characters from *That 70's Show*, which turned out to have been a generous gesture on her part because the cats were assholes.

Nora told anyone who would listen, *My cats are assholes. But at least they're my Assholes.*

She regretted it every time, but somehow she couldn't stop herself from saying it.

Just after eight o'clock that night she sat on her sofa, a thirdhand piece of furniture whose original color was lost to history and its fabric threaded through with cat hair that the vacuum cleaner never drew out.

"I hate you little shits," she told Kelso.

He arched his back and sneered down his nose before marching away.

Hyde jumped onto the sofa, walked onto her lap as if he'd barely noticed her, then curled into her lap. He knew a lie when he heard it.

Nora preferred dogs, but she spent too much time out of the apartment to be a dog owner. In truth, she disliked other people's cats and other people's cats disliked her, but she loved her three Assholes.

Sometimes, though, they watched her with more than typical feline interest. On early mornings when she stumbled out of bed or on exhausted late nights when she fell asleep watching television, she would mutter accusations that the three of them were hatching some sinister plot. Joking, mostly.

Hyde purred as she stroked his fur.

On her TV screen, Jason Statham used his fists and a sharp knife to avoid being killed by a trio of grim men with guns. Nora had been channel surfing when she stopped at the sight of Statham's chiseled features. She had no idea what the movie might be, but it didn't matter. After a full day at work, she needed to unwind with something that did not demand much of her attention.

One thing she refused to do was watch the news. She'd spent the entire day writing about dead kids and grieving parents, with tangents into New York City politics and various criticisms of the police investigation into the Kingsbridge murders.

She'd had enough of reality.

A quick rap at her door brought Nora off the sofa. She dumped Hyde from her lap and hurried to answer the knock. The deliveryman from the Golden Lotus stood in the hall with a fat brown paper bag, redolent with the smell of Chinese food. Nora's stomach growled as she quickly signed the credit-card slip, adding a nice tip as she thanked the man.

Breathing in the delicious aromas from the bag, she began to close her door only to be interrupted by another loud knock. Nora turned to find Shelby Coughlin waiting on her threshold.

"I saw the delivery guy!" Shelby said happily, slipping inside. "So hungry!"

"Me, too." Nora closed the door. "Ravenous."

"You'd better have remembered the beer!"

"I acquired the beer as instructed, Your Majesty," Nora said archly.

"Well done, lowly creature," Shelby replied, playing along. "Although I still object to the delivery thing. The whole point of going to the Lotus for Chinese food is that they make it fresh. If we get it delivered—"

"Y'know, you keep using that word, but I don't think it means what you think it means."

Shelby smiled as Nora carried the brown bag into the galley kitchen. "Which word is that, Inigo Montoya?"

"*We.*"

"Yes, okay, *you* have been buying the Chinese food lately, and I'm deeply grateful. But it's practically on your way home, right?"

Nora sighed. "Fine. Next week, I promise I will go and pick it up myself. But you are bringing the beer."

Shelby grinned. "You are my hero. Really."

"You're lucky you're my favorite person."

"Am I really your favorite person?"

Nora opened the bag of Chinese food. "Absolutely. If you liked cats, I would give you all of mine."

Shelby tied her long red-and-gold mane back with an elastic and took plates down from Nora's cabinet. "You hate your cats," Shelby said drily. "*I* don't hate cats, but I don't want *your* cats."

They put the food out on the coffee table and then did battle with the cats to keep them away from the spread. Shelby turned off the TV and opened Nora's laptop, choosing the eighties alt-rock channel that Shelby herself had set up on Pandora radio. They'd known each other less than eighteen months, but the girl from Atlanta had been making herself at home since day one. Every time, Nora surprised herself by finding it endearing instead of intrusive. If anyone else behaved as presumptuously in her home as Shelby did, Nora would never stand for it, but whenever Shelby swept into the apartment and took over Nora's life, it never seemed to be selfish.

"I was watching that," Nora said, mostly because she felt that she should issue some sort of protest.

"Not really." Shelby settled beside Nora on the sofa and nudged Red away from the edge of the coffee table. "You just like having the TV for company, and now you've got actual company, not to mention food and beer and music."

Nora wanted to argue, but she couldn't fight the truth. Instead, she ate her kung pao shrimp and listened to Shelby detail every hour of her day, from the aggravating old-school condescension of her boss at the fashion-design company where she worked, to the constant efforts of her ex-boyfriend to get back into her good graces. Twenty-five-year-old Shelby had too much ambition to let either man get in her way, but somehow she couldn't help letting them under her skin.

They shared their frustrations over the building's unreliable hot-water heater and the landlord's delays in getting it repaired. Shelby lived on the top floor—the fifth—and had taken to showering right before bed, when the hot water was less likely to run out so quickly. But as Nora chimed in, she found her friend studying her a little more intently than usual and stopped midsentence.

"What?"

"I read your piece about the girl's memorial today. You doing all right?"

Nora dished some more rice onto her plate, letting it soak up some of the spicy kung pao sauce. She picked up her beer bottle and held it. "I'll be okay when they catch whoever's doing it."

Shelby took a swig of her own beer and looked around the room. "You've got a lot of lights on in here. All the lights, really. I noticed it right off, but didn't want to ask."

"And now that you've had half a beer, you're ready to ask?"

"Something like that."

Nora glanced around and saw that Shelby was right. Without even realizing it, as night had fallen, Nora had turned on every light in the apartment, including the little buzzing fluorescent bar above the kitchen sink and the string of white Christmas lights that stayed stapled above her picture window year-round.

"Just keeping the darkness at bay, I guess."

"Well then, I'm glad I'm here."

"Me, too." Nora was tempted to say more, but how could she explain without revealing at least some of her secrets? If she tried, she knew she'd end up spilling the whole story. She trusted Shelby, but the woman was so intent on helping that Nora feared what she might do with the truth. Eventually, it would get her hurt.

Nora couldn't have that, so she kept her concerns to herself.

She didn't explain that the shadows were starting to worry her, that whenever she wasn't exerting her control over them, she could not escape the feeling that they bore her some profound ill will.

A buzzing sound made her jump, and she felt foolish when she realized it was only the vibration of her cell against the coffee table. Swallowing a mouthful of food, she reached for the phone. Shelby and the cats gave her an array of reproachful looks, but she glanced at the screen and saw that it was Rajitha Perera, her editor at *NYChronicle*.

"Sorry," she mumbled, swiping her thumb across the screen to answer. "Hey, Raj. What's news?"

Nora listened, feeling the blood drain from her face as she turned toward Shelby. When the call ended, Nora sat for a few seconds with the phone in her hand, staring at its screen as if the phone itself had upset her.

"Hey." Shelby nudged Nora's knee. "What's happening? What did she want?"

Sadness had welled up inside Nora, but now anger rose to replace it, burning all the sorrow out of her. Despite all the lights in the apartment she could feel the shadows pulsing, reacting to her emotions, ready to lash out at her command.

"They found another one. A thirteen-year-old girl, six blocks from the stairs where the bastard dumped Maidali."

"Oh, no," Shelby said quietly. She exhaled, and all of the bright humor and enthusiasm left her with that one breath. "You've got to go. Cover the story."

Nora stood, appetite forgotten. "Yeah."

But the time had come to stop worrying about covering the story. Whatever it took, she intended to bring the story to an end.

Outside in the dark, she wasn't Nora anymore.

Night had fallen on her little block of Seventy-Fourth Street. The leaves still rustled overhead, but without the daylight the sound might not have been the wind at all. The higher branches might have been infested with inhuman things with sharp teeth, the rustling the sound of their moving lower or simply shuddering with the nearness of prey. She had faced such things before, so she knew all too well that such thoughts were not paranoia but wisdom.

The possibility did not frighten her. Not this other woman, the one Nora became when she allowed herself to melt into the blue-black shadows. Indigo, she called herself then. Indigo, now.

Three doors down from her apartment, in a deep patch of shadow where the wan yellow streetlights could not reach, she inhaled a cleansing breath and reached out her hands to summon the darkness. It wrapped itself around her, cleaving to her body and flowing outward, a cloak of shadows. To the naked eye it would have looked like an actual cloak, woven of fabric the color of night. Her face was hidden by a hood, and the darkness moved to keep her features obscured.

With a gesture she summoned the shadows closer and fed them so they blotted out all the light around her and wrapped her in a dusky cocoon. An image formed in her mind, a memory from that morning—the stairs where Maidali's body had been found, where the streetlamps were always broken. She reached out into the shadows and then stepped through . . .

. . . and emerged on that staircase in Kingsbridge.

A kid in a red hoodie dodged to his left on the way down the steps, unconsciously avoiding the deeper patch that had gathered around Indigo. She watched him go by, saw him shudder as he felt her presence without ever peering into the depths of her shadows. He hurried down toward Bailey Avenue as if he feared the darkness might follow.

Ascending to the top of the stairs, she stared for a moment at the graffitied mailbox and the detritus of mourning that still lay piled around its feet. All that remained of Maidali Ortiz were memories. The same could be said of Corinna Dewar and Tomas Soares, and the child who had been found dead in Kingsbridge tonight. The desire to find the killer felt a little like vengeance, but Indigo knew she could do nothing for Tomas or Corinna or Maidali. What she did now, she did for the child who would otherwise be next.

Rajitha had given her an address, and now she glanced around, refreshing her memory. Far up the road a white box truck sat at the curb, silent and abandoned. The shape of the truck blocked out the illumination of the streetlight behind it, throwing a strange geometry of shadow onto the pavement. With merely a thought she stepped from one patch to the next, flowed from the small shadow beside the mailbox to the one cast by that truck, a block and a half away.

In the same fashion she continued through the neighborhood, slipping from gloom to gloom, until she emerged in a patch of airless black in the service alley behind an elementary school. Grass grew up through cracks in the pavement, and the Dumpster was rimmed with rust. Blue lights flashed at either end of the alley, throwing pale ghosts against the back wall of the school and the high fence behind it. The police cars were silent, the officers guarding the crime scene just waiting by their vehicles, and Indigo knew that the detectives had not yet arrived. Except for her, only two people were in the alley, and one of them was dead.

A single police officer had been posted to guard this new body until the detectives and the crime-scene techs arrived. Tall and broad-shouldered, he must have been in his midtwenties but had a sweetness to his face that made him look younger. A good cop, though, or the others on-site would not have posted him here. They trusted that he was smart enough not to contaminate the scene by touching anything he shouldn't.

The dead girl lay on her side, wrapped in a blanket. One arm was flung over her head as if she'd just gone to sleep in the alley behind the school. Thirteen years old, according to Raj, which must mean that the police had already identified her. Or had Raj made assumptions? The detectives hadn't even arrived yet, but if a girl of this age and description had been reported missing, both the cops and Raj might have leaped to conclusions.

Nora needed a closer look.

Indigo stepped out from behind the Dumpster, some of the shadows trailing after her.

"What's your name?" she asked quietly.

The big, baby-faced cop whipped around. His hand dropped to the butt of his pistol, but he froze when he saw her.

"Holy shit," he whispered.

"You know who I am." It wasn't a question.

The cop exhaled, glanced toward the blue lights at the nearest end of the service alley—gauging how long it would take his fellow officers to back him up if he shouted for them. His chest rose and fell but the hand resting on the butt of his gun did not tremble.

"Hey," she prodded. "Officer . . ."

"I know who you are." He shifted his head in an attempt to get a look at her face beneath the hood, unaware that the shadows wouldn't allow it. "I thought you were just a story."

"Now you know better. What's your name?"

"Pacheco."

"Officer Pacheco, I need to take a closer look at the girl."

The cop stiffened. His grip settled more firmly on his sidearm. "We're supposed to secure the crime scene. You're going to want to step away now. Anything you want to know, you can—"

She took a step toward him. "I'm on your side, Officer."

Finally, he drew his gun and held it down by his side. "Ma'am, you need to back the hell up right—"

Indigo swept the deeper shadows out from behind her, and the darkness washed over Pacheco like a wave. All light fled the patch of alley around them, leaving Indigo, the cop, and the dead girl in a circle of total darkness about twenty feet in diameter.

Pacheco shouted for help, terror in his voice and etched on his features. He spun around in a panic, aiming his gun at nothing, rendered virtually blind. But Indigo could see perfectly well. She slid toward him and wrapped a hand around his wrist. He pulled the trigger, fired into the impossible dark. The sound was thickly muffled, as if they were underwater instead of lost in shadow.

"I'm on your side," she said again, ripping the gun from his hand and tossing it along the alley. It skittered out of the pool of darkness.

Officer Pacheco dropped to his hands and knees, cursing her as he scrabbled around in the dark for his weapon. He shouted for backup again, but the shadows swallowed his voice and returned it in echoes.

Indigo knelt by the body of the dead girl. Thirteen years old, if Raj had been right, but she looked younger. A mess of blond hair haloed around her head, veiling part of her face, but the blanket was what interested Indigo the most. None of the police statements had mentioned the dead children being in any state of undress, but she'd reported on enough crimes to know that the police routinely held back vital details from the public. If a suspect knew something that the detectives had kept out of the media, it could indicate guilt, or at least complicity.

A wave of unease rushed through her. She reached out and gripped the edge of the blanket. Distant shouts penetrated the gloom as Pacheco's fellow officers began to respond, his shouts not quite muffled enough to keep them from hearing.

She drew the blanket back and her heart sank. Sorrow and guilt warred inside her, and then were obliterated by fury.

The girl's eyes had been removed, yes, but her body had suffered other mutilations. Her chest had been cut open, ribs exposed. On her arms and legs, and most explicitly on her abdomen, her killers had carved arcane symbols that Indigo recognized immediately. Ritual markings.

"Oh, you bastards," she whispered.

The Children of Phonos had murdered four children. She had dealt with members of the cult several times. She had fought them, exposed individuals, even taken lives, but she had always stopped short of simply destroying them all. It would have felt like murder, and she had drawn the line. Now she had to live with the knowledge that if she *had* crossed that line, four children might still be alive.

This didn't explain all of the other missing kids in New York, but now she knew what had happened to these four. Horror. Human sacrifice.

The police were shouting and she felt them trying to enter her sphere of darkness. Numb with anger and sick inside, she stood and walked back toward the Dumpster. Pacheco cried out in relief as the shadows withdrew and he could see again at last. It was the last thing Indigo heard before she slid fully into the shadows between shadows . . .

. . . and stepped out again into that darkness just a few doors down from her apartment.

Over on Columbus Avenue, a car went by with music blaring through open windows. A chilly autumn wind caressed her and a few leaves danced along the sidewalk at her feet, and then she turned and vomited kung pao shrimp onto the concrete.

Unsteady on her feet, Nora Hesper shed the cloak of shadows and started back to her apartment, knowing she could never again hesitate. She had drawn the line, but now all the lines had been erased.

2

——

This time she kept all the lights in her apartment turned off. The place felt quiet in the aftermath of Shelby's earlier visit. Nora would normally have welcomed her friend's chaotic, comforting presence, but after being Indigo for a while, she needed some time alone.

Even with blinds drawn, light bled into the apartment from the streets, and moonlight silvered through the long, high window by her loft bed. As Nora slumped on her sofa, she drew the shadows around her. It took no effort to feed and expand them, and as total darkness enclosed her, she saw so much more. To anyone opening the door, her apartment would have looked like a void, endless and depthless, a hollow in the world.

Even her cats allowed her this time to herself. Assholes they might have been, but they also recognized and respected this aspect of who Nora was. She could sense them now, Red and Hyde hunkered down on her bed close enough to touch, Kelso alone in the small kitchen, flat against the base of the oven, purring softly against the night. They understood that when Indigo was in the apartment, it was safest for them to stay low, quiet, and unseen. The primeval part of them allowed this. Their instinct for self-preservation insisted upon it.

She often talked to them about who she was and what she could do. They were surrogate friends, listening but not understanding, accepting her heartfelt monologues without passing judgment or questioning the choices she had made, the actions she had taken.

Just over a year before, she had returned to her apartment splashed with someone else's blood. It had been her second encounter with members of the Children of Phonos—who also called themselves Phonoi. From what she'd gleaned, they were a worldwide black-magic cult with a number of chapters in the United States. Her first run-in with them had involved the theft of an occult artifact from the New-York Historical Society. Simple enough. But that second time had included the kidnapping of the husband of a high-powered corporate attorney, some kind of blackmail scheme. Indigo had never discovered exactly what the scheme had been, because although she'd brought the husband home alive, they'd arrived to find his wife dead, her Phonoi assassins waiting for them.

Indigo had killed three of them that night. The story the dead attorney's husband had given the media had fueled the legend of the city's nocturnal vigilante, but all it had taught Indigo was that the Children of Phonos weren't just socialite fucks dabbling in magic—some of them were vicious, highly skilled killers. She'd kept her eyes open for them ever since.

That night, covered in their blood, she had emerged from the shadows inside her apartment and gone immediately to scrub her sins clean in the shower. Kelso, ever the loner, had come to sit on her lowered toilet-seat lid and listen to her confession.

"There were three of them." Nora's eyes were closed as scorching water cleansed her face. "They bore the mark behind their right ears, and the abdominal branding. I've been tracking them for a while, you know that, I've told you all about it. What they did to that woman—the lawyer—it was so brutal I couldn't let them get away with it. I just . . ."

As Indigo she had opened her eyes and stared at Kelso, and the cat had hissed and darted from the small bathroom. She'd reached across the sink and swiped her hand across the misted mirror. Shadows were leaking from her pupils and running down her face, like eyeliner melting in the heat.

"I slit their throats," she'd said to herself in the mirror, unsure who was talking to whom. She could practically still feel the shadow knife in her hand. "It was the right thing to do."

She had believed that then, and she believed it now. She did.

Nora had been careful not to be the one reporting the story of the murdered attorney and the wild story her husband told about Indigo. That had been Sam Loh's last job before he'd left the newspaper. She'd tried not to take pleasure in the reaction to her deeds. *"Indigo,"* some people had said, *"Indigo gave those killers what they deserved."*

If she felt a swelling of pride or satisfaction, she tamped it down quickly. Murder was nothing to celebrate, no matter how deserving the victims. In the long, lonely evenings she spent in the apartment with only her cats for company, talking to them was an effort to alleviate her guilt, or perhaps to lessen its impact. But she held on to the memories of her violence, of her victims' blood gushing over her hands, the light dying in their eyes as her shadows danced around her in glee. She was Indigo and Indigo was her, but Nora refused to allow murder to feel ordinary.

Because sometimes the shadows were malevolent. Sometimes Indigo thought they hid something deeper and darker. She had always been able to control this malevolence, drive it down with her own will and lock it away in the deeper, more complete darkness from which it seemed to originate, a place marked not only by an

absence of light but by some heavier presence, an anti-place where
darkness was the norm. But a few times lately she'd felt this separate presence rising, rebelling against her efforts to contain it.

Four times, in fact.

Now that she had examined the fourth dead child and realized
that the Phonoi were responsible for these murders, she could place
the occasions of these shadowy incursions approximately along-
side the murders.

That frightened her and made her think of long ago. Her memories of that time were like a movie viewed over and over, spooling
through her mind while she watched as an outside observer. They
were painful times to dwell upon, but she had to understand them—
because the power that had made her might also have brought into
being that presence in the shadows, reveling in murder, preparing
to attack.

*The man at her parents' funeral is short and thin, of an indefinable
age, and with a face she has never before seen—but that shouldn't matter.
Plenty of strangers are here, people her parents encountered during their
working lives, but whom they never mentioned. She's never met them.
It's nice that they have come to pay their respects. Hundreds have done so,
and now Nora stands in the midst of a large group of black-clad people,
a vast slick of shadows in the blazing sunlight of this fine summer day. They
stand on the grass and paths; they rest against other gravestones, lean on
each other for support.*

*Nora has no one to lean on. She is almost at the center of this crowd,
but only almost, because its true center, its focus, is the two rectangular
holes in the world. Everything she knows and loves has been lowered
into those holes. At nineteen years old, a gunman's random bullets have
stolen away her family and security and left her floundering in a world
she does not understand.*

*Dust to dust, the dull thump of soil, of wood, hugs and kissed cheeks
and hands held tight, and then Nora is being led back across the cemetery*

by an uncle she doesn't remember meeting before. He's sad and stern, but he doesn't pretend to be in true mourning for his estranged brother. She respects his honesty.

"There's a sizable sum in insurance money coming to you," he says. "I'll stay in the city for a few days and help you through the process. Matt would have wanted that."

Matt would have wanted to not be dead, *Nora thinks.*

The tears come again as she thinks of her father down there in that hole in the world, eight feet from her mother but an eternity away.

As they reach the parking lot and her uncle Theo guides her toward his Mercedes, the short, thin man is waiting beneath a tree. The smoke from his cigarette curls up in the still air, and it looks as if it comes from the barrel of a gun. Uncle Theo is opening the car door, and as Nora crunches across the gravel toward the tree, he calls after her. She ignores him.

The man smiles as she approaches. He leans back against the tree, taking a long drag on his cigarette. Its end crackles and glows.

"Who are you?" Nora's voice breaks because she hasn't said anything since the burial, and tears are still stuck in her throat.

"My name doesn't matter." The man drops the cigarette and crushes it out on the grass. It seems like such an improper gesture in this place of somberness and death. "What I have to say does."

"I don't know you." Nora is nineteen and confident, fit and strong and fast, but now she's afraid. Perhaps this fear is a new thing that will stick with her, now that her mother and father are gone.

"Nor will you. But you'll know my words, and heed them. You were meant for more than this, Nora. I'm sorry for your grief, but it is also your freedom. There are places you must go. Things you must learn. Hide from the glare, take to the shadows. Find your path."

Her uncle calls her. Nora glances back and waves, and when she turns again, the man is walking away.

"Where? Learn what?"

"You'll know soon enough," the man says without turning around. As he strides off, he lights another cigarette.

Nora does not follow. She trudges back toward the Mercedes and her uncle. He seems angry, and as she approaches, he berates her for wasting time. "There's a wake. We should be there first to welcome people. Hurry, Nora."

Her hand burns. She holds it before her, fingers splayed, and her fingernails have grown dark. Black. Something leaks from beneath them, like black ink except more ethereal—

Wait a minute. It wasn't like that.

Uncle Theo's eyes go wide with fear, his mouth drops open—

That didn't happen.

She reaches for him. He cringes back against the car, reaching for his phone as it begins to ring—

No, no, not like this at all. I got into the car and went home, waited for the life insurance payout, traveled the world and went to Nepal, hid from the glare, took to the shadows, never saw Uncle Theo again—

Nora jerked upright on her sofa. Shadows retreated like startled creatures, darkness faded, and weak light filtered into her apartment from outside. On the coffee table, her phone was ringing.

One of the cats hissed somewhere out of sight, and the light of the waxing moon touched her skin.

"Fucking hell." Nora snatched up the phone. Her heart galloped, and her back and armpits were damp with sweat. Sam Loh's image grinned at her from the screen. She answered, and his voice had never been so welcome.

"Hey, sexy."

"Sam. You . . . startled me." She glanced at the digital clock on her DVD player. "It's after two in the morning."

"The news cycle's twenty-four hours."

"Bastard. Okay, what's up?" She always liked hearing from Sam. In the time they'd worked at *NYChronicle* together—sometimes in the same vehicle, on the same story, for days on end—a pressure had built between them that had no real avenue for release. They'd found that release in many sessions of great sex. Eventually they'd said they loved each other, though Nora had never been sure.

Then Sam had left. He'd fallen out with Rajitha over his handling of the kidnapped-woman story. His focus had been more on the weird rumors of Indigo rather than the gritty truth, and their editor had questioned his commitment to serious journalism. He in turn had questioned her commitment to the truth, and it had blown up into a furious confrontation, an argument that took place in the paper's main office at a time when most people were at their desks. Voices had been raised, names called. Rajitha had been left with no recourse but to fire Sam. Luckily, he saved her the trouble by resigning on the spot.

Such events inspired by Nora's secret life should have made her relationship with Sam complex and troublesome, but they had since become the best of friends. Her stated belief in his Indigo story had endeared her to him more than ever, and his childlike fascination with the character pleased her.

Of course, she could never tell him the truth.

"Got a tidbit I thought I should throw your way," he said.

"A tidbit?"

"A curious coincidence. Maybe. Call it a favor."

Nora frowned and ran her hand through her hair. Her dream lingered, its dregs echoing even as she sat here in her silent apartment. The cats slept. She heard one of them snoring softly from somewhere out of sight, and she wondered what *their* dreams were like.

"At two a.m.?"

She could hear his cheeky smile through the phone when he

said, "It's not the first favor I've given you this time of night." She wished he'd facetimed her instead.

"Okay, you've got me intrigued, so out with it." She walked to the kitchenette with the phone to her ear, and as Sam started talking, she poured a glass of water.

"You're reporting on these child murders, right? Another one tonight?"

"Yeah." She blinked and saw the mutilation, the horrors inflicted on the girl's innocent body.

"I've been working on a piece, too, for the *Indie*. More directed at the police investigation than the murders themselves—the cops' inability to catch the killer, drifting off into politics and bureaucracy. Whether or not there's a human-trafficking angle to the abductions of these kids who end up dead."

"I'd been wondering the same thing. But I don't think they're related. These kids . . . there's a ritual element to this, I think. Just between us, not for print. I don't think traffickers were behind this."

"Ritual . . . like that cult stuff with Indigo last year?"

"Maybe." She hesitated. Sam was fascinated by all things Indigo, and she didn't want him digging too much. "I'll keep you posted. But unless it's a smoke screen, disposing of the bodies like this, I don't think it's related."

"Maybe not. But you know I've got some decent police connections—hell, some of them are your connections, too. They don't like me too much after all the focus I'm throwing on the trafficking stuff, the vanished kids, but with these murders . . . well, they're putting everything into trying to catch the bastard."

"So far 'everything' isn't enough."

"Anyway, a name came up last night: Bullington. One of the lawyers who repped the cultist couple who abducted Andy Chesbro last year."

Nora almost dropped the glass. Chesbro had been the fancy attorney's kidnapped husband. Police had arrested a Scarsdale couple for the actual kidnapping but could never link them to the cult assassins who'd murdered Chesbro's wife—the ones Indigo had killed. The Scarsdale couple had gotten off after a grand jury inquiry showed police misconduct in the investigation—the lead detective had botched the whole thing.

A month later, the Scarsdale couple had been murdered in their home.

Indigo hadn't been responsible for those deaths. She had assumed it was the Phonoi, cleaning up their mess.

She leaned back against the kitchen worktop and blinked rapidly a few times, trying to shake the memory of blood gushing across her hands, and fear in the faces of the assassins as she put an end to them.

"Nora?"

"Yeah, I'm here. Tell me about Bullington. He was part of the legal team for the kidnappers?"

"After the Newells were killed—"

The Newells. The Scarsdale couple. Somehow she'd managed to forget their name, but there it was.

"—Chesbro sued the estate in a civil case, figuring it was like O. J. Simpson. Jury found O.J. not guilty, but he got clobbered in a civil suit by the families of his victims. Chesbro sued, and I guess he was pretty surprised when they settled almost immediately. The lawyer who represented the Newells' estate, who negotiated that settlement, was Bullington."

Nora frowned. "I don't see where you're going with this."

"Thing is, prior to that, Bullington had a rep as just some sleaze-bag ambulance chaser. And when the case was over, he went back to being exactly that."

"So why's his name come up again now?"

"He's showing an interest in these killings, talking to the uniforms who found two of the kids' bodies. There's evidence he's been tracking the case electronically, though he's good at covering his trail."

"Has he approached the families? Maybe he wants to represent them, get them to sue the city?"

"That's what's weird—no approaches that I can uncover, at least."

"If he's out to make a quick buck, that's who he'd talk to."

"So I figured," Sam said. "Thought I should tell you, in case you've got more influence with the investigating officers than I do. It's Mayhew and Symes."

The names rang a bell. "Wait, Mayhew as in the detective who fucked up the Chesbro case?"

"One and the same. Way I hear it, this is her shot at redemption. You should ask her about Bullington, see if they're looking at him for anything. Worth a shot, right?"

Nora smiled. "And worth working on together, I suppose?"

"If you insist. I mean, I know you'll do anything to spend more time with me."

Nora drank some water, taking the quiet time to think about what Sam was saying.

"So, are we going to catch up soon?" he asked.

"Yeah. Yeah." But Nora's mind was already spinning. Bullington had represented the Newell estate, which meant he'd been hired by someone connected to the Children of Phonos. Now he was sniffing around the murdered kids in Kingsbridge. If she wanted to root out the core membership of the cult, it looked as if the lawyer would be the best place to start.

"You sound tired."

"Two a.m., remember?" She tried to inject some humor into her voice, but knew he could hear through the façade.

"Let's do lunch tomorrow," he suggested. "Noon, Lucy's on the Square."

Nora smiled, and this time it was genuine. "It's a date."

"We don't do dates. We're friends."

"With benefits."

"Hmm. Don't get me going."

"Thanks, Sam."

"No problem. Get some sleep. Kick a cat for me." Sam hated her cats. He was allergic to them, and he swore that they homed in on him if he ever came to visit. That was why most of their overnight meetings were at his place in Brooklyn.

Nora placed her phone carefully onto the worktop and reached for the kettle. Sirens rang in the distance. Muted voices came in from elsewhere in the apartment block. Horns honked. The sounds of the city ensured that the night was never silent, and soon she would be back out in it.

Dawn was still few hours away, and in that time Indigo would get to work.

The skills one acquired as an investigative journalist. Even though Bullington didn't advertise his services as a lawyer, it only took her five minutes and three databases to scare up his address. After that, she spent some time considering what she already knew; then she showered, dressed, ate a light breakfast, and made a big mug of coffee.

Forming a plan always gave her a sense of control, even if she couldn't shake the idea that her level of control was far more nebulous than she wanted to believe.

Indigo traveled through the predawn gloom, stepping into a shadow in her apartment and emerging again on West Forty-Ninth Street. A squirrel scampered away, squealing in shock and rustling through a pile of refuse bags lying torn open across an alleyway. She shrugged away the darkness drawn to her and moved out onto the street, intending to confront Bullington as Nora. Though her blood was up and her fury ignited, killing was always a last resort, even if the lawyer turned out to be connected to the Children of Phonos. The temptation to just pitch him off a roof would be far greater if she went to him as Indigo.

So Nora it was.

In the hour before sunrise, the Manhattan streets were already busy. Delivery trucks rumbled along concrete canyons, a couple of police cruisers rolled by, taxis driven by tired drivers wended their way from one place to another. Pedestrians walked with a purpose, to or from work. Vagrants still huddled in a few doorways, and Nora felt eyes upon her as she walked from north to south on Ninth. She was cautious, but not worried. She carried her press card, useful in case of questions from a curious police officer.

If danger came from another quarter, Indigo was ready to spring from the shadows.

She had intentionally emerged several blocks from Bullington's address, so she could gather her thoughts while walking. The slayings were ritualistic, which meant human sacrifice in some sort of perverted black-magic bullshit. The Phonoi thought themselves servants to the gods of murder, but they were really only paying homage to the gods of blood and death, sickness and perversion.

She hated every one of them. The trouble was that she was constantly struggling with the desire to hate herself, as well. She kept murder as a final option, and she had a life of her own to live. She was more than a vigilante, more than the shadows she wielded as Indigo. Nora Hesper had a job, she had joys and responsibilities. Yes, of course, she had used her work as a journalist to poke into the Children of Phonos, but without much luck. Now she could only wonder whether things might have been different. If she'd put everything else aside, if she'd dedicated every moment to tracking down and exterminating all of the members of this chapter of the cult a year ago, would these four children still be alive?

Maybe, she thought. *Or maybe you'd have just pulled more chapters to New York and there'd have been even more twisted bastards sacrificing kids to the murder gods.*

When she reached Bullington's address, she crossed the street and entered a diner. Even at seven in the morning it was busy, and Nora found comfort in the gentle hubbub. A radio played in the background, some people ate breakfast and drank coffee alone, others sat in pairs or small groups, laughing and chatting as they prepared for their day ahead. Most of them would live a normal day with few surprises. She envied them.

But as she drank her coffee and looked across the street, she reminded herself that Indigo might be making things better. It was how she maintained her sanity.

Bullington's office was on the fourth floor above a launderette. Just after Nora had ordered blueberry pancakes for breakfast and settled down to wait for opening hours, she saw movement in his office window. She frowned, shielding her eyes from dawn light reflected through the diner's windows, and she concentrated on the building opposite.

The movement came again. A flicker of curtain, then a shadow passing left to right. Someone was in Bullington's office. The light was on inside.

Nora chewed on her pancakes, but she was no longer hungry. Maybe Bullington was already at work, or perhaps he actually lived up there. Either way, she would not have to wait for an hour as she'd expected.

The bathroom was at the back of the diner, close to the busy, noisy kitchen. The chef sang, loud and tuneless, and a waitress good-naturedly berated him. They were entirely too immersed in each other to notice Nora as she moved quickly past the open door, and along a narrow hallway. At the end, a fire door stood propped open.

The alleyway beyond was silent, still, stinking. This, too, was a place of shadows. They shimmered as Nora stepped out from the building, as if inviting her in. She accepted the invitation, submersing herself in darkness.

For a moment, she felt lost in the dark. That had never before happened.

I'm Nora Hesper, she thought. Shadows hung around her, doubting her name. She breathed heavily, struggling to push them away or draw them back in. Reveal herself. Become once more the person she had always been. *I'm Nora Hesper, and there's something . . .*

She found control once more. She shrugged her shoulders and stepped from the darkness in the anteroom of Bullington's office. Alone, she exhaled and closed her eyes, remembering what one of the monks at the Nepalese monastery had told her on the day she left.

"You carry the weight of the night with you, and darkness is heavier than light. Be strong. Never weak. Never give it a vulnerable face."

"I'm Nora Hesper," she said, louder. From behind the interior door she heard a surprised voice, but gave it no time to call out a challenge.

She turned the knob and stepped inside.

It might once have been a presentable office—the furniture was decent quality, with a large desk and a leather chair, a more informal seating area close to the windows, and several tasteful prints hanging on the walls. But such finery had been subsumed beneath old fast-food cartons and wrappers, sheaves of paper and files, discarded clothing, and bizarrely, several bikes in various states of dismantlement.

In the middle of the room, standing in front of the desk, was the man himself.

"I'm not open."

Nora almost laughed. Almost. Because even in those three words, she heard and sensed something in him that she didn't like. Immediately on the defensive, here was a lawyer who saw no need to provide a presentable office for his clients to visit—a man instantly suspicious of anyone who might seek his help.

"Don't worry, I'm not hiring." Nora closed the door behind her and plucked her press card from her pocket.

"What the hell do you want?"

"I've got a few questions. But it looks like you're busy tidying up."

Bullington glanced around the office, unconcerned.

"Moving your office?" Nora saw the mattress in the corner, almost hidden from view beneath twisted blankets and piles of clothing. "Or moving house?"

"None of your concern. No one comes here without an appointment."

"I'd have made one with your assistant, but the outer office was empty."

He snorted. "Just get out."

"Or?"

"You're trespassing." He sneered as he skirted around his desk and pulled open a drawer. The gun was dark and ugly in his hand. He held it like a rock, not a firearm. He didn't threaten her with it, not directly. Whatever he looked like, he knew the law.

"You've been asking a lot of questions about the murdered kids. What's your interest?"

Bullington froze, then tried the sneer on again. This time it seemed forced. "A lawyer on his own always scouts for work."

"You on retainer?"

"None of your business."

"I bet you are. I bet you've got a decent sum in the bank, paid to

you by people you'd never dream of talking about. I bet you're trying not to even think about them right now, aren't you?"

Nora stared into his eyes. He glanced away, then moved around
his desk again, dragging the gun's barrel across the oak surface. It
struck a bottle lying on its side and shoved aside a messy sheaf of
paper. He moved as if he were unaware that his hand held the gun,
that it scraped across the desk.

"This is not a public office. I don't know how you got in here,
but you need to leave. I'm busy."

"Weird definition of *busy*." She backed to the door and almost
mentioned the Children of Phonos. But that was not a name for
Nora to utter. "I won't be the only one asking questions, you know,"
she said instead. "I'll bet you have to be guarded about who you talk
to. Careful about what you say. Or there'll be repercussions."

His lips pressed together, a mixture of anger and fear. But he
said nothing.

Nora took one last look around the office, then left without another word. She moved through the reception area, exiting into a
short hallway that stank of neglect and pessimism. She held her
breath until she was down the stairs and unlocking the front door
to get outside, into the relatively fresh air. She hadn't entered the
building that way. The locks took a while to open.

Once outside, she knew she wouldn't have to wait long. Bullington would be on the move, packing what he needed to run. Maybe
he'd go to the Phonoi first, maybe not.

Fifty yards away she found another alley, where she drew the
gloom around her as a cloak. She wrapped herself inside it, slipped
through the shadows, and emerged outside his office once more.
Unlike the last time, she felt no hesitation in the darkness. The tran-
sition was almost instantaneous, a moment of weightlessness and
timelessness during which memories assaulted her in a rush—her

parents' death and funeral; her journeys across Europe and Asia, learning, experiencing; that mountainside in Nepal, shunned by the monastery yet never, ever turning her back or giving up in her efforts to get inside.

Then she gulped in a breath and smelled the rank office. From behind the door, Bullington mumbled to himself.

Indigo pushed the door open.

The lawyer turned, crouched, and fired his gun twice.

She flinched, although there was no need. The bullets were swallowed by the night she brought with her. Perhaps somewhere infinitely far away they continued to travel, piercing a darkness never intended for the likes of humankind . . . but they did not touch *her*.

She flowed across the room, snatching the gun from Bullington's hand and knocking him aside. In the far corner she plucked open a fuse box and tore out several fuses. Beside the box was a burglar alarm. She quickly disabled it.

She turned around and saw Bullington struggling for the door. He tripped in his own mess, sprawling in an avalanche of musty fast-food wrappers and faded papers. Indigo was on him in a second, and her shadows swallowed his screams.

"You know who I am."

Bullington squirmed beneath her, head twisted to one side and eyes squeezed closed. He had to have heard of Indigo. If he was involved with the Children, he would be all too aware of the things she'd done. Maybe he had been expecting this meeting for some time. If that was the case, she saw no reason to disappoint him.

She breathed in deeply, then out again slowly. As she exhaled, the darkness spread, enveloping the writhing, petrified man, drowning him in eternal black nothing.

Indigo kept it that way for a few breaths, then stood and stepped back, taking the shadows with her.

Bullington scrambled to his feet and staggered away, gasping, sobbing like a child. He stumbled against his desk, trying not to take his eyes off the shadow-clad figure before him. She denied the sunlight slanting through broken blinds on his windows. If the sad room had contained any shred of hope or optimism, she would have swallowed it all.

"The Children of Phonos. I need to find them."

Bullington's eyes went wide. He shook his head and drooled.

"You're afraid of them?"

He nodded.

"Scared of what they'll do to you if you tell me about them?"

The nodding became more enthusiastic.

"Imagine what *I'll* do to you if you don't." The threat hung in the air, working on the lawyer as he fought to catch his breath. He slumped slowly onto the desk, deflating, his shoulders shaking as he silently sobbed.

Indigo flowed forward and slapped him, rocking his head to one side. She ran her hand behind his ear, then turned his head in the other direction, checking that ear, too. There were no sigils, no signs of the cult.

"You think they'd welcome me?" he whispered. All his defiance was gone. Now he only sounded sad and pathetic.

"Tell me what they're doing."

"Or what?"

"Or I'll show you the darkness again and leave you there."

He breathed heavily, weighing options. He was not brave. "Another sacrifice. Three victims this time."

"I don't believe you."

Bullington shrugged.

"Why three? And where?"

He stared directly at her, and for the first time she felt some grudging respect. Few people could gaze into such darkness without seeing all their own ugliness glaring back.

"Castle Hill. A warehouse on the point."

She nodded and started to turn, thinking, her mind racing forward to the horrors the cultists were planning. "Do they already have the children they need for the ritual?"

Only in the last instant did she realize her mistake. He could stare at her like that, no longer fearing for his life and sanity, because he had nothing left to live for. He'd already decided on that.

Bullington shoved himself back across his desk, pivoted, and leaped at the nearest window. The blinds broke, the window smashed.

Indigo reached out with a tendril of shadows and missed grabbing hold of his flailing foot by inches. As she heard the impact from below, the squealing brakes, the screams, she gathered herself and probed outward for a safe place.

As ever, the shadows took her there.

3

——

*S*afe was relative.

The shadows deposited Indigo in an alley behind her own building, where two guys were arguing over money. One of them had a gun. She felt it more than she saw it, a concentrated heaviness in the darkness, a weight hanging on the man's belt—where the firearm's cold metal had grown warm against his belly. She wondered if he'd yelped when he jammed it there in the first place, cold steel connecting with skin. She wondered if he'd felt stupid for the uncomfortable macho gesture.

She wondered, but she didn't care. And she didn't intervene.

Indigo had bigger problems than two day-drunk assholes with a gambling disagreement; she had a cult with plans to take three more children and perform three more sacrifices, probably sooner rather than later. She withdrew again, dragging the early-morning shadows fast behind her—and leaving a chilly breeze in her wake.

The men stopped arguing and shivered. Nervously, they glanced back and forth, from corner to corner—and agreed with bobbing heads that, yes, they could finish the conversation someplace else.

Good, Indigo thought as she retreated farther into the alley's piss-smelling depths. *Go argue under someone else's window.*

She debated her options, but she debated them swiftly. If the Children of Phonos hadn't already gathered their intended sacrifices, it wouldn't take them long to scare up another victim, or two, or three.

With this unhappy thought in mind, she closed her eyes. With a quick twist of the gloom, she arrived home, de-cloaking with speed enough to scatter the Assholes.

"Sorry, guys," she mumbled to the cats, jerking herself free of the murk and letting it evaporate. Gossamer tendrils of the unreal stuff floated ceiling-ward, reeled backward, and coiled in the corners. A small wisp clung to her ankle. She kicked it loose and staggered into the living area, feeling shaky and short of breath . . . feeling as if she'd awakened too fast from a dream that was too awful to recall.

But that was ridiculous, because the shifting darkness was something more profound than a friend or a partner. It was an extension of herself, a projection of her own mind, and her own intentions—a power learned with years of effort and discipline, guided by the monks on the mountain.

Wasn't it? She probed the memory, feeling its edges like a tongue exploring a spot where a tooth ought to be. Yes, there it was. The snow. The wolves. The mountain. The heavy doors that had swung open at long last, to let her inside. She was the master of this power, and not its slave.

So why did she eye the edges of her apartment with such suspicion? Why did she feel queasy as Nora, when as Indigo she felt all-powerful?

She shook off the gummy feeling between her ears and grabbed her laptop—flipping it open so fast that the screen wobbled on its hinge. She beat the keyboard with her fingers, willing the stupid old device to boot faster, and wishing she had access to all the necessary databases on her phone—which was much newer and smarter.

But wishing wouldn't put a new MacBook on her coffee table, and it wouldn't pull some hapless kid's ass out of the fire before the Phonoi struck a match.

Finally the screen flared to life, and then Nora's keyboard strokes became more focused. First she opened NamUs.gov, because she might get lucky. If she could nail down a missing victim without calling in any favors, then so much the better. She refined her search and scrolled as fast as she dared, but the sheer volume of missing young people turned her stomach, and there had been no relevant new additions in the last couple of days.

Of course, NamUs wasn't always swift to update; they were good about making sure all the listed cases were verified. It was helpful for weeding out false positives, but a pain in the ass if you wanted to find someone who'd gone missing quite recently.

What about the cops, then? They'd notice anyone missing or endangered before the national database got wind of anything. But she sure as hell wasn't going to contact Mayhew, the lead detective on these child murders. Not when the woman's incompetence had made the criminal case against the Newells unwinnable.

Nora's pass code for the precinct's caseload log-in wasn't working, so either someone was onto her or someone had jiggered the settings. The two possibilities were equally likely. She'd score another log-in in a few days, but the Children of Phonos wouldn't wait that long, so she couldn't, either.

Good thing she knew a cop in the right department and he owed her.

It was also a good thing that Harry Beale worked early. She scanned the contacts on her phone, tapped to call him, and dove right in.

"Harry, I need a lead on a missing person. Probably a kid. Probably taken in the last twenty-four hours. Maybe less than that."

After some hemming and hawing, Harry admitted that she'd have to be more specific. "We've got seven new ones on deck since yesterday afternoon."

"Seven?" Nora felt sick.

"Busy night."

"All of them minors?"

"Five of them are."

"Can you run them down real quick? Brief descriptions?"

"Two gangbangers, one probably dead, one probably in hiding— if you ask me. One girl who might be a runaway—she has a history of that sort of thing, so it wouldn't be the first time. The other two are boys—neither with any known gang affiliations or behavioral problems. None on record, as far as I can tell."

Nora chewed on her thumbnail and tapped her boot on the coffee-table leg. "The two boys, where were they last seen?"

"One of them at school," Harry said vaguely. Maybe he didn't have the particulars right in front of him, or maybe the report was incomplete. "The other one . . . his friends said he'd been down by the Whitestone Bridge on his skateboard."

She popped her nail out of her mouth. "That one!"

"What's he to you?"

The bridge was close to Castle Point, and the boy could've been a grab of opportunity. It wasn't much to go on, so she didn't share it with Harry, who was probably still on his first cup of coffee—and surely didn't care about the answer. All she said was "I've got a feeling, that's all. Working an angle on something I've been poking into. What's his name?"

The cop sighed. He probably wasn't supposed to tell her, but that wouldn't stop him. She wouldn't let it. "Luis Gallardo. Age sixteen.

No record, no history of truancy or petty crime. Reported missing yesterday afternoon, when he didn't come home for dinner."

"Gallardo. Sixteen. Whitestone Bridge. Got it. Thanks." She almost closed by saying she owed him one, except she wasn't sure it was true. Luis might not be the next victim, and even if her gut was right and he was the kid in question . . . then Indigo might not be able to save him.

She hung up fast and checked her phone before stuffing it into her pocket. It was quarter to eight in the morning. The shadows would be long and sharp, but shallow in the Bronx. They would carry her anyway.

She glanced at the nearest patch, one studiously avoided by all three cats—a dark place between the refrigerator and the undersize cupboard that served as a pantry. Her throat was dry. She swallowed. It didn't help.

Indigo was raring to go, but Nora was afraid.

"This is stupid," she declared to herself and the cats. She rose to her feet and rolled her neck from left to right—cracking it loudly. "It's time to get to work," she announced, but she didn't move. Her boots were stuck to the floor. A lump was stuck in her throat. The shadow was stuck to the wall, to the cheap vinyl, to the side of the refrigerator.

"Luis is counting on me," she whispered.

And if it wasn't Luis, it was someone else who needed her help just as badly. Several someones, if Bullington's intel was good.

Steeling herself with this certainty, she took two long steps and slipped into the blackness that pooled in the kitchenette. It swallowed her whole and the world went dim. Then it went cool, and comfortable.

Indigo was back, and Indigo wasn't afraid.

Indigo was in charge.

Her strength had returned, and her confidence along with it—as she moved through the margins of the world, ducking in and out of the crevices no one but her ever noticed.

Neither Nora nor Indigo knew the Castle Hill area of the Bronx well, so she hopscotched a few blocks at a time—popping out of a doorway here and emerging from an underpass there, getting her bearings.

She rolled out from under a stationary cargo car in the railyard, then tumbled underneath one parked beside it, only to hesitate in the murk, trying to remember how this end of the city was shaped. When she thought of the bridge, she mostly though of the toll lines, and the long metal cables that stretched toward the sky; she had to think of it another way, from underneath—where the skater kids ground their boards on the cement and scraped their wheels along the curbs.

Was she close enough to touch it with her powers? She shut her eyes and used the billowing dark to feel around—the tentacles of gloom working like fingers, prying apart the nooks and crannies until she found what she was looking for.

There.

A smooth place, where three young people huddled together and whispered about a friend nobody'd seen in too many hours.

She sighed, exhaled, and clung to a dark place behind a jumbled pile of concrete dividers discarded by the city. They made a crude stack with thick shadows, thick enough to let Indigo hide and watch, and listen, and draw her conclusions.

Two girls and a boy. None of them older than eighteen, and all of them still awake from the night before. They'd been scouring the streets looking for Luis, so they were way ahead of her—except they didn't know there was a cult, and a warehouse, and a place where Luis or someone very much like him would certainly die before long, if Indigo couldn't find him first.

She darted away again, letting the shadows whisk her to the old sanitation plant. She hid herself in the gloom of its thick brick walls and the spires of its three spindly towers—then she found an alley behind an apartment block. She had to find the Children of Phonos, but she had so little to go on . . . a warehouse on the point, somewhere in Castle Hill. If Bullington's last words could even be believed.

There wasn't much industrial work in the area anymore, but she knew of a few old places along Zerega Avenue, beside Westchester Creek. She'd find warehouses there. A handful of them, maybe more. Her phone said it was almost eight thirty, so workers would be arriving for their jobs.

The blocks should be bustling. It might not be easy to hide.

Trial and error brought her to a makeshift fort made of shipping containers—all of them empty and reeking of rust. Indigo wrapped herself in the darkness there, cocooning herself from head to toe in its protective bubble . . . and she watched.

Mostly men came and went from the two businesses in her immediate line of sight. They wore jeans and light jackets and carried lunch pails or sacks. They cast away cigarettes, throwing them into the dew-damp grass by the door before going inside to work.

Nothing suspicious, and nothing abandoned.

Up on the nearest warehouse roof, a water tower offered enough shade to carry her, and to give her a better vantage point. She gulped at the height, then calmed herself and climbed to the edge in full view of anyone who might've looked up into the morning light.

No one did.

None of the drones who trudged to work, none of their bosses who exited cars while chattering on cell phones, toting their hard hats. None of the heavy-equipment operators, warming up their machines and sparking up cigarettes to warm their hands. Not even the stray dogs, sniffing at the edges of the properties—scavenging for discarded crusts and apple cores. No one looked up, while Indigo surveyed the district. No one noticed her on the roof's edge, leaning over like a gargoyle and watching the world wake up.

One by one, she dismissed the larger buildings as they bustled to life. But farther down the queue—beyond the edge of her vision—were several others. She crouched down and pulled the shadows over her head like a blanket.

Two blocks down, she found another shipping container. They were ubiquitous, empty and decaying, all corroded edges and jagged sheet metal. They couldn't hurt her. Not while she wore the shadows for armor and peered through a hole in the rust that was big enough to crawl through.

She wrinkled her nose. The container smelled like pennies at the bottom of a well.

In her new line of sight was another working factory with the usual staff of bored-looking people in blue-collar clothes, and a warehouse in the midst of being converted to loft spaces. At the warehouse, a fleet of construction workers arrived in pickup trucks, and foremen strolled around with blueprints tucked under their arms.

Then, out of the corner of her eye, Indigo saw a flash of red.

Not the brownish red of the rust around her, and not a bloodred or an orangey crimson. It was more like a proper high-class scarlet, and it stood out like a sore thumb in this world of gray scale, denim, and mud with a smattering of yellow hard hats.

She craned her neck to get a better look, then spied a big-rig trailer much closer to the object of her interest, about fifty yards away. She breathed into the darkness, and it took her like smoke, draping her and moving her, giving her permission to slip through the yard unseen—and into the spot beside the truck, where the morning light couldn't quite reach.

Her feet squished in mud and God knew what else, but she

didn't flinch. She hunkered down and followed with her eyes as the swatch of red walked past.

The splash of red was a dress—expensive, made of linen or raw silk, Indigo couldn't tell from where she was hiding. It was tea-length with three-quarter sleeves. A church dress . . . the thought flickered through her head. Yes, a church dress. Somebody's costly Sunday best.

The woman was walking away, showing a narrow backside and seams on her stockings. Her heels sank into the gravel and mud, but she hauled them out and kept going toward firmer ground. A gravel path turned into a sidewalk. A sidewalk led into a blocky old building so dull, so outstandingly ordinary, that it was almost invisible.

Indigo shook her head and blinked hard to clear her eyes. It might be magic, or it might be the clouded sensibility of a city woman, all too accustomed to sights like this one. But she didn't think so.

Another woman, equally well dressed, joined the lady in red on the sidewalk. This one wore a cream-colored suit, a hat with a tasteful white feather, and knee-high boots made of leather so soft that it clung to her calves and stretched gently with every step.

Then a man came along. His suit was a shade of blue just too light to call navy, and the heels of his shiny dress shoes clicked happily on the concrete.

A Lexus pulled up, its chrome details sparkling, and its dark gray finish slicker than oil. Four people got out, a black couple and two white women. A BMW pulled up beside it, wheels grinding in the half-paved surface of the lot that was swiftly filling up with gleaming late-model luxury cars.

Under her breath, where only the darkness could hear her, Nora whispered, "Found you."

Except that she hadn't found Luis Gallardo—she'd found a bunch of fancy people dressed for a service of some kind. But this was no church, and these were no benign parishioners bound for a potluck. These were the New York chapter of the Children of Phonos. Indigo knew it in her soul.

The warehouse's windows were covered with a light, filmy fabric or paper that let only shapes and motion show through—but she detected a number of figures drifting back and forth inside. It was hard to say how many people were already present for whatever ceremony the cultists were cooking up, but it didn't matter. She could handle them. All of them, and with great prejudice. The time for caution and leniency had damn well passed.

Nora might've hesitated, but Indigo was finished with whatever mental bullshit had kept her from wiping them off the face of the earth when she'd had the chance.

Well, here was another chance.

She sensed them as she crept closer; she heard a low hum of chatter and song . . . chanting, she thought. People chanted in church, didn't they? This congregation was no different, not in that one small way. They were all dressed for the occasion, too—high heels, high style, and high-end everything, even though they gathered at a warehouse that no one would've looked at twice. Not even someone who was looking for it.

The place was shielded somehow, with some spell that kept it from standing out in any way, or looking like anyone's obvious destination. Indigo frowned. The cult dabbled in black magic, ritual sacrifice, that sort of thing, and she was well aware that this group was only one chapter, but she'd never sensed this sort of real magic around them before. Through the shadows around her she could practically feel the magic vibrating, burning with its own dark power. This wasn't bullshit dabbling—this was sorcery. It occurred to her that other chapters of the Phonoi might be more advanced with their magic, but to her—from this group—this was new.

Two more cars pulled up in the lot, for a total of sixteen by Indigo's count. Dozens of people could be inside.

Dozens of happy worshippers, and one miserable victim. *Three victims*, Bullington had said. *Three at once. So Luis isn't likely to be in there alone.*

But his was the name she knew, and she kept it in mind because she didn't know his face. She hadn't thought to look up a photo. She imagined him a thin kid if he was the skating type. Puerto Rican, if he was local to the neighborhood—or that was as good a guess as any. Lost and trapped among people who would do to him . . . the kinds of things they'd done to others before.

But not again.

Indigo raged, and smoky tendrils clung to her tighter than perfume, a black cloud that sought out cracks and overhangs, stairwells and closets and unused rooms sealed shut in a building so unremarkable that no one had even condemned it yet.

She squeezed the darkness and told it where to go—somewhere quiet, somewhere safe. She stretched and felt for some crevice and found it behind a door in an empty office. With a flick of the morning shadow, fast and thick, she took a deep, furious breath.

She emerged inside.

She exhaled and winced.

It was louder here, where all the voices mingled into a weird soup of conversation. Her ears rang, and it was so hard to make out the words—but they sounded eager, and excited. Somewhere, a huge door clanged shut. Indigo thought of the monastery, with its huge doors. *Wood, with metal rivets and hinges. Oh, how they creaked on those hinges.*

She shook the thought away. It went easily, slipping out of her attention—as if its appearance had been perfunctory, and not some sweet function of nostalgia.

There was no time for any reverie, much less nostalgia. All the faithful were assembled; that was what the door meant when it clanged like that. No one else would be allowed in, and no one wanted out except for the kids who never asked to be there in the first place.

She slinked around the door, holding the gloom tight around her and praying it would hide her. She wasn't praying to anyone in particular. She never prayed to anyone in particular. Except . . . whom had the monks prayed to? She couldn't remember. Buddhists, they must've been. Something like that? She'd studied with them for years, so why couldn't she remember? What a stupid thing to forget.

Let it go, she commanded herself. It wasn't important. Luis was important. Wiping the Children of Phonos off the face of the earth, *that* was important. Nothing else.

Closer she came, drawn by the voices now hushed, now quivering with excitement. She flowed toward them, as near as she dared. Soon, only a thin corridor wall separated her from the cultists and their shuffling feet, their giddy whispers.

She reached her senses out through the shadows and felt the shape of the room where they had gathered—a large, open space with a loft above, overlooking the warehouse floor. Easing into darkness, she rose upward, pushed herself through the unseen spaces until she emerged high overhead. She perched on an oversize I-beam and glowered down at the ceremony about to begin.

The Phonoi were dressed too fancy for folding metal chairs, but they sat upon them anyway, in three shallow rows—twenty-five eager believers by Indigo's count—all facing an empty lectern in front of a table covered with a black cloth.

Footsteps rang out, amplified by the cavernous space and the poured-cement floors, gritty with dust and grime. Along with the footsteps came a tall woman wearing white.

Her dress was not quite frilly enough to be called a gown, Indigo could see that. Her shoes were white, glistening patent leather that cost a month of Nora's rent. Hell, the woman's hair was nearly white—that washed-out blond sometimes called platinum until an old lady wears it, and then you call it silver.

The woman stepped up to the lectern with a burgundy-lipstick smile.

No one fidgeted anymore. No feet tapped, and no one even cleared a throat or cracked a knuckle.

This had to be the high priestess, or so Indigo concluded. She wasn't fully versed in the hierarchy of the cult and its clandestine ways, but what else would you call a woman like that? She'd hushed a crowd with only a smile and a lectern. She was deaconess, not acolyte. She was power, and that power was as dark as her clothing was bright.

"Ladies and gentlemen," the priestess purred. Her voice was unexpectedly low. It sounded educated and confident, with a whiff of money around the edges. "I'm so glad you all could be here. We need everyone's support."

Indigo's first impulse was to leap down off the I-beam like freaking Batman and smash the woman to the ground. She restrained herself, but barely. Come to think of it, hadn't Batman developed his ninja-style skills at a monastery, too?

She rubbed her eyes and rolled her shoulders, forcing herself to concentrate on the scene below.

"I regret to confirm what most of you have suspected—our previous efforts were met with failure. Not *perfect* failure," she corrected, raising one finely manicured finger. "For we are absolutely making progress. The demon is awakening, and remembering himself. He will rise to join us soon, but we must show him the way. Not in a single ceremony, brief and rushed as we've tried before. No, not like that."

The faithful bowed their heads and murmured fervent agreement.

"He will take his rightful place, and we will help him. We will serve him." She reached back to the table behind her and seized the black cloth by a corner—yanking it free.

Indigo gritted her teeth to keep from gasping. The cloth didn't cover a table at all—it concealed a large box, some kind of shipping crate by the looks of it. Inside the crate, bleeding and bound, was a naked boy. Cuts crisscrossed his skin in whorls and lines, but if they were letters or signs, she couldn't read them from so far away. She watched him long enough to tell that he was breathing.

He *was* breathing. It *wasn't* her imagination. She *had* made it in time.

She trembled with anger, crushing her hands into fists so hard that her nails left gouges in her palms.

The priestess gazed down at the boy with a look that was positively fawning, for all that she must've been the one who did this to him. "All hail and bless the first of three, this bleeding gift."

The first of three, Indigo thought. Did that mean they hadn't taken the other two sacrifices yet, or only that they weren't to be executed today?

"All praise to our great Father, whom we would see freed from his prison and loosed upon the world. We will finish what began a dozen years ago. We will atone for our failings."

"The hell you will," Indigo growled, just loud enough that a few of the seated worshippers caught her words.

She drew the shadows together until they were dense and heavy, and she shaped them into something like a shield, thick enough to crush. Solid enough to kill.

She shoved it off the beam—plummeting down behind it.

Three or four of the Phonoi looked up in time to see the thunderous black circle fall from the ceiling and crash through the assembly. The weight of the shadows and the velocity of Indigo's temper crushed three cultists on impact and badly injured another. She felt their bones shatter, and she heard their skulls pop and leak.

It happened fast, but it happened loud. Two more victims strayed within easy reach, too stunned to run, too blinded by panic to save themselves.

This time Indigo molded the darkness into a blade, something long enough to touch them and sharp enough to slice them into ribbons. She pivoted, and she whirled. Her shadow sword swung hard. It stabbed deep.

From somewhere, a shot rang out. It missed by a mile, but the cultists were rallying a defense, or at least a hasty retreat.

Indigo drew the gloom around herself for cover, burying herself in its comforting buffer.

Now those who remained could not see her. They could not touch her. Their guns would not help them in the slightest.

Squeezing the murk in her fists, Indigo formed arrowheads with edges like razors . . . and hurled them with the force of bullets. The arrows pierced everything they hit, bursting through eye sockets and blowing through torsos, leaving gaping wounds and twitching corpses in their wake.

The violence made her want to scream, half in horror and half in relief. Rage burned inside her, fury directed inward, so angry with herself for the innocent lives that had been taken by these people because she had been afraid to destroy them before now. Afraid to unleash the dark and let the shadows have their way.

The remaining Phonoi scrambled blindly in any direction that might save them. More shots rang out, but the clips were soon emptied and the guns went silent. Not so the cultists, who screamed and cried as they searched for a way out.

Any way out.

Indigo cut them off, one exit at a time.

She stretched the darkness harder, farther, rolled it into a terrible tendril and wielded it like a whip. The whip was good for snatching and strangling, but choking took too much time. It was much faster to seize them by the throat and break their necks with a yank, then toss them aside and move on.

She cut them all down in turn—with her deadly whip, a spray of arrows, or the swing of a sword made from blackness as solid as stone. She killed them efficiently, and creatively, and entirely without mercy.

Mercy had never gotten her anywhere. Mercy had gotten several young people tortured and killed, so there was no more room for it. There was only room for Indigo—angel of death, knight of New York City. Guardian. Sentry.

Not a single one of these assholes was leaving alive.

She worked her way around the room, picking up stragglers as they cowered and fumbled for the doors. One man in an Armani suit flung himself through a window. The jagged glass took care of him before Indigo could reach him. He lay in the gravel against the warehouse, one foot hanging on the shattered frame.

Armani Man was not the last. Half a dozen others scuttled weakly, hurt and terrified, away from the inky, deadly vortex.

Indigo rode it like a whirlwind. She picked them off and scanned the space for anyone else—*everyone* else. Luis would never be safe until they were all wiped out, or if it wasn't Luis in the box, then whoever the child was—and whoever the next child would be.

The Children of Phonos had to go. Every single one of them. This chapter would only be the beginning.

When the room was finally silent, except for the dribbling bubbles of crushed lungs and spraying arteries, Indigo reined the shadows in—drawing them closer, making herself smaller within the cavernous room with its terrible echoes.

The high priestess had left her lectern, and she'd abandoned the boy in the box. He was now half-covered by the black cloth. It tangled damply around his legs, where his blood had glued it to his skin.

Indigo gazed around the room.

The woman in white was running toward the corridor.

Indigo swallowed her up with the shadows, dragging her back, immobilizing her, paralyzing her with pressure and darkness, but not yet killing her. This dark prison bought Indigo time to check on the boy, who was still breathing, wasn't he?

Wasn't he?

She pulled him gently into her sphere, and she gave him plenty of air, plenty of comfort and warmth. He shuddered when she touched him, even as she used the black shroud to swaddle him like a baby in a blanket.

"Hang in there, kid. Hang in there. I'm going to get you out of here."

The priestess gargled some objection, but Indigo ignored it.

"Luis?" She ran a hand across his forehead. "Can you hear me?"

The boy was dead, from fright or from blood loss, she did not know.

Indigo gulped down a cry and let the boy's body drop back into the crate, free of the shadow. She turned her attention to the priestess, who was on the brink of death herself. The woman writhed, her white hair and clothing a pale silhouette in the angry gloom, but Indigo had no pity left to waste on her. She loosened her grip enough to let the woman remain alive, and not enough to give her any real relief.

Looming above the struggling priestess, all Indigo's horror and anger made manifest in the shadows she wore like a halo . . . she let her grief and her guilt do the talking.

"Why?" she demanded. "Why these children?"

"Because . . . of . . . *you*," squeaked the priestess.

Indigo snorted and bore down hard—pushing with all the weight of her misery, and hoping that it hurt like hell. "For me? What the hell is that supposed to mean?"

The priestess tried to reply, but she was fading.

Indigo withdrew and let her speak.

The priestess gasped and gulped. "You mustn't hate us . . . ," she whispered hoarsely. "You . . . your mother . . . if it'd happened right the first time . . ." Her words were sandpaper on stone. Her larynx was crushed, and her time was nearly up. "None of these children . . . would've been necessary."

"What about my mother?" Indigo shouted. She didn't mean to. It felt too much like giving something away.

The dying priestess said, in a single rattling breath, "It should've been . . . you."

"Liar!" Indigo shouted, and shook her—trying to wring another breath out of her, another word. "Liar!" she cried again, when the priestess's head lolled back and her eyes went blank. "You don't know anything about me . . . or my mother!"

Indigo shook harder, but her murderous rampage had been too successful. The priestess was dead. *And so what?* Indigo thought with disgust—and more than a little desperation—as she dropped the corpse.

The bitch was lying. Obviously.

Except . . .

Indigo sent the shadows away and stood there, in the midst of the carnage.

Nora stood alone and wrapped her arms around herself. She surveyed the oozing bodies, the splayed limbs, the scattered cultists in their ruined churchgoing finery. She kicked at a stray shoe with a broken heel. It skittered across the concrete and stopped against a man's thigh.

She tried to picture her mother, but she recalled her uncle Theo instead, vaguely, without details. A man in a car, waiting while someone else spoke cryptically beneath a tree. Was his hair black? Blond? Gray?

Again she thought of her mother, or she tried to. She strained to recall anything at all. A birthday party. A breakfast. A sleepover with friends. She could summon nothing precise—nothing that wouldn't make a lazy background for a low-budget sitcom on a third-tier network. Here was a ticket to the school's Christmas play, in which Nora was North Pole Elf #2. There was a case of chicken pox. And they'd gone to Disneyland that one time, and Nora got to meet Mickey and got her picture taken holding his big white hand.

So where was the picture? And where was her mother, that missing ghost in the background of every mental snapshot?

For that matter . . . "What about my dad?"

Matt, she thought. Uncle Theo had called her dad Matt.

Nora didn't remember her mother's name.

From every corner, down every corridor, inside every closed, locked room in the warehouse, the shadows answered her with a fierce, unpleasant tugging that yanked at her soul. When she listened hard, she thought she heard them moving.

No. When she listened hard, she thought she heard them laughing.

4

———

Shadows swirled along the edge of the sidewalk, and Nora swore they were whispering, wondering why she didn't embrace them or, at the very least, let them carry her home. She had wandered the city most of the day, burning off anxious energy instead of going home and succumbing to exhaustion. The shadows had nudged and tugged at her all afternoon, and now that evening had arrived they were growing stronger, urging her homeward. But she didn't want the shadows right now. Didn't want the easy way home. It was all she could do to keep her pace measured and not break into a run, racing along the empty streets, racing to . . .

She didn't know. But she walked until she saw the yellow beacon of a cab and then she hailed it, even as the ebon tendrils twisted around her feet, more urgent now, promising a faster, safer ride. She climbed into the car anyway and gave the driver an address, and even then she paid little attention to what she was saying. She actually thought she'd told the driver to take her home, until he pulled up in front of a building that wasn't hers.

"This isn't—" She stopped herself. She let out a soft sigh of relief, as if the shadows themselves had deposited her here, exactly where she wanted to be right now.

She paid the driver. Overpaid him, shoving money his way and saying, "That's fine," and ignoring his effusive thanks. She hurried to the door and caught it behind another resident, one who'd clearly had a good night—too good to notice her grabbing the door before it closed behind him.

She took the stairs because the elevator would surely be too slow. She flew up the flights and then down the hall and—

And that's when she stopped. Outside the apartment door, her hand raised to knock.

It's late. Do you even know how late it is?

She checked her watch and started, surprised at the hour. Still, she didn't retreat. She hovered there, wanting to knock, not hard, not enough to wake anyone. She glanced down the hall, then back at the door. Her knuckles rapped softly—barely a whisper—before she had time to change her mind. No, this was wrong, it was too late and she was only upset. There was no good reason to inflict her woes on anyone else. She ought to turn around, walk away, and let the shadows carry her home.

She started down the hall, feet dragging, like a child being hauled off for discipline by an exasperated parent.

A lock clicked behind her. She heard the soft whoosh of a door opening.

"Nora?"

She glanced over her shoulder. Sam stepped into the hall. His hair was brushed back, bits standing up at odd angles, as if he had been fighting off sleep while he worked. He smiled at her, a genuine smile that brushed away the day, just for a moment.

"I thought I heard someone out here," he said as she returned slowly to his door. "But I didn't hear you knock."

"I'm sorry . . . sorry about lunch. I know I said I would . . . I shouldn't . . ."

"I texted you half a dozen times," he said, more concerned that admonishing. "You had me worried, Nora."

She glanced back down the hall where the shadows stretched from the corners, urging her to join them.

Don't bring him into this, they seemed to be saying. *Don't take the chance. Come to us. We'll get you home. We'll take care of you.*

It was over. The Children of Phonos were done in New York. Eventually others would come and try to reestablish the chapter here, but for now—for a while, at least—they were done. Dead. No more black magic. No more human fucking sacrifices.

It was a win, right?

Sure as hell didn't feel like one.

She looked back at Sam.

He was moving toward her, his face drawn tight with worry. "Nora, hey. Seriously, are you okay?"

"I . . ." She exhaled. "Long day. And I really am sorry I stood you up. I shouldn't have just turned up like this."

"No, you absolutely should have." He steered her toward his apartment. "You look like you were out chasing a story. Did something happen?"

Did something happen. She bit through her cheek not to laugh. *No, not much, really. I found a boy about to be sacrificed. I couldn't save him. I tried, but I couldn't. Then Indigo killed . . .*

Indigo killed? No, *Nora* killed. She was Indigo, and as much as she might like to blame the events of the day on some separate part of her, she couldn't start down that path or else she'd never stop, and every terrible thing she did as Indigo would be justified. Because it wasn't really *her.*

Except that it *was* her. It was always her.

And it *was* justified, wasn't it? When she thought of those people, and what they tried to do—what they would've done again—she knew she'd done the right thing. So why did she feel sick every time she thought about it?

Because you're weak.

She tensed at that, startled by the venom in the words—and wondering where, exactly, they'd come from.

"Nora?" Sam said.

She'd barely been aware of his ushering her inside his apartment, and now she blinked, looking around at the living room. Numb and confused, she lowered herself onto the sofa. Sam disappeared and returned with a bottle of red wine in one hand and a fifth of Scotch in the other.

He hefted the wine. "It's left over from the last time you were here. I'm not sure if it's still good or . . ." He shrugged. "I'm not really a wine guy."

He wasn't really a Scotch guy either, as evidenced by the faint layer of dust on the bottle. It'd probably been a gift.

Beer was more Sam's style, and he didn't drink much of that either—but he knew it wasn't her thing, so he'd dug up these alternatives. He'd done a good job. It settled her nerves a little, the comfort of the familiar, of being with someone who knew her.

Even though she hardly knew herself anymore.

She pointed at the Scotch.

"On the rocks, right?"

She stretched her memory and recalled that they'd once had Scotch at a party, and, yes, she'd taken it on the rocks. He'd remembered a distant, onetime event. God, he really was too good for her. "Please," she begged.

He disappeared to get some ice, and she made herself comfortable. *Just breathe in and out.* She was safe now.

Only home is safe.

She ignored the inner warning. It was time to relax with someone she knew, someone from her "real" life. She needed to be Nora again and forget the priestess's words.

"You . . . your mother . . . if it'd happened right the first time . . ."

She shook her head sharply and murmured, "That's not *forgetting*."

"Hmm?" Sam said as he came in with the glasses.

"Muttering to myself. First sign of old age."

He handed her the glass and plopped down beside her on the couch. "More like the first sign of a really long day. You want to talk about it?"

She shook her head and sipped the Scotch.

He didn't press. He knew she wasn't the type who'd say no but only to be polite when she really wanted him to drag it out of her. Nora didn't play those games. Except tonight . . .

Tonight wasn't about "being polite" and not wanting to burden him. Tonight she desperately *did* want to talk, to pour it all out and work through it with someone, and the someone most likely to understand was sitting right beside her, waiting.

No. She couldn't do that. She could *never* do that.

She gulped the Scotch, not even realizing what she'd done until the burn hit and she sputtered.

He laughed, then quickly sobered. "Whatever happened . . . if it's that bad . . . I don't want to push, but . . ."

She drained the last few drops. "Then don't. Let's talk about something else."

"I can do that, too." His arm slipped around her shoulders . . . carefully, in case it wasn't welcome. But when she collapsed against his side, he tugged her closer.

She settled in there, feeling the heat of his body and smelling the faint scent of his soap. She couldn't identify the spicy fragrance and didn't want to, because to her, it was just *him*, his smell, that familiar scent that made her think of his bed.

And damn, that sounded good right about now. The perfect distraction.

Sam was saying something, but she'd missed it. She gave her head a sharp shake and asked, "What was that?"

"You wanted to talk about something else?"

Well, no, actually, now that she thought of it, something far more enticing than talking was on her mind. . . . She slid her hand toward his leg, but before her fingers touched down, she heard the word "Indigo."

She stopped cold. "What?"

"I *said*, there's been another Indigo report. I found an online post by an anonymous officer saying Indigo was spotted—"

"I don't want to talk about Indigo." She meant for the words to come casually, even softly, but they came rough, even harsh.

Sam's arm loosened around her shoulders. "Okay . . . I just thought—"

"You thought wrong," she snapped.

Jesus, Nora, take it down a notch. Or ten.

She struggled to say something else, make some excuse for her outburst, but she couldn't form the words. She fought against a roiling anger in her gut that said she didn't need to apologize, that he should know she hated this subject.

Except she didn't hate it. She'd always liked hearing him talk about Indigo, batting around theories with him.

Well, that was her first mistake. Sloppy. Careless. Dangerous. She needed to fix that now. Slap him down hard, so he'd never bring up Indigo again.

"If you want to talk about something else . . . ," he said cautiously.

"No, damn it. I don't want to talk. Isn't that obvious?" *What the hell? Stop biting his head off.* "If I wanted to talk, I would have gone to see Shelby. I came to you. Which means that what I want"—

she put her hand on his thigh as she twisted to face him—"isn't talk."

He picked up her hand and moved it away, his voice cooling. "I understand you had a rough day, Nora, but—"

"No, you don't understand at all. Or you wouldn't be trying to *talk* to me. I don't come to you for fine conversation, Sam."

What the hell am I saying? Stop. Just stop.

But she couldn't. It was as if she were standing outside the door banging to be let in as she listened to herself berate and insult him.

"All right." He stood, his voice icy. "I think we'd better end this evening right about now. I'm going to give you a ride home—"

"Not really the ride I'm looking for." She got to her feet. "Don't act so shocked, Sam. Isn't this what we do? We have sex. That's it. So don't act like you're insulted that I came over here for exactly that. It's what you usually want from me, and tonight, it's what I want from you."

She reached out, and he caught her by the wrists. "Okay, this is more than a bad day. Where were you, Nora? Did you go anywhere that someone could have slipped something into your drink or—"

She cut him off with a harsh laugh. "You think I was roofied? Why? Because I'm being honest for once? Honest about what we have and about what I want?"

His mouth tightened. "This is not what we have."

"Could have fooled me. Once upon a time we pretended it was something else, but these days I'm pretty sure that every time we get together, we end up in bed. Sure, we talk, but that's just the preamble. Pretending we're friends so we don't feel skeezy about the whole thing. Tonight, I'm cutting through the bullshit."

She jerked her hands up hard to throw him off, but his grip was too tight, and when he didn't let go, she lashed out—a surge of panic filling her, and she blacked out for a moment, blinded by that panic.

When she recovered, he was on the floor, his hand to his mouth, blood seeping through his fingers.

She moved forward to—to say something, anything. To explain. To apologize. For what she'd done, what she'd said.

Why? That's what you feel. Deep down, it's what you feel.

No, it wasn't. It really wasn't.

She moved forward, but Sam scrambled up and backed away. The look in his eyes, that was the worst of it. Not the anger or confusion or outrage from a few moments ago. This was fear.

No, this was more than fear. This look said he didn't know her, didn't know whom he was looking at, but it sure as hell wasn't Nora.

It was Indigo.

She was Indigo. Nora was Indigo. She'd done this to Sam. She'd said those things to him. No one else was to blame.

Her. All her.

Nora opened her mouth to apologize, and this time it wasn't that something blocked the words. She simply couldn't find any. *Whoops, sorry,* didn't cut it here. Nothing did.

She turned and ran.

Behind her, she heard Sam say, "Hold on!" His feet pounded as he came after her, but she was already flying out the door, and when he called, "Nora! You shouldn't be—" she dove into the welcoming darkness before he could finish.

She imagined him darting into the hallway, mouth agape as he looked both ways, wondering how the hell she'd got down the stairs so fast.

Stupid, she thought. *So stupid.*

The shadows deposited Nora in her apartment. She sat on the cold linoleum, her back against the fridge, knees drawn up. The cats slunk in and circled, not so much concerned as curious. When Hyde nudged her hand, the shadows swirled and all three raced off, hissing.

It's for the best.

Sam knew too much. He was—like the cats—too curious. She was vulnerable right now, and when you put those together, she risked spilling everything to him, and that would endanger not only Nora but Sam himself.

It was better this way. For him. She could protect him by scaring him off. By pushing him firmly out of her life.

Except that wasn't what she wanted. Not at all.

Did it matter what she wanted?

No. It couldn't matter. She had to put others above herself. That was her mission, and it extended to Sam.

Yet all that self-talk didn't help. She was embarrassed and shamed by what she'd done, how she'd treated him. He might deserve her consideration and protection, but he hadn't deserved *that*.

This was the only way.

Wasn't it?

The problem was that now, having fled Sam, she couldn't stop her thoughts from returning to the priestess's words.

Then maybe she should let herself think about that. Focus on that, rather than push it aside and tell herself it was bullshit. Instead, she should *prove* that it was.

But you know it is.

Not good enough. She was a reporter, and she needed more. This was how she'd banish those words from her mind: not by seeking solace with Sam or by chasing him away. No, she would be logical and prove that her memories of her mother—of her life with her family—were exactly as she remembered.

She took her laptop to the kitchen table, opened it, and sat there, staring at the screen.

Start at the easiest point: her parents' murders. Look them up.

If only she could remember her mother's name. What the hell was wrong with her?

Matt, she thought. Matthew Hesper. Matt and . . .

Stella!

Relief washed over her. She'd been afraid that using her powers had begun to erode her memory. Her mother's name . . . that was a huge thing to have forgotten. It wasn't a birthday or an ex-boyfriend's address. But there were so many other fragments of memory now. When she tried to focus on them, they slipped away from her, blurred out of focus. She needed to rebuild them, to confirm them, or risk letting them deteriorate further.

And there was what the priestess had said about her mother. She couldn't let that go unchallenged. The idea that Stella Hesper had anything to do with the Children of Phonos . . .

She poised her fingers over the keys, but hesitated. What exactly would this prove? They'd been murdered. There'd been hundreds of mourners. It obviously happened, so what was she going to do when she found the proof? Tell herself it was good enough, her questions were answered?

That was a cheat. Reading those old articles would only falsely reassure her or, even worse, bring those memories tumbling back at a moment when she was already reeling.

If she was going to do this, she'd do it right. Find some less "public" memory of her family life. A private one that only she'd know, and research that.

No, find *several* memories and prove they were true. Eliminate all doubt. Treat this like a proper investigation—you don't contact a single source for verification and say, "That settles it." Not for something of this magnitude. She'd need multiple proofs.

First, pick a memory . . .

Easier said than done. How exactly would one research personal memories? She flipped through her mental filing cabinet and dredged up images of sleepover parties . . . for girls whose first names she could barely recall. She remembered family vacations . . . to places such as beaches or campgrounds or Disneyland, locales so generic or well-known that kids could probably picture themselves there even if they'd never visited.

Wait! Her parents had taken her to see *The Nutcracker* when she was eight. She distinctly remembered *that*.

Nora confirmed the year with a calendar check and then typed in the search terms and, sure enough, the show had played that holiday season in New York . . . as it did *every* holiday season. She squinted at a blurry photo of the theater façade, but it didn't ring a bell. All she remembered was holding her mother's hand and being led through a forest of people, the crush overwhelming. Oh, and it had been snowing, which a fact check told her it had done most of December that year.

Think, think . . .

She switched to her e-mail. Checked her contact list for someone she could ask . . .

Like who? Everyone in that list had come into her life after her return from Nepal. No one knew her before her parents had died.

As she was about to close the e-mail program, she saw that she'd gotten an autoreply from a colleague she'd cc'd on an e-mail, who was apparently out of town attending his high school reunion.

High school . . .

That would work. She could pull up high school memories and then check the school Web site. She hadn't thought of her school in years. While she remembered a generally uneventful time spent there, she had no desire to revisit that time in her life. Too connected to her happy family life, she supposed. But she'd been on the school paper and she'd won an athletic award—volleyball, wasn't it? She could probably verify that on the school Web site.

She found the site, clicked the link, and the screen filled with a notice that the site would be down for the next forty-eight hours for maintenance. Well, there went that idea. Time to find another.

Nora sifted through files on her laptop, hoping to spark some memory she could track down, but she kept thinking of high school. Such a simple check, one that would have taken just a few minutes, and then she'd have been able to relax, maybe even get some sleep on this endless day. But she'd been thwarted and that frustration pecked at the back of her mind.

She wasn't going to be able to rest, much less sleep, until she had answers. If the Internet couldn't provide them, she had another route.

Time to go into the shadows again.

Nora stood in a darkened corner, just inside the doors of her old school, and it took everything she had not to double over and puke out whatever remained from dinner. She could blame too many shadow rides in one day, upsetting her stomach. She could blame it on not having slept. She could add on the hell of everything that had happened in the last few hours. But all that felt like an excuse. The truth . . .

The truth was that the very smell of this place made her want to throw up.

It wasn't a bad smell. It was probably like the odor of most schools—a mix of sweaty teenage bodies, a musty old building, and the chemicals used to keep both at bay. She'd been in plenty of schools before, chasing some story or other. She'd smelled these scents. But this particular mix—the strength of each element and the myriad other scents that swirled through it—was a concoction that went straight to her gut. She could have been transported here in the pitch dark, sniffed that, and known exactly where she was.

She ran her hands over her face and told herself to get a grip. It was high school, for God's sake.

She laughed a little at that, the sound echoing through the empty halls.

Just high school.

Such loaded words for so many people. She'd never thought of herself as one of them, but she supposed she hadn't been completely immune to the agony of those years—of struggling to fit in and managing it quite well, but always feeling as if she was, in some way, cloaking herself in shadows even then . . . and hoping no one paid too much attention. That was probably how most kids felt, even those who'd pulled it off as well as she had.

After a deep breath, she headed down the hall. If someone had asked her to pull up a mental map of her old school, she would have sworn that she couldn't even find the front door. But now that she was here, there was no question of where to go. Muscle memory took over, leading her down one hall and then another until she saw the sign for the office, and across from it the display of photographs for graduating classes.

It wasn't a large school. There were maybe sixty graduates a year, so this hall was dedicated to those photos, one large frame with a full set of small portraits dating back over two decades. Nora found her graduating year easily and . . .

And there she was. Looking exactly as she remembered from her own senior photo. It wasn't the most flattering shot—a little bit wide-eyed, as if the photographer had startled her at the last second. It made her look skittish, nervous. Hardly the confident grad she'd wanted to be. No matter, it was the photo she remembered, exactly where it should be. And if she'd expected otherwise, well, it'd been a long day and night, hadn't it? Her brain wasn't firing on all cylinders.

Now go check for that athletic award.

Seriously? She shook her head at the urge. A crazed cult priestess suggested her past wasn't what she recalled, and she actually believed the woman? That was nuts enough. Tracking down an endless parade of proof was a complete waste of time. Nora had better things to do. Such as make sure that cult was stopped. And, you know, get some sleep.

But you're here now. What's the harm in checking?

She sighed and shook her head at the thought. The harm was giving credence to madness. The harm was in doubting herself.

But even as she mentally sighed, she found herself heading for the gym. She hauled open the heavy metal door, and fresh smells hit her, making the hairs on her neck rise.

No. Not this. Get out. Get out now.

She shook off the ridiculous sense of foreboding and walked in. The door smacked shut behind her. The clang made her jump. She rubbed her neck and peered into the near darkness. The halls had decent emergency lighting, but here all she got was the red glow of the exit signs.

She took out her phone, turned on the flashlight app, and made her way toward the side wall, where she remembered all the plaques listing athletic awards. They were arranged by year, and she found the right ones easily.

Which year had she gotten the award? She wasn't sure, so she started at the first and read each name. None were hers. On to the second, the third, the fourth . . . nothing. She even checked the year before and after, in case there'd been a mistake. But, no, her name wasn't listed for anything, and she'd been so sure she'd gotten an award. She could remember getting up on stage, her parents in the audience, smiling, her team cheering . . .

"Oh, look, the freak thinks she's going to try out for the volleyball team."

Laughter echoed through the gym as Nora spun toward the voice. She flashed her light beam around, seeing nothing.

"*You really think we'd let you join?*" another voice said, from her left now. Nora turned that way and stared at the empty gym.

"*But I'm good at volleyball. I really am.*"

Was that her? It sounded like it, but it was so soft, almost whispery. A timid voice, better suited to the girl in that terrible grad photo than how Nora remembered herself.

"*Here,*" that almost-hers voice said. "*Just give me the ball—*"

"*You want the ball, freak? Take it.*"

An invisible ball hit Nora in the gut and she went down, gasping. When she looked up, she could see the girls, ghost memories of them encircling her.

"*You think we'd let you on our team, Nora?*" the dark-haired girl in front said. "*We don't care how good you are. You'd embarrass us, you and your Jesus-freak mommy.*"

"*Her mom's not a Jesus freak,*" another said. "*She's into some weird pagan shit, that's what my dad says. He said I should stay away.*"

"*Which is exactly what we're doing. Staying away . . . by not letting Freak-Nora on our team.*"

"*B–but I'm not like that. And I am good at it. Let me show—*"

"*Okay, girls. Let her show us. Someone, give her a ball.*"

One of the girls pitched a ball at her. Then another whipped one at her head, and a third scrambled to retrieve the first, and soon they were pelting her from all sides, throwing the balls as hard as they could as Nora huddled on the floor, screaming for them to stop, screaming for someone to come and no one came and—

The memory snapped and she jolted up, still on the floor, tears streaming down her face, her whole body shaking, throat raw as the last strains of her screams reverberated around her.

"That's not what happened. That's not what happened at all."

She huddled on the cold floor, hugging her knees to her chest, whispering the words over and over . . .

5

———

Nora slept, long and dreamless. But when she finally awoke, she did so with a gasp, as if someone had whispered to her in the dark. The first things she saw were the shadows, pressing in from all sides like a black-clad coterie of deathbed attendants stealing the air from the soon-to-be deceased.

She jerked upright and flailed, but caught only empty air. She panted, shivered. Looked around in confusion.

What was she afraid of? The darkness was her friend, the shadows her servants. So if it wasn't the shadows that had unnerved her so badly, it must've been the memory—the one that'd hit her with such force in her old high school.

No, not a memory. That frightened, bullied girl hadn't been her. It couldn't have been.

Still shivering, she swung her legs over the side of her mattress. In the gloom, something slithered or scuttled across the wall to her left. She jerked her head in that direction, but saw only a solid mass of shadows.

What was wrong with her? Why couldn't she see into the blackness? She concentrated, made a psychic adjustment, and instantly the darkness was hers again—a protective cloak, a womb that enfolded and cradled her.

Still, the uneasiness remained . . . the recent and increasingly familiar sense that, for a moment, the darkness had not been her friend. Instead it had seemed like . . . what? Her enemy? No, but a cold and watchful presence perhaps. Sly. A keeper of secrets.

She shook her head. These were dark thoughts. Stupid thoughts. Clearly she was still rattled by what had happened earlier. The massacre. The cult priestess's words. Her loss of control with Sam. The memory, vision, whatever, at the high school . . .

She needed to orient herself. Figure out what time it was.

She switched on the little floor lamp beside her mattress, ignoring the shadows that slunk away into the cracks and crevices like snakes or rats.

Her old-fashioned alarm clock, the one with the Mickey Mouse hands, read 6:45. Was that a.m. or p.m.?

She groped for her jeans, which lay in a rumpled heap on the floor of the loft with the rest of her clothes, and fished her cell out of the pocket. She blinked at the display: *p.m.!* She'd been asleep all day. Several noncommittal texts from Sam asked her what the hell was going on, but the ones that worried her were from her boss. Yesterday had been Sunday, so wandering in a daze all day hadn't been an issue. But this was Monday, and Raj was not at all happy that Nora had been AWOL.

She didn't remember arriving home, getting undressed, crawling into bed. She had no recollection of anything after the barrage of memories—*not mine, those were not my memories*—that had assailed her at the school.

There were a few voice mails as well, from Sam and Raj and from Casey Santiago, the fashion editor at *NYChronicle*, who'd become Nora's closest work friend. She couldn't face listening to any of them right now.

Crawling to the ladder in her underwear, she descended to the living room and looked around for the Assholes. The cats were nowhere to be seen. She couldn't decide if that was a good sign or a bad one.

She padded to the picture window, clicking on lights as she went. If there'd been anyone out there, they'd have been treated to a view of her in her undies and tank top, a tantalizing glimpse through the mostly bare branches of the tall trees that stood sentinel along the street.

Nora started. Something was squatting on one of those branches, peering inside at her. It was a dark, hunched shape. Her heart quickened as she looked again, staring into the night-black tangle of branches. No, she had been mistaken. There was nothing.

She exhaled. Her own reflection was wan and sickly in the glass. Her hair was lank, her eyes dark hollows in her thin face. That thing in the tree—that thing she'd *thought* was there—had reminded her of something. In light of recent events she grasped at it almost gratefully, though the recollection was far from pleasant.

It was the night her parents had died.

She'd been nineteen. She and her parents had been celebrating something—a promotion for her father? Her memories of the night were somehow both vivid and hazy, certain details standing out with stark and unflinching clarity, others shrouded in a fog of forgetfulness.

Selective amnesia they'd called it. The therapists, the experts, her parents' friends and colleagues. She couldn't remember any of them now. Once it was all over—the initial trauma, the funeral, the aftermath—those people had melted away, though she suspected it was partly *her* doing. She'd wanted to be alone, to escape her grief and seek out some sort of . . . meaning, or solace. And so she'd . . .

But no. She was getting ahead of herself.

That night. Focus on that night. If only to prove the lie in the priestess's words.

The celebration is at a restaurant. An Italian place. Family-run affair, small but classy, in the theater district. Maybe West Forty-Fourth Street. Somewhere around there.

They're happy. Drinking champagne. Laughing a lot. Her dad is square-jawed, handsome in his double-breasted suit, his dark hair slick and neat. Her mom is wide-mouthed as she laughs, bright red lipstick framing gleaming white teeth. She's elegant in an off-the-shoulder number, which shimmers like gold.

Checked tablecloths. Candles. Music. It's all as hazy as a dream. But Nora carries the images within her, enclosed in a fragile bubble of happiness.

Then . . . the dark night. It's drizzling. The streets gleam like black metal. Light reflects off passing cars like white shards of endlessly shattering glass. Everyone is bundled up in coats and scarves. Her father opens an umbrella, holds it over the heads of his wife and daughter.

"Got to keep my girls dry," he says. It isn't particularly funny, but they all laugh.

Stepping from the warm restaurant into the cold air, Nora shivers. The soles of her shoes crackle on the gritty pavement. But the car isn't far away. Her dad has parked it in an almost-empty lot owned by a company he does business with.

"Special privileges," he'd told them earlier that evening as he cut the lights and he engine. And Nora thought how important, how respected, he must be among his colleagues, and how proud that made her feel.

The quickest route between the restaurant and the parking lot is an alleyway, little more than a cut-through. Too narrow for even a single vehicle to negotiate and made narrower still by the Dumpsters lining its walls on both sides.

Alone, she might be scared, but flanked by her parents, she feels safe, impregnable. Even when a black, hunched shape detaches itself from the dark block of a Dumpster ahead and glides along the alleyway toward them, she feels not a flutter of unease. Only when the figure raises its arm and she sees light slither along the barrel of the gun in its hand does she realize with a jolt what terrible danger they are in. Even now, though, her overriding emotion is not terror but indignation.

You can't do this! *she thinks.* Not to us! How dare you!

She looks at the man's face but she can't see it. He is nothing but a void in her mind. Later she will be no use when the police question her about the incident . . . or at least . . .

She blinked, coming back to herself for a moment. A faceless man? Of course not. He was only faceless either because he kept to the shadows or because she's blocked his features from her mind. As for the police, the truth is, she remembered nothing of the evening's immediate aftermath simply because she was—quite understandably—deep in shock.

The gunman's voice is a generic bad-guy growl. He demands her father's wallet, her mother's jewelry. How the mugger knows her mother is wearing a diamond necklace beneath her thick scarf Nora has no idea. Perhaps he's been watching them through the window of the restaurant.

What happens next happens so quickly that to Nora it's like a series of flash images, like movie stills:

The mugger makes a grab for her mother's throat.

Her father yells and steps forward, arms outstretched.

A flash of gunfire, and her father reels, arms outflung, head back.

Then he is on the ground, sprawled, perhaps already dead, and Nora and her mother are screaming.

The gunman panics, the gun blazes again, two more shots ring out.

Now Nora's mom is on the ground beside her husband, arms and legs outflung obscenely, bloody holes in her forehead and chest, rain falling into her open eyes . . .

Time slows, to shift back on track. The movie camera in Nora's head clicks and whirs back into life. All at once the movie stills are once again replaced with real-time footage, and Nora sees . . .

. . . sees herself leap at the man, both in a desperate attempt to save her own life and to prevent him inflicting more damage on her parents. Hands curled into fists, she slams into him before he can bring the gun to bear on her, knocking him backward.

Down they go, the two of them, in a sprawl of limbs. The impact with the ground causes the mugger to let go of the gun, the weapon spinning and clattering away.

In an instant Nora is up again, quick as a rabbit, chasing after the gun. Slivers of light wink and flash on its metal surface as it skids across the slick ground.

By the time she's scooped it up, the mugger is back on his feet. But he doesn't close in on her or attempt to retake the weapon. Instead he turns and flees, his feet splatting in the rain, his elongated shadow stretching behind him.

Nora raises the gun and levels it at his back, her finger tightening on the trigger. But she can't bring herself to kill him. Not in cold blood. And so she lets him get away. Lets the man who killed her parents slip into the darkness.

The instant he's gone, her hand drops to her side. The gun that ended her parents' lives suddenly feels heavy. With a cry of revulsion she opens her fingers. The weapon hits the ground with a thud. A second later she's dropping, too, her legs folding beneath her, no longer able to support her weight.

On her knees, rain darkening her hair and running down her face, she stares at the bloodied, broken bodies of her mother and father. At their blank, openmouthed faces, their glazed eyes, their fine clothes soiled with blood and grime.

A few minutes earlier they had been laughing. Life had been good. Now, in seconds, it was all gone.

It's incomprehensible, impossible. Unreal.
Like an animal she raises her face to the sky and begins to scream.

Nora came back to herself with a jerk, surprised to find she was no longer standing at the picture window, but at the sink of her little kitchenette. She was shaking. Tears blurred her vision, pouring down her cheeks.

She grabbed a glass from the drainboard with one hand and turned on the tap with the other. Having filled the glass with water, she tilted it to her lips and downed the cold liquid in three huge swallows.

As soon as the glass was empty, she refilled it and gulped down this one, too. She emerged gasping, but she felt better—marginally, at least.

Putting the glass down, she washed her face and thought once again about her parents. The memory of how they had died was vivid and distressing, but for the first time she felt that it was also . . . strange. She wasn't sure why, but she couldn't help but think of her mind like a wall, and of the memory of her parents' death like a thick layer of wallpaper, concealing cracks in the plaster beneath.

What might seep out of those cracks if she could only get at them she had no idea. But she wasn't sure that she *wanted* to get at them. Indeed, she recoiled inwardly at the thought.

When she turned from the sink, something dark flittered at the edge of her vision . . . something that seemed to scurry out of sight the moment she focused on it. One of the Assholes, or merely a shadow?

"Kelso? Hyde?" she called, but was answered with nothing but silence.

Crossing to the sagging sofa, she plumped into it, raising a cloud of cat hair. Almost immediately she jumped up again.

Photo albums. Where were her photo albums? *They* would prove her memories were real! She shook her head. How come she hadn't thought of them before? She was sure she had them stowed somewhere. In her mind's eye she could see the spines, dark blue and red. But when she tried to focus on exactly where she'd seen them, she couldn't remember.

For the next few minutes she searched the apartment, feverishly rooting through drawers and cupboards. It didn't take long; her apartment was small. Finding nothing, she switched on her computer and looked through her files for old photos that she might have forgotten about.

Five minutes later she slumped back from the screen, defeated. That she couldn't find a single photograph of her parents—or even of a time before her present life—troubled her greatly.

What was going on? And why had these things never bothered her or even occurred to her before? More to the point, what about her time in Nepal? How come she didn't have any photographs from her trip? It could be that she hadn't had a camera or a cell phone back then. Or maybe, in her quest for serenity, she had abandoned such worldly goods.

Balling her hand into a fist she knocked on the side of her skull, as if seeking access. Why couldn't she remember? What was *wrong* with her?

Physical evidence or not, there was no way Nepal hadn't happened. Nora could vividly remember her time there. She had traveled from one end of the country to the other, seeking enlightenment. She had utilized all forms of transport: boat, train, ramshackle bus, horse and cart. And on many occasions—through the subtropical jungles of the Terai region, and the hills and valleys of the Pahad region—she had traveled on foot, sometimes in a group or accompanied by a guide. Sometimes alone.

Her mind was a montage of amazing memories: the bustling

streets of Kathmandu, the beautiful Hindu temples of Patan, the calm friendliness and generosity of the brightly clothed Nepalese villagers. Time and again these wonderful people, to whom she would forever be indebted, had taken her into their homes, shared their food with her, provided her with a straw mat on which to sleep.

On other occasions, Nora had found shelter among the many traditional teahouses along her route. She retained a vivid memory of sitting on the sunny balcony of one such establishment, eating *dal bhat* and looking out over a spectacular view of the distant snow-covered mountains. She even remembered the tiny green lizards that had scampered around her feet, and the breathtakingly colorful butterflies busying themselves among the local flora. . . .

From the grandmother of the owner of a teahouse in the Manaslu Himal region, Nora first hears of the monastery. The grandmother is tiny and ancient, her spindly limbs making her wrinkled hands and feet appear overlarge, her face as creased and brown as a walnut shell with a kindly face carved into it.

Despite her age, the old woman's eyes are still young, still bright. She speaks no English, and Nora speaks little Nepali, but somehow the two manage to communicate.

Nora conveys her story to the old woman, and the old woman, in turn, tells Nora about the monastery in the mountains. There she will find what she is looking for.

The encounter, although certain details of it stand out starkly in Nora's mind, now seems like little more than a dream. As does the solitary trek into the mountains, the lush greenery gradually giving way to rockier outcrops, the air becoming thinner and colder the higher she climbs.

Had she carried provisions on her journey? Did she have a tent? The answer must be yes, but she can't remember.

One thing she does remember, though, is fighting off the wolves.

She has been trekking for five days, perhaps a week. She is nearing the summit—she must be—but she is also nearing exhaustion. She builds her camp in the shelter of some rocks and is sitting beside the fire, warming herself. The land around her is dark and silent, though the moon and stars, unsullied by light pollution, bathe the surrounding snowcaps in a minty-blue luminescence. The first signs that she is not alone are the glints of light she sees in the darkness, which she initially thinks are fire-flies. Then she realizes that the lights are in pairs, and suddenly it occurs to her what they really are.

Eyes.

Sitting up a little straighter, heart thumping hard, she reaches for a length of burning wood. Drawing it from the fire, she stands up slowly—and all at once, as if knowing that their presence has been detected, the glints of light converge on her as the wolves close in.

Nora can hear them, growling softly in the darkness. She sweeps her gaze from left to right, counting the eyes. Seven pairs. Seven wolves.

A pack.

With a snarl, two of the animals rush forward. Nora swings the burning brand, a slash of orange flame in the darkness. One of the wolves yowls and veers away. The other skids to a halt at the edge of the firelight.

It is lean, its fur pale, its jowls crinkled back to reveal long yellow teeth. It snaps at the flame, but when Nora thrusts the brand forward again, it yelps and retreats.

Holding the flaming branch at arm's length, moving it slowly from side to side, she wonders what to do. Should she yell at the wolves in the hope they will take fright and flee, or should she remain silent? Should she turn aggressor, rush at them with the brand, or stay where she is, close to the fire?

In the end she decides that discretion is the better part of valor—

Or does she? Is that really how it happened?

Looking back now, Nora couldn't rightly remember the outcome of the encounter. She had a vague notion that the wolves had stuck around for a while, and then, discouraged by the fire, had slunk away, never to return.

And after they had gone? What had happened then?

"Come on, you idiot, *remember*," she muttered.

But she couldn't, no matter how hard she tried, and in the end she decided to move on. Decided to concentrate on the monastery itself, and what had happened when she had finally got there.

She tried to picture her arrival, but all she could remember was collapsing on the steps, half-dead with hunger and exhaustion. But after trekking all that way, had she *really* been unable to make the final effort to climb those steps to the top and knock on the heavy wooden doors? It seemed unlikely, even a tad melodramatic.

She screwed her eyes tightly closed in the hope that darkness would let her unearth the memories.

She sees the huge double doors of the monastery opening, orange-clad monks hurrying down the steps toward her, lifting her up, carrying her inside. She is delirious, only half-aware of her surroundings. The monks tend to her. They nurse her back to health.

And after that . . .

After that . . .

She trains with them. They teach her how to manipulate shadows. How to forge weapons out of darkness. How to—

No!

Her own denial shocked her. Her eyes snapped open. Something inside—something that seemed, for a split second, as if it was independent of her—recoiled. Nora felt overwhelmed by panic, felt her mind attempting to backtrack. Once again she thought of wallpaper covering a crack-filled wall, hiding a multitude of sins.

But *something* nagged at her. Something about her own story. Something that simply wasn't right.

It had to do with when she'd been a little girl. To do with something she'd done. Something she'd liked.

So why did she have a sudden memory, dredged from deep within her, of sitting in a dark place?

She probed at the memory, focusing on that dark place in particular. Could it have been . . . a *wardrobe*? Yes! But why did she have a memory of sitting huddled in a wardrobe, scared and alone, wishing she could be invisible, finding comfort from books she read by the glow of a flashlight?

No, not books . . .

Comics!

Yes! Comics! She loves them, doesn't she? Her mother disapproves, but Nora reads them anyway. She sneaks them into the house, conceals them wherever she can find hiding places—behind the wardrobe, under her thin, ill-fitting bedroom carpet . . .

"Oh!"

Once again Nora snapped back to the present. The recollection was so vivid she was amazed she hadn't remembered it before, was amazed that she could ever have forgotten.

Even now, though, she sensed her mind trying to squirm away from the subject. Saw the brightly colored comic-book panels— such an escape from her own miserable existence—blurring and fading in her mind's eye, as if some part of her brain was attempting to deny her access to her past.

She concentrated again, concentrated *hard*, squeezing her eyes shut, screwing up her face until the comics came back into focus, and with them particular images, particular stories, popped like hatchlings from her memory. . . .

Her heart thundered and her breath hitched in her throat.

It was impossible, but at the same time she knew that it wasn't. The past she remembered, the death of her parents, the monastery in Nepal . . .

It wasn't her past. It wasn't *real*.

Bruce Wayne's parents had been shot by a mugger in an alley, leading to him becoming Batman. Danny Rand had learned his skills in a mountaintop monastery after fleeing a pack of wolves and later became Iron Fist. She had adopted their stories as her own.

And don't forget Doctor Strange, an insidious little voice muttered. He, too, had studied the mystic arts in some mountaintop monastery in Asia, hadn't he?

"Holy shit," she whispered.

Panic and confusion overwhelmed her and the strength drained from her body. If she hadn't already been sitting down, she would have fallen. Slumping over her desk, she buried her head in her hands.

Somehow she had taken the stories of a bunch of superheroes, twisted them, and adopted them for herself. It wasn't wallpaper that covered up the cracks in the wall of her memory, but the pages of comic books. But if her past was false, what had her childhood *really* been like? Why had she blocked it from her mind?

In the corners of the room, the shadows whispered, the sound almost like the giggle of imps. "No photos," she whispered. "No records."

Brainwashed, she wanted to tell herself. *Or maybe you've blocked out the truth.*

A truth worse than her parents being murdered in an alley and wandering Nepal in search of enlightenment and nearly being eaten by wolves?

Maybe.

But she felt sure there must be more to it than that. After all, if none of that was true . . .

If none of that was true . . .

"Oh, my God," she whispered.

Heart slamming inside her chest, Nora jumped up from her desk chair and retreated until she could put her back against the wall. The chair continued to glide backward a few feet as if nudged by a ghost, then came to a halt. She stared into the dark corners of the room for a moment, then rushed around switching on the rest of the lights in her apartment—the table lamp, the floor lamp. But even with all of them blazing, the room was still full of small shadows.

If none of those memories were true, then where the *fuck* had the shadows come from? How could she do the things she could do as Indigo?

What the hell *was* she?

Her panic and confusion gave way to a rush of terror. Her throat went dry and she opened and closed her fists as if she might be attacked at any moment. If the shadows weren't some mystical power she had been trained to control, then what were they? What might they do to her? What kind of control over them did she *really* possess?

Forcing herself to breathe, listening to the thunder of her heart, she tried to calm down. Normally she liked to be alone, but now she could not stay by herself. Not now. Not when she was on the verge of screaming. She desperately needed to talk to someone. Solitary by instinct ever since the death of her parents—however that had *really* happened—there was only one person she could trust with her secrets.

Shelby.

Reeling like a punch-drunk boxer, still barefoot and wearing little, she staggered to the door of her apartment and pulled it open. The stairs up to Shelby's floor swayed in front of her. For a moment shadows amassed there, forming a barrier to block her way. Then she blinked and the shadows dispersed, skittering in all directions like roaches exposed to the light.

She was halfway up the first flight when one of the now-exposed cracks in her mind gaped open and another long-buried memory slammed into her like a fist to the stomach.

She is young, still in her teens, naked and bound, rough cold stone pressing into her back. Someone is looming over her—a woman. Marble-

white skin. Burning eyes. A skull-like face bisected by a red, wet grin. She is clutching something in her hand. Something sharp. Something that flashes in the candlelight . . .

Nora staggered, spun, grabbed the handrail, and sat down hard on the steps. The memory was there and gone in an instant, but the image was so awful, so terrifying, that she thought she would pass out. She felt nauseated. Beads of cold sweat appeared on her skin, making her shiver. Clinging to the metal strut of a banister rail, she willed herself to stay conscious, to take slow, deep breaths.

At last she dragged herself to her feet and plodded up the stairs again. By the time she reached the fifth floor she was exhausted, as if she had run a marathon. She stumbled across the landing to Shelby's door, balled her hand into a fist, and raised it to knock . . .

And then she was no longer outside her best friend's door. Instead she was sitting at her desk, fully dressed, in the bustling, open-plan office of *NYChronicle*. Her fingers were poised on her keyboard, a half-finished article on the screen before her. Perched on the edge of her desk was Casey Santiago, a Starbucks coffee in her hand, her dark curls swishing as she tossed back her head, plump red lips stretching wide as she laughed.

Nora jerked back in her seat as if her keyboard had bitten her. Disoriented, she looked wildly around.

"What's going on?" she muttered.

Casey stopped laughing and frowned. "You all right, girl?"

"How did I get here?"

Casey blinked. "Well, I dunno, honey. The subway maybe?"

Nora stood up so fast that her chair glided back on its casters and crashed into the wall behind her. A few people looked over to see what the commotion was about, curious expressions on their faces.

The room spun in front of Nora's eyes. The strip lighting above her seemed overbright, piercing her vision, awakening pain centers in her brain.

"I shouldn't be here," she muttered.

Still bewildered, Casey asked, "Is that right? Then where should you be?"

"At home. I should be at home."

Casey nodded. "Maybe you're right. You do look a little pale. Like maybe you're coming down with something?"

Nora staggered from her office cubicle, heading for the exit. The room was still spinning and swaying. She felt eyes on her, watching her weaving progress. Some of her colleagues might think she was drunk, but she didn't care. All she cared about was getting home, talking to Shelby, trying to make some sense out of what was happening.

A dark shape loomed in front of her. She cried out.

"Hey, hey," a voice said. She felt hands on her arms, steadying her. "It's just me. Are you okay?"

She blinked until her vision cleared. Staring down at her with concern was Sam Loh, his lower lip cut and still a bit swollen from the punch she'd thrown at him.

"Sam, I . . . I gotta go."

"Go where? Look . . . I came by to talk about what happened the night before last. You're not yourself. I don't think you should be going anywhere right now, Nora. You look terrible."

"I'm fine, I'm just . . . not feeling too well."

"Look, Nora, there's obviously something going on with you—"

"There isn't," she insisted, pulling away from him. "I'm fine. Well, except for the fact that I think I'm coming down with something . . . flu maybe."

"Flu?"

She scowled. "You don't believe me?"

He raised his hands. "The way you've been behaving recently, I don't know what to believe."

She saw the hurt on his face, the concern. She reached out a trembling hand and touched him on the shoulder. "Look, Sam, I'm really sorry. You're right. I haven't been myself and I was . . . stressed. It's this story I'm working on. The murders. It . . . well, it got to me, that's all. But I'm so sorry, and I'm fine now. Other than . . ." She wafted a hand.

"The flu."

"Yeah. The flu. I just need to go home, get some sleep." She was already edging past him. "Look, I'll call you, okay?"

"You'd better."

"I will. I promise."

And then she was past him, and out the door. Running down the stairs as if something were after her. Her thoughts churning, churning.

6

—

Nora's rush of confusion and panic took her almost to the sub-way station before she managed to stop beneath a bodega awning and take a deep breath. It was as if a section of her memory had been snipped out. She'd been standing at Shelby's apartment door, about to knock, and then it had been morning and she'd been working at her desk without any recollection of the events in between. She'd been blackout drunk at least once in her life, but an episode like that wouldn't have impacted her ability to remember getting up in the morning, taking a shower and getting dressed, and commuting to work. Besides, she didn't feel hungover. And she'd never heard of a drug that could cause such a memory lapse.

So what. The fuck. Was this?

Her heart hammered in her chest. Her skin prickled and she glanced around, wondering if anyone might have noticed how oddly she was behaving. Certainly her face must be flushed. Nora took a deep breath and pushed through the doorway into the bo-dega. She bought a bottled iced tea, conducting the transaction more to feel normal than anything else, then stepped back outside.

Home, she thought, uncapping the tea and taking a sip. Maybe she really did need sleep, but that felt too simple. Whatever had happened to her, it hadn't been normal. She needed to be home, behind a locked door, safe. She needed to think. She also needed to call the office and make her excuses, then figure out a way to make everything right with Sam. It didn't matter how worn-out or confused she felt, he was an important person in her life and she had to make it right.

As she started toward the subway station, she thought about the look on Sam's face when she'd brushed him off just now, and guilt washed over her. Distracted, she took another sip of her iced tea and started down the dark, narrow steps into the subway station.

The moment she reached the landing, something moved just at the edge of her peripheral vision. Reflex alone saved her from a blow that would have crushed her trachea, if not outright killed her. She jerked back enough to take the worst of the impact on her shoulder, and her arm instantly went numb from the force. Her assailant charged forward with a flurry of devastating blows that she barely managed to block, each of them sending jolts through her arms.

Mugger? No. This was not random and Nora had nothing on her worth stealing. This had to be the cult. A Phonoi assassin. Nora felt a momentary panic, but then she reached out for the shadows and everything seemed better.

Alone in that subway stairwell, at least for a moment, Indigo turned toward her attacker, a woman in her early to mid forties, dressed in a simple black outfit, no jewelry to catch the light. No earrings or bangles to get caught on obstructions in the middle of a mêlée. She moved with regal grace and her face offered no emotions. This was a warrior, someone to respect. Maybe someone to fear.

The woman moved in a low circle and swept Indigo's feet,

knocking her on her ass before she knew what happened. She'd dealt with Phonoi assassins before, but never one this fast.

As the woman stepped closer, dark eyes assessing her, Indigo struck. The wave of shadow stuff caught the woman in the stomach and sent her staggering backward even as Indigo rose to her feet and drew the stairwell's gloom in to cloak her.

"Bad choice, lady."

"No choice." The note of regret in that voice didn't keep the woman from coming for Indigo like a cat stalking a mouse.

Indigo didn't like the idea of being the mouse in that scenario and moved in hard and fast on her enemy. Shadows wrapped around her fists and she struck four rapid blows, each aimed at the woman's rib cage.

None of them connected. The blocks were hard sweeps of hands and forearms that knocked the attacks aside, and before Indigo could recover, the older woman had struck her twice in her stomach. Neither blow was devastating, but they kept Indigo off-balance. The assassin slammed a knee into Indigo's abdomen hard enough to make her stagger and cough as she wrapped shadow tendrils around the woman and hurled her against the wall, shattering the filthy tiles that made the subway steps look like the entrance to a public bathroom.

Indigo caught her breath as the shadows around her faltered. She started down the steps toward her enemy and tried to remember how to breathe past the pain. The assassin had slid down several steps, but now she sprang up again, hatred in her eyes.

"Did you think you could walk the earth and no one would know?" the woman sneered. "That no one would try to stop you?"

"Can you translate that babble for me?" Indigo's body ached in ways she hadn't known were possible, but not enough to distract her from the nonsense words of her attacker. Whatever she was talking about, the words didn't sound like the usual Children of Phonos screed.

"When you fall into hell, tell them Selene sent you."

Selene?

The woman ran up the steps, leaped onto the handrail, and launched a kick that forced Indigo to dodge, caused her to stumble, bought the assassin a precious moment of advantage. The first blow struck Indigo in the skull and had her wobbling. The second caught her just behind her ear and made her see lights.

The third she stopped with a coil of shadows. It was close. Indigo's entire body was shaking. The darkness gathered her in comfort. Early afternoon in New York, but here in this rare private moment, no one had yet noticed two women trying to kill each other. That wouldn't last. Any second now someone would come up or down these stairs and would find themselves in danger. Indigo couldn't allow that. This had to end now.

She reached out a hand and forged a sword from the shadows. "I don't know who you think you're fighting, and I don't know who sent you, but I think maybe you're as confused as I am. You caught me off guard. Come at me again, and I will cut you in half."

The assassin paused, brow knitted in confusion. She stared at Indigo as if searching for some deception, then Selene took a step backward.

"You're not him," she whispered, seemingly to herself.

"Hell, lady, do I *look* like a 'him'?"

Selene took three steps down into the station. "What does this mean?" she said, glancing around at nothing. When she glanced up at Indigo again, her eyes glittered with dark intellect, as if she'd just experienced an epiphany that had enraged her.

"I suspect we'll meet again," Selene said. Then she turned and raced down the narrow stairs and vanished into the subway's darkness.

Indigo watched her go. "Oh, I can't wait."

Laughter bubbled down the steps from above, echoing off the tile walls. Indigo drew the shadows around her and hid as a pair of college-aged women passed her, descending into the station. She ought to follow them, ought to have followed Selene, but she couldn't imagine herself jammed onto public transportation right now. Not when she had another way home.

She felt as if she were falling, and for once she let herself go. Her body knew where it wanted to be, her unconscious mind did the work for her. She slipped from the gloomy subway stairwell to a pool of darkness outside her own apartment, where the landing light had burned out, and Indigo became Nora again.

Her key was already in her hand.

The door opened and swung inward with a creaking of hinges, and Nora stepped inside, staring at the little studio as if every solid thing were now in doubt. This was her apartment, okay, but who the hell was she, really?

And if the woman who'd kicked the shit out of her had really been a Phonoi assassin, then why hadn't she finished Indigo off when she had the chance?

Nora's mind had already been reeling, but now she was more confused than ever.

What is happening to me?

She paused a moment to listen, as if she expected Indigo to answer. As if Indigo weren't just herself, cloaked in shadows. Her gaze fell on the cats' bowls lined up in the tiny kitchen. Where were the Assholes? She remembered wondering last night, before she'd rushed up to Shelby's apartment and then . . . blacked out, or whatever, until she came back to awareness at work this morning. What kind of person was she if she didn't even take care of the three animals she'd adopted? *Maybe I'm not a person at all,* she thought, and that was so terrible that she shut the thought down completely.

Nora forced herself to search. She was aware that despite all the people she—*No, Indigo!*—had killed in the warehouse, she would feel that she had gone past the point of no return if she had killed Red, Hyde, and Kelso. With shaking hands she began to move items around, looking for the cats. She even lifted her mattress, which was crazy. But she'd gone far beyond crazy, now.

Then she heard a little noise. It was undeniably a cat noise, and she even recognized that it came from Hyde. She sagged with relief. With faltering steps she followed the sound to the tiny galley kitchen. The storage space below the cooktop had a sliding door. Now that she was right in front of it, she could hear scratching. Nora slid the door open, and three insane cats rushed out in the blink of an eye.

A light was on inside, which was so strange that Nora knelt to check it out. Flashlights. She'd stuffed the cats in the storage space on top of her pots and pans, and she'd put two flashlights in with them. One was burned out, but the other still glowed weakly. No wonder she had scratch marks on her hands. She couldn't believe she'd done this.

Nora sank to the floor in the cramped space. *The shadows,* she thought. *I was afraid the shadows would get them. How long did they spend in there?* The Assholes were in a semicircle by their water bowl, lapping steadily, but keeping their eyes fixed on her. They were deeply suspicious, and rightly so.

"I'm really me," she said, and Red spat at her and backed away. She found tears were running down her cheeks. They were assholes, but they were hers, after all. How could she save them from herself? Would it be more humane to keep them and pray she didn't hurt them? Or should she open the window onto the fire escape and let them make their own way in the cruel world? They would starve and get ill, with no one to watch out for them. Sam was allergic to cats, and Shelby didn't want them.

These cats are not the most important problem I face. She knew that was true. But this was the only commitment she'd made that she hadn't failed at. She'd been horrible to Sam. She'd run out of her job. Who knew if they'd trust her again? Nora glanced at the clock on the wall. From the light coming through the window, it was still daytime. It wasn't even three in the afternoon. Shelby didn't usually come back to her place until at least six thirty, sometimes later. The fashion industry was demanding.

Nora got to her feet with some effort. The cats backed away as far as they could. She made pathetic amends by giving them some kibble and sharing out a can of fish-flavored smelly stuff on top of each mound of hard food. After a long moment of staring at her, the three glided to their bowls and began to eat, still keeping a close watch on her.

Aching from the beating the psycho bitch with the ice-cold eyes had given her, she lay down on the sofa and fell asleep.

Sometime later, she woke to the sound of footsteps on the stairs outside her door. *Shelby,* she thought hopefully, though it might be the man who lived on the fourth floor. She went into the tiny bathroom, washed her face and brushed her hair, the mirror reflecting a face that was surprisingly normal. Her hair covered a cut on her neck and some bruises, and her clothes covered the rest.

She tried a smile. *Well, no. That's a dead giveaway.* But it felt good, felt everyday, to plan to walk up the stairs to see her friend. She had to decide what she could share with Shelby, what story line she could piece together out of the confusion. By the time she knocked on Shelby's door, she still hadn't made up her mind.

To Nora's relief, the door opened almost immediately. Shelby looked delighted to see her, and that made Nora feel even better.

"Come in! Hey, I was going to come down to talk to you. Want to go out to Desiderio's tonight?"

Nora stepped inside. Shelby's apartment made Nora's look like a dump, not because Shelby had more money to decorate, but because she had a decorating talent that had completely passed Nora by. Shelby could even make a straight-backed chair picked up from the curb look good.

Nora sat down gratefully. "Did you win the lottery today? Because I didn't hear that on TV." Desiderio's, three blocks away, was not terribly expensive, but neither of them had much extra money.

"The old fart gave me a raise." Shelby's smile broke out like the sun after a storm.

Nora was so pleased to hear good news that she almost started crying again. "That's wonderful! What triggered this generosity?"

"I saved his bacon," Shelby said smugly. "His little assistant figured the amount it would cost to make a dress wrong. We would have been in the hole by a hundred thousand dollars if we'd gone with that estimate. But *little old me* can do basic math, and I caught it."

"What happened to the little assistant?" Shelby called each handsome young thing who came to work at the fashion house by this slighting term.

"Not enough. But it's okay, since I got a raise and a regal nod."

"Cool. Okay! Desiderio's it is! You ready?"

"Let me freshen up. Be ready in two."

Soon they were clattering down the stairs, and Nora went past her own apartment with extra speed.

"The landing light is out," Shelby said. "You need to tell Mr. Carriker."

"I will," Nora said, though she knew she wouldn't. She was too worried about what would happen to Mr. Carriker if he tried to change the bulb.

In Desiderio's, they sat at a table by the window, and the evening darkened as they ate and drank. It was a happy moment, and Nora felt like an ordinary human being . . . for about thirty minutes. Then she dropped her napkin, and as she bent to retrieve it, she realized that the tablecloth was red-and-white checkered . . . like the tablecloths in the restaurant where she and her parents had eaten on the night they were killed.

Which had never happened . . .

Nora caught her breath with a gasp that frightened Shelby. "What is it? Did you hit your head on the table as you came up?"

"I just remembered something." Nora tried to sound normal, though she wasn't sure what that meant any longer.

"Are you thinking about when your parents died?"

Nora was shocked. "Why would you ask that?"

"I know that look."

Nora was sure her mouth was hanging open. She was also sure she'd never told Shelby what had happened to her mom and dad. Of course, she couldn't be certain of *anything* now, could she? Nora glanced around, wondering if anyone else had done something equally strange. The waiter was standing with his back to them, looking into the kitchen hatch. The receptionist talked on the telephone, responding to a query. The busboy cleared dishes and detritus off a table in the corner.

"Shelby," Nora said, fumbling through her confusion, "I don't think we should talk about that here." They were sitting under the bright restaurant lights, but outside, night had fallen.

"Honey, how can we not?" Shelby leaned forward, her red-gold hair swinging with the movement, and her pretty face looked more serious than Nora had ever before seen it. "It's haunting you. I can see it in your eyes."

Suddenly Nora couldn't bear to be in Desiderio's any longer. She leaped to her feet and was out of the restaurant, into the shadows of the next doorway. Abruptly, Nora emerged outside the place on Forty-fourth, the Italian restaurant her family had loved so much. Dad in his handsome suit, Mom in her gold dress, and Nora in a short skirt and lace blouse with some high-heeled shoes she'd saved her allowance to buy. Her parents had agreed to indulge her if she paid half the price. She'd scrimped and . . .

Then they were together in the alley, taking that odd shortcut. Together as a family for the very last moment.

Indigo expected to see the hunched shape lurch out of the protection of the trash bin, and the flash of the gun.

But nothing was in this alley. Nothing but her. Again she saw a flash, but it was not the gun, it was a raised knife, and it was not a man holding it, but *her mother*. Indigo sank down to her haunches, trying to see this fragment of memory more clearly, slow it down, stretch it out. But she could not capture it long enough.

Her life—her mind—was tearing itself apart, and the two halves of her were merging in some way she did not understand. Nora didn't know how to divide her two selves again. Shelby knew something she could not possibly know, unless Nora had revealed that to her and forgotten.

What else had she told Shelby that she no longer remembered? How much of her memory of anything might be false? And what if the psycho bitch came back to finish the job? Either way, just being Nora's friend might be putting Shelby in danger.

Nora might not be able to unravel her own mysteries, but she had to try. The Children of Phonos, the psycho bitch, the missing time last night, these murders . . . she had to figure it all out, and she had to make sure Shelby was safe in the meantime. In the midst of her own panic and confusion, Nora could do that, at least.

As Indigo, she stepped out of the shadows beside Sam's apartment building. As Nora, she walked around the front of the building, but before she could approach the front door, she saw Sam coming along the sidewalk toward her. She smiled. That was good. She wanted Sam to see her, to know she was waiting for him.

Nora's heart ached when he slowed down, his face revealing suspicion, even fear. She couldn't blame him.

"Sam," she said in as calm a voice as she could manage. "I know we need to talk . . . about a lot of things. But before we can do that, there are some things I need to figure out. You know I'm covering these child killings."

"If Raj doesn't fire your ass after the last few days." Sam's gaze was hard. "If you won't tell me what's going on, Nora, you've at least got to talk to her. I covered for you as best I could, but she's pissed."

Nora nodded. "I'll call her right after I leave here. But look . . . this case, these child killings . . . I do think they're ritual murders. I do think they're connected to the cult from last year, the Children of Phonos."

"I think so, too. The more I pursue the missing kids and the human-trafficking circles they've vanished into, the more I think the whole thing is connected. That lawyer, Bullington—"

Nora blinked. "Bullington's involved in trafficking?"

"He defended some of the sicker bastards the cops have picked up this year, a couple of the procurers they've got evidence on but were unable to put away."

"Unable why? If there's evidence—"

"Bullington got the judge to rule stuff inadmissible. I'm still looking into it, but there's something else. Bullington's dead."

Nora forced herself to look stunned. "How?"

Sam searched her eyes. "Someone threw him out his office window on Sunday morning. Dead on impact."

"Shit," she whispered. "Is this really all connected?"

"I think it is. Now tell me what's going on with you." Sam's expression softened. "The way you took off—"

Nora exhaled. Memories flooded her mind . . . and she thought these were real. They were recent enough that she remembered the feel of Sam's sheets, and his hands on her. She remembered the smell of the orange tea he made in the mornings and the taste of burned waffle, the morning he'd tried out the new waffle iron. That had all been well over a year ago, before he'd left *NYChronicle*, when they'd been more than friends with benefits, when they'd still said the words *I love you*. It had been Nora's suggestion after Sam left the *Chronicle* that they just be friends with benefits. It had been a relief to push away their growing intimacy. She'd started to hate keeping secrets from him, yet found herself unable to tell him the truth. He was fascinated with Indigo, had made her his pet project, but he was frightened of her, too. Loving Sam had been too complicated. Sleeping with him occasionally had been much simpler.

Until now.

"Look, I know I've been really weird. I know you're worried, and I was a bitch and I lashed out." *I hurt you. I'm so sorry.* "If I felt like I could tell anyone, I swear I'd tell *you*. But if I talk too much, I put other people in danger."

Sam was really concerned now, concerned for her. Nora could read that in his open face. She was touched that he still cared, after her bizarre and hurtful behavior.

"Listen, I'm on the track of something that will change . . . everything."

"Something on this story?" Sam took a step closer, intrigued.

She flashed back to the bloodbath inside that warehouse, the way Indigo had slaughtered the cultists who'd gathered there.

"It's starting to click together in my head," she said, grasping at that straw. "If I'm right, that whole trafficking operation might fall apart now. I've heard whispers that maybe this cult is going out of business." That was the damn truth.

"But you said you're in danger because of what you know. If that's true, you have to tell me," Sam said urgently. "If they're really at the center of all this and they get wind of the fact that you know about it, the only way you're safe is if you expose them. You can't keep this to yourself."

The reporter in Sam was on the alert, as well as the friend. Nora had to smile at him, though she couldn't manage to put much cheer into it.

"I won't. I swear I'll tell you everything as soon as I verify a few things. But in the meantime, I don't think I'm going to be home much. I'm doing some digging, maybe out of town. Can you stop by and check on the cats from time to time? It's important to me. I fed them, but if I haven't come back for a day or two, you might just open the window onto the fire escape."

She didn't know what else to do. The only way she could think of to keep Shelby safe was to stay away until she could figure all of this out, answer the questions she had about herself.

"Nora, you're scaring me. You can't—"

"Sam, please. *Trust me.*"

He frowned, wanting to share whatever risk she'd taken on herself. Wanting to know, the way reporters always wanted to know.

"Well, you're scaring the shit out of me, but okay. I can do that for a while," he said with marked reluctance. "Allergies or not, I'll check on the cats. But if you're gone for more than a couple of days without at least sending me a text, that's it. I call the cops."

"Fair enough. But I need one more small favor. When you stop by there, can you check in on my friend Shelby?"

Sam looked puzzled. "Have I met her?"

"You've heard me talk about her. She lives two floors above me. We have girls' nights pretty regularly. She comes in and out of my place enough that if someone means me harm, they might focus on her—"

"Nora, if it's that serious—"

"Sam," she said sternly. "Do this for me. I will keep in touch. If anything happens or if you haven't heard from me in two days, call out the cavalry. But do this."

He exhaled loudly. Then he nodded in surrender.

"Thanks so much!"

Sam arched an eyebrow. "You hit me."

Nora felt that same flicker of guilt, but pushed close to him and kissed him on the corner of his mouth. "So you look a little beat-up. It's kind of sexy."

"You're not funny."

She gazed into his eyes. "I really *am* sorry. And I swear I'll explain it all to you soon. I'll make this up to you, Sam."

Nora turned and walked away. She knew he would be watching her go and had to fight the urge to vanish into the shadows until she turned the corner. Then, at last, she let all of the tension bleed out of her. Whatever was going on—with her memories, with her powers, with the Children of Phonos—Nora couldn't unravel it all herself. She couldn't force the world to give her the answers she sought.

Only Indigo could do that.

She flickered through the shadowpaths until she emerged across the street from the warehouse where so many people had died at her hand. She hid in the darkness of another derelict building, surprised to see no crime-scene tape, no police presence. *It all looks exactly the same. Is it possible that no one's looked inside yet, two days later?*

Indigo could scarcely believe it. She waited, examining the other shadows in her line of sight. Surely someone was staking out the warehouse? But no one moved. She waited even longer, the eerie silence stretching her suspicion to the breaking point.

No one had come. The expensive cars waited for owners who would never slip into the drivers' seats. Indigo had a Nora thought: *It's like going back to a scenario in a computer game. Until I find the magic hammer, or I find all the hidden mirrors, nothing will change.* The silence was profound. Nothing had been altered since she'd left after her vain attempt to rescue the abducted boy.

Since she'd killed the Children of Phonos.

Indigo was like a ghost, revisiting the scene of her crimes. *No, not my crimes. Theirs.* Indigo was the avenger. She was in the right, and she must never forget that or doubt it.

She took a deep breath and went to the body of Armani Man, lying as she'd left him—his foot caught in the window, his body sprawled on the weeds and gravel. She went through his pockets. *They were all so arrogant, they came with their identification intact. They expected to return to their lives. What did they imagine they'd gain from killing those kids? Why did the priestess tell me that my own death should have been the sacrifice?*

The driver's license in the wallet had been issued to Marshall Winston, age forty-two. Indigo recognized the area where he lived— she was sure it was one of the co-op buildings overlooking Central Park. After a moment's thought, she took his keys as well.

Bracing herself, she entered the warehouse. It smelled of death, and though everything looked exactly the same—the corpses hadn't moved, of course—the bodies now seemed to have fallen so that they looked at her accusingly. *Murderers,* Indigo reminded herself. *They deserved the hand I dealt them.*

She frowned deeply. Something had bothered her on Sunday, when all of this had played out. So many things had bothered her,

but now she realized that one of them had been the absence of assassins. These were the wealthy and not-so-wealthy members of
the chapter, the ones who financed and benefited from the cult's
activities in the New York area. The dabblers in black magic—and
maybe more than dabblers. But she knew from experience that they
had trained killers in their employ, such as the assassins she'd killed
in the Chesbros' living room last year. Maybe like the psycho bitch
who'd tried to murder her this morning.

Why hadn't any of them been here?

There was so much she didn't understand about the Phonoi.
Maybe only the real practitioners of their occult bullshit were
invited to rituals like this. But if those assassins were still out there,
if she hadn't destroyed the entire chapter the way she had thought,
then why hadn't anyone discovered these corpses?

You're an investigative reporter, she reminded herself. *Do your job.*

She could not bring herself to look at the body of Luis, the only
innocent person in this whole building. Her failure to rescue the
boy still ravaged her. Only obliterating the Children of Phonos—
the entire global cult, not only the chapter that had gathered here—
could alleviate the guilt Indigo felt for not arriving in time to save
the boy.

It would take a long, long time to rifle the pockets and hand-
bags of all the dead. So Indigo, her fingertips wrapped in shadow
to blur her prints, concentrated on the discarded handbag of the
white-clad priestess, now identified as Charlotte Edwards. Indigo
pocketed Edwards's keys and identification. She also examined the
wallets of an Ovidio Bogdani and the purse of a woman whose
license read Bonnie Alessio. Bogdani and Alessio were both younger,
and more cheaply clothed. Their addresses were not fancy. In fact,
Bogdani's was in Kingsbridge . . . and his name was ringing a bell
in Indigo's memory. She couldn't remember where she'd heard it
before.

Indigo spent a few moments deciding where to go first. The priestess's wallet contained a picture of the woman with two children and a man, so Charlotte Edwards's apartment would not be empty. Indigo found it disgusting that the woman had a family of her own when she had been involved in the deaths of other people's children. She didn't harbor a scrap of guilt or regret for sending Charlotte Edwards to hell.

Winston's personal effects gave no hint that he had a family, so she'd try the co-op across from Central Park first.

Indigo stepped into the deepest patch of blackness in the warehouse, danced through inky nothing, and emerged among the trees in the park. With one glance across the street, she flickered back into the dark and slid out into the shadows beside Marshall Winston's apartment building.

It made her a little uneasy when she thought about the increasing ease and speed with which she moved from shadow to shadow, as if she had somehow graduated to an entirely new level of intimacy with the darkness. The logic seemed reversed. Indigo had never been less confident, never been more confused, and yet she felt as if she had only begun to tap the potential of her power. The temptation to surrender completely to instinct, to shadow, was almost overpowering. If only she could make sense of it all.

Now's not the time. Now's the time to find out who these bastards really were and if there are more of them. In her previous skirmishes with them, she'd learned of at least seven chapters of the Children of Phonos in the United States, including those in New Orleans, Los Angeles, and Houston, and she assumed their high priests and priestesses all reported to one who was above them all—some national or global figure or secret council or something. But those larger mysteries were for later. Right now she wanted to find out if some members of the local chapter were left alive.

Charlotte Edwards, the dead priestess, had claimed to have

some secret knowledge about Indigo—and she needed that knowledge. Yes, she wanted to unravel and expose the entire cult, and, yes, she knew that if they were trafficking in abducted children, they had to be stopped. But her fear and confusion drove her tonight. It was selfish, but she didn't care. How could she help anyone, how could she expose them to the light, if she couldn't even be sure who or what she was?

She hid in the darkness outside the luxury apartment building. Through the glass of the lobby, she could see the doorman standing behind a high desk. The lobby gleamed with glass and chrome, well lit. Indigo didn't like well lit.

Fortunately, shadows were everywhere. Wherever there was light, she could find darkness.

In a heartbeat, Indigo was inside, swathed in the shadow of the high desk, rising up behind the doorman. She drew that bit of darkness around her, hiding inside it, practically invisible. A few seconds later, he opened a door to admit a resident. Indigo took the darkness with her as she went into the elevator with the elderly woman and her dog. A light in the rear corner of the elevator winked out. The Pomeranian knew Indigo was there. It sniffed the floor and backed away, staring into the corner, but Indigo's shadow cloak concealed her. The Pomeranian pressed against the legs of its owner, but whether to protect her or to be protected, Indigo couldn't tell.

"What's wrong, Plutarch?" The woman bent to stroke the dog's head. "You're shaking like a leaf."

I never had a dog when I was a kid. Or a cat. Any pet. Indigo didn't know where the piece of knowledge had come from, but she recognized it as the truth. Real truth, not some blurred bit of untrusted memory.

Indigo got off the elevator with the old woman and Plutarch, and as the woman unlocked her apartment, Indigo took to the stairs. Low and fast, the shadow streaked up the gleaming marble.

It was too well lit. It felt as though she were running in a spotlight. On the next floor, Indigo found the apartment number she'd been seeking. Two keys, two locks, and she stepped inside, taking the precaution of locking the door behind her.

The foyer was a hallway, not wide, lined with bookshelves on one side. The flooring was wood, and she used a shadow below her feet to cushion the sound of her steps. The short entry hall led into the living area and the kitchen, and she stood still for a moment. A single light burned within, a tiny lamp on a narrow table behind the couch.

Though the ever-present sounds of the city provided a background hum, Indigo could not hear any other living thing breathing within the apartment. It was as silent here as it had been at the warehouse. Her hand found the light switches, and in an instant the luxury of the place flooded her senses. Though it wasn't large, it was expensively furnished. It looked like a dream after Nora's scruffy place. The colors harmonized, the floors gleamed, and there was no clutter. The surfaces were dusted and orderly, the furniture modern. It didn't look like the apartment of a man who'd been part of a child-murdering black-magic cult.

Demon worship pays well, Indigo thought. For the first time, she wondered what the Children of Phonos gained by the deaths of the children. She'd simply been ascribing the murders to "evil," but there had to be some kind of profit in it for the cultists. *Does sacrificing the real children reap tangible rewards? Are they all this prosperous?*

The bedroom was as elegant and orderly as the rest of the place. Winston's clothes were all name brand, and he must have had twenty pairs of shoes, which amazed Indigo. She opened a box in his closet to find a collection of watches, which simply bewildered her. Who needed more than one watch? They all told the same time, right? She shrugged and continued her search. The bureau held nothing out of the ordinary—clothing, medication, a few books. All novels. No grimoires or satanic Bibles. She couldn't find a safe.

In the office area, part of the living room, she found a few paper copies of Winston's financial dealings. A real estate broker, he had made a great deal of money. She was sure most of his records were on his computer, and though she turned it on, everything was password protected. She had some small skill in that area, but she was no expert. Should she take it with her, try to find someone who knew what to do and might be able to break into the files?

She looked at the paperwork she'd found more carefully. They were sales documents, mortgage papers, all items associated with his line of work. But as she shuffled them one last time and was about to push them aside, a shudder went through her as she realized one particular address was familiar to her.

The warehouse where the Children of Phonos would have sacrificed Luis Gallardo. Winston had been the broker on the sale, and the attorney had been Andrew Bullington, the prick who'd hurled himself out a window rather than face the vengeance of the cult he served.

As she was considering that, she kept going through the desk.

She found a printed directory.

It was in a file marked "Donors: At-Risk Children's Intervention," which sounded noble. But a quick glance told Indigo that the priestess's address was in there, as were Bogdani's and Allessio's. She folded the document and slid it under her shirt. If she was going to work with Sam and both of their employers and blow the lid off the cult's entire organization, figure out their connections to human trafficking and other crimes that had nothing to do with the occult, this list would be the beginning of that.

She heard a ding down the hall and the sound of the elevator doors opening. Another apartment adjoined Winston's, and the newcomers could be going there, but Indigo had a feeling that her time had run out.

She clicked off the lights and concealed herself in the entrance hall, in the corner where the open door would hide her. She wrapped the gloom around her until she was swathed in darkness and waited. A moment later she heard the snick of a key in the first lock, then the second. It would have been simple enough for her to flee, but she had come here for answers. Marshall Winston was dead. She had to know who else had a key to his apartment.

In the light from the hallway, she saw a flash of red hair and glimpsed a face she recognized. Detective Angela Mayhew.

Like a bad penny, Mayhew kept turning up. For the first time, it occurred to Indigo that the detective hadn't botched the criminal case against the Newells at all. That maybe Detective Mayhew was on the cult's payroll, or even a member.

Tonight, the woman was trailed by her partner and junior, Hugh Symes. Detective Symes was thin and pale and looked unhealthy, while Mayhew was bursting with vigor. As she went down the short hall to the living room, she was saying, "Hugh, we have to call the captain after we're through here. He's going to want to know."

"This guy Winston was a buddy of Captain Mueller's?"

"Close enough that the captain knew exactly where to get an extra set of keys."

"Well, we ain't gonna find a body in here," Symes grumbled.

Detective Mayhew wandered through the living room and the kitchen, flipping on the same lights Indigo had used.

"You haven't even looked around," Mayhew said.

"We woulda smelled it, Ange."

Indigo wanted to get out of there. It would be simple enough to slip into the shadowpaths. But she wanted to know what had drawn the detectives to this place. If they thought they might find Winston's corpse here, then the bodies at the warehouse had still not been discovered—at least not by the police—but what gave them the idea that the man might be dead?

"Must be nice to have that view of the park, to say nothing of the doorman," Mayhew muttered. "Check the bedroom," she said more loudly.

The detective had said her captain, Mueller, was friends with Marshall Winston. Could the police captain be involved with the Children of Phonos as well? Was that so hard to believe? Maybe the bodies had been found, but not by the police . . . or by police who were in league with the cult, or a part of it.

Indigo's head spun. How far did the cult's influence reach? How deep did their corruption run? Indigo could hear Mayhew rummaging around. It sounded to Indigo as if the detective was hurriedly looking for something while Symes was out of the room.

"Hey," Symes called. "Ange, come look at all the watches this guy had. He lives alone. You think his estate'll miss one?"

Indigo held her breath while she waited.

Finally, Angela Mayhew's steps clicked as she stepped off the area rug in the living area and went into the bedroom.

Time to go.

Remembering the dearth of shadows in the hall, Indigo pictured the darkest moon shadows in Central Park. The next instant, she was there, in the center of a clump of trees. Two men were doing the nasty about a foot away. They were so intent on their pleasure that she was able to slip away again without their noticing either her arrival or departure.

Her next stop was the apartment of the high priestess, Charlotte Edwards.

Indigo knew the address was on the Upper East Side, and not far from an art studio she'd written about in her early days at

NYChronicle. She shadow-walked to the studio, or rather to the alley behind it. After her encounter in Central Park she felt lucky that no one was peeing against the wall. Presumably even in the Upper East Side that happened.

Indigo stepped out, then set off at a brisk walk, searching for the right address. Soon her steps slowed. Edwards's address was not a condo or a co-op, by all the signs. She and her husband owned the whole house. Nora had lived in New York long enough to know what that meant in terms of investment, so Indigo knew it, too. For a moment, Indigo felt a moment of dizziness. Did she know everything Nora knew? Did Nora know everything Indigo did? What if the answer was no?

The question terrified her, and she forced herself to focus on the task at hand.

Charlotte. Dead evil priestess. *Who told me that all the children's deaths were my fault.*

Indigo wished she could kill the woman again. Once wasn't enough.

The whole house was dark, with the exception of a dim light glowing somewhere in the tiny backyard. Indigo went there in a thought. The garden had been planted for privacy, with a brick patio outside the ground floor, right up to the kitchen door—at least, Indigo assumed the kitchen was at the rear.

In the middle of the city, this spot was peaceful and relaxing. And dark. Indigo went up the rear steps like a cloud of smoke. She looked through the windows, locating the source of the light, a small lamp on the counter of a kitchen she could only gape at. No one appeared to be home.

Everything was locked up tight, but Indigo couldn't let that stop her. If someone had sent Angela Mayhew and Hugh Symes to search for the corpses of the cultists Indigo had killed, other detectives might show up here at any moment. She tried all the keys on Charlotte's key ring, and none of them fit. This puzzled her, but she couldn't take the time to figure it out.

Indigo became pure shadow and slid through the keyhole.

On the other side of the door she paused, shocked and delighted and more than a little bit frightened. She'd never done that before. Been *pure* darkness. Noncorporeal. It bore contemplation, but not here. Not now.

Indigo moved swiftly through the house, as quietly as she could manage, which was very quietly indeed. The children in Edwards's wallet picture had grown up. Their rooms were the lairs of affluent teenagers. Marijuana was in the boy's bedside drawer. The girl had a closet full of high fashion. But Indigo gave their rooms only the most cursory of examinations because she wanted to dig into all things Charlotte.

Charlotte and her husband, Graham, shared a beautifully appointed study, with his and hers mahogany rolltop desks. For a moment Indigo almost ignored the room, thinking Charlotte wouldn't have hidden anything related to the Children of Phonos where her husband might easily discover it. But that was assuming Graham wasn't also been a member. He hadn't been at the warehouse, true enough, but was that conclusive proof that he did not belong to the cult along with his wife?

Something gave her pause. She hesitated, sensing something in the room.

At times in the past she had felt the presence of magic, of the occult. Until now she would have attributed that to the training she had received in Nepal. But that was all bullshit, wasn't it?

She drifted toward Charlotte's desk. There were built-in drawers and one had a lock. Indigo's fingers turned to shadow, flowed through the tiny keyhole, unlatched the lock from inside.

Ahhhh, this is worth finding, this is what I need. She opened the drawer. *Though I'm not sure what it is.* It was pale gold, a symbol she'd only seen once before. She had a sliver of a memory—that knife raised above her. *This symbol was on the blade of that knife. The blade meant to kill me.*

I should have died.

7

———

Indigo stared at the golden object. It seemed as cloaked in shadow as she was herself, beckoning her closer to it, to touch it, take it. Deep inside, Nora squirmed, but the part of her that was Indigo was ascendant now and leaned closer. The emblem, on a chain, was of pair of stylized, down-sweeping wings with a circle resting above them, endless and somehow filled with shadow. Big for a pendant, but what else could it be? It had an odor—an aura almost—faint, grim, like burned flesh and running blood. She reached for it.

The psychic weight of the old brownstone had been so oppressive, but now its strong current seemed to flex and shift against her, as if something had immersed itself into that current with her, disturbing its flow. Indigo whipped around, flicking the drawer closed. She expected to find someone else in the room, but all she saw was a light on the security panel. Someone was home, but who? *Not Killer Priestess Charlotte, that's for sure.*

The front door slammed hard enough to be heard upstairs, and then the ARMED indicator blinked off. Indigo left the emblem behind and slipped shadow to shadow until she came to the stair landing. She gathered the gloom around her and gazed down into the ground-floor entryway.

The man in the foyer growled and flung his keys onto the hall table. They rattled against an antique bowl as he shrugged out of his overcoat and threw that aside, too, with the same angry disdain.

"Son of a *bitch*," he spat, and stalked out of view. From this angle, Indigo couldn't make him out him well enough to compare him to the photo she'd seen, but he had to be Charlotte's husband, Graham Edwards.

Where are the kids?

Indigo drifted down the staircase to an ebon patch beside a longcase clock that was probably older than the house. She drew closer to the swinging brass pendulum as it slowly ticked . . . ticked . . . Glassware chimed nearby and Indigo looked toward it. Graham had gone to a sideboard in the dining room and made himself a drink. He had to be over fifty, tall, and handsome in the sleek, groomed way of rich men, his body trim from the constant attention of expensive trainers and displayed by the art of even-more-expensive tailors. He swallowed about half of the contents of his glass in a gulp and started to refill it. *Well, that's not a handsome habit, though I'd drink, too, if I were married to that bitch.*

The doorbell rang. Graham flinched, then slammed his heavy crystal tumbler down and stalked to the door. Indigo drew the cloak of darkness closer around her, easing into the gloomy corner created as Graham opened the carved front door. Inches away from him. Close enough to hear his breathing.

He was silent a moment, then: "What the fuck do you want?"

"Why, yes, it really *is* a lovely evening, isn't it?"

Indigo couldn't see the sarcastic man, but his voice seemed familiar.

"I said, 'What do you want?'" Graham held on to the door, issuing no invitation.

"I *need* to speak to Charlotte. About the blessed event."

"What, you and my wife don't *talk* while you're *fucking*?" Graham shouted.

The other man scoffed, "Oh, grow up, Edwards." He moved into the house and pushed against Graham's chest with one hand. "It's circle business."

Graham recoiled from the man's touch, backing up until he could rest one unsteady hand on the hall table as the other man turned to close the door. This one was younger, slimmer, casual in a hipster sort of way that wasn't totally obnoxious. If he noticed the unnatural darkness in that gloomy corner, he gave no sign. Indigo studied the scruffy beard first and then the brown eyes, and realized she knew him.

The connection jolted her. *The stairs at Heath and Bailey. Maidali Ortiz's death scene, the memorial. What was his name . . . ? Rafe! Rafe Bogdani—no wonder the dead cultist's name had rung a bell—he had to be related. Brother, maybe? Holy shit. This guy had been Maidali's teacher! He'd stood there laying on the guilt with those doe eyes. . . .*

Nora had thought his eyes warm and sad, but at the moment Rafe Bogdani's expression was anything but.

"Charlotte's not here," Graham said through clenched teeth.

"I guessed that. I'll settle for the list."

"You're missing the point. I haven't seen her since Sunday."

"From what she said, the two of you had quite a dustup."

Graham barked a hollow laugh. "A 'dustup'? Is that what she called it? A fucking 'dustup'? She wanted to use our own children for—"

Rafe held up a hand. "I know, Graham. And I understand why you're furious. I understand why you sent them away—"

"Damn right I sent them away!"

"—but the thing is, I asked her to wait for me to return. I was three thousand miles away on Sunday, and Charlotte chose to go ahead without me. I spoke to her after that fight you had and she told me you'd . . . shall we say, withdrawn from our circle. That you weren't going to attend the rite."

"Of course I refused to attend, knowing what she planned!" Graham snapped. "I took my children and got them out of town. I've only just—"

"Yes, yes . . . we've both only just come home, haven't we? But the thing is, I've been back in New York an hour and cannot find hide nor hair of Charlotte, or any of the other members of the inner circle. I've made phone calls, but this is my first house call. Before I continued my search, I thought I would make absolutely certain you don't know what's gone wrong."

"With your plans for the so-called blessed event? I couldn't care less."

Rafe stepped in close. Graham stiffened, as if remembering that he really ought to be afraid of the other man. Rafe inhaled deeply, as if drawing in Graham's scent and studying it, as if he could learn something from that smell.

"All right," Rafe relented. "Fine. But I want the list."

"I don't have it. And I won't have you rummaging through my wife's things without her consent. Get it from Winston." Graham's posture was stiff and he groped along the table edge as if he were searching for protection.

Rafe's eyes narrowed until they gleamed like chips of dirty ice. He closed the gap between them and stared into Graham's face. "You're weak, Edwards. You're not worthy. That's why *I'm* the one in Charlotte's bed, not *you*. No matter what asinine excuse you make for yourself."

Graham's lip twisted with revulsion, and he took a sudden step away from the hall table. He held a blocky, black automatic in the hand that had moved so nervously. He wasn't nervous now. Graham swung the gun up and pointed it at Rafe's face. "Get out."

Rafe chuckled and stepped back. "You have no problem living with the fruits of assassination, extortion, and trafficking, but *this* suddenly makes you grow a spine—"

Graham shoved the muzzle into Rafe's left eye. "Get. Out." Graham's voice had gone silky cold. "Or I'll put a bullet through your head and make somebody very happy."

Rafe spread his arms, still chuckling, and walked backward to the door. "Fine. I'm going. I'll see you at the event. You will be there, my friend. You can't step away from the circle. You know how this goes." Rafe's gaze passed over Indigo in her shadows as he reached to open the door. He frowned for a moment, but that vanished as he stepped outside the doorway and turned back to Graham. Rafe grinned. "Give my love to the kids—especially that adorable daughter of yours."

Graham slammed the door in Rafe's face and spat, "Smug, twisted little motherfucker." Graham rearmed the perimeter alarm and turned away, still muttering to himself about Rafe Bogdani and the "bloody *blessed* event."

Blessed event, Indigo echoed. *It's gotta be whatever these sick bastards have in mind for the other two kids Bullington mentioned.* And from the sound of it, Charlotte Edwards had offered up her own offspring for the ritual. Her husband might be an evil son of a bitch, but at least he had balked at that.

She toyed with staying and seeing what she could get out of Graham, but it seemed more likely Rafe had the information she wanted. Before she left, Indigo tucked Charlotte Edwards's keys into an ornamental box on a bedside table. She couldn't be caught carrying them, but she might need them again if she could figure out what they unlocked. *I guess Nora will have to "run into" Rafe— ever so coincidentally, of course.*

She left Graham Edwards alone with his bottle and his gun and hoped he'd blow his own brains out—saving her the trouble of coming back. Indigo reached for the deepest shadows outside the brownstone, felt the pathways available to her, and sensed the shifting night come alive at her touch. She stepped from the apartment onto those dark paths and reappeared on the street, following Rafe. He didn't head across the park on foot toward Winston's co-op, but toward the nearest subway station.

Perfect.

From patch to patch, she slipped along behind him and down into the station, coming to rest in the murky gray space behind the stairs. She watched Rafe pace on the subway platform until his train pulled in. Once he'd stepped aboard, she hurtled forward, out of the darkness, shedding her shadows, shedding Indigo.

Nora darted through the gap just ahead of the closing doors. They groaned shut as she tumbled into him, saying, "Sorry, sorry, ohmigod, I'm so sorry. . . ."

Rafe caught her, holding on for maybe a second longer than a gentleman should have before he set her back on her feet. He frowned, while the shadows in the corners of the car reached toward them, trembling. A darker feeling inside her twisted, pulling away while the rest of the shade seemed to want the opposite. The shifting patches inside the train car behaved as if they had more than one master. It made Nora queasy, and Indigo curious. She stood still, blinking as if surprised.

Rafe gave her one of the sweet smiles he'd used at the memorial. "Don't I know you? Sorry, that sounds totally creepy, doesn't it? But I'd swear—"

"Oh. Yeah." For a moment it was a struggle for her to sound like innocent Nora and not like someone who knew Rafe Bogdani had been banging the Queen of the Kid Killers. She shook off the weird feeling that her shadows were divided, then dropped her gaze as if the memory of their first meeting hurt. The only hurt she was feeling was the restraint of not whacking the dirtbag right here and now.

"Maidali Ortiz. We met at the procession for her."

"Right!" He snapped his fingers. "Shelby . . . Coughlin. Right?"

Nora repressed a shudder. *Damn it. I gave him Shelby's name. Fuck. Now they'll come after her for sure if I don't play this right. And Sam . . .* "That's right. Look, I know I may have seemed insensitive at the time—"

"You and half of New York." She glanced up. He'd let his smile cool, but it wasn't gone yet. "I understand the impulse."

"No, no. I . . . wasn't quite honest with you. See, I contribute to a news blog and I wanted some pics for the memorial page—the guys can be such pricks about that stuff, so I said I'd do it. I was trying to be discreet. Respectful. I guess I screwed that up."

Being disingenuous chafed. What she really wanted to do was smash in the bastard's face, then drag him into darkness, cutting and tearing into him with shadow knives and needles until he started screaming, begging to tell her about the "blessed event."

But not yet. Not yet.

"It's still haunting me, to be honest."

"Yeah, I can't seem to let go of it either," Rafe said, looking at the floor as the train rattled on. *Yeah, you'd better look away.* "It's really ruined the way I feel about the city. People talk about the crime and the violence, but they don't live here and it's not really like that. Or I thought it wasn't. I mean, if something like this can happen to a sweet kid like Maidali, what sort of monsters are we?"

Just the question I want to ask you, Teach. She let the silence clatter along with the sway and rush of the subway car for a while. He started to raise his head again, pulling in a breath to speak, and she beat him to it. "Hey—" she started, as he said, "Look—"

They both faked embarrassed laughs and argued who should talk first. Nora took the lead. "So . . . I was wondering if I could buy you a drink. To apologize. Y'know."

Rafe gave a bullshit boyish smile, but she knew he didn't buy her excuse for a hot second, so he plainly had an agenda of his own. "I was going to ask you the same thing. Some friends of mine hang out at a jazz club a couple of stops away—it'd be pretty mellow this time of night. If you're okay with that."

Oh, yeah, she was fine with that. They'd stroll along and she'd wait for some place dark. . . .

They made stupid conversation until Rafe looked up and said, "This is it!"

They exited the train together and he led the way up to the street.

The neighborhood at the edge of El Barrio was rougher than the one they'd come from—but pretty much every neighborhood was rougher than the Upper East Side, one way or another. Rafe offered her his arm—as if this were some kind of date—and they started walking east. A couple of old buildings under renovation stood on their left, ringed with construction scaffolds and those plastic slides for skipping rubble down into the industrial Dumpsters below. A lonely neon sign clung to a railing across the alley from the reno site, flickering an unsteady arrow toward a basement entrance. "There it is," Rafe said.

". . . There?" Totally Nora, that hesitation. From within, Indigo stifled her. "Well . . . okay."

As they started into the alley, puzzle pieces clicked into place in her head. This street, this block—another address from Marshall Winston's real estate paperwork. Rafe Bogdani hadn't brought her here on a date.

Eyes narrowed, she turned toward him, but as she did, the shadows began to undulate around them, a nest of snakes at war with itself. Some of those serpents looked darker than the rest—hell, they felt darker—and for a moment Nora could only focus on the twisting, writhing, warring shadows. *What the hell—*

Rafe yanked her sideways into a pitch-black staircase on the renovation side. His eyes flashed, pinpoint flares of white. Nora cried out, and for half a moment she felt Indigo inside her, trying to take over. They were one and the same person—she'd created Indigo as a separate identity in her mind to make it easier for her to keep her two worlds apart—but now she felt power there, down in the dark. Power, hunger, even malice. In that half a moment, she fought Indigo and paid for that hesitation when Rafe smacked her forehead against the blackened basement door.

"No!" Nora shouted, sagging dramatically.

Quiet, Indigo said inside her. *I'll make him pay for that. Right after he tells me what I want to know about the other kids and whatever the cult is planning for them. Just be still for now. I am the power. I am the shadow. He's nothing but scum.*

Her mind whirled. This was her own internal voice, or the part of her that she'd ascribed to Indigo. It came from her own mind. A fractured mind, yes, but her own. The power she'd felt, the grasping hunger that had reached up from the darkness within, that had felt like something else.

Rafe unlocked the door and dragged her into a gloom-shrouded small space, a small antechamber that led to a larger room beyond. The darkness yearned toward her. *Toward Nora or Indigo?* There shouldn't have been a difference.

Indigo, she told herself. *I'm Indigo.*

I am.

In the murk she could see every detail. Shelves and a desk. Lamps unlit. A doorway ahead, into that larger space. Through that open door her Shadow Sight picked out the gleam of golden sigils on the floor. The odors of dried blood, candle wax, human waste, and bitter, oily herbs filled her nose, nearly overpowering the building's lingering old-age reek of ancient tobacco smoke and water damage.

"I heard you at the Edwards house just now," she said as Nora. For that was how he saw her, wasn't it? As Nora? "Searching for Charlotte and the rest of your circle of murdering fucks. Well, I know where you can find them. I—"

He flung her toward the shining symbols that formed a circle on the floor. Tendrils of true ebony shot up from those symbols and wove together to form an open cage, a pen to hold some type of shadow animal—and she knew which animal it would be.

Indigo came forth, twisted away from Rafe, and spun into the gloom. The disquieting blackness of those darker serpents seemed to reach for her, but she dove into the softer shades of familiar power. She *knew* she had to avoid falling into that hungry circle. Into that cage.

Rafe flicked a switch and a single light shone down from the low ceiling to spotlight the ritual circle. He scowled in frustration when he saw that circle was empty. Then he grinned and stepped into the ring himself, turning widdershins round and round, as if he were winding a spring tighter and tighter before unleashing it. Dark power crackled around him. Who the hell *was* this guy?

"So where are they? Charlotte and the others. There are half a dozen addresses I planned to search, but go ahead, save me the trouble."

"They're in hell," she snarled. "Every last one of them. Dead as you're about to be."

He chuckled as he watched the shadows. "I knew you the moment I first touched you, there at the top of the stairs when we were both pretending we had come to grieve for a dead girl. If you hadn't tracked me down, I'd have hunted for you eventually. Did you really think I was so stupid that I wouldn't know you, *Indigo?* Me, of all people?"

Indigo wrapped a tendril of darkness around the lightbulb and crushed it.

"And who the fuck are *you* that I should be impressed?" she whispered, though by now of course she knew. Sorcerer. Magician. Not any ordinary cultist, that was clear.

She circled him clockwise from shadow to shadow and taunted him, hoping he would expose some vulnerability. "Child of Phonos?" she sneered. "I've killed dozens of your breed. Adulterer? Laughable. Betrayer and murderer of the children placed in your care? Only makes me itch to spill your blood sooner."

"Then why don't you?" Even in the renewed blackness, he still turned, looking for her.

Can he see in the dark, like me? Unlikely, but the thought gave her a qualm. He was too confident, and that circle only made him more so. And something was wrong with the darkness as well. As if it warred with itself, not a whole nest but two great snakes, twined together in battle.

"We're alone here. I'm unarmed, unprotected, corporeal as dirt," Rafe continued, as if they were just talking. As if they were friends. "Easy prey. Come get me."

"Now you think *I'm* stupid?"

The seething darkness of that ritual cage made her nervous and she kept away from the shining symbols on the floor, certain they were vibrating. The air was charged, as if some force were building under the floor, in the walls. . . .

"Of course you are. After all, you're standing in *my* lair now. My ritual circle." His gaze seemed to light on her at last, and he stared in her direction with a wolf's smile, as if the darkness could not hide her at all. "Only an idiot would walk willingly into a chamber like this." He laughed. "So, yes. I think you're the stupidest bitch I've ever met, *Shelby*. You want to spill my blood? Give it a try!"

Fury burned red and hot through her body, and the ugly shadows rushed to fill her. She did not stop them this time. "Fuck you."

She surged toward the circle, forged sharpest ebony into a terrible spear, and flung her weapon.

No!

The voice crashed inside her head like thunder, even as it cut like a whisper. It wasn't her own voice. Not Indigo. Not Nora. She felt the dark snakes of the sinister blackness twine around her, piercing deep as daggers. *Fool!*

Rafe swept his hands out, and the force that had resonated in the walls and floor shouted, bursting out from the circle of gleaming symbols, and *reflecting her own weapon back at her!* She dodged left, leaping for another pool of darkness, but the spear whipped past, slicing into her right shoulder. Indigo gasped in shock. *Never! The shadows are mine! No one has ever—*

A star of her own bright blood struck the floor and it *rang!* Rafe's circle of shining symbols blazed into a wall of golden light, banishing every shade and shadow. Nora felt the icy darkness draw into her, racing to her core and binding her still and silent. She toppled across the burning line of sigils and they died down to a heatless glow.

Grinning, Rafe stepped over her so his feet rested on the brightness to either side, neither in the circle nor out of it. He closed his eyes a moment and laughed quietly, shaking his head as if the entire thing had been nothing but a joke. Then he knelt, straddling her. The position didn't feel sexual as much as it felt as if she were a calf about to be branded.

"You need to learn to curb your temper," Rafe said. "And not underestimate a guy whose family was casting blood magic eight hundred years before Mary whelped Jesus." He'd slipped back into his kindly teacher persona, looking so harmless and sweet—and smug—that she wanted to kick him to death.

The blackness inside her strained against her skin as if she were too small a vessel to contain it, and she felt frozen, yet bursting with its incomprehensible movement. It was like a living thing that coiled and writhed and yearned to escape the confines of her body, but she couldn't draw it forth, couldn't use it. Indigo had been cut off from her power, unable even to reach it, as though a wall had been thrown up between herself and the shadows. But she could feel them, and when she began to sense the true immensity of the darkness of the void, she wondered why it had never simply smothered her.

"Guess what happens now?"

"You kill me," she croaked, tasting the bitterness of those other shadows in her mouth like blood.

He looked shocked. "Oh, no, sweetheart." He brushed her hair out of her face. "Now I keep you. This is where I keep all my pets. Until they're needed somewhere else, that is. Of course, *you* will never leave, since this is *it*—if you know what I mean."

"The missing kids," Nora gasped, thinking of Sam's investigation, all of those children abducted and dragged into human trafficking, into slavery. "Here?"

Her wounded shoulder ached and leaked onto the chilly cement floor, and her bruised forehead throbbed with the pounding of her pulse.

"Not all of them. Just the ones *we* need. Your ritual should have worked the first time, but someone screwed it up. This time, we'll make sure. All around the world, all at once, one great, global ritual. It should be magnificent." Rafe paused and cast a speculative glance over her. "Although with you here, I might not need Charlotte's children. This is my ritual circle—*mine*. Maybe I can achieve my goals without the rest of them. Maybe I won't even share the power that's to come."

Nora felt that foreign, unfamiliar darkness stretching itself through her, invading her. It reached out from inside her, twining into a shrieking maelstrom of power that thrummed below them, deep and black as eternal space.

Rafe frowned at her, thinking as he rubbed one finger along his lower lip. "Let's test things . . . see how much control you have over the darkness inside you."

He pinned her right wrist down inside the circle with one hand while he reached inside his jacket with the other. Rafe drew out a small dagger, golden bronze. The hilt's crossbar formed stylized wings that swept down to guard his hand. A circle, endless and empty, surmounted the wings from which sprang the blade. A channel was carved down the center so her blood would flow into the circle, into the void. *Like the emblem in Charlotte's drawer. Like the one on the knife my mother—*

He jabbed the blade toward her hand, as if to pin her flesh and bone to the circle. The darkness tore through Nora and Indigo together, bound them and ripped them, and the blackness that was neither shadow nor herselves bellowed, *NO!*—tearing through the screaming core of power under them as the knife came down . . .

. . . and carved a slit in the skin of reality.

Nora and Indigo plummeted.

Into the void.

Through nightmares of blood, death, and pain.

And out, into daylight.

Nora hit the ground at the speed of horror, and Indigo retreated deeper, huddled down inside, away from the brightness and rising heat of a dusty, pink-tinged morning. Cold blackness lay along

Nora's spine, drawing her like implacable arms into the west-facing shadow of a carved stone pillar. She caught her breath and stared around.

Broken ancient limestone tiles and lines of graceful Grecian pillars—the dusty ruins of a long-gone building. Deep-green plants peeped over the tumbled remains of a white-stone wall, and a bent old woman swathed in a shapeless black dress and head scarf stared at her from the depths of a face sun creased and withered to a walnut skull. This was no picturesque Victorian ruin, no clever construction erected on a knoll in Central Park. It was no place Nora had ever been before and certainly no place American. *Where? How? Holy crap!*

"Rafe, you asshole!" she screamed. "Where'd you send me?"

"Korkyra." The voice came from her own mouth and it came from the darkness within, black and cold as death, but it was not hers. *"And I have brought you."*

8

―――

Nora's gaze shifted wildly, trying to take in everything at once. The sun was overwhelming, rising and lashing at her eyes as she tried to adjust to the unexpected glare.

She squinted and raised her hand to block the worst of the light. Inside her, Indigo shuddered.

No, Nora thought. *She's supposed to be the brave one.*

Nora shook herself and shoved the thought aside. She and Indigo were the same person. She had to remember that, because now there was *another* voice in her head, speaking, demanding her attention. A thundering whisper inside her head that felt as if it came from deep inside her. From the shadows. From the black void at her core, where her power came from . . . the space within her that she had never understood.

But you never really tried to understand, she thought. *When any sane person would have gone mad searching for answers, you didn't even look. Why is that?*

"Who are you?" she demanded, speaking inward, to that void.

The old woman above her muttered a quick prayer and crossed herself as she backed away.

Nora's voice helped her clear her own head, but she realized she'd spoken too loudly, and as she looked around, she saw other people nearby, many of them staring at her. She stood in the middle of an area that had been roped off and nearly barricaded by heavy piles of freshly sorted dirt. Vases and fragments and columns were half-buried in the ground—some kind of archaeological dig. Nearby, two men with guns were looking her way. They wore uniforms, but didn't strike her as police. Security guards, maybe. They didn't look happy to see her.

Surrender to me, that dark voice commanded from the void inside her.

Nora shuddered and hugged herself tightly, a wave of revulsion flowing through her. It was really there—he, for she was certain the voice was male—was deep within her. His words made her insides rumble, shook her bones, thudded against her like loud music at a concert or fireworks exploding right overhead.

She wanted to be sick.

"Who are you?" she asked again, quieter now, wondering if she even needed to speak the words aloud for him to hear them.

As if in some twisted reply to her thoughts, that voice pushed upward and she felt her mouth open, lips forming words against her will. He spoke through her, but the voice was not her own.

I am Damastes. You have kept me locked away long enough. Now I will be free.

The words ripped through her and echoed and sent Nora staggering backward. A flicker of familiarity touched her mind. Had she heard the voice before, back when—

No! She didn't have time for that.

Nora tried to move and felt the world tilt madly. Her legs refused to obey her commands and her arms shuddered. Her mouth pulled into a scowl on one side, as if she were some kind of human marionette and the voice of the void—this presence called Damastes—was pulling her strings.

Idiot girl, you've stepped into my home now. You stand in my temple, and here I will finally take control.

Pain lanced through her, forced her into a shuddering convulsion. There were more words, but she did not hear them so much as she felt them. Her body seized, twisting into a spasmodic arch even as she fell to the ground. The back of her skull slammed into the dirt and her left arm slapped a clay pot that rolled and shattered.

The armed men came for her then. Their faces were lost to her, their words incoherent shouts of alarm, but she understood their intent. She had trespassed where she was not allowed. They would punish her for that. She reached out her hands to draw the darkness to her, ready to become Indigo, to fight if she had to fight. But nothing happened. The guards slowed, moving warily now, and one of them drew his gun.

Indigo? she thought. Half in confusion and half in summons. Nora had created Indigo as a separate persona, someone who had the courage and fortitude to do things Nora might not otherwise have been able to endure, but she and Indigo were one and the same. They were. Which meant the power was *her* power.

So why could she not wield it now?

Nora tried to reach out to the nearby shadows, to draw a cloak of darkness around her—and she felt Damastes fight her from the void. Just as he'd pulled her strings, he held the reins of her power tightly.

You dare interfere with me? You, who hide in your own shadows and bury your own world beneath a mountain of lies? No more.

The words slammed into her, crushed her under their weight. The first of the guards reached her, grabbed at Nora's arm, and then reeled back, screaming as Indigo lashed out. Shadows fluttered like hummingbirds and spilled from her flesh into his, cutting through his skin and muscles as they pulsed their way up to his shoulder.

Nora twisted and rolled, her body still fighting against every attempt she made at control. Her muscles jittered as if electrified, and her teeth clamped down hard enough she feared they might shatter.

Indigo screamed. Damastes roared.

A lurking presence from the deepest waters of her soul, he rose now like a tidal wave, dwarfing her, surely large enough to crush her. Nora felt herself dragged down inside herself, her mind trying to escape the presence of the great darkness that tore through her, seeking a way to break its bonds.

Set me free! the demon roared.

For what could it be other than a demon? The thought turned her blood to ice. If she'd had control over her body, she would have wept.

But how am I holding him? What am I doing to stop his escape?

She had no answer to that question, but it seemed Indigo might. A strange calm came over her, a confidence that had been inconceivable a moment before, and Nora knew then that Indigo had surfaced. Perhaps Indigo had no soul of her own, but she did have her own identity. Her own courage. Nora might call upon the darkness, caress and persuade it, but it was Indigo who had spent years mastering the shadows, turning them into her servants. Her weapons.

Nora jerked side to side, whipped her head around. Clawed at her own flesh. Fell to her knees and curled into a fetal ball. The guards shouted at her, both of them with their guns out. Others were shouting. Somewhere not far off, police sirens screamed. But the real battle was being waged inside her, a tug-of-war over the shadows of that internal void. Nora opened her mouth and two voices cried out, neither of them truly belonging to her. Indigo and Damastes fought, lashing at each other, those twin serpents of darkness twisting and diving, two shades of black. Nora lay on the ground and did her best to breathe.

The second guard shouted orders she could never hope to obey. In the space between heartbeats, she saw him begin to squeeze the trigger on his gun.

Nora saw him, but it was Indigo who reached out with a tendril of darkness and whipped at the guard, intending to knock him backward. That other presence, so large and potent, magnified the attack, pouring ebony rage out of the void and turning that tendril into a battering ram that shattered bone and pulped muscle. The guard sailed backward into a half-submerged column of stone with enough force to blast chunks of the ancient structure into the air.

What remained of him oozed down the column.

Nora froze, too stunned even to fight that inner war. Even Indigo was horrified.

A dark glee emanated from Damastes.

Nora stepped toward the ruined man, thinking that if she could reach him in time, it might be possible to save him.

He is beyond redemption. He is of no concern.

One good look at the meat that had been flayed from his bones and Nora knew Damastes was right. Though the man still had a pulse—easily seen as every heartbeat pumped another weak cascade of crimson from his shoulder—it was weak and fading. A thick halo of blood surrounded him.

The dying guard looked at her and spoke words that she could not understand.

Whatever he had said, Damastes responded, speaking with her lips. *"Your death offers me strength. You die for a worthy cause."* Nora's lips pulled into a cold smile that felt completely wrong. The curl of her mouth had a cruelty that was foreign to her.

Someone shouted and she managed to glance toward a half-ruined column, where the other guard had hidden himself. His gun still out, he seemed much more interested in barking fearful orders into a radio or cell phone than in confronting her now.

The other onlookers were gone, wisely fleeing for safety.

Greece, she thought. *Is this Greece?*

This was my home. The glories offered here in worship of me were grand things, indeed. Worthy. But greater glories will be mine when I am in control of your body, as I was meant to be.

Her eyes moved, but they did so without her intention. She saw the walls of the dig site, the half-ruined frescoes that showed fragmentary images of a vast black shape. One fresco depicted an army dying in a tide of blackness. Another showed some kind of ritual taking place in a temple that seemed to be the palm of a gigantic hand, complete with claws that nearly doubled the length of the fingers, towering above the worshippers within.

The voice of the void rose up, its deeper shadows beginning to fill her gut, her chest, reaching out to her extremities. Damastes flooding through her like an ancient, dreadful poison.

Indigo screamed and Nora's body shuddered, vibrated as her other self fought Damastes's control. Darkness rippled across Nora's flesh like waves smashing into a rocky shoreline, and she groaned as her body collapsed again. Whether it was Indigo or that other presence she did not know, but the closest image on the wall— a winged shadow that cast lightning from its claws—shattered.

Nora tried to rise again and saw the police officers coming toward them. These were not rented guards. These were hardened men— soldiers perhaps, or police officers, what did she know of Greek uniforms?—and they approached with weapons drawn.

The needles of a Taser punched into Nora's right forearm and the meat under her left breast.

The current ran into her body, raced through her, spreading faster even than the ebon poison of Damastes. Her vision blurred and her mouth let out three separate, distinctive screams as she flopped to the ground, incapable of any further motion, any real thought.

The world buzzed in an electrical storm and then silence reached out and dragged her under.

Her body still aching and buzzing from the pain of being hit by the cop's Taser, Nora snapped back to consciousness in the back of a police van. Her wrists were bound behind her and she lay prone, seeing nothing but the padded walls of the van and the screen that let her view the backs of the heads of the two police officers up at the front of the vehicle.

Everything hurt.

She tried to summon Indigo, the darkness, to wrap herself in shadows and slip away, but nothing happened. The void within her—that well of blackness—was still there, but when she attempted to draw it to her, to influence it and muster some control, the void did not respond. She paused, expecting some backlash from the presence there, but seconds ticked by and she felt no sign of Damastes. His voice had fallen silent and whatever power he'd wielded to turn her into some kind of puppet before, it was gone. But so was her control of the shadows. Whatever Damastes had done to her, she was powerless.

Inside her was a silence that she had not felt since before her parents were shot.

No. Those were lies. However her parents had really died, her memories could not be trusted.

A fresh brand of panic swept through her. Handcuffed and locked in the back of the van, she realized she was truly a captive for the first time in her memory. She had always had the freedom to slip into a patch of nothing and fade away. Now, she was a prisoner. What if that cop back at the archaeological dig had died?

Of course he died, she thought, remembering his injuries.

Nora bit her lip and curled into a tighter ball as the van bounced over ruts in the road. Hot grief swept through her. She had killed a security guard, an innocent man who had been trying to secure the safety of the people at the dig. Trying to protect his city.

"Oh, my God," she whispered, and felt tears well in her eyes.

The cop behind the wheel glanced in the mirror and muttered something to his partner. Something, she was sure, about the killer they had handcuffed in the back.

A dreadful calm descended upon her. A strange surrender. She had not been in control of the shadows that had struck out and killed the security guard, but how could she have even begun to explain that? If any of them even believed their own eyes, or the testimony of witnesses, they would see her as a monster, a witch. To ask them to also believe she had been momentarily possessed by something even more monstrous . . .

Momentarily, she thought again, wondering how long Damastes had been lurking down there in the void within her. Recently, the shadows had been malevolent to her, as though they meant her harm. Had that been Damastes's influence? Could he have been there all that time without her being aware of his presence? And if so . . . where was he now?

Nora wondered if he might still be in there, quiet now, perhaps in hiding. Or just waiting.

The van bounced through potholes and her head banged against the floor. The impact cleared her thoughts for a moment, broke her focus on Damastes long enough for her to remember the man responsible for her ending up here. Damastes might have had something to do with it—after all, he'd said that temple was his home, that people had worshipped him there—but it had started with that son of a bitch Rafe Bogdani. Magician or sorcerer or whatever the hell he was, if anyone had some kind of answers for her, it would be Rafe. The trouble would be in finding a way to get back home so she could beat those answers out of him.

The trouble will be in ever going anywhere again, she thought. *Once you're in a Greek prison, convicted of murder.*

She needed her powers. Needed the shadows.

Nora mustered up the courage that she so often associated with her alter ego. Without the darkness, she didn't feel as if she could be Indigo, even for a second, but she could tap into Indigo's strength and determination. She closed her eyes, breathed deeply to calm herself, and looked into the void.

Damastes. Are you real? Are you here?

Nothing. Not even a twinge.

Her bones still ached from being hit by the Taser—maybe more than one—and for the first time she wondered if Damastes wasn't hiding at all. Had his malignant presence been burned out of her by that Taser strike? She had done research on Tasers for several articles and understood the basics: current without amplitude. Ten volts with a thousand amps would kill a person. Ten thousand volts with no amps would shock a brain into a stupor as long as the current went on. It would hurt. It would paralyze, and as long as it wasn't abused, it would usually cause little permanent harm.

If the voltage had quieted Damastes—and even, it seemed, Indigo—what did that mean? If they could be silenced by a few seconds of electricity coursing through her body, through her brain, were the voices ever really there at all? She wondered if they were just symptoms of some brain disorder.

Of course, a brain disorder couldn't transport a body across thousands of miles and an ocean.

The silence inside her ought to have been comforting. Instead it was unsettling. Though she sometimes thought of Indigo as a separate entity, she knew better. But it was easier to put up a wall between her daytime self and her nighttime self. Indigo played in darkness and Nora preferred to stay where she could see the light. In some ways, Indigo was her best friend.

Ugh, how sad is that?

But the truth was that she didn't have many friends and couldn't stand the idea of having none.

She felt a flash of guilt then, unwanted, unwelcome, a quick reminder of how she'd treated—

Sam.

"No," she whispered, as the dark presence rushed up from the void again. Damastes had returned.

Sam. Your mate. Your plaything. What is he to you? Does he know who you really are behind your shadows and lies?

Fingers of darkness pushed at her brain, dug through her consciousness, and Nora fought back as best she could, blocking those questing probes into her mind because they would surely find secrets she needed kept. She tried to escape from the black, cold mind that examined her, but it wasn't easy and the effort had her body shaking and spasming again. Her limbs jittered and danced in a half dozen petit mal seizures.

"Get out of my head you freak!" her voice screeched, and her words slurred past teeth locked together and lips peeled back beyond her control.

You don't know, do you? How perfect! How utterly delicious!

Damastes's peals of laughter pounded through her skull and rocked her body even harder.

Oh, little Nora, how very foolish of you! You don't understand anything at all!

"Leave me alone! Leave me the fuck alone!"

Nora tried again to summon her shadows. The cop in the passenger seat had turned and was staring nervously at her, and now she saw that the Taser was back in his hand. Flurries of ice cut through her stomach as panic started pulling at her mind. Without her shadows, what was she?

The shadows are not yours, little Nora. They are mine! I am as a god, and you are nothing but weak, human flesh.

Nora screamed and her body bucked, her legs kicking hard enough to knock one shoe completely off. Spittle flew from her too-dry lips and her eyes rolled back into her skull.

You're nothing but a failed sacrifice. Your own parents offered you to me, a promise they failed to keep. You will die at my hands and I will make this miserable world my own.

"Go fuck yourself! You're nothing!" Her voice sounded different, deeper, colder. The shadows in the back of the van coalesced, weaving around her, and she laughed. Indigo laughed.

Then she saw the guard push the Taser through the grate that separated the front of the van from the back and pull the trigger. The barbs hit her and voltage arced through her. Nora went rigid with the pain, bones on fire, and consciousness fled. In the last eye blink of awareness, she felt herself tumbling into the void. . . .

And then she was gone.

Her body ached everywhere, from her toes to the top of her head, with the sort of dull throbs that normally indicated she'd pushed herself too far when exercising the day before. Muscle strain, and possibly a few torn ligaments.

Petit mal seizures. Possibly grand mal. Was it her cousin Becky who'd had epilepsy? She frowned. Did she have a cousin Becky? There was someone named Becky, back in the days before her parents died.

Her arms were wrapped uncomfortably around her body.

Hard straps pinned her to a cold metal surface.

Nora opened her eyes and looked at a cracked plaster ceiling.

She lifted her head, despite the way the motion pulled at her neck muscles, and saw that she was strapped to a table and locked inside a straitjacket. Her head fell back and bounced on stainless steel, and she felt a groan merge with a laugh. There it was. She was crazy after all.

The memories came hammering at her mind and Nora recoiled. For a moment, as the Taser had shocked her for the second time, she had seen into the utterly vile core of Damastes. There was nothing human there, nothing redeeming within that endless blackness. The mind she'd accidentally touched was an endless chasm of loathsome urges and dark desires. No matter what else happened, Damastes could never be allowed to escape into the physical world.

You cannot keep me, little Nora.

"Watch me, you sick bastard." Her voice was barely recognizable.

Nora looked more carefully around the room. Medical equipment was in the room—the cell?—but none of it was being used on her. She was here for the table, she suspected, and nothing else. The police wanted to make absolutely certain she didn't have a chance to kill anyone else.

Please, kill more of them. Take their lives and offer me their essence. I might even let you retain some semblance of life in gratitude for your worship. I have been far too long without proper sustenance. Murder, little Nora, and feed me.

Murder. The word resonated. Her mind had been spinning ever since Rafe had attacked her in that basement, but now it all began to click together for her. Rafe Bogdani was some kind of magician and a high-ranking member of the Children of Phonos. The way he had talked to Graham Edwards, it was as if Rafe operated separately from the New York chapter of the cult. He certainly hadn't sounded as if he answered to Charlotte Edwards, the local high priestess.

Graham had as good as said he was a member, but that he'd

withdrawn when he learned that his wife intended to sacrifice their children to the gods of murder. Three children were to be killed as part of a ritual, not simultaneously but in some kind of specific, pertinent sequence. Luis Gallardo was meant to be the first, and though Indigo had interrupted the ritual, she hadn't been in time to save him. Would his death count toward the rite? Would the murder gods consider it a proper sacrifice?

Indigo had killed every member of the New York chapter's inner circle in that warehouse, but she knew that didn't mean the chapter had been completely obliterated. There would be Phonoi assassins, at the very least, though she had no idea who would give them orders now that their high priestess was dead. Rafe Bogdani, perhaps. The man had real magic at his command, not the kind of dabbling that the Phonoi typically engaged in. Was he some kind of sorcerer-for-hire, or was he truly a part of the cult? She tried to recall his exact words, the things he'd said before she'd dropped through the shadows in the ritual circle of that basement, where he'd tried to kill her. Or capture her, or whatever he'd intended. Had he said anything that gave away the nature of his relationship to the Children of Phonos? She didn't think so.

Maybe it's over, she thought. Not her tussle with Rafe, which obviously required a rematch. But she wondered hopefully if killing the high priestess and the inner circle had torn the heart out of the cult, at least that chapter. Maybe Graham Edwards's children were safe, now. Maybe whatever had been planned would never come to fruition.

She had so many enemies now, worst of all this evil cancer of a demon that had taken root inside her. It would have been nice to think that the Children of Phonos weren't her problem anymore.

But that felt too easy.

The cult was global, and they worshipped the gods of murder. If she'd erased one cell, others would arrive to fill that void, particularly if they were involved in the somehow more mundane criminal horrors of human trafficking. And then there was Rafe. Whatever the magician had done to her in that basement before she'd been transported here, it had ended up with Damastes locked inside her. Or given him access to the dark void inside her.

"You're one of the murder gods," she whispered.

Damastes laughed inside her.

I have worshippers throughout the world. My followers are legion.

"I've met a few. They die easily enough." Bravado.

Even now my followers seek to serve me. They seek to win my favor. They know what you refuse to know, that I will eventually climb free of you or seize complete control. A foolish mistake on the part of your parents and the high priestess that night. A miscast summoning, that is all you are. You were meant to be my offering, a promised body to climb into and take as my own.

Nora shook her head. Lies! Her parents would have never done anything of the sort. Her mom and dad loved her! Still, she felt the sting of tears at the corner of her eyes, unshed but threatening to fall.

A gathering of fools tried to claim my power as their own, and the end result is a trap, a gateway that was sealed with me halfway through it. That will change soon enough. I will bend you to my will or Bogdani will find a way to release me. His friends hoped to summon and enslave me, but only a fool would attempt that a second time. His only hope is to separate me from your flesh. Then perhaps I will allow him to serve me the way he and his cult wished me to serve them. Or I will kill him, and so many others.

Her thoughts were scattered in so many directions as she tried to pull all of these threads together.

"So I was meant to be, what, a vessel?"

A doorway, nothing more. But I am trapped on the threshold. I fought their summoning because they wished to bind me as their slave, like a genie they might use to make them rich or fetch them water or seduce reluctant lovers for them. I fought . . . and somehow, so did you. And in fighting . . . we became one.

Ice flowed through her, a cold, calculating hatred that soothed her and helped her focus. She could feel the shadows breathing in the corners and beneath the table. Rafe's magic, the shock of being shifted thousands of miles in a moment, the tumorous presence of the demon in the void . . . something had stripped her of her powers, broken her ability to concentrate and to touch the dark. Now, for the first time since Damastes had tried to seize control of her, she felt that connection to the shadows again. They knew her. They yearned for her.

For Indigo.

"Rafe's gonna die," she said.

If he is loyal to me, he will live. If he ignores my commands, he will die. The same could be said of you, Nora Hesper. You, who have siphoned your power from me while I lay dormant within. But now I am awake . . . now that the Phonoi have been trying to summon and enslave me again, from afar. And the time has come for me to walk the world in this flesh.

She could feel the darkness hiding at the edges of her awareness as if trying to decide whom it should obey, Nora or Damastes. Now she called and the darkness fluttered, whispered closer to her.

"It's my body. You're nothing but a virus. Poison in my veins."

And **you** *are little more than a corpse too foolish to die. Oh, little Nora—*

"Not Nora," she said quietly. "Indigo."

And what is Indigo? A mask on a frightened girl.

"Flesh and blood. Solid and alive, which is more than you can say. You need your precious sacrifices and your cult of killers! You need their worship. I need nothing and no one!"

To prove her point she ripped the darkness closer, wrapping herself in the reluctant shadows and slithering free from the restraints that tried to hold her. She could move through a keyhole; what possible chance did a straitjacket and leather straps have?

Are you so sure about that? Are you certain there is no one and nothing that you need?

Nora stood and felt her legs under her, once again hers to command. There were no seizures now. He blood pumped and her nerves sang and her fists clenched until she felt the crescents of her nails biting into soft skin.

Indigo sneered.

Nora asked, "What do you mean?"

Can you so easily live without Shelby or Sam? Even now Rafe watches Shelby's domicile. Even now he waits for Sam to arrive, the better to kill them both without having to hunt either of them down. Give me free rein, surrender control of this body to me, and I will stop him.

"I'll kill him. And then I'll kill you." The words were whispered from a cold throat, choked by rage. Her friends were half a world away and she wasn't even certain how she'd gotten here. Rafe had done something to her with that ritual circle, used some kind of spell, but had he chosen this destination or had Damastes pulled her to his seat of power, to the place he'd once called home? One or both of them had broken the laws of physics, strained the ties of reality, and cast her a few thousand miles through the darkness. How the hell could she hope to match that task?

You are not powerful enough to save your friend, your lover, or yourself. Surrender to me, little Nora, and I will spare your friends. Offer yourself to me willingly and they will be safe.

Nora shook her head. She had seen inside of Damastes and knew better. He'd hunt them down and make them suffer to satisfy his petty need for revenge over whatever indignities he believed Nora had caused. More than that, she sensed he was still hiding something, some secret that he was holding close to his wretched heart, waiting to use against her when the time was right.

Indigo shook her head.

How had Rafe done it? Or had he done it at all? She traveled through shadows all the time, moved from place to place as if there were no distance in between. It had always been short distances, mostly to places she had already been or at least seen, but if Damastes had somehow dragged her to his home, she knew one thing— he had done it through the shadows. And if that was true, then she could surely find her way back.

All she required was a path.

She commanded the shadows and they obeyed. The light failed to fall in one corner, and as she stared, a patch of darkness grew there, deepening into a black, inky maelstrom that pulled at her. There, her pathway home.

Damastes seemed to fight her, but only for a moment before he stopped struggling. Nora thought it might be a bluff, a lie to make her think she was winning. Still, there was no choice. Sam needed her. Shelby needed her. And she needed the both of them.

Inside her, Damastes laughed. *Go where you like, girl. Fight as long as you can. In the end, I will have my freedom. Before that day comes, I will make the ones you love suffer. I will feed on them as I fed on the souls of your—*

Indigo shoved aside his voice and leaped into the darkness. The maelstrom longed for her, welcomed her, swallowed her. The shadows swaddled her and she heard the familiar whispers of the endless void, sounds and voices she would never be able to interpret. For a moment, memories seemed to flicker at the edges of her mind, but they meant nothing to her now. Only one thing mattered at that moment. She had to get to Sam and Shelby before it was too late. She had to.

Without them she had no reasons she could think of to live, save for revenge.

9

——

Revenge.

What was the phrase? *Revenge is a dish best served cold?*

Nora didn't know who said it. She remembered it from a Klingon warlord in one of the Star Trek movies, but she thought it was older than that. Maybe a French writer, maybe Shakespeare. Maybe Genghis Khan for all she knew. And what did it matter? It was wrong. Revenge, she knew, should be hot. As hot as blood. As hot as the rage that flared inside her heart.

Hot enough to burn that evil bastard Damastes out of her soul.

As Indigo she came out of the shadows, staggered, reached for a wall—any wall, anything sturdy and upright and real—and leaned against it. Her knees buckled and she sagged drunkenly against the cold stone. She placed her forehead against it. Nora's forehead, not Indigo's.

The tears that seared her cheeks, though . . . did they belong to her or her shadow self? What was the difference now? Who was she after all?

A betrayed child of human monsters?

A slave to a demon?

A woman whose entire life was a lie?

Where was Nora in all of that? *Who* was Nora?

And what was Indigo? How much of her was hers, and how much was the demon who moved within her like a virus, infecting her, controlling her, feeding off the things she did?

Too many questions.

Too many.

Nora wept against the cold stone, not knowing or caring where she was.

Unsure if she wanted to know who she was.

And dreadfully afraid of what she was.

The voice said, "Are you all right?"

But those were not the actual words. It took Nora's numbed mind a moment to realize that the question had been asked in Italian.

"Stai bene?"

Those were the words she'd heard . . . but she'd understood them in English. She raised her head and looked at the figure standing a few feet away. It was a nun. Ancient, her face a labyrinth of deep wrinkles, mouth thin and trembling, nose bulbous and a bit crooked. But her eyes were strangely young. They were bright green, like cat's eyes, with no trace of glaucoma, no rheumy redness to the sclera.

Nora licked her lips. "I don't understand," she told the nun.

But her mouth said, *"Non capisco."*

The nun smiled. A thin smile, oddly knowing. *"Da dove vieni?"*

"Where am I from?" Nora looked around. The wall against which she'd been leaning was a massive structure, broad though only a few stories high, made from massive rough brown stones. A sloping grade of stony concrete swept down to a narrow, crooked cobble-stoned street. A handful of people sat at sidewalk tables, drinking tiny cups of coffee and eating croissants. The sign on the wall of the little restaurant read CAFFÈ DELLA GALLERIA. "Where the hell am I?"

"Dove credi di essere?" Where do you think you are?

Nora said, more as a question than a statement, "Italy . . . ?"

The nun shook her head. *"Firenze."*

Nora blinked in surprise. "Florence? How—?"

She stopped, unwilling to have that conversation with a stranger. She knew how. Shadows. The real question was "Why?" or . . . "Why here?"

She had no connection with Italy beyond a love of pizza, cannoli, and a good Chianti.

Continuing to speak in Italian, the nun took a tentative step closer. "Are you lost, my child?"

Nora began to turn away, to wave her off, a denial forming on her lips, wanting to end this conversation so she could find another doorway into shadow and get the hell out of here. Instead, she stopped and her mind replayed the question.

Something was wrong.

Her confused mind had heard the nun ask if she was okay. A kind question, spoken with compassion by a woman whose job description required compassion. But then the actual words came through the fog in Nora's mind. The nun hadn't asked a question at all. No. She had made a statement. Two words.

"Sei perso." Nora turned back to the nun. "You are lost."

That was what the old woman had said.

And she hadn't said it nicely.

"Wh-what did you say?"

"You are lost. So lost."

"What do you mean? You don't even know who I am."

"I know."

"Prove it."

The smile on the old nun's face widened, revealing yellow teeth that were wet with spit. "I know you, Nora Hesper, born of shadows, fattened on lies, blood traitor, daughter of fools, slave and whore of the Butcher."

Each word struck Nora like a physical blow, pummeling her, driving her back step by step until she sagged gasping against the wall.

"Who *are* you?"

Instead of answering the nun spat on the ground at Nora's feet. The spittle glistened on the stone and then began to sizzle like fat on a griddle. Nora yelped and scuttled sideways.

None of the people at the café across the street had noticed. They were all caught up in their envelopes of privacy, talking, laughing, hunched over coffee cups and cell phone screens.

All traces of humor were gone from the old woman's face. Her smile crushed downward to become a heavy sneer of disgust. The mass of wrinkles tightened into a lupine leer as the nun raised a liver-spotted hand and pointed one thin and twisted finger at Nora and rattled off something else in a language that sounded so familiar and yet which Nora could not understand. Even though Indigo's powers had somehow allowed her to understand and speak Italian, this language eluded her. And yet . . .

And yet . . .

It was so strangely familiar. Nora was sure she *should* know this language, and that was certainly as strong as anything in her mind. She'd heard this language somewhere. Some . . . *when,* but it was hidden back in the damaged darkness of her mind. Fumbling for it was like trying to pick up pieces of broken glass. It hurt her to try. It made her want to scream.

The woman spoke at length, hissing and snarling her strange words, pronouncing them like an accusation. Or a curse. Then Nora heard a single word in the midst of the tirade. A name, spoken with such intense hatred that it sounded as if it must have drawn blood in the nun's throat.

Damastes.

"Stop!" shrieked Nora. Her voice was a cry as sharp and high as a gull's.

The nun's words faltered, slowed, and stopped. She stood, panting with the effort of spewing her hatred, fists balled, eyes blazing with a heat that was almost palpable.

"Who are you and what do you *want* from me?" pleaded Nora.

The nun fixed her with a deadly and icy glare. "Did you think that your crimes would go unnoticed?"

"What . . . ? What crimes? You're not making any sense. I haven't done anything to you. I don't even know where I am."

"You are awash in blood. You reek of murder. You are *his,* body and soul. You are the Butcher's instrument on earth, and yet you stand before an Androktasiai—before a righteous maiden of slaughter and think you can *lie.* To me? To us?"

Nora had no idea what was going on or what any of this meant, but when the old woman spoke that word—*Androktasiai*—something within Nora's soul recoiled. The word itself echoed like a shriek in her mind.

Androktasiai.

Then a voice spoke—no . . . it screamed at her.

The witches have found you. Foolish girl, run. Flee now while you still have breath and life.

It was the towering voice of Damastes, but in that moment the demon's voice was filled with an emotion other than hatred, contempt, or bloodlust.

Nora could hear, could *feel,* the demon's fear.

"I don't understand this," Nora cried, saying it outward and inward at the same moment. "You have the wrong person. Whoever you think I am, you're wrong. I'm an American. I'm a reporter and—"

"You are the vessel of the demon of murder," interrupted the nun. "You give reach to his arm and dexterity to his hand. You wield his knives and you bathe in the blood spilled in his name. You are slave and consort to Damastes, and you pollute even the meanest ground upon which you stand."

"No!" snapped Nora, her anger rising to match the levels of fear and confusion. "You're wrong. If you think I'm *with* Damastes in any way, you're out of your goddamn mind. I hate him. He's a parasite and—"

The nun struck her.

The simple slap was so hideously fast that her withered hand became a blur. The sound was like a gunshot. Pain exploded across Nora's cheek and seemed to echo all the way down to her blood and bone. She staggered backward, struck the unyielding stone, rebounded, and fell hard to the ground. The pain was enormous and she could feel damage in her neck muscles and tendons. Any harder and that blow would have snapped her neck. The power and speed were too much, too big. It was not possible for a small woman, especially one as old as this, to hit like that.

Run, you stupid cow, screamed Damastes, *you cannot win this fight. Go, I command it. Go!*

"Fuck yourself," snarled Nora, and again it was to both the inner and the outer monsters. Inside her mind Indigo also screamed at her, telling her to flee. Not out of fear but because of the safety in shadows. *Power* was in darkness. Right now the sun was almost directly overhead. The wall seemed to stand on its own shadow, hiding them beneath skirts of stone.

"Please . . . ," said Nora weakly as the nun grabbed a handful of her shirt. With no sign of effort, the tiny woman jerked Nora to her feet. "You're making a mistake. I'm not who you think I am."

"You smell of blood and you stink of murder."

With a sudden move of her own, Nora slammed both palms

hard against the nun's flat breastbone and drove her backward. Surprise flickered on the old woman's face, though no trace of pain. If anything she looked mildly impressed, even amused.

"So, the Butcher's bitch has spirit. But it will not make your death worthy of song."

"The Butcher?" demanded Nora. "You mean Damastes? You're trying to kill me. What makes you any different?"

"Damastes is the spirit of murder, of needless death, of slaughter for its own red sake."

"I know, he's a total asshole. What does that make you?"

The nun straightened, and she seemed momentarily to appear taller and almost regal. "The Androktasiai are the sacred and eternal sisterhood of battlefield slaughter. Of *righteous* slaughter."

"How the hell is that any different? Or any better?"

The nun's eyes filled with loathing. "To ask such questions is to reveal yourself as soulless and foul, whore of the Butcher. You bathe in blood spilled without art or honor, without purpose or—"

"Shut it," growled Nora, and she swung a punch at the nun's face. Nora was tired and heartsick, confused and terrified, and all of that went into the punch. The blow came all the way up from the ground, gathering power and speed with the torque of ankles and knees, waist and shoulders, channeling out through the muscles of back and biceps, into the hard knot of bones of her clenched fist.

No! bellowed Damastes. *That is not the way to fight these witches.*

The punch . . . missed.

The nun, laughing, ducked backward and let the punch burn the air instead of smash into skin and bone. The force of the punch twisted Nora, and the momentum—unchecked by impact—spun her off-balance and toward the ground. The nun hooked her in the gut, catching floating ribs and mashing them against liver and lungs. That blow lifted Nora completely off the ground, drove the air out of her lungs, then dropped her like a bludgeoned ox. Nora landed in a fetal ball, wanting to scream, needing to, but unable to force even a choked whisper out of the spasming wreck of her body.

The pain was so bad it felt like dying. She felt ripped apart as she lay there under the unrelenting noonday sun. Through the tears in her eyes, Nora saw that the people eating at the café were oblivious to the fight. They talked and laughed and ate, and not one of them looked in her direction. As if none of this were real. As if none of it mattered. Not her life, not her death.

Then something obscured the sky, and Nora looked up to see the nun standing over her. The old woman's face was calm, almost serene, confident in her complete dominance of the moment. Her shadow fell across Nora's face. The nun reached into a pocket of her habit and drew a slim knife. The straight blade was four inches long and tapered to a thin stiletto point. Nora could see strange words and symbols etched into the metal.

"Slave of the Butcher," said the woman in a voice that was almost gentle, "you tried to fight, you tried to do battle, and so I will accept you as opponent rather than victim. This is just. May the Gods have mercy on your soul. May your blood wash clean the stains of—"

And Nora dove into the shadows cast by her own killer.

Not dove.

No.

Fell.

The tiny patch of darkness was all Indigo needed. She tumbled into it as surely and certainly as if she'd rolled off a cliff. And in the falling, the battered, weak, and helpless Nora went away and in her place was Indigo.

The damage of the slap and the punch were gone. Or, perhaps, irrelevant. The weakness of ordinary humanity had been shucked.

Indigo summoned the winds of darkness and rode them far

away from that place. Whoever this madwoman was, now was not the time to fight her. Indigo needed answers and time to think it all through. There had been no time to process the enormity of everything that had happened in the last . . .

How long? Hours? Days? She did not know.

How much of what Damastes had told her was the truth? How much of her own life was a lie? Where was the safe ground between those poles? If her powers came from a demon trapped with her, then what did that make her? Was she a slave, as the nun had said? Was she a monster? Could she even swear that all the blood she'd spilled was that of killers?

No. *No.* The Phonoi were evil. They were.

And this nun, this so-called maiden of slaughter, what was she really? She claimed to be different from Damastes because she was a worshipper of battlefield killing. Was that really different?

No, growled Damastes. Then he began to lecture her as if she were a stupid and stubborn schoolgirl. *We are all killers. They are weak, though. They delude themselves with false justifications because they do not have the courage and insight to accept murder in all of its many and beautiful aspects. They—*

"Shut. The. Fuck. Up," snarled Indigo, and she threw her whole will against the demon.

Silence rang like a dark bell. She could feel its echoes in the beat of her own heart.

Up ahead the shadows seemed to swirl in a familiar way.

Home.

God. Home.

Indigo found the doorway in the darkness and stepped through into the shadows of her apartment. The shades were down, the morning sunlight blazing around their edges, and the room was bathed in a soft and soothing gloom. She staggered but caught herself, catching her balance by the closet door. She looked around.

The coffee table was there, the desk, her TV. Her asshole cats. Everything.

And there, standing by the door, was the nun.

How the hell did she—

But, no. It wasn't her at all. For a moment Indigo had been confused by the woman's battle stance, but this intruder was someone else. Instead of the habit and wimple of a nun, this younger woman wore a simple tunic and a leather belt, from which hung the scabbards of a short knife and a sword. Her thick black hair had been pulled back and tied in a long braid.

The face and hair were different, but the clothes and weapons were identical to those of the psycho bitch who'd tried to kill her after her blackout, when she'd been approached by Sam at the *NYChronicle* offices and had taken off. But the woman's stance was the same as that of the murder nun, which suggested that maybe they were all related, these bloodthirsty women. All slaughter maidens. The first one had attacked her and then vanished when she had a chance at the killing blow. This one didn't look inclined to retreat.

"Welcome, whore of the Butcher," the slaughter maiden said, her weapons gleaming and deadly in her hands.

"Look, sister," said Indigo, trying to be reasonable in an unreasonable situation, "I don't know what the hell your problem is, you and your sorority, but can we put a pin in it for now? Leave while you can. Last and only warning."

The woman settled into a more fluid combat stance, sword and dagger loose in her hands, the tips of each weapon pointed toward Indigo. Everything about this killer's posture spoke of a disheartening competence. Her knees were bent, weight on the balls of her feet, rear leg cocked to spring forward or sideways, body angled to present weapons but protect vulnerabilities, face calm and eyes sharp.

"Okay, so we're doing this," said Indigo with a sigh. "It's on you then."

Her hands were open, fingers splayed, and as she closed them into fists, she willed shadow knives to form. They became solid in her grip. Familiar. Comforting.

"Will you renounce your master and submit to the holy purity of my knife?" asked the slaughter maiden.

"Like I told the old version in Italy just now, Damastes is *not* my master. He's trying to make me his victim, but he doesn't own me." Indigo hoped it didn't sound as false or uncertain as it felt. "Second, eat me."

The maiden smiled.

And attacked.

She was fast.

So fast.

Her blades sliced like silver fire through the shadows, faking high and low, jabbing, circling, slashing short and stabbing shallow. Beautiful in a way. Like a light show. Like a dance.

Nora would have died right there.

Nora would never have had a chance.

But the slaughter maiden was not fighting Nora. She was not fighting any ordinary human woman.

She fought Indigo.

As the maiden darted in, Indigo parried and spun, but her own countercut was blocked. In the claustrophobic closeness of that studio, she half turned the way she'd come and tried to thrust under the maiden's guard, met steel, and both weapons slithered off. The steel knife trailed sparks, but flecks of darkness flew from Indigo's shadow dagger. Indigo darted sideways, catching a one-two attack on her knives, locked them in place, and kicked the woman. She aimed for stomach, caught her thigh, but drove her back anyway. Indigo lunged forward, pressing the attack with a swirl of chops and stabs, forcing the maiden to give ground, forcing her into a purely defensive battle. They locked weapons again as they crashed backward against the dresser, and this time both women kicked out. Knee met knee and they rebounded, each of them momentarily lamed by the force of their collision.

Indigo leaped high but slashed downward and in, and her shadow knife opened a long red line from the maiden's elbow to deltoid, seeding the air with wet droplets like scattered rubies. The maiden grunted, impressed and angry, and countered with a jab that sent her dagger point skittering across Indigo's ribs. Shadow cloak and flesh parted as new pain detonated in Indigo's side, but she ate the pain, used it as fuel, forced herself to close in. The motion deepened the cut, but it gave Indigo the advantage of angle, and she chopped the maiden across the face with her forearm, then checked the movement and slashed backward. Another gash spilled open, this time from ear to jawline.

The maiden did not cry out, but instead head-butted Indigo and then tried to stab her as she reeled back. But Indigo brought up her shadow cloak and whipped it around the stabbing arm. Then she kicked under it, twisting her body to bring her heel up to crunch into the cartilage beneath the woman's kneecap. Indigo could hear bone creak and tissue rip.

The maiden hurled herself forward, using the collapse of her leg to pitch her weight against Indigo and drive her against the arm of the sofa. The padded arm punched Indigo hard in the hip, and then they were falling over it, crashing onto the sofa, twisting even as they sprang back up in the air, stabbing and hissing and grappling. They fell hard onto the floor, crashed against the legs of the coffee table. One of the shadow knives went flying away, dissolving the moment it left Indigo's hand. The other was knotted in the fist of the arm that had wound the cloak around the maiden's arm. That left Indigo one hand free, and she had to whip it up and block the downward stab of the maiden's sword. She parried it with all of her strength, crunching the woman's wrist against the coffee table. Once, again, and again until the nerves yielded and the blade fell away.

Then, still tethered together by the cloak, the women lay on the floor on their hips, each trying to strike with their free hands and kick with knees and feet. The fight was savage, ugly.

The woman could fight. This was not like battling a cultist. Here was a woman who, despite her apparent age, was at the height of her physical powers and equally highly skilled with weapons and empty hands.

Yet so was Indigo. She fought with skills that she knew she had never earned. Techniques of karate, jujitsu, boxing, kung fu . . . moves that Nora had never studied. Fighting arts whose skills should have come from some phase of preparation for a life as a superhero, but which Indigo now knew had darker origins.

She fought with the masterful skills of the world's most dangerous being: Damastes, demon of murder.

Each block was followed by a killing blow, and when these were blocked, the hand reshaped itself and sought a new ingress to something that would break or bleed. It was as if Indigo's body was truly a living weapon and she was its passenger. It was beautiful to witness—and in a way both Nora and Indigo stood apart and watched the fight with the fascination of Romans at the Circus. But it was also brutal and terrifying because both aspects of her, the woman and the hero, knew that this was what Damastes wanted of her.

To be a weapon of destruction. To be the blade that would allow him to spill blood over and over and over again . . .

To be the evil thing that this warrior nun believed her to be.

The horror of it, the disgust of it, suddenly rose up like a great black snake in Indigo's mind. It swelled in her chest and then burst from her as a scream so sudden, so loud, so impossible, that it splintered windows and picture frames. Cracks whipsawed down the walls and dust coughed upward from between the floorboards. The force of it lifted the women and flung them apart. Indigo hurled the maiden against the chair tucked into the writing desk, and chair and desk blew apart.

Indigo felt herself tottering on the edge of total, bottomless blackness. She raised her head, and it felt heavy and broken and wrong. Through eyes that were filled with bloody tears, she looked across the room to where the maiden of slaughter lay, lips parted, eyes open, head canted strangely on a loose and rubbery neck.

This slaughter nun was dead.

Indigo tried to speak, to say something, to take back all of this.

She blinked once and all she saw now were fireflies burning in the air of her room.

She blinked again and then saw nothing.

Indigo fell backward into the darkness, and there was nothing to catch her fall. And so she fell down, down, down . . .

10

——

Alice in her rabbit hole could not have fallen any farther, or with any less regard for what was real and what was fiction. A world peopled by talking flowers and handyman lizards didn't seem any less likely than a world where she could have done—where anyone could have done—what she had. . . .

Shadows she could understand.

Shadows were ordinary, shadows were safe, shadows were *hers*. Even with Damastes clawing at her mind like a rat scrabbling at a pipe, the shadows belonged to her. Nothing in the shadows could scream a world to pieces. She wasn't a banshee, to wail death to the living. So how . . .

It didn't matter. It didn't matter.

Everything matters, murmured a voice, and for the first time she couldn't say whether it belonged to her or to Damastes. She was falling, down, down, down, until nothing existed but the shadows and the fall.

She could fight it, but to what end? As long as she kept falling, she didn't have to think about any of this. She could let herself go, relaxing into the comforting arms of gravity, which was only an echo of itself here in the darkness; it pulled her down, but it would never pull her all the way to the ground. She could fall forever, a perpetual motion machine of one, and nothing else would matter.

It was tempting—so tempting—and she was so tired. She didn't think she'd ever before been this tired in her life. The exhaustion ran all the way down to her bones, curling around them like smoke, making her feel fragile and thin, like a glass sculpture of herself.

Her powers should have come with an instruction manual. Better yet, they should have come with an *actual* teacher, not the half-remembered lie of one, someone who could actually understand what she was capable of and explain it to her so that she would know.

The place where Nora ended and Indigo began (or was it the other way around?) was raw. It rubbed against itself, and that small pain was enough to keep her from surrendering completely to the fall.

How was it her fault that Damastes wanted her? She hadn't asked for this. She hadn't been the one to join a cult or barter her soul to the gods of murder.

How was it her fault that the Phonoi wouldn't leave her alone? Yes, she killed them when she found them, but *they* killed *children*. *They* made their perverse beliefs *her* problem when they left the bodies of innocents scattered in the streets like trash. That stupid nun should have realized that if anyone was killing in the name of righteousness, it was Nora.

Wasn't it?

Wasn't it?

And still she was falling. Nora scrabbled at the edges of her mind, trying to find the place where she ended and Indigo began. Something was important, even here. Something still mattered; something she had almost forgotten, except as a small, nagging need to act, to perform some unremembered task. Indigo would recall.

They weren't really different people—Nora wasn't so far gone as to believe that they were—but she had been Indigo when she'd heard the bad thing, the important thing, and she wasn't Indigo now.

Or maybe she was. Maybe this was what it was like to really be Indigo, no friends, no family, no . . .

Nora's eyes snapped open, beholding only blackness. Friends. *Friends.*

Shelby and Sam were in danger. Damastes had as much as confirmed that Rafe was on his way to hurt them, and she had gotten sidelined by the murder nun and her sister, leaving her friends all alone. They didn't know what was coming.

She was so tired. She was hurt, and she was exhausted, and if her powers were ever going to give out, this was the time. Maybe her power had never been to enter the shadows; maybe it had always been *to leave* them, and now that she was at the end of her rope, she was trapped, no way out.

But they needed her.

Please, she thought, and there was no more divide in her mind. There was no more Nora, no more Indigo, only her, only a woman who needed, more than anything, to save her friends.

She wrapped the shadows around herself, pulling them tight as a veil, and she was gone.

Transitioning back into the real world had never before felt so difficult. From the outside it might have looked easy, but for her, it was a struggle every inch of the way. There was nothing between reality and the shadows—they were the flip side of each other, connected and connecting and inextricably linked—and still she struggled through the morass before collapsing into the light.

Everything ached. Her wounds from the fight with the murder nun had traveled with her into shadow, but they had somehow been inconsequential there; the trials of the flesh mattered less in a place that was defined by the absence of light. Now that she was back in a place with physical laws, every bruise, abrasion, and cut felt as if it were being delivered all over again.

Panting, Nora used the wall to pull herself to her feet and looked dully around. The shadows seemed too heavy. She couldn't see through them the way she should have been able to, so tired that even the most basic attributes of her power were unreliable.

There's the answer, she thought, with a trace of wry bitterness. *I can be normal. I just have to run myself into the ground to do it.*

Into the ground—where *was* she? After the shadows had dumped her in Florence, she was less willing to trust her sense of direction. The unshifting shadows made it hard to tell exactly where she was. It was like having a whole layer of her vision stolen, replaced by . . . what? By what normal people saw. By what she had claimed to want for so long.

Now that she had it, at the most inconvenient time possible, she didn't want it anymore.

The most inconvenient—Sam and Shelby. She was looking for Sam and Shelby. They needed her. Injured or not, she was their best chance of survival.

And if Sam finds out you're Indigo? The voice was hers, she was almost sure of that. Her own fears and misgivings lacked the poisonous poetry of Damastes. When she spoke in her own head—as everyone did, as normal people did—she used her own voice, her own inflections, and her own utter lack of murderous intent.

She felt sure that she could tell Shelby the truth and Shelby would love her anyway. But how much of the truth? If she only confessed she was Indigo, Shelby would love her for it. Even Sam—Sam, who thought Indigo some kind of superhero vigilante, who practically worshipped her—would still love her.

But what if she told them the whole truth?

They'll leave you. All that you love will be taken from you.

But they would be alive to make that decision.

Nora straightened, blinking again as the shadows seemed to clear a little. It wasn't as much of a surprise as it should perhaps have been when this change in perspective made it clear that this was her hallway, her apartment building, her home.

It was tempting to walk to her own door, to check on the degree of damage done by her fight with the slaughter nun—and more, to check on the Assholes. They had to have been terrified by all the noise and commotion. She paused. Noise. They hadn't been subtle about their fight. How come none of the neighbors had called the police yet? Why was the hall so quiet? She remembered the fight in Florence, the way none of the people at the outdoor café had even noticed them—some bit of magic that slaughter nun had managed. The bitch had done the same thing here, she felt sure. And how had the bitch even gotten here?

None of that mattered if Nora hadn't gotten here in time. If she'd already failed to save Sam and Shelby—if she'd yanked herself out of the dark for nothing—then there was no reason to stay. But if she hadn't failed them yet, she was going to if she didn't move.

She moved.

Haltingly at first, then with increasing speed, she stumbled down the hall toward the stairs. She didn't know where her phone was. Shelby, if she was alive, would have a phone, and she could use it to call Sam. She could make sure that they were both fine, and then she could . . .

Well, collapse for the better part of a year, if it were up to her. But it wasn't likely to be up to her, and it wasn't safe to stay around them anymore. Not with murder nuns and cultists on her trail and a demon inside her.

The thought of everything that wanted to kill her paradoxically made her feel stronger, as if she could go up against the entire world by refusing to fall down and die. She gathered speed, going from a walk to an uneven jog to an outright run. The shadows were back in full force by the time she reached the stairs, and she was briefly tempted to leap through them, letting them transport her to Shelby's floor.

No. That would use power she didn't have to spare right now, especially if she was about to face a cult full of people bent on killing the only friends she had left in the world.

She took the stairs two and three at a time, surprisingly feeling the muscles in her thighs burn from this mundane activity. She forced herself to keep going. It was annoying that being a superpowered killing machine didn't come with basic physical fitness, but whatever. She could hit the gym later, if she miraculously lived that long.

Shelby's hall was exactly as it had always been, save for one new addition—Sam, standing outside Shelby's door, one hand raised, as if he had just been knocking.

Sam, alive and checking on Shelby, as Nora had asked. She felt like Scrooge on Christmas morning—she wasn't too late. He hadn't noticed her arrival, and for a second she braced herself against the wall with one hand, the other hand pressed over her heart, catching her breath. Elated. Then he knocked on the door again.

"Come on, Shelby. I'm a friend of Nora's," Sam called, not quite shouting, but raising his voice enough for it to carry into the apartment. "If you're home, you need to open the door."

"Coming!" shouted Shelby's voice.

The door opened. Sam straightened, a look of pure confusion on his face. Nora shoved herself away from the wall, started toward them. Something was—

The fist hit Sam squarely in the chin, knocking him backward, away from the door. He staggered until he hit the wall and crumpled. Shelby screamed.

Nora flickered. One moment she was herself, running as fast as she could toward her friends, and the next she was Indigo, diving into the narrow band of shadow created by her own foot. It was like turning herself into a pretzel, twisting inward in a way that made her stomach lurch, but it worked. She went from the hallway to the interior of Shelby's apartment in the blink of an eye, appearing behind her friend.

The color of the apartment was almost a shock, it was so bright, seeming to snap into place in an instant as she materialized. There was no time to dwell on the ache in her retinas. Shelby was still screaming, and the Phonoi assassin behind her was raising his knife to silence her. Reflection was for later. For now, Indigo needed to act.

She thrust her hands out in front of her, sending waves of shadow to wrap around the cultist and *squeeze* until his screams drowned out Shelby's. Indigo flung him to the side, hearing him hit the wall with a satisfying crunch. When he fell, he smashed a decorative end table that she remembered helping Shelby lug home from a swap meet downtown. Indigo felt a sharp pang of guilt. Being near her was like being too close to a tornado. One way or another, everything wound up getting smashed.

A man grabbed her from the side, yanking her off-balance. She hadn't even seen him there. Another came at her from the other side. This time, she was more prepared. She grabbed the arm that held her, using it to brace herself as she kicked at the second man, landing a blow to his gut. He staggered backward, and she called the shadows, bringing them raining down on both of her attackers.

"Indigo! Watch out!" Shelby sounded strangely far away.

Indigo ducked, flowing down into the shadows and reappearing a few feet behind her original position. The fourth assassin stumbled as his attempt to stab her landed on empty air. Shelby stepped up and smashed a vase over his head.

It was a silly, cliché note, like something out of a children's movie. But it worked. The man wobbled, his eyes rolling back in his head, and collapsed to the floor. Indigo raised her head, meeting Shelby's eyes. Shelby quirked a smile and tossed the remains of her shattered vase aside.

"Very cool."

"Behind you!" said Indigo, and shoved Shelby aside with a sweep of her arm before hitting the last assassin full in the face with a blast of shadow. He staggered into the hallway, hitting the wall next to Sam . . .

Who was awake on the hallway floor and staring at Indigo in wide-eyed dismay.

Shit.

Indigo froze, not sure what to do. Shelby rushed over and slammed the door, cutting off Sam's view. Leaving him out in the hall with a dead Phonoi assassin.

"Run," Shelby whispered loudly. "Get yourself—back to yourself, and come back, but right now, *run.*"

Indigo's eyes went wide in surprise. Shelby recognized her. Somehow, she knew that Indigo and Nora were one and the same.

Reeling from this epiphany, Indigo glanced at the dead assassins, the four cultists scattered around Shelby's apartment in pools of blood and the wreckage of furniture. For the moment, Shelby was out of danger.

Indigo dropped into the floor, into the silence of the shadows beneath their feet. The world fell away.

Once again, she was falling, and once again, she didn't know what to do about it. Shelby knew she was Indigo, and Sam had seen . . . *something.* She'd been Nora when she stopped to catch her breath, but she'd been Indigo when she appeared in the apartment, and

Indigo when she joined in the fight. Shelby had never called her by the name Nora. Maybe he hadn't realized it was her.

This falling thing was getting old. It used to be that when she slipped into shadow, she slipped right back out again, arriving at her destination without any time passing between entry and exit. Now . . .

She tried to feel for the purpose that would allow her to move back into the real world. She couldn't find it.

You're weakening, little one, rumbled the voice of Damastes. *You'll give in soon enough. Why not give in now?*

I will never give in to you, she thought. She didn't speak. She didn't need to.

But you already listen to me. I told you that your friends were in danger and you moved to protect them. I told you that Rafe would wait until they were together, and you raced to beat him to their door. I told you everything you needed to know. You followed my lead. Damastes's voice dropped to a purr, low and thrumming and dangerous. *See how well we work together? I can tell you where to go. I can tell you who to kill. I can remove all question from your life and give you the freedom to act as you see fit, to do as you see fit, to* live *as you see fit. And you can keep your friends. Doesn't that make it more tempting to give in?*

No, she thought fiercely, and *yes* her heart whispered, and Nora grabbed the shadows around her and disappeared, leaving behind the nothingness, and the distant, aching echo of Damastes laughing as if he were the only source of laughter in all the universe. In all the world.

Nora toppled out of shadow and back into the hallway outside Shelby's apartment. As she came out of her crouch, she could see Sam slumped against the wall across from Shelby's door, his hands braced flat against the floor and his eyes wide. He hadn't seen her appear. She was almost certain of that.

The body of the assassin was gone. Indigo had no idea how that was possible. She also had no idea if these two attacks were connected. While she'd been trying to shadow-walk back from Greece to New York, the murder nun had somehow managed to drag her right out of the shadowpaths, landing her in Italy. Then when she'd escaped, one of her same order—that sisterhood of slaughter maidens, the Androk-somethings—had been waiting in Nora' apartment to ambush her. And minutes later, as she was approaching Shelby's apartment and Sam was knocking on the door, Phonoi assassins tried to kill Sam?

Fucking chaos.

She needed to clear her head, needed to find somewhere to breathe and pull her thoughts together, lay the puzzle pieces out and see how they fit together the way that Nora did as an investigative journalist. Right now she needed to be Nora more than she needed to be Indigo.

And it wasn't Indigo that Sam needed.

She scrambled to her feet and ran for him. "Sam, are you all right? Where's Shelby?"

"Nora?" He turned to face her, and no fear or suspicion was in his face, only dawning relief at the sight of her, as if he hadn't been allowing himself to wonder whether she was all right. He started to stand—and stopped, pressing a hand to his forehead. "Ow," he said weakly.

"Don't get up." She ran to him, dropping to her knee by his side. "Are you all right? What happened?"

Lying to him hurt, in the wake of the lies that had been told to her. He deserved the truth. But if she told him she was Indigo, he would know that she wasn't safe—that she wasn't real, not in any meaningful sense. Her entire past was a lie, and that meant that

Nora was a lie, because a person was only the sum of what the person knew and remembered.

Sam was true. Shelby was true. Everything else was a beautiful lie created by someone else, someone who had not had her best interests at heart.

"Indigo," he said, turning to look straight at her.

Her heart gave a painful lurch.

He wasn't done. "She appeared out of nowhere, just as your friend opened her apartment door. The whole place was filled with shadows. I think—I think she attacked me."

No! No, that isn't what happened at all! Nora wanted to yell, to tell him that he didn't understand what he had seen. She couldn't do it. For now, her secret needed to stay hidden, even from him.

"Shelby's okay?" she asked.

"I only saw her for a second, but she seemed fine." He pressed a hand against his head again. "Jeez. I need medical help, Nora. I think I might have a concussion."

"Shelby has an ice pack." Nora stood, running for the apartment door.

It wasn't locked. Nora let herself in and closed the door behind her. Shelby had been waiting for her, stood staring at her. The wrecked furniture remained, but like the corpse in the corridor, the dead assassins were gone. Even their blood had vanished.

"Well?" Shelby demanded. "This is fucking magic, right?"

"I know you have questions. You can be damn sure *I* have some, but right now I need your first-aid kit."

The sound of sirens split the air. Someone had heard the commotion, called the cops. Nora froze.

Shelby didn't. "You should go. I'll take care of Sam, but maybe now's not the time for you to be answering questions from cops."

"Make sure he's okay. Promise me he'll be okay."

"I promise. Now go. You can meet up with Sam at the hospital. Put yourself as far as possible from the scene of the crime."

Nora nodded. "All right. But whatever happens, do not let the cops go into my apartment. I don't think they'll have any reason to, but if it looks like they might, find some way to put them off."

"Why—"

"Later. All of the answers, I promise." Nora ran for the nearest shadow. Sam might wonder where she'd gone, but he'd had some head trauma. She could talk her way around it. As for Shelby, Nora no longer cared what her friend saw. Shelby *knew*. Part of Nora was elated to have someone she didn't have to hide herself from.

She dove into a patch of darkness and was gone.

11

———

Nora slipped through the shadows into her apartment for a moment, checking to see if everything was as it had been before she left. Yes, the body was still there.

That, at least, she could easily enough fix. There was no way to hide the signs of a struggle, but the corpse . . .

Guilt ran through her and sent swarms of icy butterflies through her stomach, freezing her guts.

Just one shadow, that was all it would take. Fortunately the room was full of them. She opened the shadowpath under the dead slaughter nun's body and watched it sink into the blackness. In seconds the corpse was gone, lost to the blackness beyond the shadows.

She heard the Assholes hissing from behind curtains and beneath furniture, reacting to the presence of Indigo as they so often did. She was too tired to think of much of anything, but their presence was another layer of guilt. How many times could she terrify the little shits before they never trusted her again?

Swaying on her feet, she fought the crushing exhaustion that had finally begun to catch up with her. She couldn't stay in her apartment right now, didn't want to deal with the police if they showed up, so she stumbled into darkness again. The shadowpaths were so familiar, so comforting, but she could feel Damastes there with her, and somehow she seemed closer to him in the dark, so she emerged again on a rooftop across from her apartment building. The pool of deeper shadow beneath a water tower hid her well, and there she collapsed. Sleep had not been a part of her plan, but weariness seized her. Nora wrapped herself within a cocoon of darkness and dropped into a heavy slumber.

When she woke, hours later, her first thoughts were of Sam. The shadowpaths were easy enough to follow now that her mind had finally been allowed to relax from the constant state of danger. The sun was well up and the morning was progressing. Indigo emerged behind the shelter of a bus stop, half a block from the hospital, and divested herself of the cloak of darkness. Nora took stock of her appearance. Her clothes were wrinkled, yes, but she smoothed the front of her coat, pushed her fingers through her magenta-streaked hair, and she was good to go.

Three minutes at the reception desk got her Sam's room number. Five more in the hospital cafeteria got her a large coffee that tasted like strained swamp water but had enough caffeine to make her eyes twitch. Just what the doctor ordered.

Sam was sitting up in his bed and picking at what had probably been breakfast sometime in the past. His fork had pushed the bits and pieces around until nothing recognizable was left. Another bed was in the room but at present it was empty. He'd won the dubious honor of sleeping alone in a double room.

"Sam?"

He looked up from the ruination of his food and offered her an expression that warred between an exhausted smile and a frown. "I was wondering where you'd gotten to. Are you okay?"

"I'm not the one in a hospital bed. Are *you* all right?"

"Finally got to see Indigo in action, but it was sort of a bummer. Mostly I sat on the floor and tried to remember my own name."

"Shelby told me. How bad is it? Are they keeping you?" Guilt rumbled through Nora. Or maybe it was hunger. She'd managed coffee but had forgotten to eat anything, and it had been a long while since her last meal.

"I have a concussion." He shrugged. "Mostly I'm good, but they're keeping me a little longer to make sure my skull doesn't implode. Know what the worst part of a concussion is?"

"No. What?"

"They wake you up every hour or so, just to make certain there isn't anything worse going on in your head." He shrugged. "I don't need worse. I have enough going on in there."

"Like what?"

"Questions about your friend Shelby. Questions about you. Questions about why a bunch of pricks were trying to kill me and Shelby, and why Indigo came along at exactly the right time to save us." The look Sam shot Nora was not one that said he had a rattled brain in his head. It was pure reporter.

"What about Shelby?"

"I went up right after you asked me, and I checked on her. I knocked on her door for a good ten minutes, and nothing. And because I was worried, I waited around, wondering if she'd show up. Nothing."

"Sometimes people go out. I mean, I would have expected her home."

"No. You were too worried about her, so I decided to look into it. I checked to see if I could get a phone number. I had her address, right? So I figured a number was easy, only there's nothing about Shelby anywhere, Nora. Nothing."

"What are you talking about?" A flurry of cold dread hit her stomach. She didn't like the way this was going.

"There's no power bill. No cable bill. No phone bill. No electricity bill. There's nothing at all under the name Shelby Coughlin. I dug as deep as I could in a few hours, and near as I can figure there is no one named Shelby Coughlin in the whole borough."

"That's crazy. She's my upstairs neighbor."

"Actually, the crazy part was finding out who it is that's actually paying for her apartment." Sam sat up a bit straighter in his bed and frowned.

"Who?" Nora's throat was dry. She had a sudden deep and irrational fear that it was Rafe Bogdani, or the slaughter nuns. Neither made any sense, but they were both haunting her life, and suddenly the one certainty she had in her world, her best friend, was not who she seemed.

"Her apartment is paid for through a trust fund set up in your name, Nora." Sam's eyes looked into hers. "It wasn't too hard to track, but I wasn't really expecting that one."

"Sam, I don't know what you're talking about. I never set up a trust fund, and if I had, I'd use it to pay my own bills before I'd worry about someone else's."

"That's the part that doesn't make any sense. There's no logic to it. But there it is. You're paying her rent, and you have been since she moved into an apartment with no utility bills at all."

"What the hell?"

"You tell me, Nora, and maybe we'll both know."

Nora thought back to her friend. Mostly it was Chinese food, beer, and old movies when they were hanging around together. What made no sense at all was that she had been in Shelby's apartment a dozen times and had seen its lamps, the TV, the stereo, and the tasteful furniture. None of which were signs that no one was paying any utilities. Mostly they watched and ate in Nora's place, but that was just because it was home and Nora preferred it. She tried to remember if she had ever had a meal or watched a show in Shelby's place but couldn't think of a single time.

Then again . . . her memories had proven spectacularly unreliable, hadn't they?

"Sam, other than you, Shelby's my best friend. But none of this—"

Nora's eyes flew wide. Shelby knew about her and Indigo. A little while ago she'd been celebrating that fact, but now?

"What is it?"

"She knows." The words were out before Nora could halt them. It was immediate and reflexive.

"Knows what?"

Nora stared at Sam. He was real. He was solid. He was something familiar, and nothing else was making sense. If what he said was true—and she never once doubted it—then who the hell was Shelby Coughlin? There was no way she could be some kind of spy for Rafe Bogdani or the Phonoi. They'd have tracked Nora by now. She'd be dead.

Nora paced to the window and looked out at the sun-splashed cityscape. Nothing she knew—nothing she believed in or thought she'd understood—seemed reliable anymore. Nothing but Sam. She needed a touchstone, something solid and true.

Nora swallowed hard.

"Sam," she said, her back still toward him, "there's something I have to tell you. I'm pretty sure you're going to be angry with me for not telling you before, but I want you to try to see it from my point of view, and understand that there are a lot of reasons why I—"

"Hell, Nora, spit it out. If you've got some big secret that'll help me make sense of all this, lay it on me."

She went and sat on the bed beside him. Nora wasn't used to feeling vulnerable, but she had nothing but questions and enemies now, and she desperately needed answers and a friend.

"I can't lose you over this, Sam."

He took her hand, gave her fingers a squeeze. "Nora. Talk to me."

She locked eyes with him. "Sam . . . I'm her. I'm Indigo."

For half a second, he seemed as if he might laugh, but they knew each other too well for him to read her eyes—read her face—and not see that she meant it.

"You can't . . ." He frowned, wincing as if from the pain of his injuries. "Nora, with all you've been going through, and this bizarre crap with Shelby . . . I mean, are you sure you're not having some kind of breakdown?"

He was good. His voice only went up a little in volume and maybe one octave.

Nora held up her hand and wrapped it in shadows. She watched his face as the darkness covered her hand, her arm, moved up to briefly cover her chest and face before she drew the inky night back into her skin.

"I'm Indigo. Always have been. I mean, since she showed up. You can guess why I never told you."

"Well, holy shit," he whispered, wincing again. He reached up and massaged his temple with two fingers. "You . . . Nora, you could have told me, y'know?"

"You were a little too focused on Indigo, and I wanted you to be focused on me. On Nora. Plus . . . what Indigo does is often pretty damned illegal, and I couldn't drag you into that. Couldn't compromise you. I didn't tell anyone, Sam. Not ever."

Long seconds ticked past as he studied her, letting it all sink in.

"Yeah. Okay," he said at last. He looked past her, his eyes going soft. She knew the expression. She'd seen it a hundred times before when he got locked into solving a mystery in his head. He was thinking over all of the details, all of the stories he'd heard about Indigo and correlating that information with what he knew of Nora Hesper.

"Fuck."

"Yeah. I know." She willed him to understand.

"So you know all about the cult? What's true and what isn't?"

She sat on the edge of his bed, her hand an inch from his, the rolling table holding his food pushing against her back. She nudged the table gently away, sighed, and then told him everything she knew about what had happened in her past and what was happening in the city and around the world that involved Indigo.

Sam nodded and listened.

A short time later, after the story had been told, Sam nodded a final time. "Okay. So where do we go from here?"

"I'm not sure. I mean. I need to talk to Shelby, obviously—"

"Carefully."

"Yes, carefully. But that's not even my first concern. I need to—" She stopped herself and her hands patted at her shirt. "The list of names. The one I told you about."

"From when you broke into Marshall's place."

Nora's fingers pulled the folded sheet of paper she'd taken from Marshall Winston's apartment. "These are all members of the cult. Most of them are dead now."

Her voice just then was softer. It was one thing to confess to being Indigo, but another entirely to realize that meant she was also confessing to killing people. Bad people, yes, but still, murder was murder and she was placing monumental trust in Sam.

He took the paper and looked it over carefully. Concussed or not, his mind seemed to be working fine. "I know some of these names, I think. I have to go home and check my files, but I'm pretty sure they tie into some of my cases on missing kids and trafficking."

"The last couple of days, it's been pointing that way. Plus the Phonoi are skeezy. I can see them trafficking in kids to pay their bills. Anyway, I have a lot more notes. I'll get them to you when you get out of the hospital."

"What about your investigation?"

"Right now, I have bigger problems. I'm going to need you to handle the research if you can, Sam. I think it's obvious your investigation and mine at least cross paths. But there are things I can look into as Indigo that I really can't touch as Nora. And right now, being Nora isn't the safest thing in any event. They've been to my apartment. One of them was waiting for me when I got home."

"Was that a Phonoi? Or one of these . . . slaughter nuns? The Andro-whatever?"

"See? This is my life right now." She shook her head. "Slaughter nun at my place. Phonoi at Shelby's."

Sam nodded and then froze for a moment, wincing as he waited out a wave of nausea. "I didn't even like bed spins when I was a partyer."

"Do I need to call someone?"

"No. I just have to remember I've got a concussion." He smiled to make light of it, but Nora felt a wave of guilt again. "So I'll look into those names. And I'll let you know what I find."

Nora was about to volunteer to wait until he was ready for a ride home when the door to the hospital room opened. Any positive feelings she'd been fostering were destroyed as Detectives Symes and Mayhew walked across the threshold. Mayhew was a perfect vision of health, as always, while her partner, if anything, looked sicker than ever.

Symes frowned when he saw Nora.

Mayhew smiled. "Some days the universe is on your side. Know what I mean, Hugh?"

Symes nodded. "Doesn't get much easier."

Sam tried sitting up in bed and went pale, as if moving made him nauseated. "What can I do for you, Detectives?" he managed. "You can't be here over a little assault case."

Mayhew shot Sam a withering glance. "Somebody get assaulted?"

Symes stuffed his hands into his pockets. "We were actually coming here to question you about the whereabouts of Nora Hesper. Seems she's not been seen at home for a couple of days, but then, here we are and here she is."

Nora shook her head. "Why were you looking for me?"

"We have reports of you being seen at the scene of a recent crime, Ms. Hesper." Mayhew moved closer, menace in her gaze. Nora's instinct was to fight, but she was not about to reveal herself to these detectives—not unless they crossed the line. She believed Mayhew worked for the Phonoi, but as long as she was operating within the parameters of her job, Nora would have to behave.

"What crime?" Sam demanded. "Maybe you should explain yourself, Detective."

Mayhew stopped just out of Nora's reach and rested her hand on her hip, right next to her service pistol. "There was a recent multiple homicide at a warehouse. We have witnesses who claim you were there when everything went down. We're going to have to ask you to come with us to the station."

That smile again, as pretty as you please and filled with malice.

"That's ridiculous," Sam said. "Who are these supposed witnesses?"

Nora gave him a dark look, urging him to be silent. Better that he be ignored than dragged into the mess. She needed him doing the research she could no longer take the time to do herself.

"Do I need a lawyer?" Nora asked, pulling the focus off Sam. She wasn't worried about herself, but she wanted any ugliness that might result from this encounter to unfold somewhere else.

Symes answered with a shrug of narrow shoulders. Mayhew might have a shady purpose here, but her partner was at least pretending to be nothing more than a cop doing his job.

"It's just routine questions, Ms. Hesper," Symes said. "No one is making accusations at this stage, but we'd like you to come down to the station with us. You're a reporter. You know how this works."

Nora looked at Sam, and he carefully nodded. He knew where she was going. He also knew, now, that she was Indigo and could handle a couple of police detectives if she had to.

She wondered if Mayhew had invented the witnesses, and if Symes knew about the cult. Were they working for Rafe Bogdani? She'd told Rafe her name was Shelby Coughlin, but he might have found out the truth. Just as it was possible that Shelby had been the one to tell him that truth.

You don't even know if that's her *name,* Nora thought.

Too many questions, and only one easy way to find the answers she needed. Demand them from the one person she could lay her hands on who might know something useful.

It was Nora's turn to smile. "Happy to be of whatever help I can. Lead the way, Detectives."

The police precinct house, she suspected, was the last place the detectives intended to take her, but Mayhew smiled and Symes nodded.

"I'll talk to you soon, Sam."

Sam smiled. "Count on it."

"Jesus. It's just some questions, kids," Mayhew said. "Don't worry, Mr. Loh. We'll get her back to you safe and sound."

Mayhew led the way, but Symes stayed where he was until Nora preceded him out of the room. Part of her wanted to run, but she knew the answers were here if they were anywhere.

"So what are these murders you're talking about?" Nora asked as they walked along the corridor.

Mayhew shook her head and looked over her shoulder at Nora. "You're a reporter, right? Where have you been? The murders that *everyone* is talking about. Some kind of cult thing gone wrong."

"Cut her some slack. I never watch the news either. It's too depressing," Symes said with almost no inflection and certainly without malice.

Mayhew chuckled. "That's what I like about you, Hugh. You have empathy. You always see the bright side."

They reached the elevators in silence and stayed quiet all the way out to the unmarked police car. They'd left the vehicle in the no-parking zone and had a red-cherry light on the top of the car to warn away anyone who might think they'd earned a ticket.

Symes helped Nora into the backseat and even made sure she didn't clock her skull on the low door. She wasn't wearing cuffs. There had been no arrest.

Nora closed her eyes, still nervous. Indigo opened them again, calmer and prepared.

Symes drove and Mayhew looked back from the passenger seat. "So how did you miss the news? Were you out of the country?"

"I don't watch the news much. I'm too busy following leads and writing articles."

Mayhew stared at her, that damned smug smile still on her face, as if she were the only one in the car who understood the joke going down. "Investigative reporter, isn't it? You should see the scene of the crime. It was grisly. Lots of corpses. Lots of blood. One minor marked and cut and murdered with a bunch of rich folks who were maybe out of their league."

"You still haven't said who's trying to link me to the crime scene?"

"I guess you'll find out at the station. We have pictures as well as witness statements."

Symes was driving, yes, but Nora could see his eyes in the rearview, and he was looking at his partner and frowning. "What are you doing, Ange?"

"Don't worry about it, Hugh. This is what we're here for."

"We're here to bring in a suspect for questioning."

"Who's the lead detective here, Hugh?"

"You are. Don't mean I like it when you act weird. If you really thought she was dangerous, she'd be in cuffs."

"It's all good, Hugh. Shut up and drive," Mayhew said with an edge to her voice. A warning. As she talked, she opened the glove compartment and stuck her hand in carefully, fishing.

Still wearing Nora's face, Indigo tensed. Something was wrong. Seriously wrong.

"Handcuffs wouldn't hold her. Isn't that right, Ms. Hesper? Or do you prefer your other name?"

"Ange, what the hell?"

"I said I've got this, Hugh!" Mayhew's smile was still there, but the redhead was glaring past her little smirk. "Everything's as right as rain, and we're all just going along for the ride."

"Ange, seriously."

The dagger in Mayhew's hand bore a hilt made of wings and a circle, a symbol that Indigo knew all too well. Indigo slid across the broad backseat as Mayhew lunged for her, trying to stab her.

The dagger cut through the cheap vinyl cushion.

Indigo cursed under her breath.

"Stay still, bitch!" The detective pulled back and released her seat belt, turning her body to try again, ready to lunge into the backseat if she needed.

"Ange, what the fuck?" Symes reached for his pistol as he slammed the brakes and shook all three of them in their seats. Mayhew slid and fell into the footwell, but the dagger was still in her hand.

"I told you to stay out of this, Hugh!" Mayhew shrieked, and lunged.

Before Symes could finish pulling his sidearm, the ritual dagger rammed through his sternum. His foot came off the brake and jabbed at the accelerator. Symes gasped and coughed, and Indigo could hear the wheeze coming from his chest. His lung instead of his heart. That was a good thing.

"You've seen enough dark shit, Hugh," Mayhew said. "You should've played along."

Symes glanced at the dagger lodged in his chest, at his partner's hand on its hilt, and his wide-eyed shock turned to fury. He jerked the steering wheel to the left, right at a retaining wall. Mayhew screamed and aimed her dagger at her partner a second time.

Enough.

The darkness exploded from Indigo, consuming the interior of the car. Through the shadows, she saw Symes fall back against the driver's-side door as Mayhew plunged the dagger down again. The way he'd fallen, the blade would open him from sternum to crotch.

Somewhere in the back of Indigo's head, Damastes chuckled deep and low.

She flexed and the darkness flexed with her. At her command, the shadows hauled Symes into the backseat, even as she slipped forward. Indigo had jumped continents. Moving to the front seat of a careening car was easy as opening a door. Tendrils of blackness grasped the steering wheel and hauled it to the right. Mayhew grunted as she was shoved sideways in her seat, her aim thrown off. The dagger stabbed the headrest next to Indigo's shoulder.

Indigo drove her feet into the detective's face as more darkness pushed the passenger's-side door open.

They were moving perhaps thirty miles an hour. Mayhew sailed from the open door and crashed into the asphalt, bouncing and rolling, the dagger clutched tightly in her hand. The bitch had a death grip on her weapon.

The brakes locked as Indigo pushed a column of darkness against the pedal. The car shuddered and stopped. She flowed out of the car, a cloak of shadow wrapping around her, hiding herself in a writhing mass of darkness.

Mayhew stood up, bloodied and crazed, her face skinned and her knuckles on the hand holding the dagger bleeding. A bakery van careened around her and tried to recover, but wound up rolling. The driver's-side window was open, and even without focusing on the man, Indigo could see his head cave in as it was pinned between van and asphalt.

Brakes screamed, and cars behind Mayhew and the squad car veered madly to avoid the situation, but only a few of them succeeded. A blue Prius swerved between the detective and the car as Indigo slid into the road. A car behind the police cruiser tapped the edge of the right rear panel as it came to a halt.

There was no time. There was no thought.

Mayhew charged past the Prius as it slipped by and came for Indigo, the dagger held close to her side. Mayhew knew how to use a knife. She knew how to fight. That mystical dagger was trouble. Indigo could nearly feel the arcane power coming from it, and she would have bet everything she had on its ability to carve her darkness away.

Mayhew's face exploded.

The detective was almost in striking distance when everything above her left eye bulged backward and then sprayed away from her in a cloud of red hair and bone and blood.

Nora nearly screamed.

Indigo spun around and saw Symes holding his service pistol in the shooting stance he had likely practiced for years. His face was as pale as ever, and his mouth was pulled down in a rictus of agony, but he held his place as his partner flopped dead on the road amid the chaos.

Then he coughed blood and tried to holster his weapon. He missed and the pistol hit the ground. He was bleeding badly. The entire front of his dress shirt was black with blood, and his pants looked wet.

No time. None.

Without asking, without consciously worrying about her decision, Indigo moved to Symes and her cloak swarmed over him, burying him in the depths of midnight.

The effect on Symes was immediate: He went stiff and whimpered.

"I know it's scary. I know it's cold. But I am here, Symes. I'm going to protect you from the shadows. We need to get you to the hospital now, and there's no other way you live through this."

Symes screamed as she started down the shadowpaths. His hands clutched at her arms, and he wailed and moaned like the damned on the pathway to hell itself.

It was only seconds for Indigo, but for Symes it might as well have been an eternity. Tears fell from his eyes and his body shivered as if wracked with arctic cold.

"They're going to fix you up, Symes. They're going to mend you. When you're taken care of, go find Sam Loh. He can explain everything."

Symes had saved her life. She had saved his. Now she had to hope that she'd made the right choice. He knew her secret, that Nora was Indigo. If he betrayed her, she was as good as dead. But if he was with her, if he chose to help with her crusade, she had gone from being alone to having a team to back her.

No time. None at all. She had to find Shelby. She had to know what was going on with her best friend. Indigo would have answers, no matter the cost.

12

If Nora didn't get some real sleep and a real meal soon, she'd end up in the morgue. Ever since she'd met Rafe Bogdani at the vigil for the Ortiz girl, the fights and the revelations had been coming in a never-ending stream, and it was all catching up to her.

On her way to her apartment, she spared a moment to imagine how Hugh Symes was going to explain his arrival at the hospital within seconds after he'd shot his partner. She couldn't think of anything he could say that would sound halfway sane, but she figured Symes would rather be alive to answer questions than eviscerated by Mayhew.

Nora worried about her own vulnerability. Sam had been the only witness to Symes and Mayhew's asking her to come down to the precinct with them, but some of the hospital staff might have noticed her departure with the two detectives. Maybe someone had seen her getting into the backseat of their unmarked car. She'd have to have a story ready, if—when—other detectives came calling. But she didn't feel capable of making up a credible account at the moment. Indigo had other things on her to-do list, and they all seemed more urgent.

Sam had told her Shelby Coughlin didn't exist . . . at least not under that name. Maybe "Shelby" knew who'd created the trust fund that paid her bills. Nora smiled. It would have been nice if this trust fund in her name had paid her own bills.

But at that thought, a bell began chiming in Nora's head. Hadn't that been what Uncle Theo had discussed with her? At her parents' funeral?

Trying to remember, she bought a cup of coffee and a pastry at the counter of a neighborhood coffeehouse and sat down at one of the tiny tables. As she ate the pastry absently, she poked at the memory, trying to recover more of the conversation. Her eyes closed, and she concentrated. The day of her parents' funeral had been gray; Nora found she was now sure of that. She remembered wearing a coat, so it had been cold, but no snow was on the ground. Most of all, she remembered her overwhelmingly bleak mood, but of course she had been grieving. Hadn't she?

Now that she understood her parents' assassination in the alley had been a fiction, real images were beginning to seep in.

"You'll never run out of money," Uncle Theo said. *"Matt and Stella were insured, and they had some savings. Your folks left enough to make your life comfortable. Of course, you'll need to work, Nora. But maybe you can pick the job you want most, rather than the job that pays the most."*

Nora could see Theo's face clearly now, but she still didn't know where he'd come from or where he'd gone after the funeral. Why hadn't she ever seen her uncle again? She had become an investigative reporter. Why hadn't she used her skills to track him down? Theo Hesper was not a common name . . . assuming he had been her father's brother.

So the trust fund might be a reality. Nora had never placed a high priority on making every dime she could, but it would have been pleasant to enjoy a few things she'd wanted: a new laptop, maybe an apartment with more than one room. Instead, apparently, she'd rented an apartment for Shelby. And paid her utilities.

Nora made herself finish the pastry and the coffee, but inside she was panicking. Before she left the table, she looked down at her hands on the plastic table. She took a deep breath. *Are you there?*

I'm always here, my host, the sneering voice replied.

How long have we been . . . merged? Nora didn't know how else to put it.

Since your parents died. You don't remember yet?

Not exactly. Nora shuddered. Something about chatting with yourself was fundamentally wrong. Or whatever the voice was.

The thing inside Nora laughed. **You saved me, though you didn't intend to. In return, I saved you. I gave you strength and courage when you needed it the most.**

Courage? Nora couldn't understand why she'd needed courage.

Maybe "survival skills" is more accurate.

So much for the monks in Nepal. How could she not have seen the absurdity of that scenario?

"Miss, are you all right?" The voice was not the horrifying one inside her, but that of the young waiter from the counter where she'd paid for her coffee and the pastry. Now he was standing anxiously by her table, studying her with concern.

Nora emerged from her reverie with some bewilderment. Quite a few faces were turned to her, and they were all curious or frightened. She wondered what she'd been doing to cause such apprehension. She had to get out of there.

"So sorry." Nora forced a smile on her face. "I sat up with a friend at the hospital last night." She stood hastily, gathered her bag, and nodded to the waiter.

It was time to confront Shelby.

Nora was so unsettled that she didn't want to use the shadows to travel. Walking like other humans would be fine.

Fifteen minutes later, Nora was knocking on the familiar door. She'd delayed this confrontation by stopping at her own apartment to feed and water the Assholes, who had ventured out of their hiding places when they'd decided she was Nora, not Indigo. She was going to have the most messed-up cats in New York, which was saying something. Then Nora had taken five more minutes to change their litter box. It seemed like the least she could do.

She did not feel in any way ready for this conversation, but she had to have it. When the door opened, Nora jumped.

"Hey." Shelby sagged against the doorframe, her red-gold hair in a tangled mass. Nora had never seen Shelby so disheveled. "That was crazy, huh? How's your friend Sam?" Shelby stood aside and gestured Nora into the apartment.

To Nora's eyes, Shelby looked exactly the same. Her apartment was the familiar, charming blend of attractive odds and ends. But when Nora stepped through the door, she slipped into Indigo and looked again. The view through Indigo's eyes staggered her. She stared at Shelby, shaking her head, and took a step back.

"What are you?" Indigo snarled.

Shelby looked shadowy now—almost translucent—and the rosy-pink love seat behind her flickered in and out of Indigo's sight, as if it both existed and did not.

Sorrow shattered Shelby's expression, along with a kind of shame. She slid down to her knees. "Don't look at me like that. Don't look from the shadows."

"*Who* are you?"

Shelby began weeping. "Don't you get it? I'm *you*, Nora. At least, you and Damastes created me."

"What?" Indigo's resolve faltered. "What do you mean?" she asked, her voice shaky.

Shelby pulled a green-and-gold vase off the little table next to the love seat and threw it at Indigo. Inhumanly fast, Indigo reached out to catch it . . . but it was air. The vase had vanished.

"Ask the demon," Shelby said, and closed her eyes, her anguish painful to watch.

Time for you to know, Damastes rumbled inside Indigo.

She did not even need to formulate a question.

You have so much of me in you. I occupied you so . . . unexpectedly. And you were so strong. My power is manifesting in you, Indigo. My child.

I'm not your child, Indigo thought. *You're a demon. I fight the bad guys, asshole. I fight evil.*

You do not just fight the people who wanted to control me. You leave bodies strewn in your wake. You can create what you need most. You pave the way for my return.

Indigo looked down at the spot where Shelby slumped against the table. For a second, Shelby's legs vanished.

"What are you?" Indigo asked quietly now, sadness sweeping over her.

"I'm your friend," Shelby whispered. "Because that's what you needed the most."

She's your Heykeli. If she were mine, I would use her to kill people who need to die, including the ones you named. Damastes laughed. *Friend, indeed!*

Indigo stared at Shelby, the demon's words echoing in her head. "I don't know what that is. Heykeli?"

Shelby hung her head. "You do know, because I know. And the only way that's possible is if somewhere inside, you have all this information already."

Simmering with frustration and anger, sadness and confusion,

Indigo crouched by Shelby and reached out to take her hand and felt reassured by its solidity. Whatever she was, she wasn't just a figment.

"Talk to me," Indigo said. Or maybe the words were Nora's.

Shelby shook her head. "Let Damastes tell you. He won't lie about this part. He wants you to know."

Indigo felt a warmth in her chest, a feeling of pleasure, and she knew that in some shadowy hell, the demon was grinning.

Tell me, then, she thought.

Damastes laughed softly inside her head. *Your power comes from me, woman, and I am a **murder god**. The shadows you control are only one tool I have at my disposal. Another is the creation of a Heykeli. The word is from the Turkish language and myth. Heykeli is a thing sculpted from air and light, a manifestation of pure will. The shadows are **only** that, but a well-forged Heykeli can appear as real as—*

No, Indigo thought. She said it aloud. But the word didn't make it any less true. She felt it. She knew it. A thing sculpted from shadows the way the golem of Hebrew legend had been sculpted from clay. Which made a Heykeli some kind of murder golem.

In ancient times, the murder gods would have used this power to create champions to fight and die for them. It takes such power that it is only possible to forge and maintain one Heykeli at a time. Unaware, unknowing, you've been giving Shelby life for years.

Indigo stared at Shelby, saw the tears streaming down her friend's face, and shook her head. It was unthinkable. Impossible. And yet . . .

"So, you're what?" Indigo said quietly. "My—"

"Imaginary friend." Shelby glanced up, wiped at her tears, and looked away. "More or less, yeah."

"But you're right here! Right in front of me!"

"Only when you're near. When you're too far away, or you haven't thought of me in a while, I'm just . . . gone."

Indigo could barely breathe. Trying to come to terms with this revelation, she looked around the room. As she did, items began to fade to black and white, and then to vanish.

"What are you doing?" she demanded, focused inward.

Nothing, Damastes said. *This is your doing. You've been hiding the truth from yourself, and now it is unraveling. Shelby is three-dimensional, full color, but the things in this apartment are only shadows that you've seen the way you want to see them. Like so much else.*

"Or the way you made me see them," Indigo snarled.

Damastes kept silent on that point.

"I'm a crazy person," Indigo whispered to herself. "All of this lunacy. Have I really even been out there, fighting crime, or is that all in my head?"

You are a great fighter. Better than I ever expected.

Praise from a demon. Indigo shuddered.

Unexpectedly, Shelby said, "You're more than Indigo."

"What?" She was already shaken, and talking to someone who kept flickering in and out was absolutely unnerving.

"You've taken and *taken* from Damastes every time you go through the shadows, as you hide, as you attack. You're a leech on him. He never planned on you getting so strong when he entered you, but you did. Only someone very strong could have created me."

"What about the money?" Indigo asked her Heykeli. Her murder golem. "The trust?"

"Maybe Sam can find out. It's not something I have to worry about."

Indigo shifted back into Nora, who pointed out something that had been bothering her, eating at the edges of her new knowledge. "How could I see you eat pizza and drink beer? How did you create all those stories about what happened to you at work? It seems impossible that you aren't real."

"And yet, I am." Shelby seemed more sad than angry now.

"Please don't kill me, Nora. Please don't erase me. I know keeping me around is sapping your power. But you need me."

"I'd be stronger without you?" Strength . . . Indigo certainly needed as much as she could muster.

Shelby started to cry. "I love you, Nora. I've been your friend through all these trials. You confessed who you were to me."

Shelby looked completely solid now, as if she were mustering the remnants of energy Nora had channeled into maintaining her. Nora stretched out her hand, laid it on Shelby's shoulder, warm and solid. Nora's heart ached and she still couldn't quite believe any of this, but if she was going to be able to defend herself against the Phonoi and the murder nuns and even Damastes, she knew she had no choice.

"I can't let them kill any more children. And I need to know who I really am. How this all happened to me." Nora could feel tears running down her cheeks. "I'm so sorry, Shelby. I have to let you go."

Shelby shrieked, and Nora drew the shadows close, transforming once more into Indigo. She knew how to expend power. Now she experimented with absorbing it. *Like a vacuum cleaner,* she told herself. She felt the moment Shelby became part of her. Indigo felt the surge of strength, an incredible jolt of power. She closed her eyes to revel in the feeling, and to fight off the guilt and shame that swept through her.

When she opened her eyes, Shelby was gone. The closet door hung open, the rack inside it vacant. The apartment was bare and silent, aside from a dripping tap in the tiny bathroom. And an empty space was inside Nora. But even as the Nora part of her acknowledged this loss, the Indigo of her felt invigorated and leaped into the shadows.

With an unprecedented swiftness and ease, she emerged behind the open bathroom door in Sam's hospital room.

"Before I come out, I want you to know I'm here," she said, and Sam squawked.

When Indigo emerged, she saw that Sam was half-sitting on the bed, his hair rumpled and his expression startled.

"I was asleep," he said in protest. "Could you not do that ever again?"

"Sorry. I see you got your laptop."

"Yeah, my neighbor has a key to my apartment, and he brought it over for me."

"What have you been doing in your waking hours?"

"Mostly battling a killer headache," Sam said sourly. "But I started looking up the names on the list you gave me."

"And?"

His sourness deepened.

"Wow, Sam, I'm so sorry you got hurt because you are my friend. I'm really devastated that you're missing work and running up a hospital bill."

Indigo felt ashamed. But only briefly. Children's lives were in the balance. She hadn't lost sight of the missing children of Graham Edwards. Edwards had told Rafe Bogdani that he was through with the Children of Phonos. Bogdani might dispute that, and he was both a powerful and a violent man.

"I'm sorry, Sam," Indigo said with as much contrition as she could summon. "You shouldn't have been hurt, and I hope you recover in record time." She kissed his forehead lightly.

"You don't smell like Nora."

Shocked, Indigo flinched backward. They stared at each other for a long moment. Then Sam shook his head, dismissing his own words with visible effort. He winced when the movement made his head swim.

"Okay," he said. "I checked all the names. Some of the people on the list are dead. In fact, at least eighty-five percent of them. They were killed in that massacre in the warehouse. Maybe you read about it." He eyed Indigo narrowly. "Maybe you were there."

Indigo did her best to look blank.

After a moment Sam went on, "The real shocker on the list was Captain Fritz Mueller, of the NYPD. He's alive and well and raging in the press over the death of his detective, Angela Mayhew. She was apparently gunned down by her partner, Hugh Symes, whom she'd stabbed with a knife. One witness said he saw a dark cloud in their car. And the last time I saw them, you were leaving this room with them."

She took a breath, then told him about Mayhew's being a member of the cult, about how the detective had tried to kill her, and Symes had intervened and been stabbed for his efforts.

"Symes had to shoot his own partner," Indigo said. "I don't know how he'll come out of the inquiry. I can't make it up to him, but I can at least ensure that all the pain and trauma were worthwhile by saving kids' lives. And in ridding this city, and maybe even the world, of the Children of Phonos."

For a fraction of a second she was Nora, looking at the man she'd loved, maybe still loved, and he was looking back at her with a whopping dose of doubt.

"Assuming I accept your point of view," Sam said deliberately, "and that's a big assumption . . . what do you plan to do next?"

"I plan to find out where Graham Edwards stowed his children. He indicated in a conversation that his wife, Charlotte, had been preparing them for sacrifice. Edwards hid them, and because he was busy taking them away, he missed the slaughter at the warehouse where his wife died."

Sam had pulled the laptop toward him and he began to type. "I think I can answer one question, though not the one you asked.

Look." He turned the screen to face Indigo, and she bent closer. Graham Edwards, looking ten years older than the man she'd watched confronting Rafe Bogdani, was standing at a bank of microphones. A handsome blond man was standing at Edwards's elbow, and Indigo had no trouble pegging him as the family lawyer. The man at Edwards's other side was a uniformed police officer. As long as the cop in charge wasn't Fritz Mueller, Edwards might keep his children safe.

"My wife died two days ago," Graham Edwards told the cameras, looking suitably shocked and grieved. "I have received revelation after revelation about her secret life as a cult member. I thought I had hit rock bottom, until my children were taken from me. I have contacted the NYPD, the finest police force in the world, to help me to get them back."

One of the reporters yelled, "Ransom demand?"

Edwards shook his head. "Not yet."

"Don't you think calling the police in on this will make the kidnappers think twice about giving them back?"

"I hope, by going public, I'm enlisting the eyes and ears of the good citizens of this city." Edwards appeared to start crying, and his lawyer gently turned the distraught father away from the microphone.

He took Edwards's place. "If any of the cult members have survived the mysterious massacre in which Mrs. Edwards died, we plead with you to please come forward to share any information you have concerning the whereabouts of Anastasia Catherine Edwards, age twelve, and Andel Raymond Edwards, age ten. We beg you to come forward. I'll be distributing recent pictures of the children at the exit doors."

"Any reward?" called a voice.

The police officer stepped forward and almost shouldered the lawyer out of the reach of the microphones. "I'm Captain Ray

Delaney. In situations in which a reward has been posted, the flood of information becomes almost impossible to wade through. But it's still under consideration."

"But if you don't offer a reward, you might miss the good tip that leads to their recovery!" a young woman said.

She could have been me a few years ago, Nora thought. Voicing the unpopular thought, trying to get an honest answer.

Captain Delaney looked at the reporter with distaste. "For now, we rely on the goodwill of the people of New York to save the lives of these two children. Thanks for coming. Good-bye."

And the press conference was over. Sam had pulled his laptop back, and he was typing as he talked.

"What do you think?" Sam said. "Sincere, or staged?"

"Little of both. It makes me suspicious that they emphasized New York City so much. If that's sincere, it's smart, but maybe Edwards is trying for misdirection. Maybe he knows where his kids are, but in case something happens to them, he wants all eyes watching."

"Does he really think the cult took them?"

"He has good reason to wonder."

"Get this," Sam said. "The kids' weird names? At a quick glance at one of those baby-name Web sites online, Anastasia means 'resurrection,' and Andel means 'God's messenger.'"

"That's unsettling." Indigo thought of Rafe Bogdani getting possession of those children, and she shuddered. She wouldn't leave an earthworm in the care of Bogdani, especially if the earthworm had something Bogdani wanted.

Such as a life to sacrificed.

"I have to go," she said abruptly.

"What are you going to do?"

"I'm visiting Symes. He's here in this hospital."

"How do you know?"

I brought him here. Through the shadows.

She shrugged. "I heard the nurses talking about it."

"They may not let you in."

Indigo smiled. "They can't stop me."

She found the right floor on the directory, but when she got off the elevator, she was confronted by a nurses' station at the hub of a wheel of intensive-care rooms. The rooms didn't have conventional walls, just plate glass, so the nurses could keep an eye on their patients. Light curtains could be drawn across the glass, though, probably to allow the patients some privacy when they were being bathed.

Indigo scanned the people in the rooms. She had never visited an ICU before. For the first time, she realized what a desperate place this was. And how bright. She could not find a single shadow.

At first her eyes passed over Hugh Symes without recognition. The detective was propped up, unconscious or asleep, and he'd clearly had surgery. There were tubes and bandages, wires running to machines. Sitting outside the room was a police officer. At Symes's bedside stood a handsome woman in her forties, who looked down at Symes with mingled despair and pleading. Indigo could see the woman's mouth was moving. She was talking to Symes, though she didn't get any response that Indigo could detect. The woman patted Symes's hand and left the room, pausing to chat with the cop on duty, who'd pulled up a chair to flank the door.

Indigo had been intent on speaking to Symes. She'd wanted to thank him. She'd wanted to be sure he was going to recover. Though not true allies, they had saved each other's life. Symes had stopped Mayhew from killing Indigo. And Indigo had gotten him to the hospital faster than any ambulance, giving him the best survival chance he'd had.

"Can I help you?" a sharp voice said.

Indigo started and looked down at the short woman standing in front of her. She ought to have been in the shadows, but this woman had seen her. Somehow, in a moment of distraction, she'd become Nora again.

"I'm sorry," she said, trying to gather some composure. "I think I got off at the wrong floor. I'm looking for Pediatrics."

Short Nurse didn't believe her for a second. "Not here," she said crisply. "Please get on the elevator and go to third floor, if you want Pediatrics."

"Thanks." Nora punched the elevator button. Short Nurse made it clear that she was going to wait until Nora got inside, so the minute the door pinged open, she stepped aboard. She nodded and smiled at the nurse, who did not nod and smile back.

Nora wanted to go home and go to sleep. She wanted to wake up to the life she'd had before. But Indigo knew that was never going to happen.

As she made her way out of the hospital, she decided to return to the Edwards house. She would interrogate Graham Edwards, determine if his children had really been kidnapped or if he'd trumped up the story to explain his kids' absence so Rafe Bogdani wouldn't go after them. She could avoid wasting time if she knew the truth.

It was midafternoon, and shadows were to be found. In an alley a block from the hospital she saw a slice of darkness to the side of a green Dumpster, and she made for it like a homing pigeon. She wanted to feel she was moving forward again, something Indigo did well.

She flowed through the shadow world until she emerged in the Edwards backyard. It had never before been so easy, so painless, to travel. *And all I had to do for it was kill my best friend.* But that was a Nora idea, and Indigo banished it.

She focused on the questions she'd ask Graham Edwards. And while she was in the house, she'd retrieve the keys she'd taken from Charlotte Edwards's corpse. It had occurred to Indigo that since the keys hadn't unlocked the Edwards house, maybe they opened

Rafe Bogdani's apartment. After all, Charlotte had been having an affair with the magician. Or wizard. Or whatever he called himself.

As she went up the steps to the kitchen door, she extended her senses into the house, but she could not feel the presence of another human inside. Maybe she would wait for Edwards's return, or maybe she'd get the keys from the ornamental box and start searching for Bogdani's apartment.

Having a plan felt good. She flowed in through the keyhole as she had before. This time it was easier, less frightening.

She took shape in the middle of the kitchen . . .

Just in time to catch a blow to the jaw.

Indigo staggered back, which was involuntary but fortunate. The swipe of a knife barely missed her throat.

She hit the kitchen door and righted herself, ducked to avoid another knife, and turned her own hands into blades of darkness. The ability to see in the dark gave her a slight advantage, because no matter how they'd been disguised from her detection, these were human beings. They weren't all women, which meant they were Phonoi assassins. She swung her blade across the arm of a man, who screamed and fell, clutching at the flayed meat of his biceps. That left four more, and they were skilled.

After the events of the morning with Symes and Mayhew, Indigo was not in any condition to win a fight of this intensity. She wanted to flow out of the keyhole as she'd come in, but the Phonoi were on her every second. All of her attention had to be focused on parrying, thrusting, dodging.

Finally, to her relief, she managed a well-timed stab that took out another assailant. But that still left three, and they were fresher than she was.

Indigo found her back pressed against the door again, and she launched a twisting side kick at the man in front of her. The kick took him in the chest and knocked him flailing backward across the floor . . . into the arms of a new arrival, a woman who hadn't been there a moment before. This new arrival caught the man and twisted his neck with an audible, nasty crack. He collapsed on the floor like a bag of rice.

The face was familiar: Selene, the nut job who'd attacked Indigo on the subway steps.

Selene was here. But this time, it appeared, she was on Indigo's side.

Having an ally gave Indigo a surge of strength, and she cut the throat of another man who'd turned to stare at this new twist of events. Indigo had mustered her last reserve of strength, so she was grateful that Selene, still only another shadow in the gloom of the kitchen, dispatched the last Phonoi with another neck-breaking twist.

Indigo let herself slide to the floor and sit with her back pressed against the door. She took a few moments to catch her breath. Her heart rate gradually slowed to normal, and at last she didn't feel like a scared rabbit.

"Thanks," she said finally. "I don't know what changed your mind about me, and I hope you're not going to pick up the job they started."

Selene laughed. "If I'd wanted you dead, I would have let them wear you out before I took over. It would have saved me some trouble."

"I guess you'll tell me why you helped."

"If you'll tell me why you pulled such a foolish move, coming back here."

Indigo didn't even try to deny that she shouldn't have revisited the Edwards house. "I wanted to question him. He says his kids were kidnapped, and I want to know if that's true or if he's keeping them hidden from Rafe Bogdani. Their mother promised Rafe he could sacrifice them."

"Anything else?"

"Yes, I wanted to retrieve some keys."

"What do these keys unlock?"

"I don't know. But I figure if Charlotte Edwards had them, the keys must open something interesting."

Selene thought for a moment, her expression unreadable. "You and I need to go somewhere and have a heart-to-heart," she said finally.

"About this?" Indigo waved her hand at the corpses.

"Not our problem, are they?"

"I guess not." Indigo felt better immediately. Exhausted, she accepted Selene's hand to rise from the floor.

"So go get these keys. And then we'll find a safe place to have a conversation. You need to tell me what happened in New York today, and I need to explain why I helped you. It's a story you'll find interesting, I promise you."

13

———

They had to keep moving. Selene wanted a safe place to sit and talk, but Nora knew that the moment she paused, she'd be out for the count. She was beyond exhausted, both physically and mentally, and she felt hopelessly carried along on a tsunami of events, borne aloft by chaos and conflict. At present she was barely swimming with the flow. If she paused to catch her breath, she would be subsumed and drowned.

Blotted from existence, just like Shelby.

I'm in control, she thought in Indigo's voice. *I'm steering things from here on in.* As long as she kept believing that, maybe she could keep the exhaustion and desperation at bay.

Of course, she wasn't the only one listening to those thoughts. She felt *him* there, deep and dark, and Damastes's sly confidence chipped away at her resolve.

"So talk," Nora said.

"We need to find somewhere safe," Selene said. "There's too much to say, too much for you to learn."

"Nowhere's safe. Does any of this look safe to you?" They'd left the Edwards place ten minutes earlier and were now walking along a New York street, cars parked at the curb, others passing on the road, pedestrians strolling alone or chatting in groups. Nora hoped that Selene saw the same dangers she did—the windows, the parked cars, the alleys, the countless places that could hide people who wished them harm.

The memories of blood on the sidewalk. The echoes of screams, long lost beneath the sounds of the everyday, yet still reverberating through these concrete canyons for those willing to listen long and hard enough.

"No," Selene said. "Not safe."

"So we keep moving. There are places I have to go."

"Bogdani's apartment?"

Nora had found the keys she sought in the Edwards house and pocketed them. "Soon. But not yet."

"Good. You need to be much stronger before you face him. You need to control the thing you have inside you."

Control? Nora's surprised thought was in harmony with the same word whispered by Damastes.

"There are ways and means," Selene said. "There's more going on here than you know."

"Tell me about it," Nora quipped.

"More than *it* knows, too."

For a moment Nora thought she meant Indigo, and she felt a moment of sharp anger at this strange woman who'd intruded into her life. But when she glanced sidelong at Selene, Nora saw a strange look in the woman's eyes. She was staring *through* Nora's eyes, deeper, seeking something darker. Seeking Damastes.

"Can you really help me?" Nora asked, hardly daring to hope.

"I think so. There's more information we need about the ritual when you were . . . infected, and how such a thing could happen. I know plenty about the murder god's nature."

Liar, Damastes drawled.

"If we discover everything about what was done to you, I believe I can help you combat it."

Witch.

"But you have to let me help you, Nora."

Bitch!

"I *will* let you," Nora said, enjoying that Damastes sounded rattled. It seeded a newfound confidence in her. "But it will have to be on my terms."

"So what's first?"

"First, I need to settle something from the past. Something that might also help you help me. Sam's been working on this for me, and hopefully soon I'll be able to start looking for some answers." Nora checked her phone screen, but there were still no texts. She couldn't let it worry her, not yet. Trapped as he was in the hospital, it might take Sam longer than normal to track down the information she needed.

"The names from the list," Selene said. "Yes, good. That will help us both."

Nora felt an unexpected rush of confidence and well-being, one of those clear, bright moments that always came as a surprise and rarely lasted long enough. It was doubly surprising that it should sweep over her now, and she glanced again at the woman who had first fought her, then fought with her.

Witch, Damastes said, his voice tinged with humor this time.

"But the very first thing is coffee. I'm asleep on my feet." Nora nodded at a coffee shop at the corner. "Best in town."

"I don't drink coffee."

"Freak." Nora walked into the coffee shop ahead of Selene, breathing in deeply and enjoying the warm, heady aromas of freshly ground beans. How could someone not drink coffee and still function like a normal person? It would be like not breathing.

Damastes started to say something. She felt him draw breath, even though he didn't breathe. She sensed him gathering his words, preparing to speak, and she paused by the coffee counter, hands fisted, eyes staring straight through the barista as the young man asked what he could get her.

She tried her best—

I'm going to kill her with your hands, and you'll feel the meat of her as I tear her apart.

—but Damastes was too strong. His words broke through, their presence heavy and dark, warm, intimate.

"Miss?" the man asked again.

"Double espresso," she said, breathing hard. "No . . . triple."

"Need a pick-me-up, eh?"

"More than you know."

While her coffee was being made, she looked at Selene standing outside on the sidewalk. Nora needed this stranger's help more than anything else. If only Selene could deliver on her promises.

As Nora paid, her phone buzzed. A text from Sam: *Got one and he's close,* followed by an address in Brooklyn. She scanned the address twice, downed her espresso in one, and hurried outside.

"Brooklyn. We'll get a cab. You're paying." Traveling through shadows would be quicker, but she knew she couldn't take Selene with her. Although leaving her behind was tempting, she knew that this woman had quickly become part of her life.

Selene hailed a cab while Nora checked the text again. While she stood on the street and New York continued breathing and pulsing around her, Nora and Sam had a brief, hurried text conversation. Sam had found an address for a name on the short list of survivors from the ritual twelve years ago. Matt O'Hagan lived on a street she didn't know in Brooklyn. Sam had dug up more info, too— unmarried, a teacher, O'Hagan had been unemployed for several years following some sort of accident. Sam was still digging to see what that might have entailed, but right then Nora didn't care. She could question O'Hagan about her past, the ritual, and what had happened to her there. Indigo had seen to it that many other people who might have been able to reveal such information were now dead, so Nora was determined to make this attempt work.

"You might have to torture him," Selene said, touching Nora's arm and steering her toward a cab.

Nora bristled at the comment, shocked and afraid. Indigo did not. Deeper down, Damastes seemed to swell with delight at the idea.

"After everything that's happened, maybe he'll be ready to talk," Nora said. She and Selene sat in the back of the cab, and Nora told the driver the address.

"More than likely ready to throw himself from a rooftop," Selene said.

Nora leaned back and stared from the window. New York crept by outside as the cab stopped and started south along Park Avenue. The city had been her home for a long time, but being closed off inside a cab made the outside seem like more of an alien place than ever. People went about their business with no idea what dangers dwelled around them. They walked from light to shadow and back again, too wrapped up in their day-to-day lives to discern the greater, deeper events going on in the wider world. The city wore a mask, and they were constituent parts of it.

In truth, though, the true alienness existed inside this cab, not without.

"So tell me about them," Nora said. "Twice they've come for me, now. Who are these slaughter nuns, and why do they want me dead?"

"It's Damastes."

"They think I serve him?"

Selene shrugged. "Whether they do or not, that's not their

concern. They want him dead and gone. Except . . . they want that for all the wrong reasons."

"What do you mean?"

"The 'slaughter nuns,' as you call them, are an honorable group."

"Could've fooled me."

"Their real name is the Androktasiai."

Nora nodded. The nun had mentioned that name back in Florence, before trying to rip out her spine.

"They believe themselves to be inhabited by the spirits of the Androktasiai. In Greek mythology these were female spirits of honorable killing, such as on the battlefield. They have pride and commitment."

"Great. More gods of murder and death. Why couldn't I be possessed by the god of orgasm? Or ice cream?" Nora knew she wasn't making sense. She felt hysteria lurking around the corner, and now that she was sitting and resting, tiredness allowed it closer. She squeezed her eyes shut and felt the caffeine blasting through her system. But it wasn't enough, and it would not last for long.

"In a way, they're on your side," Selene said. "They despise the Children of Phonos and what they're trying to do."

"Trying to kill me is a funny way of getting me on their side."

"Well, their hatred of Damastes is strong."

Nora sensed him shifting within her, and she glanced around the interior of the cab. The temptation to pick a shadow and flee into it was great. She could fall into darkness and seek somewhere safe. But where was safe? Home, stained with the blood of a dead slaughter nun? Sam's hospital room?

Anywhere?

"So they want me dead because they think that'll kill Damastes."

"They think it's worth a shot."

"How do you know so much about them?" Nora asked, but she

didn't need telling, and Selene's raised eyebrow said it all. Nora sighed. "So let me guess . . . they want you dead, too, because you left them."

"Other way around. I left because they wanted me dead."

"Huh?"

"Because I knew the truth. They know it, too, most of them, but they won't admit it."

"So what's the truth?"

Selene eyed Nora for some time, and she'd never felt so analyzed before. It became uncomfortable, then almost painful, sitting beneath the gaze of this strange, deadly woman. The lure of the shadows had never felt stronger, yet Indigo held back. She knew that the truth was more important than anything else, and she was convinced that this woman carried it. To run now could only be folly.

"I can't tell you until you've learned to control it."

"You mean Damastes? It thinks you're a bitch."

"Because it's scared of me." Selene let that lie for a while, turning away from Nora and staring from the window.

"How long?" Nora asked the driver.

"Ten minutes. You want me to take a shortcut?"

"No. That's fine." Nora nursed her phone, willing Sam to text her more information about who or what she might be about to face. The phone remained silent. She was nervous but excited, a strange combination considering the things she'd seen and done over the past couple of days.

"So how do I control it?" she asked quietly, fearing a harsh reaction from the thing she carried. There was nothing. A silence, a stillness, that of something listening and watching. Nora couldn't dare believe that Damastes was afraid of Selene, but he was certainly cautious and wary. Perhaps for now that was enough.

"There are ways," Selene said. "I can tell you and show you. But it'll need calmer surroundings than a cab in the middle of the city."

"Like a Tibetan monastery?"

Selene threw Nora a confused look, and Nora smiled in return.

The cab pulled up outside a four-story town house, and while Selene paid the fare, Nora's phone buzzed again. Sam.

Matt O'Hagan was accused of assaulting a pupil. His lawyer got him off.

Nora sighed heavily. "Lemme guess which lawyer," she muttered, and remembered Bullington leaping for the window, accepting death rather that the anger of the Phonoi.

"Okay?" Selene had left the vehicle and was holding the door for Nora, and suddenly Indigo was there, cool and calm and ready to dig heavily into the past. At the warehouse she'd displayed her fury, a rage fed by the bloody, ritualistic murders of children. Here, now, her anger was deeper, but also more in control.

This was about knowledge ahead of revenge.

But that didn't mean that revenge wouldn't play a part in what came next.

As she stepped from the car, Indigo knew that she'd need a small head start. She could not trust Selene. Indigo could barely even trust herself, with the slew of memories true and false, the self-deceptions, her confusion about Sam, her trauma over Shelby and who or what she herself had been or become. . . .

And if she couldn't trust herself, investing trust in someone she didn't know would take some time.

She had to at least start this on her own.

Indigo found the head start down beside the steps leading to the apartment block's front door. She leaped for the shadow and fell away, and as she shifted into the shadow realms, the last thing she heard was Selene's voice calling after her.

"Damastes will—"

Nothing more.

Indigo steered through the shadowpaths to where she needed to go. She felt strong and confident, and as she emerged into the third-floor apartment, she wondered what Selene had been trying to say.

Damastes will . . .

"Damastes will shut the fuck up," Indigo muttered as she twisted herself out of the shadows, and she felt the murder god recoil from the strength in her words. Selene had promised to show her how to block Damastes from her thoughts and keep him low, but right now she was doing fine herself.

The apartment stank. She noticed that first. Then, she sensed the fear that permeated the rank atmosphere. It was a ringing tension, like coiled springs waiting to whip undone. It was a stink on the air, death and piss and gone-off food. It was the fast, light breathing she could hear, coming from just out of sight in the living room. Doing her best not to wallow in the fear and make some of it her own, Indigo flowed into the living room and crouched in shadows in the corner.

Curtains were drawn across the windows, even though it was bright daylight outside. Plates and cups were piled on a small table in front of the sofa, and the TV muttered inanities with no one there to watch.

Turned away from the TV to face the door out into the hallway, a heavy leather chair was now the focus of the room. A man was seated in it. He held a pump-action shotgun across his legs. His eyes grew wide when Indigo arrived, and although he could not see her—not yet—he could certainly sense that something had changed.

Indigo knew him. The shock made her waver, almost step from shadows into view, and if she'd done that, perhaps the man who had professed to be her uncle would have blasted her to death. He'd called himself Uncle Theo, but he was no such thing. The care he'd appeared to show her after her parents' funeral must have been something else—a way to keep track of her, perhaps, or an attempt to get close and assess how damaged she was.

Now he was close to madness. He sat in his own waste, its stink rising around him and seeping through the chair. Empty booze bottles were splayed around his feet, some smashed, some still half-full as if he'd forgotten to finish drinking. He shivered in the apartment's rancid heat. The shotgun shook in his hands.

Matt O'Hagan was waiting for death to arrive.

"I'm here," Indigo said, emerging from the shadows, swinging a shadow club at O'Hagan's arms as she approached the chair from one side, knocking the shotgun from his grasp. It clattered against the wall and slipped down behind the sofa.

Matt O'Hagan turned to stare at her, then he opened his mouth to scream.

Indigo thrust a gag of shadows down his throat and pinned his head back against the armchair. She pressed a finger against her lips.

"Scream and I'll rip out your tongue." Slowly she withdrew the shadow gag.

"Are you her?" He was staring at her.

The front door smashed open, out of sight around the corner and along the hallway. Indigo held her breath.

"Are you her?" O'Hagan asked again, louder, and she could see that he was no longer afraid of anything beyond this room. Everything that scared him was inside.

"You remember me." Anger made her voice deep. She felt Damastes squirming inside her at the promise of violence to come.

"We didn't finish." He was staring into her eyes, leaning forward, looking deep as if to see something more.

"How do I get him out of me?"

"Out? You can't. And he can't *get* out. Not on his own. If he could have, he already would have. And he'd have torn you apart."

Selene appeared in the doorway. She quickly took in the scene, then entered the room, ready to intercede.

"He had a shotgun," Indigo said. "He'd have blown us in half."

Selene ignored her, all her focus on the man.

"Is he . . . does he see me?" O'Hagan asked, still staring into Indigo's eyes.

Kill him, Damastes said, and Indigo started moving toward Matt O'Hagan. In truth he was nearly dead already.

"Build a wall," Selene said. "Indigo. Build a wall."

Indigo paused, surprised at what she'd said and how much sense it made.

Step forward and kill him, Damastes insisted, his dark self swollen with desire and eagerness for the kill. He glowed within Indigo, red and hungry.

"A wall made of shadow," Selene said. She was staring at Indigo now, the man between them almost forgotten. Selene could see what was happening. "Draw it around you, inside you, and make it thick and strong. He's a thing of shadow himself, and you're using some of his power. It's made you."

"It's not mine to use," Indigo said. Damastes was guiding her hands now, controlling her body and urging her to form two shadow swords, their edges so sharp because they were made of nothing. They would slice through O'Hagan's throat with hardly any effort from her. Damastes was making his move.

And then her, the murder god said, and Indigo caught Selene's eye.

"I can help you," Selene said. Her eyes had grown wider with the realization that she might soon be fighting for her life, Indigo saw. "But you also have to help yourself!"

Her, slowly, with blunter blades.

"Use his powers against him, because he'll understand them. He'll feel the shadows close around him."

"Please . . ." O'Hagan was pleading, and Indigo saw that she'd rested one shadow blade on his shoulder. A gash had opened across his neck from its subtle touch. One twitch of her arm and his head would roll from his body, a red fountain blooming from his severed neck—

Oh, yes! Damastes said, trying to surge forward even more. For one terrible moment Indigo believed that he had the power to break away from her, and she wondered what the murder god would look like in all his unbridled glory.

"I won't let you," she muttered.

"Yes!" Selene said. "Fight! Use your own power, your humanity, to turn the darkness against him! You are his prison, now build his cell, small and deep!"

Kill . . . blood . . . feed me!

"No." Indigo heaved the blades away from O'Hagan's neck and they shattered in the light, shadow shards scattering across the room and impacting walls and floor. They left dark scars that slowly faded away.

"Please . . . ," the sniveling man said.

Indigo punched him. He snapped back in the armchair, blood spewing from his nose, and she felt Damastes revel in the violence.

Which was exactly what she wanted. Bloodthirsty and wanton, he let his guard down. She gathered everything she had—the determination, the anger, the sense that real life was passing her by and leaving her with this haunted existence—and smothered it down upon the murder god. In her mind she did as Selene had suggested, imagined her flesh a prison for him, then imagined a cell down inside the prison, deep and small and without windows or doors.

He screamed in rage, but his voice seemed to fade, and he did not fight back.

Indigo stood panting over O'Hagan, and she hated the terror in his eyes. She feared that it mirrored her own.

"Yes!" Selene shouted. "You did it! You—"

"Damastes wants him dead. Not because it's one more body, but him, in particular."

"Of course. This excuse for a human, and anyone else we can find from your list, might be able to help you."

"Because they were there when this was done to me." Indigo frowned. She couldn't remember O'Hagan being at the ritual, but he'd still played his part as Uncle Theo, making himself a fragment of her life even after destroying it.

He was looking back and forth between the two women, not sure which of them he ought to fear the most. Indigo could not feel sorry for him.

"I couldn't do it," he said. "I was told to. Your mother herself told me to, and I went through with some of it, the worst of it, but when it came time to finish, I . . ." He was crying, and Indigo considered punching him again.

"The worst of what?" Selene asked.

O'Hagan nodded toward the hallway. "In there."

Oh, no, Indigo thought. *That stench. Rot and death, and obviously not his own.* She was suddenly certain that the Edwards children had been taken and murdered after all, not hidden by their father, but kidnapped and slaughtered by Rafe Bogdani to throw her off his scent. While she'd been searching for them—certain that they would form the end of a ritual to drag Damastes fully into the world—Bogdani had created another method to fulfill his ambitions.

Selene obviously thought so, too. She went first, and Indigo was close behind, considering leaping through shadows but knowing the terrible truth was only a few human steps away.

She pushed into the bedroom behind Selene, eager to see, desperate not to. The stink in there was far worse, and Indigo's eyes watered from the stench and what it meant.

It was not a child lying dead on the bed.

Stark, red memories assaulted her, making the fear in this apartment seem stale.

Nora's being held down on the table with a person grasping each limb, and even though she squirms and thrashes, she can't break free. That's the greatest terror. She is helpless, and the woman approaching the table—

(Altar, they have me on an altar, and there's smoke and something else in the air around me, like the promise of horrors to come)

—can afford to take her time. She, too, is chanting, and holding aloft a knife whose polished sheen will soon be marred with Nora's blood.

Indigo staggered a little at the memory. The woman's face was clear in her mind for the first time ever, a memory made solid.

Now that woman lay dead on the bed. Selene moved in for a closer inspection, but Indigo hesitated. A hole was in the woman's chest, perhaps from a shotgun blast. She'd been dead for a couple of days. Long enough for blood to coagulate and harden, flies to gather, and for the stench of rot to fill the room.

"Oh, no," Indigo said, and even as she turned back toward the living room, she heard the shotgun sing.

She was there in time to see the gun slip from O'Hagan's hands and strike the floor. Smoke hung in the air. His brains, blood, and scraps of scalp and hair decorated the ceiling and wall, dripping.

His mouth hung open, the shadow inside deep and filled with the ghosts of the dead.

She saw something in his lap. An old-fashioned video-camera cassette, the size of a cigarette lighter. He held it palm out, as if for her to see.

Indigo took the cassette. Perhaps video of her, her younger self being prepared for ritual death.

"Just one more corpse," Indigo said. "This is what happens around me."

"Not forever," Selene said. "Come on, we should go. There's more I need to tell you, and if all goes well, we can get the beast out of you."

"I . . . can't hear him anymore. Damastes. Yet I know he's still there."

Selene smiled. The expression did not suit her. "You'll learn to control him. He's fooled you into thinking he's in charge, but he needs you an awful lot more than he's letting on."

"I don't *want* him to need me."

"Let's go. The Androktasiai will be looking for us. They want Damastes dead, and they think killing you will do that."

"And won't it?"

"I don't think that's something we want to find out."

Indigo took one more look at O'Hagan's body. Perhaps seeing her had given him the courage to do what he'd been trying. She liked to think it was guilt that finally pushed him over the edge.

But she remembered the way he'd looked into her eyes, seeking something deeper. Seeking Damastes.

Yet hadn't there been something else there, too? When he'd realized who she was, hadn't there been a moment of sadness, or even . . . wonder? Hadn't she seen a glimmer of human tenderness in his eyes?

The fear of Damastes had allowed Matt O'Hagan to take his own life. Indigo felt certain of that. But those other emotions in the man were a mystery, and they gnawed at her. She thought perhaps the tape might hold answers, but for the first time—as O'Hagan's eyes lingered in her memory—she wasn't sure she wanted the truth anymore.

14
⸻

D amastes is not the only murder god."

They'd grabbed another cab, and the women talked in low voices, their heads as close as two lovers', so the driver couldn't overhear or read their lips in the rearview mirror. Now that Nora had Damastes bottled up, at least for the time being, she'd demanded the truth about the Androktasiai and why they were so desperate to kill Selene.

Nora had frowned at Selene's answer. "I figured. But so what?"

"He's also not the only one that's present on this plane."

"What?"

"That's part of the terrible truth the Androktasiai would kill me to silence. They are meant to stand against the murder gods—they serve honorable death, remember. But they have been corrupted, controlled, by one of darker gods they fight to destroy. Their mission has been twisted into fanaticism for evil ends. I don't know exactly when it happened or how, but they have come under the influence of Caedis—one of Damastes's sister murder gods and a rival to his power. She's clever. She's managed to keep the Sisters of

Righteous Slaughter from believing what I know to be true, that she rides one of them as Damastes would ride you. She goads them to kill me, and to destroy Damastes, not for the salvation of humanity, but for its doom."

Nora had felt the shadows ripple beneath her skin. "The murder of a murder god . . . that's gotta be some kind of super power-up."

Selene had given a bitter chuckle. "The Androktasiai believe they must kill you to kill Damastes, though I have some doubts it will be that simple. Or that the power will simply return to the void if they succeed."

Nora had sat back in her seat, scowling.

"Don't dwell on it," Selene had chided. "You'll lose your mental balance and the demon can push up again. The idea is to keep Damastes in the dark—literally. Here, let me show you some tricks for holding him there. First, remember two things: power is never destroyed, only recycled; and you must balance need and effort or you can't keep the demon on his leash. Place your fingertips together and imagine the flow of shadows like an endless circle through your body."

"But the shadows—" Nora had started to object. Didn't she share her power with Damastes? Could darkness really hold him?

"Don't believe the demon's lies—uncertainty weakens you. Shadows have no allegiance—just as bricks don't care about the mason who builds the wall. Own your power. Once he's contained, it takes less effort to hold him there, and the shadows are still yours to command. Balance need and effort. Keep the cycle flowing."

Now they sat on rickety chairs in a darkened storage room. The cassette Nora had taken from O'Hagan's dead hand had been obsolete and bloodstained, but it fit in the old video-editing machine and it ran. The quality was lousy, but it would do.

On-screen, the light of candles and fire lent an ominous gleam to the blade, anointed with oil and flecked with ash. Nora's stomach lurched as she watched the video of her own intended murder twelve years earlier and struggled to keep Damastes in the darkness. She'd been holding him for a while and she was tired.

"Don't let him out during this," Selene whispered. "If you feel him rising to the surface, say so—he mustn't know what we know."

Nora couldn't spare the concentration to speak. She nodded and kept her fingertips pressed together—she nearly had the knack of doing it without the physical prompt, but not quite yet. For now, Nora-who-was-Indigo held the murder god in check and stared at the dusty old CRT.

Nora's younger self lay naked on the altar, her body covered in strange designs painted in blood, and some strange powder that sparkled like black diamond dust. *What* is *that crap? Did they drug me? Why didn't I keep fighting?* A woman stood beside the altar with her back to the camera, watching as then-younger Charlotte Edwards placed something shiny on Nora's forehead where a series of lines all came together. The object—it seemed familiar, but the video was too dark and damaged for it to be clear in such a fleeting shot—didn't lie flat, but stood proud by a half inch or so, and something flashed and spun at its heart. The lines on young Nora's body pulsed with darkness that seemed to flow toward the thing.

Charlotte's lips moved, her voice growing stronger as she continued. The language was completely foreign to Nora, but the sound raised every hair on her body and sent a twisting nausea through her gut. Selene frowned and leaned closer to the screen.

Young Nora's eyes flashed open, pupils wide and black from side to side. Charlotte continued chanting, holding out the knife and touching the point to the outstretched hand of the other woman. All the flames seemed to bow down and flicker for a moment. Then Charlotte touched the same blood-tipped blade to Nora's forehead, just above the flashing, shining object.

The girl on the altar convulsed. Her body rose like a bridge, only head and heels still in contact with the stone. Nora's present body jerked in sympathy, and she felt a sharp pain in her head and the surge of Damastes within her.

"Selene!" she gasped as the scene and the sound went on and on.

On the screen, a shiver and a ripple of motion started in the darkened ritual room. Noise swelled like a small wave moving through the cultists and toward the altar. A man was pushing his way up from the darkness near the floor, struggling against the chanting people.

"No!" the man shouted. "You can't—Stella, no!"

A couple clutched the man by his arms and hauled on them as if they would tear him limb from limb, their eyes shining like those of beasts reflecting the firelight.

Selene shoved past Nora, reaching for the editing machine's power button.

The man threw himself sideways. He lashed out with his feet against the closest captor, seeming not to care if he fell, so long as he took them down, too. His violent action freed one of his arms and he flailed as he fell. His foot connected with one cultist's knee. The three went to the floor together and vanished from sight for a moment. A cracking sound, like a tree bough snapping in a storm, broke through the chanting for an instant and the man rose back to his feet, lurching forward again.

"Nora!"

Then, like that girl on the tiny editing screen, Nora seized, her body wrenching backward without her control and knocking Selene aside. The darkness within her ripped apart, tore into multiple shades of shadow and death that clashed and tore at one another as the demon fought to free itself of her control. Damastes surged against her barriers like a million frozen quills.

Teeth clenched, she let the heat of her fury pour toward his chilly fingers that scrabbled at her mind and body as the sound from the video whirled her into the memory of that night. Her body was rigid, but her eyes were still riveted to the screen and her mind was still her own. She pushed Damastes down inside as she had before—as she had then—felt him falter. . . .

The rest of the chanting people surged toward the man, seeming to bury him in the press of their bodies. The two women beside the altar ignored it all. Charlotte nodded to the other woman with a smile and a graceful motion of her hand. "Go on," Charlotte murmured, then turned toward the struggle that inched closer and closer.

Selene scrambled up, jumped over Nora's rigid body to pass her and get to the machine's controls.

The woman with the knife continued her own turn the other way, toward the camera, toward the altar, where the younger Nora convulsed and thrashed, teeth clenched, foam and blood running from the corners of her lips. The woman's eyes were dark and hollow as she muttered under her breath, walking calmly closer, raising the gleaming, oiled blade. . . .

A flame spurted upward from the darkness and the massed bodies behind the altar, and the man rose up against the sudden light, swinging one of the thick iron candelabra, knocking Charlotte and the cultists aside and then lunging to grab the woman with the knife as the blade came down—

The black snakes within shook present Nora and pitched her to the floor of the tiny room. *Mother! No!* Nora's body was locked rigid, but her mind was wild with fragments of memory. That was her *mother* about to stab her through the heart. *Her father—no! No, he wasn't, it was "Uncle Theo"* . . .

Selene slammed down on the power button, but for a moment the images, like ghosts, remained.

You cannot hold me—why waste your strength? Bow, little Nora, and I will be merciful.

Then the CRT darkened, the scene shrinking and vanishing

into a small white dot even as Selene spun and dropped to the floor to grab onto Nora's thrashing body. But the instant the sound died, Nora went limp, stunned by the sudden, violent reversals of control. Her hold on Damastes loosened. The shadows inside her ripped apart and thrashed against each other.

Damastes's voice thundered in Nora's head and echoed from her mouth. *You cannot bind me, witch. Blind me, silence me awhile—it matters not. I will be free! And I will gorge on your screams while I tear you apart!*

Selene pushed her face next to Nora's and crooned, "Think of the shadow, the cycle. Drive him down, wall him up in the endless dark. Your power is his prison, his prison is your power."

Empty prattling! This vessel is mine!

"Fuck you, demon," Nora muttered, slamming the lid back down on Damastes, putting him back into that cell in the prison of her flesh. It wouldn't hold forever, but it would keep long enough for her to get back on her feet and make the next move. She lay against the dirty linoleum floor, panting. "I've got him, Selene. I'm okay."

Selene stared into Nora's eyes a moment, searching for a sign of Damastes, perhaps. Selene sat back on her heels, apparently satisfied, but she was holding tight to her own knife. "Is he—?"

"Back in his box for now. Still in the dark." Nora pulled herself up. "That—my mother . . . was going to sacrifice me."

"Hmm . . . I suspected the ritual used on you was different from those practiced more recently."

"Yeah, none of the kids—none of the recent victims were related to any of the names on the list. Not like me. Holy crap . . . those were my *parents*!"

"Yes." Selene looked puzzled by Nora's outburst.

"No. I don't mean back then—though all that's disgusting and freaky, too. *The dead woman in O'Hagan's apartment was my mother!* And *he*—'Uncle Theo,' Matt O'Hagan—Christ! They were never even married . . . yet another fucking lie. *He* was my *father*! They were alive all this time! Did he really try to save me? How? Why didn't the cult find me sooner? Why are my memories so . . . fucked-up?"

Clutching her head in pain and confusion, Nora collapsed into a rickety chair. She remembered the cemetery, but now she knew it had been empty, shrouded in night, as O'Hagan—her father, damn it!—had spirited her away from the crumbling old chapel where the ritual had taken place. There had been no funeral, no mourners. Only the ruin of the ritual and their escape into a cleaner darkness.

Her father had defied the cult—why? For love? That was some twisted kind of affection. He'd muttered into her ear as he'd carried her away. All the words he'd said—that her parents were dead, the assurances that she would be taken care of—those hadn't been comforting words. They were her personal catechism in the Church of Indigo:

Who are you? Indigo. Where do you come from? Humanity's darkest shadows. What became of your parents? Murdered by a mugger. How did you become as you are? Shaped by adversity, trained by monks in high Tibetan mountains, tempered in righteous anger.

Strands in the tapestry of lies. More false memories, woven from bits of horrible truth. To keep her safe. But there were still holes in her past where memory stopped short and only blackness held sway.

Somehow, O'Hagan must have stayed with the cult to keep her safe. To keep her mother safe, as well? Had he realized that letting a murder god loose upon the world could only lead to ultimate destruction? That Nora was the gateway that must never be used or replicated? She shuddered and felt the shadows within roll in her chest, almost like chuckling.

Selene sat down beside Nora again and took her hands, forcing the younger woman to turn toward her. "We have little time. If

O'Hagan and his victim were who you say, it casts new light on the ritual that was used on you and what the Phonoi must be planning—"

"You mean what Rafe Bogdani is planning," Nora spat. "He talked about taking the power for himself, that the original ritual was screwed up and that pissed him off. That old ritual's got to be some kind of clue."

Nora frowned at the floor as wild thoughts fell into place in her head. "My parents . . . the missing Edwards kids . . . Rafe's going to re-create the original ritual as he thinks it *should* have gone. That requires the sacrifice of a child—or children—by their own parents! My parents are dead, Charlotte's dead, but Graham's not. Rafe—" She had to stop and swallow down bile. "Whatever he had O'Hagan do to my mother must have been a way to salvage or extend the original ritual."

Nora closed her eyes and tried to remember what her—what the *corpse* had looked like, how it had been mutilated. If she thought of it as just a body, the roiling nausea and horror were a little easier to stand. *Think!* What damage had the body sustained? Ripped open from sternum to groin, a bloody red cavity, going black and brown as the blood coagulated, rippling with the movement of maggots—

Nora clapped her hand over her mouth and breathed through her nose. She caught a whiff of old paper and dust that clung to her hand from moving boxes and cleaning off the editing machine. Ordinary, decent odors of files, work, dull, dry fact. *Thank God.*

Nora got hold of herself. "Did you get a better look? Have you any idea what he did to her?"

"I couldn't really say. There were symbols on her flesh and organs missing, but in that pesthole . . . It wasn't anything I've ever seen before."

"Damn it. That's no help. Whatever Rafe had planned, O'Hagan—my father—killed himself to stop it." It hadn't been terror at the end . . . no. That was a relief. "They were hiding in plain sight."

Selene made a sour face. "No. He was her guard."

Nora scowled at her. "What?"

"Didn't you notice? There were drugs in the room—strong antipsychotics, opiates, depressants, and others. She was kept medicated. Given what we've seen on that tape, I wouldn't doubt she was dangerously insane. Whatever Rafe Bogdani had demanded of O'Hagan, it was a way to control *you*—their daughter."

"Well, it's not fucking working."

"That could be why Rafe's now bent on using Graham Edwards's children—with or without his cooperation. He's going back to the original ritual."

"We have to find them. We have to—" Nora made herself slow down. She took another deep breath and pressed her fingers together again, testing the shadow walls she'd ringed around Damastes. He lay like a cold stone inside her, quiet for now, but waiting for another chance, another slip. . . . But for now, she had him. "Let's watch the video again. No sound this time. I *know* there's something there that O'Hagan wanted me to see." She couldn't think of him as her father—or even as "Uncle Theo"—and she wasn't sure what she ought to feel aside from horrified and angry. But she could work with that.

The girl struggles at first as they lead her into the room—the details are lost in shadow but for a pillar here, a bit of wall there, as a small fire and a scattering of fat candles in iron candelabra flicker as if floating in darkness. Only an incomplete ring of candles around the altar creates a well-defined aura of illumination. The view swivels to follow the progress of the chanting people who accompany two women in white to the altar dais—and the girl. The camera dwells on her, like an unclean gaze.

With each step, the girl seems to grow weaker, sleepier perhaps. Or hopeless. Her expression moves from fear to submission to emptiness, until the small procession stops beside the candles that illuminate the altar. The older woman—Charlotte—steps into the circle through the gap in the candles. The younger of the two women in white—Nora's mother, Stella— removes the girl's thin robe from her shoulders to reveal the lines of blood already decorating her body. Facing the other woman, Stella speaks.

"I give my daughter, Nora, flesh of my flesh, to the service of our great master. For the glorification of Damastes, was she born. For the embodiment of the god, I give her of my own free will, asking nothing for myself."

"Your sacrifice is acceptable. For your gift, you shall be the favored of Damastes," Charlotte replies.

Stella bows her head with a solemn smile. Young Nora shivers and makes a frightened small sound, but gives only token resistance as her mother steps into the circle and pulls her along. Nora stumbles as she crosses the line.

Charlotte closes the circle by lighting the final candle, and the light within makes the darkness without deeper, as if the blackness oozes directly from hell. The other members of the procession spread around the altar, still muttering their strange chant. As they pass the camera, a moment's light illuminates each face—the faces of those who will die in a warehouse years hence, and of the few who will escape. Each expression ecstatic but one: Matt O'Hagan's, which is pale and cast down. Then he passes into the gloom, just one of the dim shapes that ring the bright altar.

The girl is pushed up onto the altar and made to lie supine. Now she gives no resistance, her eyes dim, unfocused, her body pliant and still while the high priestess and her acolyte draw the last of the incantations and sigils on her flesh in gleaming black powder. The girl seems asleep. . . .

The chanting rises as Charlotte anoints the knife and hands it to Stella, rises again as the high priestess brings forth a shining object: golden wings surmounting an endless circle filled with a spinning darkness that both draws and repels the eye. Stare too long and the darkness stares back. The shining thing is laid on the girl's forehead while Charlotte speaks words that quiver on the air and make the shadows squirm like a maggot-rich corpse.

The girl's eyes flash open, pupils wide and black from side to side.

Charlotte accepts the knife, given by Stella and blooded on her hand. The flames bow down. Charlotte touched the bloodstained blade's tip to the girl's forehead—

The girl seizes, bowing upward.

The outer shadows stir and shiver, a single voice threading out of tune through the chanting of the assembled cultists. Matt O'Hagan struggles forward.

"No! You can't—Stella, no!"

The chanting goes on, never breaking, even as the nearest pair of worshippers turn to grab the man as if they would rend him apart. Their eyes shine in the dark.

Matt struggles violently, lashes out, kicks, and falls, then rises again on the sound of bones breaking, and the chanting finally falters.

"Nora!"

The girl convulses, thrashes against the altar top, foam beginning to drip from the corners of her mouth as her lips pull back in a rictus.

The women at the altar ignore everything but their ritual. Charlotte hands the knife to Stella and smiles, motioning her forward. "Go on." Then she turns to see the cause of the commotion behind them.

Stella turns toward the camera, toward the girl on the altar—her daughter, sacrifice to Damastes. She steps forward, raising the knife on high, murmuring strange words with the soft expression of a mother singing a lullaby. . . .

Behind her, Matt swings one of the iron candelabra, clearing a path *to the altar as Charlotte steps toward him. He kicks over the candles and swipes at Charlotte, knocking her down.*

Flames lick across the ground and spread, climbing every loose fold of fabric they touch. All voices but Stella's give way to screams and chaos.

Stella holds the knife above her daughter's chest, staring into the flashing darkness at the heart of the golden object that rests on Nora's forehead. No amount of thrashing, no amount of tears, blood, or spit that run from her has dislodged it from the girl's skin.

"No!"

Pandemonium and flame stir the shadows outside the ring of altar candlelight as Stella plunges the knife down—

Matt lunges forward and swings the candelabra one more time, smashes it across Stella's shoulders, sweeping her away.

Stella screams in fury and pain as she falls behind the altar.

The view rocks, slips, falls . . .

And only static reigns. Then nothing.

It took five minutes of stopping and starting for Nora to get a single clear frame of it, and the squirming of the shadows deep inside her confirmed the idea in her mind: This was something important, something that she'd seen no sign of at the warehouse where Luis Gallardo had died. She pointed at the golden circle-and-wings that contained living darkness. "I've seen that before."

Nora and Selene leaned close to the screen to look at the gleaming shape. The circle wasn't empty as it had been the first time— the darkness at the center emanated from a glittering dark object that spun like a tiny gyroscope.

"I found that at Charlotte's house," said Nora. "But it didn't have the thing in the middle. I've seen the circle-and-wings on the hilts of those knives the Phonoi use, but this one's like a pendant— no blade."

"Death's Wings and the Circle of the Eternal Void," Selene said. "The Phonoi adopted the symbols and merged them. That spinning stone is an ombrikos—a shadow lodestone. Hung in the symbolic circle, it spins and opens a sort of hole between the realm of shadow and death, and the world of light and life. Call it a Void Portal."

"That hasn't showed up in any other ritual that I've seen traces of. Could that be how—or why—Damastes was pulled into me and trapped when I wasn't killed?"

"Yes. And it might send him straight back into the void, too. But we need both parts."

"Well, I have no idea where the whatsit—the shadow lodestone?— is, but we've got keys to both the Edwards house and Rafe's place. I saw the pendant last in Charlotte's desk drawer, but the Edwards house will be too full of FBI and cops waiting for a call from the 'kidnapper' for us to walk right in and take it—though I could go by myself."

"I'd rather that we stay together for now. So, let's start with Rafe Bogdani. He wasn't at the original ritual—"

"I noticed." Nora frowned. "But that means he may not know how it all went bad."

"No, and that may help us if we're forced to disrupt the new ritual rather than stop it before it happens. In addition, Rafe may not know about Charlotte having the Death's Wings pendant. Though if he does, he may have taken it as well as the Edwards children."

"I'm not sure about that. If he's got them, he most likely took the kids from wherever Graham Edwards stashed them, not from their house. I'm finding it hard to believe that Graham would have willingly handed them over to Rafe. That man's got a lot of dirty secrets, and I'm sure we can find something we could use against him at his place."

Selene gave a wolfish smile. "With pleasure. It'll give you something else to concentrate on before the demon pushes his way to the surface again."

Nora's momentary glee dampened. "I knew I couldn't keep him down forever."

"It won't be as bad as before. Just hold on until we're someplace where he won't learn anything he can use against us. Then he can rage as much as you can stand."

Nora ejected the cassette and put it into a file box labeled "Mount St. Helens Lava Dome 2005," sure it was safe from prying eyes in the files of such a nonevent.

Nora locked the storage room and they headed for the elevators by way of the main office. Nora could hear her coworkers talking and working and the usual clack of keyboards and the whir of printers, but the sound was weirdly distant. As she stepped into the bullpen with Selene on her left, something flickered at the edge of her vision and she spun, crouching automatically to avoid a blow to the head as a frisson ran up her spine.

Selene whirled to place her back to Nora's—to Indigo's—as she drew her blades. Indigo whipped her head up.

Like Florence, only worse: the women in tunics blocked the aisle ahead and closed in from behind, blades drawn, while Nora's coworkers chatted and typed on obliviously. One of the staffers tripped as an Androktasiai swept past her. Indigo reached for shadows to pull the woman aside before her head could strike the corner of a bulky old copier. But in the buzzing, pervasive fluorescent light of the office, the shadows huddled under furniture and drew forth as thin streams that barely shifted the woman, who stumbled and hit her shoulder. The woman's shout of pain and surprise drew others, unsuspecting, toward the impending fight.

The slaughter nuns did not come gently in ones and twos, but launched forward, offering no quarter and giving no kind of a damn if the *NYChronicle* staff got in the way.

"It's the influence of Caedis," Selene muttered, poised for battle. "They no longer care about the collateral damage they may cause."

"Shit."

15

Indigo watched as the slaughter nuns fanned out. *NYChronicle* staffers started to rise in alarm, voices erupting in an anxious chatter. They couldn't see Indigo, but the Androktasiai were visible now. They were stealthy, even mystical, but they could not fold shadows around themselves. They could not remain invisible forever.

No choice, Indigo thought, and she dropped the cloak of shadows she'd been hiding in. Kenny Ortega, part of the sports staff, swore as he shoved back so hard in his chair that he tipped over and slammed to the ground.

"Everybody, stay where you are!" Indigo snapped. She backed away, moving swiftly and skillfully across the tops of several desks, keeping the killers in sight even as they spread out through the office. "It's not you they want!"

Doesn't mean they won't kill these people, she thought. This was a gamble. Caedis might be manipulating them, but if the slaughter nuns thought they were the good guys, Indigo hoped that meant they wouldn't kill innocents at random.

"Selene? If you have a plan, now's the time to speak up!"

Nora checked over her shoulder, and spotted an emergency-access stairwell sixty feet away, at the other end of the room. Its glowing red EXIT sign shone like a beacon. Only three of the sisters had managed to block the way so far. Selene had shifted into a combat stance, but if she had suggestions, she hadn't volunteered them.

"Okay, first things first," Indigo said. "We take this fight someplace else."

They *had* to move the fray away from this bustling room full of people. The *NYChronicle* staffers were terrified, probably assuming the slaughter nuns were terrorists. Several stood up and tried to flee. Kenny Ortega climbed to his feet and barked at the nearest nun to back off. He took a fighter's stance, and the nun smashed his nose in, then swept his legs out from under him. The sisters started shoving the journalists aside, pushing them over, knocking them out of the way.

Anything to reach Indigo. Anything to kill her, and ostensibly to kill the god within her, too.

"Damn it, Selene!" Indigo shouted, nodding toward the metal exit door.

Selene glanced that direction, saw the glowing sign, and understood. "Got it! Make a run for it—I've got your back!"

Indigo pivoted and dropped into the aisle. She faced the three warriors blocking her way and charged them headlong, leaving Selene to handle the rest.

They didn't all have to die—not here, not now—but they all had to *move*.

From this position, most of the nuns were at Indigo's back. She wasn't sure if it was better or worse that way, but Selene was running point and the EXIT was calling her name. In the stairwell, there would be shadows. In the stairwell, Indigo would have options.

In the stairwell, nobody else had to get hurt.

But the first of the three obstacles was ready for her—blades in hand, and scowl on face. Indigo went in low, counting on her weight to carry her smack into the woman's knees. Indigo crashed into her like a bowling ball, knocking her hard without sending her flying. The Androktasiai flailed but rallied, snagging one blade on the rough Berber carpet and swinging the other one around at Indigo's head.

Indigo ducked, rolled behind the nun, and shoved her forward—directly into Selene's sword. Maybe the woman gasped, maybe she cried out. Indigo didn't watch, and she didn't listen. She didn't have the attention to spare, not when the second and third nuns were bearing down and closing in. When one of them tried to sweep her legs, she leaped aside, bounced off a metal desk with a loud clang, and slid on her ass to a more defensible position against a cubicle.

From there, she kicked with both feet and caught the first woman in the chest—propelling her back into the third. It was only a little save. Indigo was still on her heels, and then on her feet.

Selene got a grip on the nearest nun and seized her by the tunic, then flung her back down the aisle toward her friends. One of them tripped over her, and another jumped. They did not stop. They did not close ranks. They trickled around the mail carts and the printers and advanced at a graceful, terrible speed.

But the EXIT sign was still calling, and now it was closer. Twenty feet away, maybe.

For twenty feet, Indigo scrambled, and with Selene breathing down her neck she slammed into the emergency bar and leaned on it. IN CASE OF EMERGENCY, HOLD LEVER: DOOR WILL OPEN IN TEN SECONDS.

The slaughter nuns were going to close the gap in a whole lot less than ten seconds.

The alarm began to wail, starting at a low whistle and working its way up to a hard scream. Everyone on that floor who wasn't fighting for her life popped up and looked around. Women grabbed purses and men collected satchels. Several stayed cowering in their cubicles, but most of them made a run for the elevator alcove and the main stairs there.

Indigo wondered what they were thinking now, those people. She'd been an urban legend, and now they'd all seen her. What would they remember?

Selene sliced, chopped, and stabbed, using her body to shield Indigo's while they waited those ten interminable seconds. The press of the sisters' bodies was a crush of wild limbs and sharp blades, but finally the emergency exit door gave way, and they all collapsed into the corridor in one vicious tumble.

Indigo could breathe again. There were shadows again.

She seized Selene and pulled her into a corner beneath the stairs, gaining a few feet of distance. But it wasn't that easy, not against these women. She knew it would be bad, and she knew that Florence had almost been too much—and now she was in even closer quarters.

But she had shadows. She slipped in and out of them, popping free when she had to, slicing and thrusting unseen when she could . . . and in the face of more blades, more fury, when she couldn't.

"Up or down?" Selene asked with a pained gasp that worried Indigo as much as anything else in the stairwell.

Indigo made an executive decision. "Down!"

In the basement there would be more shadows, more darkness. Down there, she'd find the old archives in a storage space with rickety bulbs, and a boiler room, and below that a crawlspace where no one except workmen in overalls ever dared to go.

"Down?"

"Yes!"

If they went up, they'd land in the sunlight on the roof, eventually. Fewer shadows. Worse odds. Their odds were better if they headed below. If Indigo could only find a shadow deep enough, dark enough . . . if she could only steal a moment to think, to wrap herself up and build up some proper defenses . . .

"If wishes were fishes," she muttered, falling backward and taking Selene with her, into one shadow and out from another. Selene went feral, and two of the nuns screamed. Indigo didn't see what Selene had done, but those two women quit following them, so it was a big fat win as far as Indigo was concerned.

She was breathless. She was afraid, for herself and Selene, too. Selene was slowing down.

Down. Always down. Everything was going down.

Selene was bleeding. Indigo was bleeding, too, but it wasn't bad enough to drag her down yet. Not all the way.

Down. She took another shadow, and Selene hopped the banister to the next level. The slaughter nuns followed their descent, shrieking like Harpies, their tunics billowing like wings in the unrelenting chase.

"We have to get ahead of them!" Selene whispered frantically. "This is too close, too much!"

"Down!" Indigo insisted. "Trust me!"

But when she caught Selene's eye, she saw fear. When she glimpsed Selene's arm, she saw a slash. When she looked lower, she saw a puncture in her companion's left shoulder, and what looked like a wound in her belly. "Something is wrong here."

"They aren't alone," Selene agreed. "One of them . . ." She cocked her head toward the charging cluster of nuns. "Caedis rides on one of them."

"Well, shit."

Indigo didn't dare take inventory of her own situation. Hers wasn't much better, and she knew it. She refused to think about it. She insisted to herself that the fire along her right flank was just a scratch. The bleeding down her thigh was only a flesh wound. Never mind the stumbling. Never mind how Selene's hands were slipping on her blades. Or how she dropped one.

Indigo's breathing came harder and harder, and so did Selene's.

"Down won't cut it," Selene wheezed.

But they were already committed, so Indigo pressed onward, a little slower. Fewer sisters were on their tail, but it might as well have been a thousand. There were too many, and Indigo and Selene were running out of floors, running out of shadows.

They were running out of options.

They burst through one particularly dense patch of darkness at the very bottom of the very last flight of stairs, and then they were in the basement. It was dark, but not as dark as they'd hoped—and the slaughter nuns were right behind them.

"This won't work. It can't work, they're coming, they're coming," wheezed Selene.

Indigo was frozen with uncertainty. Where could they go where the sisters couldn't follow? After Florence, they seemed almost invincible and immortal. They weren't. It wasn't possible. Only the gods were immortal, and that wasn't a sure thing either.

"The gods . . . ," she breathed.

"What?"

Indigo closed her eyes. She only needed a few seconds.

"What are you doing?"

She almost responded, but stopped herself. No, Selene might not go for it. She might interfere. She wouldn't be wrong if she did, but this is what it had come to. Indigo retreated to the shadows in her mind, in her soul. She felt around on the walls and floors of the rooms she'd built, and she found the trapdoor that led some place much, much deeper than the basement.

There was always some place farther down, if you knew where to look.

Damastes, she breathed to the blackness. *I know you're in here.*

Time did not quite stop, but it stretched, slowed, and waned.

Yes. But why are you?

The ancient god of violent death, of murder and mayhem, and whatever else he was alleged to oversee . . . the powerful, sour-tempered brute of darkness . . . it swelled up and stretched and enveloped her. He swallowed Nora, not quite touching her. He filled the space in the shadows around her and observed her keenly.

I have a proposal. I think you're going to like it.

You must be quite confident of this, to arrive so boldly. You must need something.

She confessed, *You've got me there. But I've got you* here; *so we're either at an impasse, or we're in a great position to strike a bargain. It's up to you.*

He pondered this. **Name your terms.**

Help me fight your sister.

Damastes recoiled. Then he recovered and crowded around Nora again. **You need me to help fight. You think she's here.**

I know she's here. There's no way these slaughter nuns are following me so fast, so crazy, around all these shadows. They've got help. Now I need help, so are you in, or what?

What's in it for me?

You get to come out and play and wreak a little havoc. Do some murdering. It'll be fun. And then you'll go back in the box.

He bristled. She could feel it.

So she added, *But if you play nice and make yourself useful, maybe we can come to some sort of arrangement. Like a time-share or something.*

Maybe the old god didn't know exactly what a time-share was, but he got the general idea fast enough. Nora thought he sensed an opportunity and was calculating exactly how he might leverage the situation to his advantage.

He was undoubtedly planning a hostile takeover and a hasty escape when he let out a long, wicked sigh and said, *On your word, then: I defeat my sister—*

Which you'd probably do for free, let's be real.

I defeat my sister, he began again, with a decidedly peevish tone. *And the lid on the box, as you put it . . . is up for negotiation. I will . . . play nice. With you, not her.*

Outside the strange little space where time wasn't working normally, and Nora had time for a conversation with a murder god, things were about to get very, very bad. The slaughter nuns were circling. They were coming.

Indigo and Selene were screwed.

Yes—it's up for negotiation. Now hurry up and help me out, or we're both going to have a seriously shitty day!

The air went cold and the darkness went sharp.

Nora tried hard to keep from panicking. She tried to hold herself together, even as she let herself come apart—one shadowed brick at a time. When the wall was down, and the lid was cracked, she looked down at her hands. She was pressing her fingers together almost automatically. It was practically a superstition at this point, but she'd kept it filed it away in the "can't hurt, might help" column. Now it was time to hurt. She took a deep breath, and she opened her hand.

Damastes surged forth.

He rose up and filled Nora's body—he assumed control over *Indigo's* body—and then, as time snapped back into place around the pair of them, they moved together as one.

Let go, little woman. I need a word with my sister, and you'll be in the way.

"I thought I *did* let go . . . ?"

Selene asked, "What?"

But there wasn't time to explain.

Indigo exhaled and retreated, feeling the god rush through her veins like her own blood. She could still move her hands, her legs. She could still blink and turn her head and look around at the terrible scene in the newspaper's basement.

Let. Go.

"Sorry!" she squeaked. "Take the wheel, man. Take it."

You didn't have to ask Damastes twice. He reared up, and Indigo reared up. She felt him taking the reins and running with them—and it was thrilling, but appalling. She did her best to keep one hand on the controls, but he was a runaway train and she'd made a deal.

Well . . . go get 'er, she told him. But she didn't say it out loud. He had too much control, and she had to thank some other god for that. It was as if she'd been driving a Lamborghini, and she'd handed over the keys to a NASCAR driver.

The shadows jutted up higher and sharper and stronger than she'd imagined them; they rallied around her like a fortress—an armed fortress, with foot-long spikes on every brick. Damastes surged and the walls swept outward, catching the first two slaughter nuns and ending them on the spot. They didn't die, but they twitched and they stopped, broken and bent. They bled all over the floor. Indigo could watch them if she was fast, if she caught them out of the corner of her eye.

Of Damastes's eye.

No, of *her* eye.

He moved in a blocky blur, a chess rook the size of a horse. He shuffled the darkness with all the speed and facility of a ninja, and all the unstoppable force of a train. Two more sisters went down under the fresh onslaught, as the murder god seized every drip, drop, and sliver of the basement shadows. He weaponized them in an instant, lifting the dark scraps up and swinging them around, using those modified arms as big as doors, shoving and stabbing all in one brutal gesture.

One of the Androktasiai held back. The twist of her face said she was wrestling with something, and Indigo had a pretty good idea of what that something might be.

To Damastes she whispered, *It's her. Over there. Look at her. She's negotiating, like I did.*

I'm on it.

And he was. He pushed another slaughter nun aside with something that looked like ease, but came with such a rush of violence that it couldn't have been. These were the same shadows Indigo used, and she had used them to kill, but the god of murder (or *a* god of murder) did it so much more smoothly, without even the faintest hint of hesitation.

The Androktasiai's eyes changed, going so black that they bled ink. She opened her mouth and raised her arms, and she spoke with a voice so loud that it threatened to split her open. Her body shuddered and seized, even as this new power took control and lashed out.

"Brother of mine!" she roared, and she looked so much larger than she had before, even a few seconds ago. Her hair moved like Medusa's snakes, and the shadows pushed against her, around her. They outlined her like a dull black halo.

Four slaughter nuns froze. They gazed at their sister with confusion.

Selene saw an opportunity and raised her remaining bloody blade. She sent it swirling at the closest Androktasiai and nearly took off her arm. Grievously wounded, the woman retreated. The other three withdrew from Indigo and Selene and their own fellow nun. They weren't stupid. They knew this wasn't right—they just weren't sure how wrong it was. Not yet.

Selene was happy to fill them in.

"You see?" she shouted, and a stringy line of bloody drool slipped down her chin. "I told you—I told you all! Caedis wants to murder Damastes—what better way to accrue enough strength to fully manifest in this world than to murder a murder god and take his power?"

Damastes was clearly delighted. "There you are, my sister! It is good to gaze upon your face, one last time before you die!" he said with Indigo's voice.

Caedis blazed with her full and awful glory. "You first!" she shrieked, or growled, or some combination of these things. When she spoke through the mouth of the Androktasiai, she seemed to speak with the voice of dozens of lost souls at once.

She might actually *be scarier than you*, Indigo told her own demonic parasite.

He took it personally, but that was her intent. He launched Indigo's body at his sister and brought the full weight of his rage and power against her—but Caedis was no slouch herself, and she mounted a vigorous defense.

Caedis peeled off some of the shadow armor Damastes had fashioned for himself and locked it around herself in an impenetrable cloak. Her brother raged at the theft and yanked back what he could. They wrestled and rolled, and Indigo lost track of who was holding what, and which one was controlling what patch of darkness.

She was getting dizzy, and she felt herself withdrawing farther inward as Damastes took more and more control of her body. It frightened her, and she struggled to get a grip on herself—any grip at all—but too much was occurring at once. She watched it all from the inside, feeling every wrenching jerk and every thudding blow . . . and she caught snatches of the world outside her own body that told her this was working.

So far as working went.

The three surviving and unharmed slaughter nuns gazed in horror at the chaos. One had a hand clapped over her mouth, and the other two were backing away, reconsidering everything they'd believed.

Selene slipped around the fray between the gods and approached her former sisters—hands out, blade tipped down in show of peace. "I told you," she said softly, but firmly. "I told you, the order has been compromised. Now do you see?"

They nodded. One of them extended a hand. Selene took it and allowed the woman to pull her close.

Indigo couldn't tell what they said. She was eyeballs deep in a battle over which she had virtually no control. Damastes wasn't paying attention anymore—she might as well not have been there, for all the notice he gave her. While he wasn't looking, while he raged against his sister, she felt around and worked her way back into her body. She pushed her memory of hands into her own hands, and her recollection of feet back down her legs.

She took a deep breath and sought to refill her own vessel with her own essence.

Damastes noticed.

Let go!

Not all the way, she insisted. *You can't be trusted to give the body back.*

And you *can't be trusted to vanquish Caedis.*

She pressed him anyway. *I'm riding along. Don't push me out.*

Fine.

It was all the concession she was going to get, so she'd have to take it. Caedis whirled and charged, and Damastes rose to the challenge—pushing her back and shoving her into a wall so hard that she cracked it. Bricks clattered and fell along with mortar dust. Caedis shook her head, shook off the blow, and came again, and again.

But outside the circle of horror, Selene was working magic. She conferred with the remaining nuns, who were rattled beyond belief—but finding themselves, and finding understanding. Together they struggled backward and away. Selene was recovering. The nuns were firming their resolve, and eyeing the murder goddess who occupied their sister with less horror and more determination.

"Indigo!" Selene shouted. "Can you hear me in there?"

She fought Damastes for the right to respond and won with a garbled "Yes!"

"They understand!" Selene cried. "They'll stand with us!"

Caedis's attention slipped; she looked back to the women. "None of you understands anything!"

One replied with a betrayed, unhappy scowl, "We understand *enough.*"

The murder goddess swooped away from Damastes and Indigo, turning her back on them both. "I stalked this earth before the earliest generations of your kind! You will serve me and obey me!"

Damastes formed and gripped a sword of shadow. Maybe Caedis didn't really think he'd do it, but Indigo thought it was more likely that Damastes didn't really think she'd die—Indigo could hear some odd echo of mirth rattling around in their shared skull space. He leaped and swung, and in the short instant when Caedis was distracted by the nuns, he struck.

The Androktasiai's head jumped, slipped loose of her neck, and rolled in a lumpy stumble until it stopped against the oversize boiler. It creaked, steamed, and hissed. The head went still.

The body still stood, but only for another few seconds. It folded in half and flopped backward, blood pouring and pooling, and then it was still, too.

"Is she . . . is she dead? Are they both dead?" Indigo asked aloud. Her voice was her own again. It startled her—she'd fully expected to hear it buzzing in her head, and for no one but Damastes to answer.

He did, in fact, answer. *Not at all. But she's gone for now, and I keep my word.*

With that, he faded, climbing back into the box Indigo had built for him. He didn't pull the lid back on top of himself, though. Indigo had to do that herself. As she shoved it back down and locked him out of her consciousness for the time being, she heard a muffled protest—but felt no real resistance. Indigo knew she couldn't trust him, that if he'd kept his word, he must be playing a longer game, but for now she only felt relieved.

"Are you all right?" asked Selene, who did not look very all right herself.

"I'll survive." Or so Indigo assumed. Everything ached, and she was still bleeding from too many places to count, but she was on her feet—and that was something.

"Is it . . . is he . . . ?" one of the sisters asked.

"He's locked away. For now. He can't hear us or see what's going on."

Selene assured them, "She's been learning to control him."

"*Manage* him," Indigo argued. "That's the best I can do, and now I've gone and made him a deal. He kept his end of the bargain, but I suspect he's trying to lure me into a false sense of security."

"He can't be trusted," Selene said with terrifying confidence.

"I know. But he did what I asked, and now he's cut off again. So we have to move fast."

"What do we do?" asked one of the other nuns. She was a study in confusion, both impossibly powerful and every bit as lost as a child.

Indigo took a deep breath and tried to think. The boiler ticked and the mortar dust still trickled, and the pipes overhead rattled and buzzed. "Selene, can we rely on these women? The ones who've been trying to murder us all this time?"

"Now that they know they've been manipulated, yes."

"It was never our intention . . . ," the lost one said with a quiver in her voice. "We serve a goddess of honorable death, not this arbitrary carnage. Selene tried to warn us . . . but we didn't listen. We owe her a terrible debt."

"Okay, then here's the plan: You ladies track down Graham Edwards. Whatever he's doing . . . make him stop it. Park him some place safe, and don't let him out of your sight. Meanwhile, Selene and I will go to Rafe's apartment. There *has* to be something there—something we can use. Even if he doesn't have the Void Portal, we might find something we can use against him, or against Caedis. Or even against Damastes, in the long run."

"What does that long run look like, for you and him?" asked Selene with a note of dread in her words, and a crinkle of resignation on her forehead.

"I don't know yet. Obviously killing me won't get rid of him." She gestured at the headless corpse still draining on the floor. "Damastes said his sister's still out there—she's just lost a vessel, and she'll have to pick someone else to ride. So it's not as easy as suicide," she added wryly. "We'll have to pull him out of me one way or another, and once we do, we'll need a place to put him. But let's not get ahead of ourselves."

"No, you're right. First things first." Selene nodded. "The sisters will go collect Edwards—the news said he was withdrawing to the family's weekend home in Scarsdale. You and I can scour Rafe's place. We'll meet back at your apartment—Nora's apartment—in a few hours. Will that work?"

Indigo tried not to sag down into a little puddle of beat-up flesh. "It'd damned well better." She wiped at her sweaty face with the back of her hand and sighed. "It pretty much *has* to."

16

___

Rafe's apartment building was not what Nora had expected. She would almost have thought it was the wrong building, except that she had tracked the address down through Rafe's teacher's certificate and security info, and New York City's tax database— she could always be sure those guys would never let a taxpayer slip through their fingers.

She stared up at the building. *It looks like mine.* He'd made himself the most powerful of the inner circle of the Children of Phonos without their ever knowing it, yet his apartment looked more like something she'd expect from . . . well, from a public-school teacher. Obviously he knew better than to tip his hand while he was still waiting for his big payoff. Still, she'd sort of expected his place to be more . . . sinister? Flamboyant?

Whatever. His taste and motives didn't matter—it was just something to stick in the back of her mind. For now.

"You think he's home?" she asked Selene. When no response came, she glanced over to find herself alone, a side door shutting behind Selene.

Nora sighed and raced to catch the door, following Selene up the stairwell to the fourth floor. The hall outside Rafe's apartment was quiet. *Too quiet?* No, not really—she was just on edge and still a little tired from the fight at the *NYChronicle*. The trip across town hadn't provided much of a rest, and she had bruises and aches everywhere.

In the fourth-floor corridor, Nora slid into the shadows. She was about to enter the apartment that way when Selene turned the knob and pushed the door open an inch. The apartment was as silent as the hall, but that unlocked door screamed trap.

"Unlocked," Selene said. "Wait here while—"

"No." Indigo flowed into the darkness and rode the shadows through the gap. No alarm, no attack . . . Nothing moved, but there was a smell. . . .

"Impatient?" Selene murmured. "Or are you showing off?"

Indigo continued along the shadows inside the unlit apartment. Another step . . . Something plinked onto her arm. She pulled back quickly and saw a red spot near her elbow. A drop of bright blood. She looked up. There, on the ceiling was . . .

Nora as Indigo had torn the cultists apart at the warehouse, but even she winced as she recognized the pulpy mess. A clump of bloodied flesh, plastered to the ceiling. She swallowed her revulsion and pushed on, taking one more step, almost to the end of the hall- way. She noted spattered blood on walls and ceiling. She kept to the shadows and then peered around the corner—

A wheeze stopped her. Just one wheeze, but when she focused, she caught the sound of shallow breathing.

"Took you long enough," Selene whispered at her ear.

Indigo paused. The signs of blood. That clump of flesh. The la- bored breathing. It all suggested they weren't the first ones through that door. It also suggested a trap, perhaps a lure to get her racing to the aid of whoever had been hurt without stopping to think.

Preying on the same compassion that had led her into her life as Indigo in the first place. She knew better—this was Rafe Bogdani's home, and the sorcerer had already demonstrated his knack for deception and skillful traps. Even knowing someone could be around that corner, near death, while she and Selene stood here, listening to the breathing growing shallower by the second, she had to remain calm and in control.

"Do you want my advice?" Selene whispered.

Indigo didn't answer. She *did* trust Selene—knowing the woman wouldn't stand there calmly, letting Indigo take charge, if one wrong step could prove fatal to their goal. But Nora was the investigator—Selene was the sword of justice—and they needed answers as much as action. This was her domain.

Indigo slipped around the corner, into a small room—a home office, it looked like. There, across the floor cluttered with debris, Captain Fritz Mueller huddled in the corner at the end of a swath of blood. His mouth worked with a small, wet sound, eyes glazing, chest covered in blood.

His name had been on the list she had given to Sam. Mueller, the late and unlamented Detective Mayhew's commander, child trafficker, cultist, using his position to protect the guilty and line his own pockets. She felt no compassion for him. He'd sent Mayhew after her at the hospital, would have sacrificed poor, trusting Symes. He was the last of the local cabal's inner circle, the last of the people who'd attended the original ritual. So what was he doing bleeding out on Rafe Bogdani's floor?

Indigo surveyed the room. No weapon seemed to be in sight, nothing that could cause this damage. Then she spotted something on the floor. It almost looked like a speck of light, and as she watched, it faded, leaving nothing. She was turning toward Selene when she caught sight of three other balls of light, larger, sparking on the floor beside Mueller.

"Magic," Selene said. "He set off a trap. That's the shrapnel."

Indigo flowed as shadow toward the three pieces.

"Don't—" Selene said, but stopped as Indigo lowered herself to one knee, examining. "Just don't touch."

"I wasn't planning to. I've seen Rafe's magic in action before." Up close, she could see the spheres spinning almost too fast for the eye to detect. Like whirring saw blades of pure light. "Brightness seems like an odd trap to secure an office against ordinary trespassers." But not against a shadowy one. Had this been for *her*?

Damastes snorted but said nothing.

Keep your feelings to yourself, demon, or I'll slam the lid down on you so hard, you'll think you're Quasimodo in the bell tower.

Mueller wheezed again. Indigo moved toward—

Light flickered off to the side. She saw it and dropped to the floor as Selene shouted, "Down!"

Sparks flew from the air above Indigo's head, but it was more like the sputter of a short than a live wire. Only a few specks of light shot out. One struck her hand, and the speck burrowed into her shadow-clad flesh like a white-hot BB pellet. Then it vanished, leaving her with a shallow hole in her hand, roughly the size of a pinhead.

"Shit! Ow!" She stared at the hole in her hand. Powerful magic, if one spark of it could rip into her insubstantial form like that. . . . The full blast must have been horrific—and yet it hadn't killed Mueller. Yet.

You think **that's** *powerful?* Damastes chuckled in her head. *I could show you power that—*Indigo stuffed him back down in her mind, into his box, with a furious thought. She glanced over at Selene and then up at the ball of sparks, sputtering out now.

"Untriggered remnants of the trap," Selene said. "Even that could have taken your head off if you walked into it, so let's be a little more careful before rushing in where angels fear, and so on."

"I'm not rushing. This bastard is one of the Phonoi's inner circle.

I have to wonder what he's doing here now and in this state. Yeah, that trap would have taken my head off—*my* head, but it didn't take his. That trap was meant for me, but it still packed a hell of a punch against *him*. So . . . maybe we can get some answers out of this piece of shit, since he was clearly up to something here."

Selene shook her head. "And how could you trust a word he said?"

"I don't think he's a willing martyr to the cause. Maybe they had a falling out, or maybe he's had a change of heart—though I doubt that—and he's also going to die unless I help him. That's a powerful incentive to get chatty."

"He's already dead. His body just doesn't know it yet. You want information? That's why we're here. To *look* for it."

When Nora didn't answer, Selene threw up her hands. "Fine. I'll look. You try to save a man who'd happily see you dead."

"He's tried that twice before and failed. You be careful. I doubt Rafe left only one trap around here."

Shaking her head, Selene stalked back into the hall.

Nora shed her shadows as she crossed the short distance to Mueller and lowered herself beside him. He didn't react at all to her emergence from the darkness, only held both blood-covered hands clutched to his chest. When she pulled them away, she saw where that divot of flesh had come from. The magic shrapnel had ripped apart his shirt and the skin beneath.

Nora peeled off the blood-and-gore-soaked tatters of Mueller's shirt—or what remained of it. She shook her head. The wounds looked bad, and she was no doctor, but it seemed mostly surface damage. She could feel broken ribs, which probably explained the wheezing breaths. Deadly, if one pierced a lung, but he'd survived this long. He could make it a little longer.

She brought ice and wet towels from the kitchen. She cleaned him up, but he continued to lie still, eyes closed while he labored to breathe. She pressed the ice to his chest wound.

That snapped him out of his shock, his eyes rolling as he struggled to focus. "You . . . Shoulda died twelve years ago. Saved us . . . getting Bogdani on our backs. I shoulda guessed . . . Indigo . . . and the brat that wouldn't die . . . were the same."

"Yes, *me*. Never thought I'd get tired of seeing your kind surprised, but it's really getting old. So let's cut to the chase. You're in rough shape. Broken ribs. Internal damage. If you get to a hospital in the next hour, you may live. If I walk out of here without the information I want, though, you're not getting so much as a Band-Aid."

A bitter, gasping laugh. "Is that how you think this works? I talk, a doctor fixes me up, and everything is hunky-dory? It's not a lack of medical care that's gonna kill me, girl. Might as well finish the job and then turn the gun on yourself. That's all the mercy either of us is getting."

"You set off a trap, which means you weren't an invited guest. You came here to confront Rafe?"

Another snort of a laugh. "You're such a child. Or an idiot. The only way to stop that bastard is . . ." Mueller trailed off, not quite ready to complete the evolution to traitor.

She leaned into his face and raised an eyebrow. "You want to *stop* him. How interesting. Did Graham Edwards convince you to take his side, once his kids went missing, leave the Children of Phonos? You see what the cult is doing, and you want it stopped."

Now she got a long laugh, one that set Mueller gasping in pain.

"Ah, I see. You want *Rafe* stopped. Not the cult. You want the old order restored. Not Rafe in charge and taking it all for himself. Find information you can take to higher-ups. The European wing? Tell them Rafe has been a bad boy, and they'll reward you . . . by getting rid of him? Open fresh new opportunities for your advancement?"

"I don't give a shit about my advancement. There's nothing to advance in. Not here. He's ruined everything. A Johnny-come-lately who thought he could waltz in after the hard work was done and claim the rewards. His cousin brought him in afterward—the great sorcerer to fix our mess. And he lectured us like kids about how we'd screwed up the ritual, how we'd have to reclaim the god, how we'd have to *atone*, rebuild. He wasn't even there! Instead he destroyed us. Most of the American wing wiped out, from the highest ranks to the newest warriors. Gone. Dead. And for what?"

The speech drained Mueller, and he slumped, eyelids flagging. Nora pressed the cold cloth to his face, thinking about the way lust for power rotted every organization at the core. The Children of Phonos had been undone by internecine fighting, betrayal after betrayal. The Androktasiai had suffered the same, with the added influence of Caedis. Now there was almost nothing left of either group.

"You're not done yet," Indigo said to Mueller. "What were you doing here? What's Rafe up to? How were you supposed to reclaim the god?"

Mueller rolled his eyes. "You really are a child, aren't you?"

"Am I?" she demanded, letting the shadows flow over her face, letting the presence of Damastes inside her consume the light around her body as she pushed her dark-wrapped fingers into his wound. "Child of something you should fear."

"Christ," he moaned as consciousness wavered. "I'd almost feel sorry for you if I didn't know what's inside of you. That's what he wants. What he needs. . . ."

Indigo was about to reply when Selene walked in. Mueller frowned and wheezed. Nora saw a flicker in his eyes, as if he might be putting things together. Did he know Selene was an Androktasiai? He'd been inner circle, he must know about the slaughter nuns.

"Did you find anything?" Nora asked. "Like whatever the captain here was after?"

Selene scooped up a backpack Nora had missed beside the couch. "Looks like he's already done our work for us. Thank you, Mr. Mueller."

Selene rifled through the bag. Then she cursed.

"Not what you were looking for?" Mueller said with a grimacing smirk.

"He was planting evidence tying Rafe to the child trafficking. Nothing here helps us find out what Rafe is planning now."

Mueller wheezed a horrible, bubbling laugh and said to Nora, "Not such a bad guy after all, huh?"

"Right," Nora said. "It was just another way to get rid of Rafe. And save your own skin. But it wouldn't work—you're tied to the trafficking, too, Captain. So what did you expect to accomplish here?"

"It doesn't matter," Selene said. "He's failed his mission. He's not interested in walking out of here alive." She crouched in front of Mueller. "But I bet he would be interested in a quick death."

"Go to hell," Mueller said.

"Oh, I'm not the one who needs to worry about that."

"Don't be so sure. I know what you are. You've got blood on your hands. More than me, I bet."

"I do," Selene agreed. "And I'm about to spill more."

Without a word, Nora slid aside and let Selene take over. She felt the shadows roil and burn inside her, heard Damastes's ironic chuckle. For a moment, she hated what she had become, then she sank the thought the same way she sank Damastes, banishing it into inner darkness. Rafe and what remained of the American Children of Phonos had to be stopped, and if it took the blood and pain of one more Phonoi, so be it.

Selene pulled a balled-up sock from her pocket and stuffed it into Mueller's mouth. Then she poked a finger into one of the divots in his chest. He howled behind the gag. Selene tortured Mueller. There was no nice way to put it, and while Nora might recognize that, as torture went, this was mild, it was still torture. Captain Mueller was in pain. Selene didn't add to his wounds, but she manipulated that pain. Nora could not count herself innocent—she had done the same.

Selene deepened Mueller's agony. "Are you ready to answer our questions?"

Nora could see Mueller snarling and raging, but it was all in his eyes, his body growing too weak to fight.

Selene pushed deeper into his gouged chest. "Where are the Edwards children?"

She plucked the gag from his mouth and Mueller gasped, choking on his breath and blood. "Bogdani. I don't know where."

Selene shoved the gag back and went at him again.

He passed out twice. Nora roused him with an icy cloth. Finally, he nodded. Selene still didn't remove the gag.

"What is Rafe's plan?"

Mueller's gaze was eager and bright with pain. Nora plucked the gag from his mouth.

Mueller's voice was thin now. "Re-create the original ritual."

Nora looked at Selene. It made sense only up to a point—the original ritual had called Damastes forth, but left him stuck inside Nora. Was Rafe planning to call Caedis or another murder god? Or did he have a way to wrench Damastes out of *Nora's* body and into another vessel of his choosing?

Selene glared at her to remain silent. "We want to know where the original ritual was held."

He seemed almost relieved at that, as if he'd feared some larger question. Something he might not be able to answer. "Westchester.

Near New Rochelle. Old cemetery in the woods . . . Abandoned now. An old vault . . ."

Memory and nightmare shook Nora. "Yes. I know it now." She shuddered under the weight of recollection. "I know where it is."

"If he intends to re-create the ritual, he'll need the Death's Wings pendant." Selene leaned close to Mueller and rested her hands on his bleeding chest with enough weight to make blood well up between her fingers. "I know you were present for the original ritual."

"Yes. I was. Me. Not that bastard. Rafe Bogdani. He says it's our fault the ritual went wrong. He said he could fix it—restore what was destroyed. That's why the others trusted him—they needed him. He's been creating something. . . . All those kids . . . Taken him goddamned years, but it's ready. Or so he claims."

The ombrikos, Nora thought. That must have been what Rafe was re-creating. Mueller didn't know what had gone wrong—he was no sorcerer or high priest. She couldn't let Damastes know, either, or all their caution at the *NYChronicle* would be for nothing. Nora held her breath until Selene went on.

"And the pendant?"

He turned his fading glare on Nora. "Charlotte's had it since your idiot father fucked up the first ritual. When her own kids were born, the pendant was part of a ceremony to bind them over to us. To prepare them . . ."

"For the moment when their own mother would murder them in the name of her god," Nora said.

Mueller tried to shrug, but it turned into a twist of agony. "Sacrifices . . . made. Charlotte always knew that. She didn't get too close. Not like Graham. And the kids had a good life."

Nora held back her desire to scream and rage at Mueller as Selene said, "But Rafe needs them for the ritual. One of them at least. And with Charlotte dead, he needs their father to perform the sacrifice."

Mueller nodded weakly. "And the Wings. Graham's got 'em . . . explained what Rafe was doing—had been doing. Why Bogdani needed the kids, needed him. Coulda handed him over, but . . . I'll be damned if I'll give anything more to that cocksucker."

Selene looked at Indigo. "Then, wherever Graham Edwards is, that's where we need to be. Now."

Nora got to her feet, looking around. "As soon as I call 9-1-1. If he survives, he'll be useful in mopping up the details. I just need a phone." She glanced around the blood-spattered office. "Must be one around—can't use mine."

Selene grabbed Mueller by the hair . . . and snapped his neck. Then she rose and started for the door. "Let's go. You can use his."

Nora stared at her. "He could have helped—"

"He would only have died slower. And implicated both of us, just to keep you and Damastes out of Rafe's hands. Do you not understand that if his ritual with the Edwards children fails, Rafe will still have one other chance to claim a god for his personal puppet? By taking you. And we don't know how far ahead Rafe is."

Which came first: the ritual or the house? Couldn't be a coincidence that the Edwards house was only a short drive from New Rochelle, though it felt like a long one from Manhattan. Nora knew they weren't going to arrive at the Edwards place in Scarsdale and find Graham sitting on the terrace, enjoying a cup of tea and watching the sunset. That would have been wonderful, but if that was what they found, Nora would know they'd walked into some kind of trap. Rafe needed Graham, and thanks to his ill-conceived press conference, the guy wasn't exactly in deep hiding.

Still, she'd hoped they'd arrive to find Rafe handling this discreetly. Maybe a few assassins in tow, but nothing more. Instead, they were barely past the gate when they saw fighting. And the closer they drew, the worse it got. Skirmishes were everywhere. Cops versus cops, FBI, guys who looked like gangbangers, and others in paramilitary gear, all mixing it up hand to hand or with weapons at a distance. . . . She couldn't tell who were Phonoi assassins and who were defenders. It was like walking onto a combat zone, every step taking them deeper into the chaos as they made their way to the epicenter: the house itself.

They cut through the battleground as best they could, continually moving forward, even when Selene slowed and Nora could tell she was searching for her sister warriors. But there was no time to waste. They dodged knots of men struggling hand to hand, ducked, and dove through gunfire and bounded from cover to cover. Even swift and insubstantial as a shadow, Indigo felt her heart pound in her ears as bullets brushed past her.

Beside her, Selene moved like a striking snake and sliced through enemies that blocked their path before whirling onward. Finally they reached the pool house. A trio of assassins fought a handful of cops near the back doors, but otherwise it was clear.

They crouched behind the poolside cabana as Indigo surveyed the dark house. She could see Selene trying to do the same, but her attention kept shifting to the battle nearby.

"The house seems quiet," Nora whispered. "But I know better than to trust that."

Selene nodded, still distracted by the fight, but muttered, "I think the police and the Androktasiai have managed to keep the rabble of Phonoi assassins out so far, to establish and hold a perimeter within the house, but there were only three sisters left strong enough to fight, and if they should fall . . ."

A scream of agony set Selene wheeling, eyes going wide as she searched for the source, a name on her lips.

"Go," Nora whispered as they crouched behind the pool house. Selene shook her head. "My place is with you."

"No, your place is helping the last of your sisters hold the line until I can locate Graham. I can take to the shadows. I'll be careful."

Selene seemed ready to argue. Then the nun who'd screamed gave another shriek of agony and rage.

"*Go,*" Nora said. "Help her and keep them *out.*"

Selene couldn't resist rattling off a string of warnings, even as she was running. Nora drew shadows around her and slipped into the house as a wisp of darkness passing through the keyhole.

Nora had known that the battles were *not* confined to the yard and surrounding area—just as she'd known Selene's time was better spent helping the Androktasiai than guarding Nora's ass.

There was evidence of earlier fighting, but most of it had moved outside or been resolved in blood and bodies. The remaining skirmishes were small, bitter, and strategically placed: a knot of assassins pressed a single Androktasiai at the formal dining room's impressive doors, while a few one-on-one fights had developed at the edges, bleeding into another battle at the foot of the grand staircase. Indigo easily avoided most of the small clashes by slipping through the shadows and staying on guard for traps, but any traps—magical or otherwise—most likely had already been set off, judging by the bodies and furniture that had been flung everywhere.

When she reached the main staircase, she saw Selene, back-to-back with another of the slaughter nuns, blades whirling as they feinted, stabbed, and sliced, barring the way against a troop of men in black fatigues—the Phonoi's top assassins, Nora guessed by their silent and unrelenting push to break through. Indigo saw no sign of the remaining Androktasiai, but assumed she, too, was holding the perimeter elsewhere, buying time to find Graham Edwards.

That these battles continued and that combatants seemed to be still trying to make their way to the house suggested Graham was still here. *Cowering in a corner?* No. If that were the case, the last of the Phonoi would be hunting for him, slipping in under cover of the confusion.

As Indigo slid deeper into the house, the sounds of battle retreated. She could imagine only one reason for the unnatural silence that had settled on the interior: Graham *was* here and Rafe was stalking him while the Phonoi's assassins held all help at bay. The troops created a distraction while the puppet master focused on his mission.

Indigo stood in the stillness, listening, letting the shadows spin from her like sonar seeking the shapes of Rafe's magic. Then she heard it—felt it in the shadow—from the second level. A single cry of "No!" cut short, that beat on her shadow-attuned ears as sharp as the sound of breaking glass.

Up the stairs into the silence again. Then a voice, a whisper, words she couldn't catch. She followed the sibilant sounds to a closed door. A thick wooden door. Nora reached for the knob, but hesitated and bent to listen at the old-fashioned keyhole first.

"You don't *dare* kill me," Graham Edwards was saying. "You want that damned pendant, and I'm the only person who can touch it—Charlotte made sure of that. While I'd love to think she was protecting me, we both know better. She *trusted* me—she may have been sleeping with you for the power, but she didn't trust you. And she was right not to. I'll never give the Wings to you, for my children's sake."

Indigo remembered how the pendant had seemed to draw her to touch it, so it was possible that Graham was only partially right; only someone already bound to the pendant would be able to handle it, but that small group must include her, too. She wondered if Rafe knew that.

Graham continued, snarling defiance, "You can go fuck your-self, Rafe. I'm done with this shit. Do whatever you want to me, but I'm not helping you with that damned ritual."

"Graham . . . always with the manly posturing." Rafe sighed. "For *your children's sake*, you *will* help me. You will choose one child to live . . . or they'll both die in front of you."

"No. You won't do that." Graham's voice was quivering. "You need me. You need the pendant. And you need my kids and I won't give one up to save the other. You'll leave them both alone. How can you think I would choose—?"

"Then I will. Or, how about this? I'll grant you a boon—a salve to conscience—in return for your cooperation. You choose, but as far as anyone else will ever know, I did. That way, you can keep your favorite while pretending you had no say in the matter. Fair?"

"Fair?" Graham sputtered. "You're asking me to give up one of my children."

"No, no. I'm not asking. I'm demanding. One or both. You choose. I don't need both, but I'll take them, if you leave me no other choice."

"And then what? You expect that I'll do as you say once they're dead?"

"Yes. Once one has died, you'll beg me to spare the other. That's when you'll do whatever I want. I'm merely trying to avoid unnec-essary unpleasantness."

Oh, for fuck's sake. While warriors risked—and gave—their lives battling below, these two were locked in an apparently unresolv-able debate. Indigo looked back toward the staircase. Should she try to break their impasse by taking Graham? Could she? Rafe had trapped her and turned her own tools against her before. Even if she did beat Rafe, were the shadows enough to whisk Graham out unseen? She'd never moved another person through the shadow, only herself. Well, always a first time—she'd have to make it work.

But there was no sign of Selene, and there *were* signs—growing, audible ones—that the battle was moving closer. The Androktasiai must have been falling back. . . . If the Phonoi assassins broke through, they'd help Rafe take Graham, and Indigo doubted she could stop all of them. But she had no doubt that Graham would buckle in the end. So . . . she had to get Graham away from Rafe long enough to pull him into the shadows with her. That would be the tough part, followed by shadow-walking both of them far away from Scarsdale.

Damastes growled in her head, ***I want that pendant.***

And you'll help me get it?

It's in my best interests, is it not?

She nodded and slipped through the keyhole as darkness, leaping along the shaded edges and overhangs of the room. A feeling like the steel tines of a rake scraped over her skin as she passed through. She briefly noted that Rafe and Graham were in the middle of the room, fully lit, which made things more difficult. But they were still arguing, Rafe's voice losing its smarmy arrogance as his patience frayed. Too distracted to notice her oozing like smoke into the room. Excellent.

It was a dressing room—a huge one—and Nora marveled at the sheer extravagance of having so much space dedicated to getting dressed. It wasn't even an oversize walk-in closet but a fully decorated room. Rafe stood on the other side of a table lined with empty display boxes and black velvet busts. So madam could lay out jewels from her safe and contemplate her choice for the evening? Nora thought of the shoebox in her closet, filled with a tangle of cheap necklaces and random earrings.

Focus, she reminded herself. This wasn't HGTV—it was a war.

Rafe stood on the other side of that table, with a knife to Graham's throat. It was almost laughable—what did a sorcerer need with such a crude threat? But it would make getting Graham into the shadows a whole lot tougher.

Then don't try, Damastes whispered.

What?

The goal is to stop the ceremony. Without Graham Edwards, it is stopped. Therefore . . .

No. It's you *he wants to control. Edwards is just the first possible means to that end. I'm sure Rafe has more than one ace up his sleeve.*

Damastes issued a dismissive snort while Indigo surveyed the shadows. The table cast one. Not perfect, but good enough. She simply needed to get to it. She took one careful step and—

Damastes roared. A sudden roar that set Indigo staggering, tripping, slamming into the table. *What the hell—?*

She could *feel* Damastes chuckling as he squirmed free of his confinement. She had no time to put the lid back on him. Rafe spun so fast the blade sliced a thin line across Graham's neck, the older man letting out a hiss of pain.

"Indigo," Rafe said, smiling. "How nice of you to drop in. But I knew you'd have to show up sometime."

"Spare me the banter and let go of Edwards—you've lost."

"Oh, sweetheart, don't you see that with *you* here, I've *won?*" Rafe laughed merrily and the knife rose. Indigo leaped to shove Graham out of the way, but Rafe wasn't killing him—he'd lifted his hand to cast a spell. When it came down, light flew. A hundred points of light, those whirring razor-sharp balls of pure energy. Indigo dove, and as she did, she became shadow. The lights hit and her darkness consumed them. Most of them anyway. A few still struck, slicing into her as she hit the floor, hard, naked to the glare of light. Dammit! Rafe *had* been ready for her—that scraping feeling had to have been some trap he'd laid that she hadn't seen. He knew she sheltered Damastes and that he didn't need the Edwards kids if he could capture her alive. But he also knew Indigo wasn't likely to let that happen.

She spun and scrambled to her feet.

Rafe cast again, and Indigo reached for the shadows. Nothing happened. The shrapnel shards of light hit, and Indigo bit back a howl of pain. She managed to leap into the shadows along the wall, and they enveloped her.

She struggled for the reassuring strength of the shadows at her command, but there was nothing, as if the flow of darkness was restrained inside her. Was it Rafe's magic or . . . ?

You bastard.

Yes, child? Damastes laughed. **Would you like something?**

Let go or we're all dead.

I think not. Just continue antagonizing Rafael. He's overburdened. Between stopping you and holding Graham Edwards, he'll eventually break. He'll kill Edwards, and we won't need to worry about the ritual. The shadows around Indigo parted enough for Rafe to see her. He cast again, and she dove into the blackness as the balls peppered her legs, each one a pinpoint of excruciating pain.

You son of a—

I'll accept an alternative. If you agree to cooperate with me, I'll help you take Edwards.

Another power blast from Rafe, and Nora looked down in time to see the shadows had forsaken her again. She tried to run back into them, but it was like a child standing behind a pole and thinking her enemy couldn't see her if she couldn't see him. As Indigo, she tore at Damastes, trying to wrest the shadows back into her control. Why wasn't it working? Hadn't Selene said the shadows had no allegiance? What had Damastes—or Rafe—done?

Bits of magical shrapnel struck as she ran. The pain crippled her. She fell to her knees.

I don't want to hurt you, child.

Then don't!

She wrenched around and shouted to Graham, "Run!"

Rafe was in the middle of casting another magical assault, distracted by Nora, and Graham realized it. He broke free from Rafe's grasp and started for the door . . . and Rafe swung the full force of his spell on the older man.

Indigo shouted, "No!" and bolted to Graham, but it was too late. The spheres of spinning light hit him in the back, ripping through his shirt, tearing into his flesh.

Damastes chortled. Indigo leaped on Graham, taking him down and smacking the remaining spheres away, ignoring the pain.

Then she realized what she'd done. Captured Graham Edwards without the shadows' help. She was stunned. Then a hand grabbed her from behind. A blade went to her throat.

"Go ahead and run, Graham," Rafe said. "The men outside will bring you right back to me. You can hear them, can't you?"

Graham, still on the floor, heaving in pain as blood ran down his back, listened to the sounds of battle drawing nearer. He shook his head. Then he said, voice quaking, "My daughter. You can have my daughter. Leave my son. I need someone to carry on my name."

Rafe bent to help Graham to his feet, keeping an eye on Indigo and the knife raised between them, the hilt gleaming with the spell concealed in his hand. "You've made a wise choice," Rafe murmured to Graham.

As Graham got up, tears steamed down his face, which was twisted into an expression of torment. Indigo stared at him. Tears or no tears, any sympathy she'd felt for him washed away in a wave of disgust. Carry on his name? That's what he was concerned about? She started forward—damned if she'd let Rafe win—but her feet seemed stuck to the carpet—as if her own shadow had nailed her there.

Let me go!

Damastes laughed. ***You assume it is I who holds you back.***

Isn't it?

She could feel his shrug, like the churning of her stomach. And she was helpless to fight for Graham or herself, forced to watch Rafe drag him into the doorway.

Bastard!

I'm not one to let opportunity pass me by, little Nora. And you have already given your word . . .

Rafe paused in the open doorway with his knife to Graham's throat again. "Don't come after me—you'll hurt yourself trying to pass the ward. It will fade in an hour or so . . . unless someone else opens the door for you before then. Oh, and don't get any silly, heroic notions about saving poor Graham, here. Because I think you know what the alternative is, if anything happens to Graham or his adorable kids before the ritual. I'll be seeing you, though. I'm sure of it."

As Rafe dragged him out, Graham Edwards whispered, "My son . . ."

"Oh, he'll be fine," Rafe said. "I'll make sure he turns up somewhere safe after this is over. Don't worry—I'm a man of my word."

As the door was swinging closed between Indigo and the men, Graham shot her a pleading look. "Take care of him. Please. Don't let him know . . ."

As the door slammed, the shadows rushed loose, flooding to Indigo's command. She flung herself at the door, aiming to slip through the lock—

And was smashed backward like a fly. She tumbled across the

table, scattering the black velvet displays across the room with a crash.

"Bastard!"

A howl of rage echoed up the stairs as if in sympathy.

The terrible scream had heralded the death of the Androktasiai Selene had fought beside, and she had rallied the remaining two to find Nora. Nearly an hour later, Nora stood alone with Selene. They had all fought their way out of the house—no point in staying with Graham and Rafe gone—but Nora had failed. Selene might try to tell her it was Rafe's or Damastes's fault she had lost Graham, but that didn't make Nora feel better.

We have a bargain. I will honor it. Do you want my help or not? Damastes whispered.

You tricked me.

I am a god of murder—opportunism is in my nature. You did not have to agree.

Nora tried to ignore him, but he continued. *You wish to be free of me and I of you. To stride the world unfettered. We both wish to put an end to Rafe Bogdani and his schemes for power. Build me a Heykeli—what you think of as a "murder golem"—build me one I can inhabit. That's all I ask. Build it, and it will help you.*

Nora stuffed him down, but not from spite or anger this time. She needed the privacy of her mind.

"What's going on?" Selene said, peering at Nora.

She opened her mouth to answer. Then she closed it. Selene would tell her not to do this. But Selene hadn't been in that dressing room. She hadn't been caught between Damastes and Rafe. Selene didn't know how difficult this struggle had become, didn't know Nora's rage and self-recrimination. But in spite of it, Nora saw a possible light in her personal darkness. Build the *right* golem, keep

Damastes ignorant of her true intent . . . and she might trap him for good. She shook her head at Selene and opened her thoughts to the killer god inside her.

Yes. I'll make your golem. Tell me how.

17

Even as Nora had hurtled headlong from one bruising and traumatic confrontation to the next, she had been trying desperately to keep hold of a sense of herself. But in the last few days, with the revelations about her past coming thick and fast, and the reality she had previously believed in torn to shreds, the lines had become well and truly blurred.

Who was she exactly? It wasn't the first time she had asked herself that question, but even now she was no nearer to discovering the answer. Before she had found out about Damastes, there had been just the two of them—her and Indigo. She had always thought of Indigo not as a separate entity, but as an extension of her own personality, more ruthless and far less squeamish than she was, perhaps, and willing to embrace violence and bloodshed when circumstances demanded. Yet in many ways the *better*, more *noble* part of her. More daring, more courageous, more willing to fight for justice.

Had all of this now been proven a lie? Was it as much a lie as the heroic past she had concocted for herself from remnants of the comic books she'd read as a dysfunctional kid? Her powers had not come from a noble place, but from something that was uncompromisingly evil. Something that reveled in pain and carnage and despair.

The two parts of her were now three—Nora, Indigo, Damastes—and she was still trying to come to terms with it. Nora was Indigo, in all of the ways that mattered, and yet the inverse was not entirely true. Indigo *was* Nora, yes, but with all of the power she had taken from Damastes. Did that mean Indigo was also partly Damastes? Selene had told her that the darkness—the power of the shadows—was its own entity, and she clung to that as truth. She needed to believe that Indigo merely shared power with Damastes, not that they were part of each other, creatures of the same fabric. She *had* to believe that.

Yet . . . what if every time she shifted into Indigo, a little more of Damastes was in the mix? Nora *felt* as if she was still in control—most of the time anyway—but what if Damastes was using Indigo as his way in? Would creating a Heykeli and channeling him into that effectively divert him, free her of his influence? Or would it all be a terrible mistake?

She had brought Selene and the other two surviving Androktasiai, whose names were Megaira and Xanthe, back to her building to regroup and plan their next move. Nora had led them past the door of her own third-floor apartment, though. She hadn't wanted to alarm the Assholes any more than they had been alarmed already; plus, although her apartment had been infiltrated and part trashed during her fight with one of the women who were now her allies, she had wanted to retain a little bit of Nora space for herself. Instead, she had led them up to the now-empty apartment on the fifth floor.

Slipping from Indigo back to Nora after ensuring that the apartment was empty, she had thought sadly, *Shelby used to live here.*

Before she could twist the knife of blame even deeper into her own guts, however, a voice she couldn't help thinking of as Indigo's—harder and more pragmatic than her own—rebuked her sharply.

No, she didn't. Shelby didn't exist, except when I needed her to. She was merely my sounding board, my conscience, my pick-me-up. She had no independent life of her own, and therefore no personality and no thoughts, aside from the ones I gave to her.

And yet, and yet . . .

"Why are we here?" one of the slaughter nuns—Megaira—asked, looking around suspiciously. She was stocky and dark haired, pretty but pugnacious, and her smoky voice was shot through with an accent that Nora guessed was Spanish, or perhaps Portuguese.

"We're here to rest," Nora said. Her body felt pummeled, like tenderized steak. She looked at the dusty bare floorboards stretching in front of her and thought that if she allowed herself to lie down on one of them and close her eyes, even for a moment, she would sleep for a week.

The other slaughter nun, Xanthe, who was younger, taller, and slimmer than Megaira, and whose paler face was smeared with blood from cuts on her forehead and lip, flashed Nora a surprised look. "There's no time to rest. We can't rest until—"

"We can't go rushing in without a plan," Nora snapped. "If the Phonoi assassins don't cut us to ribbons, Rafe Bogdani will. All he has to do to stop us is raise a hand. We've got to think of a way to bring him down without giving him the chance to use his power."

Xanthe flushed and looked at Nora sullenly.

But Selene was nodding. "Nora is right, sisters. There are only three of us now. If we're going to defeat Bogdani and his rabble—"

"We will," growled Megaira.

"—then we need to use stealth and guile. We need to hit them before they even know we've hit them."

"How?" Xanthe asked.

All at once Nora was struck by a wave of dizziness and swayed on her feet. Inside her, she sensed Damastes's pleasure at her weakness, sensed him flexing his muscles—or maybe that was her own paranoia.

"Can we sit down?" she said. "I've had a rough few days, and I can't see things getting any easier in the short term."

Without waiting for a response, she shuffled into what had been Shelby's main room—*She'd had the sofa here, that nice glass lamp over there, a bookcase over there, stuffed with books on design and fashion*—and slumped down, her back against the wall. The gloom and emptiness of the place seemed to press in on her. Suddenly she felt Shelby's absence like an oppressive, insistent ache.

Selene lowered herself to the dusty floor beside Nora, and Xanthe and Megaira sat cross-legged in front of her, their faces grim.

"You were saying we have to hit them before they even know we've hit them," Megaira said.

"What of it?" said Selene.

"Well, there's only one way I can think of doing that, of making sure we wipe the lot of them out."

"Which is?" asked Xanthe, though she looked as though she already knew the answer.

"We turn ourselves into human bombs. We sneak in, unobserved, and then when we get close enough"—Megaira balled her hands into fists, then spread her fingers—"*boom!*"

"Suicide bombers?" said Nora, appalled.

"Why not?" Megaira's whole stance was challenging, aggressive. "I'm prepared to die for what I believe in. Aren't you?"

Sidestepping the question, Nora asked, "What about the children? And don't use the phrase *collateral damage*."

"We get them out first. Or you do. Using . . . *him*." Megaira screwed up her face, as though at a bad smell. "The powers he gave you."

Nora might have argued that Damastes was not her benefactor, and that her powers were not a gift he had bestowed on her like a kindly uncle . . . but she was too tired to argue semantics. Instead she said, "If we get the children out, you'll have no need to blow yourselves up."

"This ritual may be our best chance to wipe out so many of our enemies in one go. We have to take it."

"But I can't *allow* you to wipe yourselves out." Thinking of the murder golem, Nora almost told them there might be a better way, but then she bit back on the words, unwilling to discuss the possibility until she had had more time to think about it.

Megaira sneered. "*You* can't allow? Who are you to dictate our destinies?"

More gently Selene said, "My sister has a point, Nora. We fought for too long for the wrong reasons, and now our order has been decimated. If we get the opportunity to redress the balance, to make a final glorious strike at the hearts of our enemies, then we should take it."

Nora shrugged and slumped back. She could see where the sisters were coming from. But she had seen so much carnage these past few days—some of which she had meted out herself—that she was now sickened by it, or at least sickened that she had got used to the idea of life as a disposable commodity.

No, it *more* than sickened her; it *scared* her. She was scared not only that she was harboring thoughts that seemed to bring her closer to Damastes's philosophy, but also by the knowledge that her own life was viewed by her enemies as a worthless inconvenience. Put bluntly, to Rafe and the Children of Phonos she was little more than packaging. She was simply a vessel containing a great evil they intended to release and claim as their own, which, if given the opportunity, they would tear open and cast aside as casually as if she were the paper around a Christmas present.

What made that knowledge even worse was her awareness that the demon inside her knew it, too. If she was packaging to the Children of Phonos, then to Damastes she was simply a prison from which he wished to escape. All that concerned him was that he achieve his freedom, instead of simply swapping one prison for another.

The more her own thoughts swamped her, the more the debate among her companions over tactics, over how best to make their final stand against the Children of Phonos, seemed to recede from her. Nora lowered her head, closed her eyes, and let the voices of Selene and the others become an echoing blur. All at once she felt an overwhelming need for something good to cling to. Something to reassure her that life wasn't all violence and pain and self-centered viciousness.

She needed to know that somewhere in the world was a place she could find love and comfort if she needed it; that somewhere was someone who cared about her. The harsh fact was that she had only ever had two real friends in her life—and one of those had turned out to be imaginary.

That still left one, though. One whose importance she had underestimated until now. Switching effortlessly back into Indigo (and trying not to think about what that might mean), she opened her eyes a crack and sought out the nearest shadow.

It was not difficult. They were everywhere here, and eager to serve. Before the Androktasiai had time to realize what she was doing, she slipped into the nearest and began to move effortlessly along the shadowpaths.

She felt like a bird riding the thermals. Her choices were so instinctive it was as if her route had been preordained, as if some inexorable force at her destination were dragging her toward it, reeling her in. There was a sense of timelessness. Her journey felt both leisurely and instantaneous.

Then she flowed into corporeality once again, her physical senses rising to the fore, the weight of blood and bone and muscle settling into place inside her envelope of skin. She was Indigo, and then she was Nora. Although it was dark, she knew instantly where she was.

She was in the bathroom adjoining Sam's room in the hospital. She paused a moment in the dark, leaning forward to listen for any sounds on the other side of the door. Hearing nothing, she wrapped her hand around the cold metal of the handle and slowly turned it. She pulled the door open a crack, wincing as it creaked, and peered out through the gap, ready to become Indigo again in an instant, to flee back into the shadows if need be.

Sam's room was in semidarkness, the blinds drawn. The sound of deep, slow, even breathing told her he was asleep.

She pulled the door a little wider and stepped forward. Now she could see him lying in bed, the gloom giving his unruly dark hair and the white pillow that framed it a murky, soft-focus fuzz.

She stepped closer still, and as she peered at his familiar face, relaxed now in sleep, she felt her jagged edges softening, a sense of calmness fold around her like a soft blanket, or a hug. Sam was not exactly handsome, but he wasn't ugly either. He had what might be called a homely face, but one made attractive by the laugh lines around his eyes and mouth, by the gentleness in his almond-shaped eyes—when they were open, that was.

Right now his closed eyelids looked soft as moth wings in the dimness—so soft she had to fight an urge to lean forward and kiss them. As she took another step forward, disturbing the air, he stirred, as though detecting her presence.

Or maybe, she thought, he was subconsciously detecting the presence of the demon inside her. Perhaps it disturbed his peace like an ominous shadow glimpsed beneath the glassy, unbroken surface of a calm sea. Although Damastes was quiet inside her, she could still feel him there. She sensed that he was aware of her confusion and fear, and that he was taking pleasure in it.

She made a conscious effort to block him and was reassured to find that, even in her weakened state, she still could. With the lid on the box firmly closed, she allowed herself to think more freely about her agreement to create a murder golem for Damastes's use. Giving him any amount of autonomy was a huge risk, but with Selene and her sisters talking about turning themselves into suicide bombers, Nora didn't see she had any other choice. She needed to rescue the Edwards children—whatever their parents were, they themselves were innocents in all of this—and one way or another, she needed to stop Rafe.

It was imperative, though, that she not allow Damastes *complete* autonomy. Somehow she had to find a way to keep the murder god on some sort of mental leash. The last thing she wanted was to set Damastes free on an unsuspecting world. She would willingly die before she allowed that to happen.

Pushing these thoughts aside, she relieved her pressure on the lid of the box once again and sensed Damastes pushing back out into the light, clearly irritated that she still had the strength to shut him down.

Shielding secrets from me, are you? she heard him growl in her mind.

She kept her reply light, casual. *Not at all. You were disturbing my friend's sleep, making him restless.*

She almost imagined him snorting huffily. *That wasn't my doing, girl.*

Nora didn't grace him with an answer and sensed him sinking back into a torpid resentment. In the bed, as though something of her internal exchange with the demon had seeped once again into his dreams, Sam groaned and became restless, his head turning from left to right on the pillow. Though his eyes were still closed, his lips parted with a wet pop. His voice was thick, slurred. "Hello?"

Nora froze. Ridiculously she felt like a child on the verge of being caught out doing something naughty. The natural thing would be to go to the bed, stroke Sam's hair, soothe him with a few gentle words.

But she was reluctant to do that. She didn't want him to know she was here—though she couldn't exactly say why. Perhaps because she didn't want Damastes to get so close to him? Perhaps because she didn't want to get drawn into explanations? Or perhaps because she was ashamed of her recent actions and was fearful that Sam would see right through her mask and be shocked or disappointed in her?

His eyelids fluttered. He frowned. Although his lips were still moving, he made nothing but small, inarticulate sounds.

Then he suddenly became still, as though he was on the verge of waking and knew someone was in the room with him.

Softly he said, "Nora?"

Taking fright, Nora instantly became Indigo and twisted like smoke toward the block of shadow between the chunky little bedside cabinet and the wall. By the time Sam sloughed off the caul of sleep and opened his eyes, she was gone.

"Where the hell did *you* go?" Selene said.

Her face was the first thing Nora saw when she returned and emerged from Indigo's shadow. The slaughter nun was glaring at her, as were Xanthe and Megaira, the latter's eyes narrowed suspiciously.

"She was with *him*," Megaira said, startling Nora. Then she realized the slaughter nun meant Damastes, not Sam. "*He* controls her. I don't like it."

Nora was glad of the spark of anger that Megaira's malice roused in her. "He *doesn't* control me. I control *him.*"

"So where were you?" Selene asked. "Why disappear like that?"

"It was *not* cool," muttered Xanthe.

Nora blinked at her. "What is this? *Mean Girls?*" When her comment met with blank looks, she sighed. "Look, I needed some time on my own, all right? Time to think. I . . . I went to see Sam. My . . . friend. He's in the hospital."

Megaira still looked suspicious. "What use is he?"

"He calms me." Nora flushed. "I don't expect you to understand."

Selene put a hand on Nora's arm. "But you're back with us now? You're focused on what we have to do?"

Nora nodded. "I . . . have a proposal. You won't like it, but it's an alternative to getting yourselves killed."

The three Androktasiai stared at her, saying nothing. Nora took a deep breath. "I could create a Heykeli, siphon the essence of Damastes into it. He could fight for us. He'd fight with all the rage and power that a murder god possesses. But I'd keep a tight rein on him. Plus he'd be expendable—or at least his body would. If the Phonoi destroyed the murder golem . . . I mean, his physical form . . . I'd take him back into me again. No harm done."

She had spoken quickly, her voice getting increasingly louder as the Androktasiai had realized what she was proposing and started to protest. Megaira and Selene were shaking their heads vigorously; Xanthe looked shocked.

"Are you crazy?" Selene exclaimed. "Do you actually *know* what you're proposing?"

"Of course she does," Megaira said. "Because *he* put her up to it."

"No, he didn't. It was—" Nora fell silent because she had been about to say it was Shelby who had first told her about murder golems.

But Shelby wouldn't have existed if it hadn't been for Damastes, would she? So *was* this idea simply another trap she had been led into?

"It was what?" asked Selene, giving Nora a shrewd look.

Barely pausing for breath Nora replied, "I was going to say it was actually Rafe Bogdani who told me about Heykeli during our first tussle. He tried to bargain with me, implied that if I trapped Damastes in a murder golem and handed it over to him, I could walk away unscathed. I didn't believe him for a moment, of course."

She paused, aware of Damastes's mirth deep inside her, like a subterranean rumble. His velvety, sibilant voice—which she suspected was merely the archetypal villain's voice, one her subconscious had concocted for him in order to translate his thoughts into words—filled her head.

What a delicious little liar you are.

She closed him off, knowing how much it infuriated him. It wasn't that she wanted to keep what she was about to say secret from him, because even though she'd mean every word, she knew that in his arrogance he'd think she was bluffing simply to convince the Androktasiai her idea was good; it was that she wanted to piss him off, put him in his place, show him who was boss.

"But my thinking now," she continued after a moment, "is that I can use a murder golem to take Bogdani down. It would be the ultimate irony, don't you think?"

Selene, though, had barely stopped shaking her head. "I still say it's a crazy idea. It's far too dangerous."

"You wouldn't say that if you were me. You underestimate the hold I've got over Damastes."

"You only think you've got a hold over him," said Megaira. "He's lulled you into a false sense of security."

"Oh, so how come he hasn't broken out in the twelve or so years he's been inside me? Do you think he's been asleep? Biding his time? Bullshit. It's because I've been containing him."

"That's all very well," said Selene. "But if you release him . . ."

"*Partially* release him. Just enough to animate a murder golem. To do our bidding. To save *your* sorry asses."

"There's no such thing as *partially* releasing a demon," said Megaira scornfully. "That would be like *partially* releasing a tiger. You open the cage, even a little way, and he's going to muscle his way out. And no one'll be able to stop him."

"Oh? And what makes *you* such an expert? Got personal experience of demon wrangling, have you?"

"Can he hear us now?" Xanthe asked nervously.

"No, he can't. Because *I'm* controlling him. I've shut him in his kennel. Just as I can let him out but keep him on a leash if I want to."

"I still don't like it," said Selene.

Nora's eyes flashed. "Jeez, you're like a broken record. And one more thing . . ."

"What?"

"What makes you think I need your permission?"

Short of killing her, which they weren't desperate enough to do—or at least, Nora *hoped* they weren't that desperate—the Androktasiai could do nothing to stop her from going ahead with her plan. In the end, to shut them up, she told them if they didn't like it, she'd become Indigo, use the shadows to slip away, and create the murder golem without their blessing. Faced with that ultimatum, Selene had at last reluctantly agreed to the idea, though only on the proviso that she and her sisters could supervise what she referred to as "the summoning."

"You're not to interfere, though," Nora warned them.

"What if Damastes possesses you? What if you *become* him?" Megaira asked.

Nora hesitated. "*Then* you can interfere." But after a moment she added, "He won't, though. He's not strong enough. And hopefully this will prove it to you."

Twenty minutes later she was standing in the center of the floor in the main room of the empty apartment, facing away from the three Androktasiai, who were crouched against the wall watching her warily. She had told them she needed to concentrate to achieve equilibrium, and to gather her strength and resources—which was at least *partly* true—but what she *hadn't* revealed was that she had no idea how to create a murder golem and would have to take instruction from the demon inside her before going ahead.

For most of the last twenty minutes, unbeknownst to Selene and the others, that was what she had been doing. She had been conducting an internal dialogue with Damastes, and like a teacher to a pupil he had been explaining the principles of creating what would ostensibly be a vehicle for his rage from a combination of light and shadow.

And blood.

Her blood.

Nora had been dubious about this last part, but Damastes had insisted it was the only way. Now, having finally been convinced, she was ready to proceed.

She stretched out her hands, and without turning to look at Selene and the others she muttered, "Don't be alarmed by what you see in the next few minutes. I'm a willing participant in what will happen. It's all part of the ritual."

In the weighted silence behind her Nora imagined the Androktasiai glancing uncertainly at one another, tensing their muscles, gripping the hilts of their weapons. She tried to put all thought of them out of her mind and concentrate on the task at hand. Luckily the apartment was full of gloom and shadows, which was perfect for her purposes.

Twitching her fingers slightly, she drew threads of shadow toward her from the corners of the room, molding them even as they came. She had fashioned weapons from shadow before, on many occasions, and knew how to create blades so sharp they would open skin with the merest touch.

She created two such blades now, angling them so they hovered like a pair of black smiles over her outstretched forearms. For a second her attention drifted as she wondered how the slaughter nuns would react to the next part of the ritual—then she forced the thought away, tried to make her mind go blank. This was the tricky part and she couldn't afford any slip ups, couldn't allow herself to be distracted. Trying not to hesitate, she used her mind to flick the blades down and across the tops of her forearms, then instantly refashioned them, morphing them into semicircular bowls, which now hovered under her outstretched arms, catching the blood that wept from those wounds.

Only when this tricky bit of reshaping was complete did she allow herself to register the pain. All at once the cuts sizzled, as though hot coals had been laid across them. When the bowls were full she drew gauzy wisps of shadow toward her and used them to cauterize the wounds. Then she drew the bowls of blood together, combining them into one. It always amused her when pop culture suggested people might slash open their palms for some kind of blood sacrifice. She might have cut muscle or tendon, making the hands useless in a fight. No, this was simpler and cleaner.

Damastes had told her that murder golems were sculpted from air and light, and now that she had donated the blood that would both imbue her creation with life and also bind it to her, she set about shaping her creature. Using her shadow power, she began to untangle the light from the darkness, going about the task by reducing the complexity of it within her mind, couching it in terms she could understand and deal with. She imagined the darkness and the light not as a blended and inchoate mass, but as separate and defined objects. In her mind's eye the darkness became a thousand tiny black marbles and the light a thousand tiny white marbles, which at the moment were mixed in together, creating an overall impression of grayness. Once she started to pick them apart, however, to shift them to their opposite sides of the room, their differences would quickly become apparent.

With her mind she stared into the gloom, stared until her inner vision began to adjust. She had learned how to manipulate darkness and shadows, how to bend them to her will; now she simply needed to hone and adjust that skill. For the first time ever, she would be molding not only darkness but light, too—molding it and sealing it into a skin of blood and shadow.

Concentrating hard, and trying not to wonder whether she was up to the task, she began to sift the gloom with her mind and heard one of the slaughter nuns behind her—she thought it might have been Xanthe—gasp as the light and the dark started to separate, to flow in different directions. She pushed the blackness into the right-hand corner of the room, packing it in as tightly as she could, as though it were something solid and movable, like rubble. Within minutes the darkness there had deepened to such an extent that it had become impenetrable, the details of walls, floor, and ceiling no longer even partly visible.

The left-hand corner of the room, by contrast, grew increasingly sharper and brighter, as though the walls and the floor were glowing with their own inner luminescence. Soon that corner was so dazzling it masked the details of the room in an entirely different way, becoming a pure white sheen of brightness that was impossible to look upon.

Nora—or rather, Indigo—closed her eyes and looked into the light with her mind. She delved into its core, and once she had found it, she began to draw it out, to scoop it forth as a bear will scoop honey from the heart of a hive. Once again she felt her mind having to adjust in order to handle the elusive stuff; to picture the light not as something indefinable, lacking in substance, but as something warm and malleable, able to be manipulated—the clay of life.

Even as she drew the light out, she began shaping it with her mind, creating a form. At first it was a crude approximation of a human shape. Quickly, though, as her subconscious worked upon it, it began to acquire definition and detail.

Although she was the sculptress, even she was surprised, if not chastened, to realize that she *recognized* the form she was creating. Considering where they were, perhaps it was not so surprising, though it still unsettled her, still caused emotion to rush up through her and lodge hotly in her throat.

The murder golem looked just like Shelby. It was Shelby reborn. Unwittingly or not, Indigo had re-created Shelby as an angel, composed of dazzling light.

A little overcome, Indigo tried to alter the form, to bend it to a new shape, one that was less personal, that didn't engender such emotion within her. But she couldn't. Try as she might, Shelby was foremost in Indigo's mind and so remained the dominant form. It was obscene to think of Damastes inhabiting the shell of the woman whom Nora had until recently thought of as her best friend, her greatest confidante. But it seemed she could do nothing about it. It was another twist of the knife she was going to have to live with.

When the murder golem was complete and stood before her in its skin of shimmering light, Indigo began to build a shell around it. Calling forth the bowl of darkness that was full of her blood, she brought the light being and the shadow bowl together. As soon as the darkness, saturated with her blood, touched the light being, it began to slither over its surface, to stretch out, to explore its new landscape with an almost obscene and fervid eagerness. Watching it was like watching a parasite engulfing and overwhelming a more vulnerable organism, or an aggressive cancer crowding out the healthy cells to which it had become attached.

In this instance, though, the healthy cells didn't wither, they flourished. Shelby's light form began not merely to darken, but to fill with color. Her cheeks flushed with health; her lips reddened and glistened; her eyes sparkled; her hair became lustrous.

Shaking with reaction, but compelled to complete the ritual, Indigo stepped forward and placed her hands on the Heykeli's naked shoulders. They felt warm and solid, the skin soft and silky. Dutifully the Heykeli opened its mouth, its lips parting with a soft wet sound. Indigo hesitated for a second, then began to lean forward, looking into the murder golem's eyes—into *Shelby's* eyes.

Shelby—no, not Shelby; this thing was nothing but a construct, a robot waiting to be switched on—stared back at her guilelessly. Despite herself, Indigo found herself looking for a spark of recognition, a trace of her old friend.

She glanced over her shoulder at Selene and her sisters, who were still crouched against the wall, faces tense, clearly ready to pounce or flee should anything go wrong.

"Is it possible . . . ," Indigo said, then felt her voice falter. She cleared her throat and tried again. "Is it possible there's . . . anything left of Shelby? I mean . . . I know I created her, but she was my friend. She had identity. And I mean . . . we're all created by someone, aren't we? We're all of us the products of our . . . our parents." She thought of her own parents, and her guts twisted sourly. "Or at least, by . . . our surroundings . . . our friends and the . . . the people we know."

What was she asking here? She wasn't sure. Did she think it

possible that this . . . this *thing* she had created could really be Shelby reborn? Or did she honestly think that her old friend was still out there in the ether somewhere? Even that the murder golem could eventually become her new home?

She saw Selene's eyes soften a little in sympathy and realized how lost, how pitiful she must seem.

Warily Selene said, "Yes, it's possible. I believe so anyway. If your will, your spirit, your *love* was strong enough, then I do think it's possible that part of your subconscious could have taken root in your friend and separated itself."

Xanthe and Megaira nodded in agreement. "Maybe you should think hard about what you're about to do here, Nora," said Megaira. "Maybe you should reconsider."

Before she could respond, Indigo sensed a boiling inside her, a surge of fury. Damastes had been quiet throughout the ritual, but even in her deepest moments of concentration she had sensed him listening, observing. Now, his ire clearly raised, he was making himself known.

Pitiful wretches, he sneered, his voice no longer velvety, but jagged and harsh, like broken glass. *They're defeated already, their sisterhood torn apart, their faith destroyed by a false god. All that's left to them is to die a martyr's death, in the hope they can convince themselves they've lived worthwhile lives. They're so desperate they're prepared to lie to you; prepared to deny you your best chance of ending this once and for all.*

You think they're lying to me? said Indigo.

Of course they're lying! Any fool can see that!

But what if you're the one who's lying?

The murder god's tone was scornful. *You really think your so-called friend is still out there somewhere? Lost and alone? The friend you created? The friend who didn't really exist?*

I don't know. I . . . don't know.

You *know*. *In your heart you know.*

But did she? Who was telling the truth—Selene or Damastes? And in the end, what did it matter? Because the important thing was to defeat, if not destroy, the Children of Phonos. And to do that she had to trust her instincts. She had to do what *she* thought was best.

She looked at the murder golem again, then she looked over at Selene and the sisters. "No"—Indigo shook her head—"I still think this is the best way."

Stepping forward, she opened her mouth and let Damastes out of his box.

Although she had a tight hold on the murder god's mental leash, the sheer force with which he surged up and out of her wrenched her mind so violently that she staggered, causing the three Androktasiai to cry out in alarm. Desperately she clung to the beast she had set free, but for several long and terrifying seconds it was like holding a deadly serpent by the tail. Damastes thrashed and snarled and whipped about; he struck out at her, testing her resolve and her strength. As his essence poured into the Heykeli, it began to transform, Shelby's body twisting and elongating, burgeoning with new and hideous tentacular growths. Her beautiful features stretched and blackened until her face resembled charred wood. Her hair shriveled into fleshy stubs, and red insectlike eyes burst out like pustules on her flesh and peered at Indigo with eager and savage intent.

Indigo sensed the slaughter nuns rising to their feet, reaching for their weapons—and this more than anything else galvanized her to fight back. Fiercely she exerted her will over the murder god, allowed her rage to pour forth with crushing intent. Like a mother with a rebellious child she first smothered his attempt to usurp her authority, then reeled him back in.

In her mind she screamed at him, *Back into the box with you! Back into the box!*

Suddenly his voice was different again. Now he *was* a child, whining and repentant.

I'm sorry, I'll be good. I got too excited for a moment there. It's a long time since I've had a taste of freedom.

Bullshit, she said, remembering how she had allowed him to do battle with Caedis. *You were testing me. You can't be trusted.*

The Heykeli was settling back into the form of Shelby now, her features reemerging, all trace of the blackness at the heart of Damastes's true form sinking back beneath the skin.

I can, I can, he whined. **I won't try it again. I've learned my lesson.**

How do I know you're telling the truth? How do I ever know?

You've proved your dominion over me. What choice do I have but to serve you? He paused. **We both want the same outcome. Let's work together to achieve it.**

And then what?

Then we will . . . reassess.

She was silent for a long moment, thinking furiously. Finally she told him, *Don't think for a moment that I trust you. Or that you can catch me off guard again. Try anything else and I'll slam the lid of the box on you and keep you in the dark forever.*

His response was flat, no trace of emotion in it whatsoever. **Understood.**

There was barely time to rest, though God knew they all needed it. They had been battered, bruised, cut. They had lost blood, friends, and (for the Androktasiai in particular), some faith and hope in the past few days. But they couldn't stop. They had to force their battle-weary bodies ever onward. The Apocalypse was coming, and they had to do everything in their power to stop it in its tracks.

The first thing Indigo did when she arrived in New Rochelle, however, having emerged from the shadowpaths with her cargo in tow, was stagger across to the nearest tree and lean over, certain she was about to throw up. Unable to remember the last time she had eaten or drunk anything, she dry-heaved for a minute or two, the back of her throat burning with bile.

When the feeling eventually passed, she looked up, taking in deep lungfuls of the fresh autumnal air, and saw Shelby smiling at her. Once again she corrected herself. No, it wasn't Shelby, it was Damastes. And he wasn't smiling, he was smirking. The cruelty behind his eyes altered Shelby's features in such a way that the murder golem didn't even look like Shelby anymore. The face it wore was harder, tighter, less open and generous than her friend's had ever been. It was fascinating to see how an individual's personality could so drastically alter his or her appearance. And for Indigo (or more especially Nora) it was oddly heartening, too, in that it enabled her to accept more readily that Shelby, her gentle, beautiful, funny friend, was most definitely not in residence.

Straightening and pushing her hair out of her face, Indigo said, "You're enjoying this, aren't you?"

Now the murder golem's eyes widened, its face taking on a falsely innocent look. "I'm sure I don't know what you mean."

"I'm sure you do. You're as slippery as . . ."

"Slime?" suggested Xanthe.

Indigo glanced at the slaughter nun and nodded. "Yes, slime. That's what you are."

The murder golem pouted. "A girl could take offense, you know."

The tone was playful, but Indigo wasn't taken in for a moment.

The creature in Shelby's form was wholly unpredictable. In the past few days he had threatened her, raged at her, cajoled her, bargained with her, pleaded with her. He had shown her many faces, though only occasionally his true one—that of a savage, bloodthirsty entity entirely without mercy.

Indigo was exhausted, but she tried not to show it. She and Damastes had pooled their resources to drag the three Androktasiai along the shadowpaths with them, and it had taken a hell of a lot out of Indigo. Exactly how much she wasn't sure. Glancing at Damastes again, she saw that the Heykeli's pout had become a leer.

"Feeling tired, little girl?" The voice the demon spoke in—Shelby's voice—deepened and roughened on the last syllable, as if its throat had suddenly become filled with gravel.

Indigo felt a moment of panic, then one of anger. "Not too tired to do this!"

She lashed out with her mind, hitting Damastes like a tidal wave, swamping him, sweeping him back into the box and slamming the lid down hard. The Heykeli froze, its eyes glazing, its mouth dropping open.

Selene looked from Indigo to the murder golem, then back to Indigo. "What did you do?"

Indigo felt dizzy with fatigue. The mental energy she had expended along with her rage had taken more out of her than she was comfortable with. She forced a smile. "I've put him back in his box. He was being . . . disobedient."

Megaira said, "You don't look well."

Less accusingly, Selene added, "This is taking a toll on you, isn't it? Bigger than you're letting on?"

Indigo scanned her subconscious for a sign that Damastes might be listening in, but she could hear nothing. Her sudden burst of rage seemed to have stunned the murder god into a sort of stasis. Taking advantage of the moment she nodded. "Listen. I'm on top of this whole Damastes thing, and I'm pretty sure that nothing will go wrong . . ."

"But?" said Selene shrewdly.

"But I have a contingency plan, in case things do."

Quickly she outlined her plan to the three Androktasiai, who listened grimly and without interruption, as though instinctively appreciating that time was of the essence. When she was done, she said, "Right, I'm going to—" But before she could complete her sentence, she felt a surge of darkness inside her that sent her stumbling back against a tree.

All at once her head was filled with a booming, jagged fury that was not her own; a fury so vicious and uncontrolled that it took her reeling mind several moments before it could translate the maelstrom into words.

How dare you do that to me! Damastes's voice was like thunder now, like an earthquake, like the earth splitting open. *How dare you humiliate me in such a manner! If you attempt that again, there will be dire consequences!*

For a moment Indigo was cowed, then she lashed right back at him. *Don't you dare threaten me!*

But she didn't follow it up. Because in this instance she hadn't allowed Damastes out of the box. He had broken out of his own accord, had freed himself from her control, and that unsettled her. It unsettled her very much indeed.

She watched silently as he reinhabited the murder golem, its mouth shutting, its eyes blinking, then staring at her. For a moment, there was silence, a standoff. Then Selene, looking around, said, "Okay. I guess these are the woods. So where's the cemetery?"

Indigo tore her eyes away from Damastes. She tried to look and sound casual as she took her bearings. She squinted up at the sky.

There was still enough light for now, but the shadows were deepening imperceptibly between the trees. Dusk wasn't *too* far away.

Hoping she was right, she pointed. "This way."

Megaira took a long, deep breath, gripped the hilt of her sword, and said, "Let's put an end to this."

18

They moved like ghosts through the trees.

A large swath of woods surrounded the old cemetery in a remote corner of Pelham Manor, a piece of Westchester County, New York, that had been ideal in the 1950s but which now seemed quaint and faded. They'd passed through the town, but now the world of the living had been left behind. The woods were vibrant with autumn colors, though some of the branches were bare and skeletal. A breeze skittered leaves along the forest floor, but they were quiet, these women. No one would hear them coming.

Nora went first, keeping her human form for now, clinging to it as if it, rather than her shadow powers, was the strongest weapon she possessed. Her instinct told her this was true. Her fears shouted it.

Indigo was a thing of shadow. It—*she*—belonged to the same twisted world as Damastes. The same mad reality as the thing that walked behind her in a Halloween costume of her friend Shelby.

That was all wrong. So wrong. It was madness and Nora wondered, not for the first time, if all of this, if everything that had happened to her, was nothing more than a fantasy, as insubstantial as smoke? As unreliable as delusion?

It was a terrifying thought to carry into battle.

She cut looks around and saw the faces of the four women who were going to war with her.

Women. There was as much illusion as truth in that, too.

Selene, Megaira, and Xanthe were spaced out and fanned back, their faces set and grim, eyes searching the woods, weapons in their scarred hands. Sisters of Righteous Slaughter. Betrayed servants of a cunning murder god. And walking apart from them was the construct that wore Shelby's face, a thing of shadows that embodied another murder god. Slaughter nuns and a murder golem.

"I'm insane and the world is insane and none of this is real," murmured Nora. But she did not say it loud enough for anyone to hear.

Megaira bent low and ran ahead, taking point as they neared the edge of the forest. She ran for a few hundred yards and then stopped, dropping to one knee and holding a hand up. Everyone froze, and the forest itself held its breath, then Megaira waved them forward and patted the air to indicate that they should crouch beside her.

As Nora reached her, it was clear why the short nun had stopped. The grove ended at the edge of a small service lane that snaked its way south beneath the arthritic arms of ancient oaks. Across the road was a dusty gray stone wall whose sides had been cracked by tenacious creeper vines. Beyond the wall was a haphazard field of gravestones that were so badly weathered that the names were smeared to rumors. Many of the stones had been knocked over or stood broken, while some of the bigger monuments leaned down into the soft, wormy earth under the pull of their own weight. A threadbare crow stood on one headstone, its black eyes filled with madness. It opened its mouth and cawed softly.

Megaira pointed to the left side of an elm tree. At first Nora saw nothing, then a piece of shadow seemed to detach itself from the greater darkness: a man dressed in gray robes.

"Phonoi," whispered Selene, who crouched beside Nora. "From one of the European clans."

"He's one of the Spanish acolytes," supplied Megaira. "El Clan de Sangre. Very tough."

Xanthe crept up and studied the man. "That's one of the Garcia brothers from Madrid. They killed our sister Kaliope. Skinned her alive."

"God," said Nora, "why? Was it a blood sacrifice?"

"No," said Xanthe, her face twisted into a mask of mingled hatred and disgust. "They just enjoy it."

"We killed one of the brothers," said Megaira. "Luis. He was the youngest, though. I think this is Miguel. There are two others, Esteban and Diego. They have killed many people for the joy of it. They're extreme even for the Children of Phonos."

"Fuck me," murmured Nora, wondering how she had become the center of this insane war between people who worshipped homicide. Wars within wars within wars.

Selene nodded past Miguel, where a line of gray mausoleums stood in a long row, their granite sides choked with ivy. "The ritual is going to be in one of those."

"Which one?" asked Nora.

"I don't know. We'll have to search them."

Xanthe touched Nora's arm. "We'll have to be quiet about it. If they hear us coming, this will all fall apart."

Behind them the murder golem snorted. Nora shot it a look. "Did you have a suggestion? . . . No? Then shut the fuck up."

Damastes smiled at her through Shelby's features.

"If there is one Garcia brother around," cautioned Megaira, "the others will be close. They hunt together like wolves."

"Like jackals," sneered Xanthe.

"Whatever," said Nora. "Can you take him out without giving us away?"

Xanthe and Megaira both looked uncertain, and that scared the hell out of Nora.

She glanced at Selene, who nodded. "The Garcia brothers are strange. I don't know how they managed it, but they are faster and stronger than ordinary humans. A lot of people have tried to kill them, and from what I've heard, they have the walls of the den in their hacienda in Madrid lined with the mounted heads of everyone who's gone up against them. I even heard that they mounted their younger brother's head, too."

"Jesus Christ." Nora peered through the gloom to study the killer. Miguel Garcia had a face that was so hard and muscular it looked like a leather bag filled with walnuts. Uncompromising dark eyes and a cruel thin mouth. His strong hands rested on the handles of a pair of matched bayonets slung from a thick belt. The distance between them was about twenty yards, and it was mostly open ground. Dry old leaves and bracken were everywhere, which would make a silent approach virtually impossible. And now that Miguel had stepped away from the tree, he stood in a clear patch with no convenient shadows nearby for Indigo to step out of.

"I'm open to suggestions," she said, but before the slaughter nuns could reply, another snort of disgust came from behind her.

"Amateurs," complained Damastes, with Shelby's mouth. "The world will grow old and turn to dust before you cows make up your minds."

With that the Heykeli bent to snatch up a rock about half the size of a baseball, rose abruptly from the cover of the wall, cocked its arm back, and hurled the stone with incredible speed and force.

It flew as straight and true as a cannonball, whipping across the intervening distance faster than Nora's eyes could follow. Even so, Miguel Garcia must have heard or sensed something because he turned quickly, the blades beginning to slither out of their sheaths.

Then the stone hit him.

It struck with the force of a bullet, propelled by such ferocious velocity that it punched a big, wet red hole above Miguel's right eye and then exploded out through the back of his skull, splashing the elm with blood and lumps of gray. The impact snapped the man's head back much too far, and he fell without any attempt to cry out or break his fall. It was all immediate and messy.

But it was quiet.

There was a wet *splut* and then the soft thump of the man falling to the ground.

Everyone froze.

Everyone listened.

Everyone watched the cemetery.

Absolutely nothing moved.

Then the murder golem pushed past them all and vaulted the wall. "This is war," growled Damastes. "Act like it."

After only a moment's hesitation the four women surged over the wall in the monster's wake. For Nora this was a crucial moment because she wanted to *be* Nora, but Nora was a civilized woman without power or training. Nora was not Indigo. Nora was not a practiced and powerful killer. She wished she could retain all of Indigo's powers while still *being* Nora—and maybe there was some path unknown to her to that goal—but now was not the time for self-discovery. The murder golem was correct, damn it.

So as she landed on the far side of the stone wall, it was Indigo's feet that touched down. She conjured her cloak of shadows and the weapons that had already spilled so much blood.

This is who I am, too, she thought. *For better or worse, this is who I am. God save my soul, this is who I am.*

They went hunting through the trees and gravestones, through the forest of monuments and the neighborhood of mausoleums.

The other two Garcia brothers were there. Esteban and Diego. And nearly a dozen other men and women. Phonoi of different clans. Slavic faces, Asian faces, African faces, Arab faces, Germanic and Nordic faces.

They all bled the same color.

The slaughter nuns went in quick and low, their blades flashing into sight only at the last moment, too late for the flicker of light on polished steel to offer any warning. The murder golem moved on silent cat feet, using fists and elbows and rocks, a smile burned onto the borrowed face, mad delight in its eyes.

Indigo embraced her own nature, diving into shadows and emerging behind, beside, above, below. Appearing like the nightmare thing she was, her fighting sticks crunching through bone and pulping flesh and ending lives.

A few days ago this would have been an even fight. But things had changed and Indigo knew it. She felt it.

A dark and ugly joy was in her own soul as she fought, and with Damastes embodied in the Heykeli she could not truly blame him for that emotion. *She* felt it. Her. No one else.

That terrified her.

And it thrilled her.

The last of the Phonoi guards died, his throat smashed almost flat from a blow across the windpipe. He dropped to his knees and Indigo stepped aside, lowering her sticks as the man became dead meat and flopped bonelessly onto the dirt.

Selene snapped her fingers, and everyone turned to see her crouching by the door to one of the mausoleums. The faintest glow of light came from around the edges of the door. They all hurried over. Two dead Phonoi lay nearby; clearly they had been guarding this door.

Indigo knelt beside Selene and peered through the crack. Inside was a small chamber like a vestibule with a Coleman lantern, its light turned high. The room was empty except for a bench, which was piled high with coats and personal belongings. A second door was at the end of a short corridor, and as Indigo strained to listen, she could hear something. Strange music and the sound of voices speaking together in a cadence like a church litany.

"The ritual's already started," said Selene urgently.

"Shit," growled Indigo. The door, though ajar, was enormously heavy and had no handle, and Indigo figured it had a hidden catch or lever, but she had no time to look for it. Instead she extruded shadow into the narrow gap and then flexed it like a muscle. The door did not want to open, but its resistance was nothing compared to her desperate will.

With a rasp of stone and a protest of ancient iron hinges, it moved. An inch. Then two. The nuns all reached out to grab the edge and pull. Even the golem gripped a corner of it, and still the door resisted them. Then, with a muffled snap, some restraint broke. The door suddenly swung easily, and they moved inside. Xanthe paused long enough to turn down the lantern flame, plunging the vestibule into blackness.

They stopped at the second door, which had been secured by a stout padlock on a heavy chain, but the chain now lay coiled to one side. Indigo carefully opened the door, and the sound of the ongoing ritual became louder. They bent to look, and to Indigo it was like viewing a scene from Hieronymus Bosch, a scene from hell itself.

Beyond the door, a long set of stairs widened as it swept down to a huge chamber that must have run the entire length of the cemetery. Fat stone columns supported the ponderous weight of the ceiling, and every exposed inch of floor, walls, and columns was covered with hieroglyphs and pictograms from scores of ancient languages, most of which Indigo could not even place. She saw some cuneiform and some Egyptian symbols, and there was Hebrew and Greek, but the rest were unknown to her. All of the symbols seemed to glow as if lit from within, as if the very granite into which they were carved had come alive with some kind of unnatural and luminous vitality.

There were at least a dozen Phonoi. No, more. Many more. Too many to count because their numbers were confused by flickering torchlight. She could see groups that clustered together, each marked by different-colored robes or arcane symbols embroidered on their garments. Many were naked, their bodies elaborately tattooed. Despite their differences in race, nationality, and clan affiliation, they were united in the chant they all uttered. The inhuman language hurt Indigo's ears to hear, as if the human parts of her could not bear the sounds of those words and what they meant.

Central to the room was a stone platform, which was also covered with carvings, but these were directly representational and showed scenes of murder and rape and torture. Atop the platform was a figure, stripped naked and helpless, her wrists and ankles tied with leather straps secured to iron rings set into the stone.

It was Graham Edwards's twelve-year-old daughter, Anastasia.

Her eyes were wild with fear but also glazed as if drugged. Or, Indigo thought, maybe she had been pushed past sanity by the knowledge of what was about to happen to her.

Three people stood on the far side of the table.

One was Rafe, and Indigo wished she could tear his throat out with the power of her own desire. The second, Graham Edwards, was stripped to the waist, his body painted with the same symbols that covered his daughter. And the third was a boy of ten. Andel,

Anastasia's brother, son and heir to Graham. Like his father he was bare chested and painted. But unlike his father he was armed. In one trembling small fist he held a gleaming dagger. Indigo recognized that dagger. So did the others with her, for they all hissed and a shudder of hatred ran through them as they watched. The dagger was small but wickedly sharp, with a bronze blade and a crossbar fashioned like wings that swept down to guard the hand; and with a deep blood gutter that ran the length of the blade. Inside those sweeping wings was a black void that would send the flowing blood from this world into the next. The very nature of this abomination of a weapon was an offense against life itself. That it was held by a child made it worse, and that the child stood ready to plunge that knife into the heart of his own sister compounded the blackness of sin that filled the air with a toxic spiritual poison.

Rafe was leading the chanting, but it rose to a sharp crescendo, and with a shouted word he ended it. Silence crashed down on the chamber.

"We stand on the precipice above the abyss, my brothers and sisters." Rafe raised his hands and spread his arms wide as if to embrace everyone. "We have worked so long, buried so many of our friends, faced so many challenges, and now here we are. All that we have endured has brought us to this moment. Everything we have fought for is now within our grasp. Listen to the heartbeat of eternity . . . can you hear it flutter? Can you hear the winds of fate catch their breath?"

The gathered Children of Phonos cheered Rafe, but he waved them to silence again.

"Ours is not an easy path." His words echoed from the stone walls. "Ours has never been the easy path. Ours has never been a simple task because the easy and simple path is for the weak and the unenlightened. But we *know*, my brothers and sisters, we *see*.

We are diligent and precise. We have taken all this time because greatness is only possible when everything is done exactly right. Every detail, every step, every facet. Rituals will fail if the slightest error is made. But the locks to the treasure trove of unlimited power open if the right key is used and if it is turned with the subtlest, deftest hand."

The others nodded but kept their silence.

"And now we come to this moment and to what must now be done." Rafe gestured to Anastasia Edwards. "Only two things need yet be done for us to claim our place as the masters of this world. Of this and *many* worlds. This boy will forever earn his place as a true Child of Phonos, as a warrior of our faith, as a hero whose name will be praised for a thousand years."

Indigo looked at Andel, and the boy seemed to be feverish with excitement. Or fear. Or madness. She couldn't tell.

"Andel will sacrifice his sister, and Graham Edwards will sacrifice his daughter, for us. For all of us."

There was a massive thunder of applause and cheering. A strange and twisted smile came and went on Edwards's face. The body shivered as if he stood in a cold wind.

The girl wept and begged, but no one heeded her.

When the applause died down, Rafe smiled a dark smile at the crowd. "But before that can happen, there is something *I* must do. Something that I have spent many years preparing. So many years of study, of preparation, of research and prayer. Behold!"

Rafe reached down and took Andel's wrist, raising it and the knife high so that everyone could see it. The empty space in the knife's complex crossbar was empty only for a moment. As everyone watched, the space seemed to blink. No, it was more like an eye opening. One moment it was a hole and the next it was a perfect circle of darkness. Not shadow precisely, but a deeper and more profound darkness. An eternal darkness that was as bottomless as space but yet totally *alive*.

It was suddenly there.

An ombrikos.

It did not come quietly. It ripped a hole into the world, clawing at the flesh of reality to impose itself into the fabric of the moment. Indigo recoiled as if its existence stabbed her through the heart. Beside her she heard the Androktasiai hiss. But the murder golem murmured a word in some unknown language, and whatever it was, Damastes loaded it with bottomless venom and hatred.

The crowd in the chamber gasped, and for a moment they froze, eyes wide, mouths gaping.

Then they cried out in passionate glory, shouting, screaming, jumping up and down, waving their arms, laughing, weeping.

Andel Edwards stood holding the dagger, and suddenly tendrils of blackness whipped out of the ombrikos and wrapped themselves around him, covering him as thoroughly as the ivy covered the tombstones outside. The boy shrieked in pain, but Rafe held his arm steady. Graham shook his head like a man coming out of a stupor and stared at his son, and for a moment—for one flickering, fragile moment—Indigo thought that the man was going to stop what was about to happen. That he would slap the knife from his son's hand, snatch up his children, and run.

That hope was too fragile to support the reality of what Graham Edwards wanted from life. It could not bear the weight of what Rafe desired.

So Graham took his son's wrist from Rafe's grasp and guided it—and the knife—out so that the point of the blade hovered over his young daughter's defenseless chest.

Indigo whipped around to tell her team to go, to fight, to stop this, but she never got the chance. The murder golem threw back its head and let loose with a roar of such unbridled rage that the sound of it drowned out all of the chants and cheers and cries. The roar was so loud that the slaughter nuns reeled back, blood starting from their ears. Cracks whipsawed along the walls, and the torches flared as if doused by gasoline.

Then Damastes shoved Indigo out of the way and charged.

Indigo reached out to stop the murder golem, but even as her fingers closed around the Shelby-shaped wrist, the wrist *changed*. In the space of a single step the golem stopped being Shelby at all. The flesh seemed to boil, and Indigo heard bones cracking and tendons popping as the body changed and changed, becoming something else, something unknown. Becoming a monster.

Damastes stepped down onto the stone stairs with hooves instead of feet. His legs twisted into a parody of goat legs, and wiry black hair sprouted from the changing skin. The torso changed from female to male and blossomed with hard muscles covered by a scaled hide from which spikes emerged, their points dripping with sizzling venom. Damastes's head dropped low between muscular shoulders, and a pair of curling horns thrust outward from a broad, sloping brow, and teeth like boars' tusks filled the snarling mask.

Xanthe tried to stop the monster from rushing down and revealing their presence, but Damastes struck her a savage blow that sent the slaughter nun crashing into the doorframe. She rebounded with a deep grunt of pain and nearly toppled down the stairs, bit Megaira darted out a hand to catch her. The monster roared again and charged down the stars toward the shocked crowd of Phonoi.

Rafe saw the monster, and for a moment his face went slack with mingled fear and incomprehension, then his gaze shifted to the cluster of women behind Damastes and his eyes sharpened. Indigo saw how realization changed the man's expression into a mask of cruelty and hatred. There was fear, too, because this was such a crucial moment for him and so much of what he had worked for could collapse.

But he was also amused, as if the challenge of this attack sent a sexual thrill through him.

On the floor of the chamber the Phonoi were rushing to meet the oncoming monster, and blades, sickles, spiked truncheons, and other weapons appeared as if by magic in their hands. They had come to this ceremony armed for the murders they prized so deeply.

And murder in its more savage form rushed at them.

"Let's go!" yelled Indigo, and she charged down in Damastes's wake. Megaira and Selene pulled Xanthe to her feet and they followed, weapons drawn, cries rising to their lips.

Damastes struck the wall of Phonoi like a tsunami, and Indigo saw bodies and parts of bodies go flying, trailed by sprays of dark red. Then she was in the thick of it.

Suddenly the world fractured, becoming less a straight series of events but more a kaleidoscope of bizarre images. Or a movie montage whose sound track was screams and the clash of blades.

Selene leaped from the third step and snapped out a brutal kick that caught an Asian woman on the point of her chin with such force it sent the Phonoi into an awkward backflip. The woman landed badly and did not move again.

Two African Phonoi, both wearing Somalian tattoos, charged at Megaira, and within an instant the three of them seemed to fade inside a whirlwind of flashing silver blades.

Damastes did not stay in the form of a demonic satyr but changed and changed as he fought. One moment he was manlike, with golden skin and eyes filled with actual fire; the next he was a Gorgon, with heavy breasts whose nipples leaked boiling venom and whose head was a writhing mass of copperheads, cobras, and coral snakes; then he became a towering troll with massive arms; then a goblin-shaped imp with swords for arms. Changing over and over and over again, as if the murder god's mind had fractured. With each change someone died or staggered back with a terrible wound. And throughout the carnage Damastes laughed for the pure joy of bloodshed.

Behind the altar Graham Edwards swayed, his face twisted with fear and doubt. His chained daughter lay screaming, his son struggled to break free of his father's grip, and Edwards was clearly torn between whatever love he had left for his children and his duty to the cult who owned his soul. Rafe stood nearby, a curved kukri in his hand, eyes wild and feral. Indigo thought that he was as ready to defend the ceremony as he was to kill Edwards if the man waivered too far. Rafe's eyes roved across the sea of battle and found Indigo. He smiled an inviting smile.

"Get him!" cried Selene, but Indigo was already moving toward the madman behind the altar. A Phonoi with a thick black beard and hook nose came at her with an old-fashioned scimitar, and the curved blade sheared through the air, missing Indigo's throat by a hairsbreadth as she suddenly lurched backward. She took the fall of her weight to put power and speed into a crouching turn, and as the man checked his swing for another cut, Indigo rose up inside the arc of his attack and drove a shadow dagger into the softness of the flesh beneath the man's jaw. The blade punched all the way up so that the tip burst through the top of his skull, and she saw the lights in his eyes change from madness to surprise to a terminal vacuity.

Megaira pushed past her and raised her blade to catch the downward stroke of a knife that Indigo did not see coming.

"Thanks," gasped Indigo as she wrenched her own blade free.

The slaughter nun grinned at Indigo, but then she juddered and coughed out a pint of hot red blood. She and Indigo both looked down at Megaira's chest to see the six inches of blade that stood out from just beneath her sternum.

Megaira said, "I . . ."

Then the killer behind her tore the blade free and Megaira fell, her eyes rolling high and white. Across the room Xanthe screamed, but she was too far away to do anything but watch her sister die.

The killer, a slender woman with a dancer's body and a face like a French fashion model, came at Indigo with a series of blindingly fast attacks, wielding a long, thin-bladed straight sword with the disheartening proficiency of a master swordswoman. The attack was blinding and powerful and Indigo was forced to give ground step by step.

On the altar, Rafe slapped Edwards hard across the face, knocking some of the dazed stupidity from it and tearing a cry from young Andel.

"Do what you promised, you piece of shit," snarled Rafe. "Do it *now*."

Andel renewed his efforts to pull away, but his father took a breath and adjusted his grip on his son's arm. The blade began moving downward toward the heaving chest of the helpless girl.

Damastes was now in the shape of some kind of sea creature, with a mass of tentacles sprouting from an amorphous body. The Children of Phonos stabbed at him, and Indigo saw two of the tentacles go flying, but if the wounds hurt the murder god, his cries sounded very much like joyful laughter.

Selene dove low, rolling beneath the swing of a staff so that her at-tacker struck another Phonoi full in the mouth. The victim spun around and fell, and Selene scrambled up and whipped her blade across the staff fighter's thigh, his arm, his cheek, and his throat. The wooden weapon clattered to the floor and the attacker stum-bled sideways, trying to stop the arterial spray. And failing.

Indigo whipped her cloak of shadows up and let the Frenchwom-an's blade stab through it, then Indigo jerked her hand down and sideways, wrapping the blade in knots of unreality. The woman tried to cut her way out, but it was the wrong tactic, and Indigo made her pay for it by driving a knee into the woman's crotch, head-butting her, and then reshaping the shadow knife into a cleaver that crunched into the side of the woman's neck. The Frenchwoman's head rolled to the floor.

Gasping for air, Indigo turned toward the altar. Time was running out. Edwards was going to force his son to sacrifice Anastasia. The blade was inches away now, and defeat and even a sick acceptance was in Andel's young eyes.

So she ran, pulling shadows around her to create armor and intensifying her cloak into a battering ram. Several of the Children of Phonos tried to stop her, but Indigo willed a mass of spikes onto the front of her ram, and the resistance melted away with shrieks and splashes of red.

Rafe turned to her. She expected to see fear blossom in his eyes, but instead he was smiling. No . . . *laughing.*

Indigo slammed with full speed and force into . . .

Nothing.

She hit nothing but it was like hitting a stone wall. Her momen-tum crushed her into the unseen obstacle, and she rebounded with tremendous force. More force, even, than hitting a wall would have generated. She saw a weird shimmer in the air and realized with a sinking heart that some kind of spell, a ward or protective charm, was in place around the altar, and Rafe had constructed it to stop her. Of that she had absolutely no doubt.

Indigo was on her knees, pain detonating in her chest. Her arms and shoulders and head all felt as if she had been beaten, as if she were broken. All around her the battle raged. Her shadows seemed to collapse around her, hanging like broken things, drooping onto the floor like torn banners on the field of a lost battle. She could not move, could not rise. Her hands twitched open and her shadow weapons fell from her fingers and dissolved into ash. Up on the altar Rafe laughed with triumph.

Indigo looked around for help, but what she saw broke her heart.

Until now Indigo had thought they had a chance, however fleeting, of saving the girl and ending Rafe's mad plan. But as she knelt there, powerless and defeated, she saw the tide of battle turn.

Xanthe and Selene fought with incredible ferocity, their blades flashing like lightning as bodies piled up around them. However there were more of the Phonoi than Indigo had thought. Many more. Clearly, the only thing keeping the two women alive was that the Phonoi had to climb over the fallen bodies of their own in order to attack. That advantage could not last. Even fighters as skilled as the slaughter nuns were still human. Their bodies were bathed with sweat, and Indigo knew their arms had to be growing heavy, the muscles burning with lactic acid, chests heaving as they fought to breathe.

They're going to die, thought Indigo, knowing it to be true.

The Nora part of her whispered a darker truth inside her head: *We're all going to die. Rafe is going to win.*

Worse still, they both thought, *I can't do this.*

The ugliest word was *I*.

Immediately a dark and awful idea whispered to her through the darkness of her despair.

"No . . . ," she whispered.

Yes, said the voice inside her. Not Nora's voice. Not exactly. The voice was part of each of the two aspects of who she was. Nora and Indigo. Human and inhuman. This was the voice of the parts of each that were always connected, always one being. An essential self whispering essential truths.

She cut a look at Damastes, and for a moment the murder god paused, blinking at her in surprise. His flesh still flowed and changed, but his eyes were human enough for her to read his expression. She watched him as he looked from her to the shimmering wall of magic and back. Damastes understood that truth, too.

Rafe's magic had been created to stop Indigo. To stop the thing she was. These wards combated her shadow self, weakened her into impotency, and in doing so they made her weakness Rafe's greatest weapon because Selene and Xanthe were never going to cut their way to the altar. And Damastes was not yet powerful enough to break through because he, too, shared the nature of shadow sorcery. Rafe had set a trap, and he laughed because he knew it would work.

Indigo was never going to reach the girl. Never.

Damastes was never going to reach Anastasia.

Never.

Neither of them could.

This was Rafe's genius, and Indigo's team had no time to fall back, regroup, and attack with a fresh plan. That moment had burned off.

Her inner voice whispered its secret to her. A chance. A plan. A hope.

But it was so dangerous that Indigo knew she would die. Absolutely. No other chance. This was the end of her.

"Please," she whispered, begging the universe to offer a different choice, to take that cup of destiny from her.

The universe was indifferent and ignored her pleas.

Indigo turned to Damastes and caught the monster's eye. She saw him stare into her. She saw him come to a higher or deeper understanding of what she was going to do. The monster's face clouded for a moment with doubt, then a wild joy flared in his eyes.

Damastes smashed away one of the Phonoi and roared again. "Yes!" he bellowed.

Indigo closed her eyes.

I'm scared, she thought.

I know, said her own inner voice.

Now that voice was not a blend of Indigo and Nora. Now that voice was only Nora's. Cold. Strong.

Apart.

Indigo thought about the girl who was going to die. She thought about all of the murdered children. She thought about all of the children—and the adults—who would die once this ceremony reached its conclusion. The world would drown in blood.

What then did hers matter?

Indigo licked her lips. "Please . . . ," she whispered, then let go of the shadows that defined her. They bled from her, dripped from her, pooled around her. It was like having her skin peeled off because it was not merely her Indigo self. It was *all* of her shadow.

Every.

Last.

Bit.

Nora knelt there in a lake of darkness and slowly collapsed forward, bowing her head to the floor as the darkness lapped like water around her.

"Go," she said, and for that last moment the spoken voice was both hers and Indigo's.

She felt the darkness move, recoiling from the power of the ward, moving backward, and as it retreated from Rafe's spell, the darkness became stronger. The outer edges of the pool became whole again, regaining its strength as it disentangled from the complexity of the ward spell. Only the slightest tether remained between her and her shadow self. The ritual that had merged her with Damastes all those years ago made it impossible for her to divest herself of that last trace of the darkness, so she felt it when the shadows flowed, felt it along that thin, thin thread. Her darkness rose up in a wall of shadows, and Nora half turned to see it, and for a moment she wanted to crawl toward it and reclaim it.

She did not.

That would only put her back in the same place, and that place was on the crumbling edge of the abyss.

The shadows deserted her, rushing away from her with such force that it stretched that thin thread almost to the breaking point. It hurt so bad. Not physically but all the way down to the center of her soul. It was like having her heart cut out. She could feel so much of herself go with it. Power and confidence, hope and . . .

The sound behind her was unbearably loud and indescribable. It hit everyone and everything in the chamber like a shock wave, knocking combatants apart and tearing chunks of masonry from the wall. Pieces of the ceiling crashed down on the Phonoi. On the altar one of the leather straps holding Anastasia broke, and she rolled partly away as the dagger plunged down, the blade biting deep into the stone instead.

Graham Edwards and his son stopped fighting. Rafe stopped laughing. Everyone turned toward the *thing* that now stood in the center of the room.

Nora looked, too, and with horror she saw the last of her shadow melt into the rippling flesh of the god of murder. Damastes seemed to swell with it, his skin stretching outward as he grew and grew, towering into a giant nearly a dozen feet tall. His legs were like stone columns—human in shape but so heavily muscled they were freakish. His torso was manlike, but the scales had grown back, and on each separate plate was a hooked barb that was as dark and sharp as the claw of a cat. Thousands of these appeared all over him, as if the shadow within him wanted to rend and tear with every possible angle of contact. Damastes's arms grew long and powerful, with broad hands covered with longer spikes. A wreath of spikes grew out like a collar below the jutting chin, and above that was a face as strangely beautiful as the rest of him was hideous. It was like the face of a statue of Adonis, god of beauty, and yet this was a terrible beauty.

Nora knew that she now beheld something she had never before seen. Not in its true form. This was Damastes, the god of murder, in the full flush of his power.

When he spoke, it was in a voice of thunder.

"I am alive again!"

"Nooooo!" screamed Selene, breaking free of her shock and impelled by horror. She shoved a Phonoi killer aside and hurled herself at Damastes, a knife held in two hands as she sought to plunge it into the murder god's heart.

Damastes swatted her aside.

As if she were nothing.

The spiked back of his hand tore through Selene's flesh, and the strength of his arm flung her thirty feet through the air. Nora screamed as Selene crashed down out of sight behind the heaped dead.

Damastes turned toward Nora.

"*Thank you,*" thundered the god.

His laughter broke the world.

19

—

Pain.

Inside, outside, it didn't matter. Her body hurt. Her heart hurt. Her *soul* hurt, an aching, sucking wound where the shadows should have been. She had been their prison and their prisoner for so long, so long, and now—

Now they were loose, running wild and rampant, and there was so much blood, so many broken bodies, and *Selene was dead* and everything was lost and the child—the child—

The children were still alive. She had done this, she had opened this terrible wound, unleashed this impossible beast upon the world, for the sake of the children. This was her fault. This was her crime, her sin, her unforgivable transgression, and unless she found a way to make it worthwhile—unless she saved the children—she might as well have let the slaughter nuns have her. She might as well have died on that first altar, the dagger to her heart, because she'd done what the men who'd killed the children had wanted all along, she had unleashed the end of days, she had broken the world, and for what? For *what?*

For the children. Without them, she had done it all for nothing, and so she had done it for them.

Pain singing hosannas to every twitch, every thought, Nora pulled herself to her feet. It took . . . forever. It took no time at all. Dully, through the agony of her own body, she heard the roars of Damastes. He was doing what he did best: he was making murder. In his hands—claws—in his grasp, it was an art form, like a painting, or a song played on an impossible instrument. The Phonoi assassins weren't having a great day.

No one was having a great day. Great days were no longer on the menu.

Fuck the menu, said a small voice at the back of her mind, sharp and sardonic and a little sweet, as if it understood what she was going through, even though it couldn't help. *I'm going to order à la carte. Who's with me?*

Shelby wasn't real. Shelby had never been real. But that meant Shelby was the better part of Nora, maybe the *best* part of her. The girl she would have been if she hadn't had a murderer for a mother and a cultist for a father, if she hadn't been promised to a murder god, if she had been allowed to grow *up,* instead of just getting older one day and one death at a time.

If she couldn't do this for herself, she could do it for Anastasia Edwards. She could do it for Andel Edwards. She could do it for Shelby.

"Fuck the menu," Nora agreed, in a voice that was virtually a sigh, and broke into a run.

The pain stayed behind, in the place where hero had become human. Everything was running. Everything was screaming. There was no *time,* there was no *time* to stop and see who was screaming, there was no *time* for anything but running as if her life depended on it. Because it did. Her life, and Anastasia's life, and everyone's life, they all depended on how quickly she could run.

Nora understood running. Indigo's powers came from Damastes, fueled by shadow and demonic magic, but the physicality behind those powers had always come from Nora. When she punched, her knuckles were the ones that got bruised. When she kicked, her toes were the ones that got broken. And when she ran, when she leaped across the rooftops of the city like the comic-book chimera Damastes had worked so hard to turn her into, her legs were the ones powering the whole thing.

She might not have shadow powers or magic or a giant-ass sword—she would really have appreciated a giant-ass sword right about then—but she could *run*.

She ran straight for the altar, where Anastasia was struggling against her remaining bonds, tears running down her face and snot hanging in ropy strings from her nose. The girl looked so *young*, because she *was* so young, and she should never have been forced into this position. She should have been thinking middle-school thoughts, not wondering whether her brother was going to slice out her heart and offer it to a murder god.

A murder god who, while he would happily have bathed in the blood of the world, had no interest in the blood of this particular girl. He didn't want to be bound to the Phonoi. He didn't want to be bound to—

"Forget something?" taunted Rafe, positioning himself so that he was between Anastasia and the running Nora. He was scarcely on the other side of his wards, a twisted delight in his eyes. Damastes was still cutting an unstoppable swath through the guards, rending and slicing without hesitation. Rafe didn't seem to care. He was safe inside his own protections.

That was how he had always been, Nora realized, her heartbeat speeding up from the mixture of adrenaline and rage. Her pain had been entirely forgotten, replaced by the need to justify her choices, to make the things she had done for the sake of her soul worthwhile. Rafe, and the people like him, had always been willing to let the world drown in a sea of its own blood as long as he could be sure of being safe.

"This is for my *father*," Nora snarled, and threw a hard right hook through his magical barrier. His nose broke against her fingers with a satisfyingly squishy sensation. It was one of the best things she had ever felt. She hauled back to do it again.

Rafe staggered backward, out of her reach, and grabbed for Andel again, getting the boy into a headlock. *"Do it!"* he howled at Graham Edwards, voice thick with blood and agony. *"Kill the little bitch! Do it now!"*

Graham Edwards looked between the struggling Andel and the terrified Anastasia, and at the knife lying forgotten on the altar. Slowly, as if against his will, he bent and reached for the handle.

"We're all dead if I don't do this, princess," he said in a voice like lead. Anastasia whimpered and struggled to the limits of her bonds, shying away from him as best she could. "I'm so sorry. Daddy tried so hard to save you. Daddy did everything he could."

"Liar!" shrieked Anastasia.

Rafe was watching the pair now, a grin painting his face, terrible through the veil of his own blood. Andel was struggling, but he was a ten-year-old boy, scrawny and held captive by a man three times his size. He was never going to break free.

The wards had been designed to keep Indigo out. They would hold against Damastes for a time. Maybe even forever. Rafe clearly thought he'd come too close to the edge, that Nora had been lucky, or he wouldn't have been standing there so exposed, so *vulnerable*.

Nora lunged.

Her shoulder impacted with his side, knocking him off-balance and loosening his grip on Andel. Rafe snarled. Andel yelped, the sound high and sharp and somehow carrying over the sounds of the one-sided battle that raged outside. Some of the Children of

Phonos had realized that they couldn't possibly win against the monster of their own making. They were running, scattering like leaves in a stiff wind, and Damastes was more than happy to pursue, gleeful as a cat disemboweling mice. They were junior members, the tattered survivors of a dying cult.

"Run, you stupid boy!" snarled Nora, and jabbed her stiffened fingers into the hollow of Rafe's throat.

He howled. He loosed his grip.

Andel ran.

Save your sister, Nora thought—but there was no time to voice it. Rafe squirmed against her, directing a quick, sharp punch at her face. Nora twisted to the side, letting his hand whish harmlessly past her. Then she turned, slamming her forehead into his so hard that stars blossomed inside her skull like fireworks, bright and beautiful and transitory.

Rafe squealed.

"This is for *Shelby!*" she howled, and punched him in the nose again.

Rafe raised his hands, not to hit, but to move his fingers in a complicated pattern that only made fucking sense if he was trying to speak ASL or trying to cast a spell on her. Since she doubted he had suddenly discovered a passion for silent communication, the latter seemed more likely. Nora abandoned her punching strategy and slammed her elbow into the hollow of his throat, bringing her knee up to his groin at the same time.

Rafe's hands stopped moving. He made a small, choked sound and fell, collapsing unconscious to the ground. She felt a sizzling sensation, as if she had brushed against the edge of an electric fence, and her skin drew tight in terrified goose bumps as Damastes laughed again, this time in sheer, unbridled delight.

The wards were down.

Nora spun to see the nightmare Adonis bearing down on her.

Edwards shouted and flung the knife aside, supplicating himself to the murder god he had worked so long and so hard to subjugate. It was too little, too late—if there had ever been a chance Damastes would see the Children of Phonos as a useful tool, it had ended when Rafe Bogdani became their guiding hand.

And now Rafe Bogdani ended, as Damastes smashed a heavy heel down on Rafe's skull, pulping the sorcerer's face with a hideous crunch. The murder god never slowed as he powered forward and fell upon Edwards, tearing the man limb from limb in an explosion of entrails and unspeakable fluids that showered the scene in a rainbow of gore. Anastasia screamed, high and shrill. The girl's mind would have been shattered forever, of that there was no question, had Xanthe not suddenly appeared between her and the body of her father. Xanthe used her thin frame to shield the girl from the bulk of that terrible tide.

Damastes snarled and batted Xanthe aside, much as he had Selene—but this slaughter nun received far less of his attention: his claws were sheathed, reserved for a better target. Anastasia, still screaming. Anastasia, whose death would complete the ritual, not to bind him, but to free him completely into the world. Without Nora. Without the guiding hand of justice. Without anything to hamper him.

"I've won!" he howled, delighted malice in his voice. He glanced over his shoulder to the woman who had been his home for so many years, eyes narrowed and calculating. "When you're dead, I'm going to fuck your corpse until it screams."

Trite, snapped the voice of Shelby.

Nora, frantic, cast around. Weapons were useless, she knew that, but it was better to die with a knife in her hand than with nothing but the blood that coated her fingers. At least then she could say she'd tri—

Damastes was moving, Damastes was bringing his claws down

toward Anastasia's throat, and the girl wasn't screaming anymore, the girl was frozen in her fear at her impending death, the girl was a rabbit ripe for the slaughter, and this could not happen this could not happen *this could not happen.*

"*No!*" howled Nora in a voice that could have rivaled Damastes's own.

The murder god froze.

Trite and stupid, murmured the Shelby side of her.

"What?" Nora's voice was a whisper or a broken scream.

You made him. You shaped him. You own *him.* Shelby's voice was matter-of-fact, and so real that Nora could have wept. *He let you do exactly what he feared because he wanted so badly to be free. He's your Heykeli. He's your puppet now.*

"Release me!" snarled Damastes, struggling to move.

"No," said Nora again, more softly this time. "No."

"I'll spare you if you release me!"

"No."

"The world—the universe—you could be a queen! You could have your revenge on everyone who ever wronged you!"

"No."

"I'll kill you. I'll rip your entrails out through your crotch and swallow them like spaghetti. I'll—"

"No," said Nora again, soft and steady. The pain was back, arcing through her like ice. She welcomed it. She welcomed the darkness it represented.

He's been yours since you said hello, whispered Shelby, and Nora knew it was true. More, she knew that if it was true, then everything that belonged to him was hers as well, from the greatest atrocity to the smallest transgression.

Everything.

Calmly she stepped past the frozen, snarling demon and picked up the ombrikos. The void surged within it, and the void within her answered. She could send him back. She could banish him back to whatever it was that waited for murder gods whose time was finished.

"Do it," hissed a familiar voice. Nora glanced to the side, startled, to behold Selene staggering toward the altar, one hand clasped over the wound at her ribs. "Kill the bastard."

Nora nodded, not quite capable of speech, and began, through the void, to pull the power away.

Damastes howled. The sound was rage and pain and fury, and Nora quaked to hear it. She kept pulling, letting the shadows spool back into the core of her, letting them wrap tight around her heart.

You can't send him back to the void, whispered Shelby.

Why not? Nora demanded silently, of no one but herself.

He's too big. Put him back and another cult will free him. His sister is already banished, and she'll be looking for some payback. If you banish him, he'll be on her *side.*

As much as murder gods had sides, beyond "drown the world in blood." Nora kept pulling, feeling the strength and confidence—the Indigo-ness—fill her lungs.

But we'll have time.

No. Shelby's silent voice was soft, almost apologetic. *We won't.*

I'm sorry. I didn't mean to—

I don't mean me.

Nora hesitated, the shadow strands nearly slipping through her fingers.

She knew.

She'd known.

She'd known since she saw the video, saw her own teenage body bound and struggling, seen the trauma and the shock. People didn't *walk away* from something like that. They didn't *survive* it. They didn't *live* and *thrive* and become *superheroes.*

She'd been dead since the ritual that bound her to the demon she was now struggling to control. She couldn't banish him without killing herself—and that might have been worth it if she'd been sure the banishment would take. But she wasn't. She couldn't be. Ripping him out of her entirely would wrest the ombrikos from her control, and Damastes would be free despite everything. It was the last trap.

There had to be another way.

He roared. She yanked as much power as she could, wrapping herself in shadows, and was Indigo once more, even as he broke free.

"Foolish *child*!" he howled, and lunged for her.

Damastes was the source of her power: he was the coal that burned in the furnace of her heart. But the engine was not the machine and never had been. His claws closed on empty air as she shoved the ombrikos into her pocket and leaped, lithe and swift and unstoppable. She yanked again, pulling more of the power out of him, into her.

"Mortal fool!" he shouted.

"The fight doesn't go to the one who yells the loudest!" she replied, and slammed both feet into his temple, knocking him sideways. For a moment, he staggered, reeling, subject to the limitations of his mortal form. He snarled. He grabbed for her.

She was gone.

The shadows spat her out behind him. She grabbed for his power again, pulling harder and harder, until he began to dwindle, borrowed body warping toward the familiar, beloved shape of a woman who had never existed. He shouted in horror as his claws melted into Shelby's soft, clever fingers, as his fangs retracted.

"No!" he snarled. "I won't be stopped! I won't be contained! I wo—"

His words cut out as his mouth vanished, covered by a shell of hardening flesh. Nora had a momentary glimpse of his eyes, widened in something that looked almost like respect, before he folded in on himself like a puzzle box, becoming small and square and almost inconsequential.

I'll be back, whispered a voice that was neither hers nor Shelby's, and the box fell to the ground, landing with a soft splash in a puddle of blood.

"I know," Nora said, releasing Indigo and staggering forward under her own power to scoop it off the ground.

It seemed so small. It was the largest thing in the world.

"What did you—?" asked Xanthe.

"He's mine. He made that clear when he let me build him a body. You own what you build." Nora's hand involuntarily tightened around the box. "He's not going to hurt anyone for a long fucking time."

"And you get to stay a superhero," said Xanthe.

"It's a decent consolation prize, since it seems I don't get to be a human anymore." Nora wrapped herself in shadows again, making the box disappear into a place where no one else would ever even dream of finding it. Her smile was a knife slashed across the throat of the world, and for a moment—just a moment—Xanthe looked afraid.

"All right," said Indigo. "Let's mop this shit up."

EPILOGUE

—

Unlike most of the narrow galley kitchens Nora had seen in New York City apartments, the one at Sam Loh's place had a little window that looked out on a small courtyard. It had always seemed a bit magical to her, that quiet space behind the building in an otherwise relatively typical, anonymous sort of New York neighborhood. The courtyard was walled in by apartment buildings that cast their shadows, one upon the other, and so sunlight only fell through that small window for a brief period each morning. Even so, on the windowsill stood a little plastic hula girl with a bright pink hula skirt, ticking side to side like a metronome, powered by the sun. The opposite of Indigo, really. Yet today, Nora felt more energized by the morning and the sunlight than she had ever felt by the shadows.

She touched the stone that hung from a string around her neck—the ombrikos, once warm but now just smooth and cold and dormant. Nothing but jewelry now, and a dreadful reminder of the malevolent power that could be brought to bear upon the world— the reason she had to remain forever vigilant.

The dusty Keurig on the counter finished trickling Sam's coffee into a chipped *NYChronicle* mug, and she added cream, then picked up her own mug and carried them both out into the living room. Unlike her own cramped studio, Sam's apartment had two closet-size bedrooms, a bathroom with an antique claw-foot tub she'd always figured must be haunted, and a living room that seemed large only because he used the second tiny bedroom as a home office, which meant no desk jammed in with the sofa, chairs, and the little dinette setup where meals were eaten when Sam had company. Any meals he ate when he didn't have company, she knew, were taken exactly where he was now . . . sprawled out on the sofa in front of the television set. Nora had made him shut the TV off when she'd arrived this morning, and now he had music playing from his laptop, the elegant, jaunty sort of classical music that he'd tried to interest her in when they'd officially been dating. She'd never tell him, but she'd listened at home more than once. The music had a soothing quality unlike almost anything else, and she needed soothing more than most.

"I've never noticed that little hula girl by the window," she said as she crossed toward him. "Is she new?"

Sam groaned as he shifted to a sitting position on the sofa. He knitted his brows, obviously uncomfortable as hell, but still managed to seem bemused by the question.

"Sort of. I used to have another one there, but with a green skirt. Her battery died, but I like seeing her there. Makes me smile. I ordered another one online. You really can find just about anything for sale."

Nora frowned. How many other things in her life had she never noticed? How much had she missed?

"Drink your coffee," she said, settling onto the sofa beside him. She tucked one leg beneath her, close to him, and aware of that closeness. "Doctor's orders."

Sam took a sip and sighed. "My name is Sam Loh, and I am a caffeine addict."

"Welcome, Sam. You're among friends."

For a short time they sat like that, with the music and their coffee and a chilly breeze dancing in through the slightly open living-room window, and the bright autumn day outside, the way only real friends did. Sam had always been good company, no matter what Nora's mood might be.

"All right. Shall we get to work?" he asked.

"All work and no play makes Sam a dull boy." Nora smiled.

Sam shifted on the sofa and winced. The hospital had sent him home and he'd been eager to go, but he still had healing to do.

"It may be a while before I'm up to playing."

Nora arched a suggestive eyebrow. "And then?"

Sam sipped his coffee, arching an eyebrow to mirror her own. "Why, then I imagine I'll get up to some mischief."

"I'm in favor of mischief."

"Oh, I'm well aware."

Nora gave a quiet laugh and took a gulp of her coffee before setting the mug down. "So, are you going to tell me what you learned from the files I brought you from Bogdani's place?"

Sam grimaced. He looked a bit paler than she liked, and Nora wondered if he'd been taking the painkillers he'd been prescribed. It would be so like Sam to try to tough it out to avoid taking the drugs.

"I'm still pretty tired and it's hard for me to focus. Y'know, concussion and all. But from what I've looked at so far, the information in there is pretty explosive. Captain Mueller intended to blow the whole thing wide-open. If Bogdani were still alive, there'd be an indictment for sure. Federal. Human trafficking is not something the FBI or local authorities can ignore. Once I can focus on all of this, I'll start quietly looking into how many of the people in these files are even still alive—"

"Not many." Nora didn't add that she'd killed some of them herself. Sam knew that, and she didn't feel like reminding him.

"—and then I'll bring in some state and federal contacts. Not only is this story going to be big, it's going to lead to a ton of arrests and save lives." Sam coughed and winced at the pain it caused him. "Are you . . . I mean, this story is really yours, Nora. You sure you want to give me all of this?"

She dragged a blanket off the arm of the sofa and draped it over her legs. "You take the parts that you were already investigating. I'll cover the cult and the core story about the kids they murdered. I owe that to those kids—to Maidali Ortiz and the others. If I'd gotten my memories untangled sooner . . ."

Averting her eyes from him, she leaned over and picked up her coffee mug again. The open window let in the crisp, refreshing air of fall, and the chill felt cozy and good, but still she wanted the warmth of the coffee and the blanket and being here with Sam. Maybe she didn't deserve it, but she wanted it nevertheless.

"You did all you could," Sam said quietly. He nudged her with his elbow so that she would meet his gaze, then he held her with his frown. "Don't be like that, Nora. You went deeper into darkness than anyone ever has, and you found light there. You've done so much good."

She let the gaze linger a moment longer than was comfortable, even for them, then she looked away.

"Good news about Symes," she said.

"Yeah? The dash-cam video exonerated him?"

"That and street-surveillance video. The footage clearly shows him being attacked by Angela Mayhew and having to fight back to protect himself and a civilian—"

"Who is you—"

"Who is me, yes. Fortunately anything that looks particularly . . . shadowy . . . has been blurred so much you can't tell what's going on there."

Sam raised his coffee mug in a toast. "Here's to Indigo, then. How'd you pull that off?"

"Just the way it is. There are surveillance cameras all over this city. Indigo never shows up as anything more than a dark blur or a bit of smoke."

"I'm sure that's come in handy more than once."

Nora nodded slowly. "The important thing is that Symes will get off. There will be questions for me, no doubt. Symes tells me one of the investigators is already trying to tie me to Indigo, since I was in the car, but we've got our story together. Indigo saved me, whisked me away through the shadows, the same way she brought him to the hospital."

"It's weird that you keep talking about her like she's not *you*. I mean, you told me already. Why keep doing that third-person thing?"

Nora glanced out the window, smiling softly. "It's a beautiful, sunny day, Sam. Peaceful. Your hula girl's dancing in the kitchen window. There's a time for me to be Indigo, but this isn't it, and when I put her away, I like her to stay there, at least for a while."

"Fair enough. But speaking of putting things away . . ."

She held her coffee mug in front of her like a shield. Took a sip. Stared at him over the rim. "You want to talk about Damastes."

"We don't have to."

"I don't mind, I guess. Not much to say. I put him in a box and hid him away where he won't be found, and I feel lighter for it."

The coffee seemed to have revived Sam a bit. He shifted on the sofa and didn't look quite so pained this time. "So you put the genie back in his bottle, but how long does that last?"

"Forever, if I can help it. And I think I can."

"And while he's there, you still have access to his power."

Nora nodded. "To the darkness, yeah. I'm still Indigo. Stronger and more controlled than ever, learning new skills, understanding how all of this magic works. Xanthe is helping."

Sam studied her thoughtfully, then reached out for her hand. Nora held her coffee mug in one hand so that she could take the comfort he offered. Their fingers laced together, solid and familiar.

She didn't tell him that sometimes she could still feel Damastes in the shadows within her. Why worry him unnecessarily? Nora didn't want to tell Sam because then she would have had to explain. She couldn't hear Damastes voice, and it wasn't as if he might influence her or break free, only that she could sense him there. What she sensed was his fury. Fury and despair. And it made her smile.

Sam tugged gently on her hand. "Hey. So, I'm in pain and it hurts if I move a lot, but otherwise I'd be putting the moves on you right now. Y'know, turning up the charm, blasting that seduction wattage."

"Excuse me, 'seduction wattage'?"

"Oh, yeah. Fifty thousand volts."

Nora snickered. "And somehow electricity metaphors are sexy?"

"Wait, they're not?" Sam looked stricken.

Nora finished the last of her coffee. She moved to put the mug back onto the coffee table, but Sam didn't let go of her hand. Nora felt her heart quicken a bit and turned to look at him.

"What I'm saying, in my incredibly sexy way, is that if you promised to be careful not to hurt me any more than necessary, I might be persuaded to let you kiss me."

Nora's mouth had gone dry. She wetted her lips, lifted his hand, and kissed the big bruise on the back of it. Then she extricated herself from his grasp and pushed aside the blanket, stood and faced the sofa.

"That's not really what I—"

"Sam, stop."

He blinked, giving her an uncertain smile. "Okay."

Nora exhaled and turned away, pacing a moment, trying to figure out what words ought to be coming out of her mouth. Finally she faced him again.

"You weren't talking to me in a 'friends with benefits' way just now." Sam started to deny it, but Nora waved the protest away. "No, it's okay. It's . . . it's good, in fact."

"Which is weird, because it doesn't seem like you think it's good."

She perched on the end of the coffee table but did not reach out to him. Instead, she fixed her gaze upon his. "It's only been a few days. You're still recovering. Maybe your brain's addled by painkillers or your concussion, and I want to know that you've thought this through."

"I have, Nora," Sam said in that business-y tone she'd always thought of as his grown-up-people-talking voice. "I have."

For a few seconds they sat looking at each other. Then she nodded once and stood up again. "I've got to go."

"Nora . . ."

"No, really. I'm not ditching you because of this. There's something I need to do, something I've got to do or I'll never feel right again."

She picked up her coffee mug and walked it into the kitchen, rinsed it in the sink, and put it in the drainer, then made her way back into the living room, where Sam still sat with his own coffee, watching her the way she imagined novice lion tamers watched their charges the first time in the big cage.

"Nora?"

"I'll be back later to look in on you," she promised, "but we're tabling this discussion until the doctor gives you an all clear. No way I'm letting myself get involved with you right now."

"Define *right now*."

Nora pointed a finger at him. "I'm not kissing you until I know you're no longer concussed."

Sam grinned.

Nora wrapped the autumn shadows around her, stepped into them, and vanished.

When Indigo stepped from the darkness, it was into the apartment two floors above Nora's. The space remained empty. The fall sunlight beyond the windows barely seemed to reach into that dusty space, which only days before had been filled with light and laughter, with furniture, and with the kindness of a woman who had fast become her best friend . . . all of which had existed only because Indigo had summoned it into being.

All of which had existed because Nora had wished it. Needed it. She had created an imaginary friend for herself, but that light and laughter and warmth, that friend, had become real and true. Of all the things she had done wrong, all of the things the darkness had taken, it had given her one true thing in return.

Indigo let the shadows go. She needed to be Nora right now.

Nora opened her hands and closed her eyes. She searched her memory for the lamp in the corner, for the big plush chair with the chocolate stain on the arm, for the spider plant hanging by the window.

With her eyes still closed, she heard a familiar laugh, and she grinned as an unfamiliar joy filled her.

"Woman," she heard, "you look like hell swallowed you down and then spat you out."

Nora opened her eyes, her smile growing. "Shelby. Welcome home."

ABOUT THE AUTHORS

——

KELLEY ARMSTRONG is the author of the Cainsville modern gothic series and the Casey Duncan crime thrillers. Past works include Otherworld urban fantasy series, the Darkest Powers & Darkness Rising teen paranormal trilogies, the Age of Legends fantasy YA series, and the Nadia Stafford crime trilogy. Armstrong lives in Ontario, Canada, with her family.

CHRISTOPHER GOLDEN is the *New York Times* bestselling author of *Snowblind, Ararat, Tin Men*, and many other novels. He cocreated (with Mike Mignola) two cult favorite comic book series, *Baltimore* and *Joe Golem: Occult Detective*. His work has been translated into many languages and published around the world.

A native of the Mississippi Delta, **CHARLAINE HARRIS** has lived her whole life in various southern states. Her first book, a mystery, was published in 1981. After that promising debut, her career meandered along until the success of the Sookie Stackhouse novels. She is married with three children and two grandchildren.

TIM LEBBON is a *New York Times* bestselling writer from South Wales. His latest novel is the supernatural thriller *Relics*, and other recent releases include *The Silence*, *The Family Man*, and The Rage War trilogy. He has won four British Fantasy Awards, a Bram Stoker Award, and a Scribe Award, and has been a finalist for World Fantasy, International Horror Guild, and Shirley Jackson Awards.

JONATHAN MABERRY is a *New York Times* bestselling suspense novelist, five-time Bram Stoker Award winner, and comic-book writer. His books include the Joe Ledger thrillers, *The Nightsiders*, *Dead of Night*, *X-Files Origins: Devil's Advocate*, as well as stand-alone novels in multiple genres. His *Rot & Ruin* novels were included in the Ten Best Horror Novels for Young Adults. Jonathan lives in Del Mar, California, with his wife, Sara Jo.

SEANAN McGUIRE lives and works in the Pacific Northwest, and writes a genuinely horrifying number of books. We're pretty sure she doesn't sleep. Keep up with her at www.seananmcguire.com.

In the last twenty-five years bestselling author **JAMES A. MOORE** has written over forty novels, from his first novel, *Under The Overtree*, to the critically acclaimed Seven Forges Series. His latest novel is *The Last Sacrifice*.

MARK MORRIS has written over twenty-five novels, among which are *Toady*, *Stitch*, *The Immaculate*, *Fiddleback*, *The Deluge*, and four books in the popular Doctor Who range. His recently published work includes the novellas *It Sustains* (Earthling Publications) and *Albion Fay* (Snowbooks), and his Obsidian Heart trilogy, *The Wolves of London*, *The Society of Blood*, and *The Wraiths of War* (Titan Books).

CHERIE PRIEST is the author of twenty books and novellas, including the recent haunted-house thriller *The Family Plot*, acclaimed gothic horror novel *Maplecroft* from Roc, and the award-winning Clockwork Century series from Tor.

Bestselling author of the Greywalker novels, **KAT RICHARDSON** lives in Washington and currently writes science fiction, crime, mystery, and fantasy. Richardson is a former journalist and editor, with a wide range of nonfiction publications on topics from technology, software, and security, to history, health, and precious metals. When not writing or researching, she may be found malingering with her dogs, shooting, or dabbling with paper automata.